LINDSAY BUROKER

STAR KINGDOM

PLANET KILLER

BOOK SIX

Planet Killer

Star Kingdom, Book 6

by Lindsay Buroker

FOREWORD

GREETINGS, GOOD READER! AS YOU'LL SOON SEE, PLANET Killer starts up shortly after the events in Book 5, Gate Quest. I did want to let you know that I wrote a side novel called Knight Protector that takes place in another system around the time the two previous books (Crossfire and Gate Quest) are occurring.

Knight Protector introduces the characters of Tristan and Nalini (and Prince Jorg), who also appear in this adventure. If you're curious about their story, I hope you'll check out their novel. That said, I tried to write this in such a way that you won't be confused if you didn't pick that one up.

While we're chatting and before you jump into the story, let me thank my team for their help: my editor, Shelley Holloway, and my beta readers, Rue Silver, Cindy Wilkinson, and Sarah Engelke. They're all great about making time for me, even though other things are going on in their lives. Also, thank you to Jeff Brown for the cover illustrations for this series, and thank you to Kim and Tarja at Deranged Doctor Design for the print formatting.

Planet Killer is the longest book in the series to date, so you may want to grab some popcorn or chocolate or whatever your pleasure is, and settle in for the read. Thanks for following along with my Star Kingdom adventures!

CHAPTER 1

CHASCA SNIFFED LOUDLY, STUCK HER SNOUT BETWEEN CRATES overflowing with compost, and thwacked her gray tail against the potting bench like a teenage drummer trying out for one of Zamek City's street bands.

"The robot groundskeeper cleans in here every morning," Princess Oku informed her dog. "I'm *sure* there aren't mice in the greenhouse."

Thwack, thwack, thwack.

Oku smiled, glad the war in the system hadn't dulled her girl's hunting instincts. Oku wished she could so easily find distraction. She kept thinking about the conference she was supposed to be attending this week in Shango Habitat and the bags of her new hybrid triticale seeds that she'd promised to bring, seeds proven to germinate and grow well on space stations.

Princess Tambora would forgive her for not coming, since System Lion's wormhole gate was currently blockaded by a hodgepodge army with an alarming number of ships, but Oku knew Shango Habitat had been struggling with the rising costs of food from the agrarian planet in their system and needed to decrease their reliance on outside sources. Her seeds were needed and would have been appreciated.

Oku drifted to her dirt-smudged tablet and pulled up her inbox with a swipe of an equally dirt-smudged finger. If nothing else, the war had caused the cancelation of the Tidal Waters Ball that week, so she wouldn't have to spend hours primping to make a suitably royal appearance on some nobleman's arm. She had numerous technologically advanced scrub brushes and body cleaners, but as a soil and seed specialist who preferred gardens to parlors, she struggled to keep her fingernails clean. Much to her father's chagrin. King Jager was certain that no prince, king, or emperor would agree to marry a woman with dirt under her fingernails. Which was perhaps one of the reasons Oku spent so little time with those fancy scrub brushes.

It had been three days since an armored fast-courier ship had made it through the blockade to deliver mail from the rest of the system. Unfortunately, that was still the case, so there was nothing new from Princess Tambora. Or Casmir.

Oku had stopped thinking of him as Professor Dabrowski sometime after the third or fourth message they'd exchanged. She hoped he didn't mind. Her finger strayed to his last message, one she'd already played several times.

Chasca snorted at something and shifted position, trying to find a route around to the back of the crate. The thwacks turned to pawing sounds.

Oku glanced at the closed door, ensuring her bodyguards were outside the greenhouse instead of standing inside where they could watch, then tapped the video file. It wasn't as if Casmir sent her anything scandalous—she doubted it would even cross his mind—but their exchanges tended to be light and playful, and she could imagine the dour-faced men who trailed her around thinking them silly. Even her loyal female bodyguard of many years, Maddie, would quirk an eyebrow.

The video played, showing the empty deck of a spaceship cabin and then a circular robot vacuum whirring across it. She grinned in anticipation of what was coming.

The vacuum started depositing purple flower petals on the deck, spelling out the words BEE MINE? with slow precise consideration.

Oku wondered if that meant Casmir and Scholar Sato were finding time to work on her bee project. She couldn't imagine it, not from the snippets of information she'd managed to inveigle out of Chief Superintendent Van Dijk of Royal Intelligence, who walked through the courtyard and passed the greenhouse on the way to meet with the king in the castle every morning.

Civilian advisor Casmir and the warships that had been sent to System Hydra had been *very* busy. But Oku did hope to deploy bees on Shango Habitat, as well as the other stations and habitats in the Twelve Systems that could benefit from natural pollinators. The triticale didn't need insect pollinators, but the stations' orchards of dwarf fruit and nut trees craved them. Oku wished her father were willing to negotiate with the invaders and do whatever it took to get them out of the system and restore travel and trade, but the last she'd heard, he'd sent the Kingdom Fleet to the gate to do their best to annihilate them.

"Are you sure that's not too forward?" a female voice said in the video, the speaker off-screen.

"No, it's charming and clever," Casmir's familiar voice said.

The robot vacuum finished spelling out the words, stopped, and started quivering on the deck. In Oku's imagination, smoke wafted from its belly and steam whistled from the little orifices that looked a bit like ears.

"What's wrong?" the woman asked—Oku was fairly certain that was Scholar Sato, though she never appeared in the video.

"I'm not sure." Casmir sounded concerned. "I had to override its foundational programming to convince it to *distribute* debris rather than pick it up. I may have put it at cross-purposes with itself."

"Casmir, are you saying that robot is having an identity crisis?"

"Something like that."

"It is difficult when one is asked to disobey one's foundational programming," a new male voice said—Oku was certain that robotic baritone belonged to Zee, since he'd been featured in several of the videos. "Such as when the human that one has been programmed to protect insists on repeatedly putting himself in danger while ordering a particularly fine crusher off on some menial task."

"I was trying to save lives by having you keep the mercenaries and marines from shooting at each other," Casmir said.

"They are lesser humans," Zee said. "My creator's life is of paramount importance."

"Ah," Casmir said. "Thank you, Zee."

"Did your crusher just call himself particularly fine?" Sato asked.

"I believe so. He's not wrong, is he?"

"No," Zee said firmly.

Oku grinned.

The robot quivered harder, then hopped slightly, and vroomed back across the deck, slurping up the offending petals until there was no trace of the message.

"Hm," Casmir said.

"Did you get it recorded first?" Sato asked.

"Yes." For the first time, Casmir leaned into view of whatever camera he'd used to record. He smiled at Oku and waved. "I hope you're doing well, Your Highness." He always kept things formal, and Oku wondered what it would be like to hear him say her name. "I apologize for being punny, but it was difficult to resist. Uhm, if you felt that was too forward—" Casmir waved to the now immaculate portion of deck where the petal message had been, "—then you may assume that the message was from the robot vacuum to Zee, who is looking particularly fine today, as he said."

The camera shifted over to focus on the six-and-a-half-foot-tall tarry-black crusher. Usually, Zee looked like a walking wrecking ball ready to destroy space stations and fleets of soldiers. Today—or when Casmir had recorded this—Zee wore a blue-and-green plaid beanie and a tie made from some officer's sash. The costume failed to make him look less like a killer, but Oku wouldn't say so aloud.

"As you can see, Zee is currently dressed well enough to attract all of the robots, androids, and smart appliances on the ship." Casmir smiled again, but it faded, his expression growing more somber. "I wish we were there with you to help with things at home. I mean, I don't know what *I* would do, but maybe I could do something small. I hope you're safe and that the warships don't make it to Odin and threaten the capital or anyone there. Do you think the Fleet can handle them? I would like to think so." Casmir paused and his eye blinked a couple of times in what Oku believed was a nervous tic. "There's also something I wanted to ask you, assuming this message gets to you before we're able to find a way home…"

Casmir paused again, and Oku waited. The first time she had watched this, she'd felt a tingle of nervous anticipation in her belly, because she'd thought he might ask something else, like if she wanted to go on a date when he got back. She wasn't sure *why* she'd thought that, since he'd been discussing the war, but she'd been trying to figure out what her answer would be in the seconds before he'd gotten to his question.

She enjoyed the messages they had been exchanging, and Casmir seemed like a fun guy, even a little quirky like she considered herself, but it wasn't as if they could really… *do* anything. *Be* anything. She'd always known, because her father had made it clear, that she would be married off for some political alliance. And her mother had agreed that was the way it was, since her own marriage to the king had been arranged for political reasons. So there wasn't any point in Oku having a relationship with anyone else, even if the various single knights and nobles who came by the castle and tried to woo her hadn't gotten that message.

She shook her head as the Casmir in the video continued on, and reminded herself that he *hadn't* asked for a date.

"I know I don't have any right to impose on your time or ask for favors, but if things seem like they're going to get hairy in the capital there… and if you have the power and the opportunity, would you mind checking on my parents? There's nothing wrong with their health or anything, but I don't think that old apartment building they live in would hold up to modern warfare if there was an attack on the city. I…" Casmir shrugged. "I guess it's not right to ask for special privileges. Maybe I'll just record them a message and beg them to be safe, not stubborn. They can be stubborn, you know. Staying to help people instead of taking cover. Kim's father and brothers would be like that too." He rubbed his face, looking distressed as he envisioned unpleasant scenarios.

Oku imagined Casmir might *also* be stubborn and one to prioritize helping others over himself. Especially if… She thought of Zee's earlier words. What ever had Casmir been doing to find himself in the middle of a firefight between mercenaries and marines?

"Just take care of yourself, please, Your Highness. I do hope to see you again in person one day." Casmir looked down as the vacuum whirred between his legs, then smiled and waved again and ended the video.

Oku paused it before his face faded away.

He looked so much more haggard in this last video than in his earlier ones. Wan, tired, maybe even sick. Had he been wounded in that battle?

Her fingers twitched, as if she could smooth his brow on the video. She wished they could talk in real time, so she could find out what he'd been doing. It bothered her that her father had ordered him out with those Fleet ships, even though he was a civilian. She still didn't know what her father thought a robotics professor could do out there or why Casmir was even on his radar, other than the obvious reason.

"Oku?" her mother asked from the doorway, stepping into the greenhouse.

Oku turned without closing the video, and her mother's gaze drifted toward it, her neatly plucked eyebrows rising. Her black hair was swept up in a perfect bun with a pair of carved-ivory prongs keeping it in place. Whenever Oku tried that with her own hair, the prongs drooped like flowers wilting in the heat. It took a few thousand painfully tight pins to make it conform into something elegant.

Her mother's gaze lingered on the video, her dark eyes difficult to read, and heat crept into Oku's cheeks. She doubted her mother would care if she was pen pals with Casmir, but faint horror burgeoned at the idea of her discussing it with her father. He had a tendency to overreact when it came to men. He liked to remind Oku that virgin princesses were a lot more enticing for arranged marriages. She'd never had the courage to tell him that he couldn't honestly assign *that* product feature to the wares he planned to peddle, though she found it puzzling that he wouldn't presume she would have experimented at some point during her twenty-six years. For some reason, he trusted all of his knights to be gentlemen who would never dally with a woman out of wedlock.

"Is that Casmir Dabrowski?"

"Yes."

Oku had almost forgotten that her mother knew Casmir, probably better than she did, if from a distance. Oku had only learned of his existence when she'd chanced across one of his publications years earlier and shown it to her mother, wondering at the author's resemblance to the deceased David Lichtenberg. Oku and her brothers had visited the Lichtenbergs several times when she'd been growing up, and Jorg had raced bikes with David, driving Jorg crazy because he refused to bow to custom and let the prince win.

Oku's mother had told her about the cloning and how David had been survived by a twin brother. A twin brother who had numerous medical issues that would have made it, her father believed, a waste of time to invest anything in him. Oku remembered immediately feeling a connection, since *she* had medical issues and her father also hadn't wanted to invest anything in *her*. Girls weren't important, he'd always implied.

But Oku had forgotten about Casmir after that, until he'd startled her by walking into the courtyard with Sir Asger that day. For a few seconds, she'd thought there'd been a mistake and that David *hadn't* died. It hadn't taken long for her to realize the truth—and that Casmir was a very different person, despite the strong resemblance. Oku hadn't disliked David, but she found Casmir much more affable and appealing.

Her mother pursed her lips. "After I realized the terrorists had discovered who Casmir was cloned from and were after him, I'd meant to bring him to the castle and tell him everything, but he was chased off the planet before I had a chance. At least Asger was able to track him down. I understand Casmir was trying to arrange an appointment with me while I was on the southern continent, but the political situation kept me busy down there longer than I expected, and Jager sent Casmir off on this current mission before I returned." Her mother strolled across the greenhouse, pausing as dirt from the previously packed earth floor flew across her path.

"*Chasca.*" Oku clapped her hands.

A mouse scurried from the opposite side of the crates where Chasca was digging. It darted to the door her mother had left open. Chasca's gray head jerked up, long ears flapping, and she sprinted out after the mouse. One of the bodyguards cursed as she bumped him on her way past before disappearing into the courtyard.

"Some botanists keep their compost outside," her mother said mildly.

"I'm putting it in pots, not the castle gardens." Oku waved to the potting bench where she'd been mixing soil, compost, and fertilizer earlier. "Do you know why Father sent Casmir with the Fleet? Van Dijk has been evasive with me when I've asked."

"Probably because you've never previously shown interest in military matters."

Oku still had no interest in military matters, though she supposed she should change that attitude now that they were at war, but she was curious about Casmir. And worried about him, she admitted, glancing again at his wan face in the paused video.

Her mother tracked the glance. "I hadn't realized you two knew each other and were exchanging messages."

There went that heat to her cheeks again. "We met briefly here in the courtyard and again at the clinic when I was getting my beta cell treatment."

"Ah."

"Do you think he's being treated all right? He's lost a lot of his… vibrancy."

Her mother's eyes flickered, and Oku shrugged, looking away from her assessing gaze.

"The latest report I saw said he had the Great Plague and barely survived," she said. "He had something to do with a change of regime on Tiamat Station, which Jager isn't pleased with. And there's been another incident since then that—well, it's not quite clear where his allegiance lies. I do wish I'd been the one to speak with him and not Jager. He does *not* have a diplomatic touch. But what's done is done. Under the circumstances, you may want to avoid sending further notes back and forth with him."

Alarm flashed through Oku, both at the idea of losing these exchanges and because Casmir's allegiance was in question. He had family here. A career. A home. Why would he do anything to jeopardize that?

"How did he get the Plague?" Oku asked because it was horrifying—no *wonder* he was wan—and also because it seemed safer to discuss than allegiances. "I didn't think anyone could get that anymore."

"I'm not sure of all the details. Casmir hasn't told you anything about that or why your father sent him on the mission?"

"No. We talk about dogs and robots."

Which Oku realized sounded silly as soon as it came out of her mouth. Like she was six, not twenty-six.

But maybe that was why she enjoyed the messages. The knights were always so serious, talking about galactic politics and their ambitions to improve their rank and earn a place in the Senate. Oku's female acquaintances from the nobility were just as bad, gossiping and spreading rumors about who was doing what scandalous thing with whom and how it would change the social landscape of the capital forever. Thankfully, Oku had less dramatic friends in academia, but even they trended more serious than Casmir. He was easy to be around. Comfortable.

"I assume our messages can be monitored," Oku added, "and he probably does too. As has been made clear of late, I don't seem to have been granted a top-secret clearance or the right to know what's going on around here."

Her mother sighed and patted her shoulder. "Our government is a bit of a men's club, but Van Dijk clawed her way into an important position, so that's not the only factor. I think it's more a mix of your father wanting to keep you innocent and that you've... not exactly cultivated an image of a concerned and politically astute individual who should be kept in the know. I don't blame you for that—I remember that odious Baron Forsberg approaching you for that scheme against your older brother when you were what, thirteen?—but you can't now begrudge that you're not anyone's confidante."

"I suppose," Oku said.

"I can let Father know you're interested, if you wish. But I came to advise you to pack your work up. He may wish to move the family to the Basilisk Citadel since it's far more defensible than this rambling old castle."

Oku gripped the edge of her workbench. "Are we truly in danger here? I'd thought—I'd assumed that the Fleet would meet the invaders at the gate and keep them far away from the inner planets. I'd been worrying about my research friends in Ve and Vili Habitats."

"So far, we're not in danger, but they've got ships that have broken away from the blockade and popped up at militarily significant stations and refineries to do damage. It's possible some will angle for Odin. Since many of them have slydar technology, it's difficult for the Fleet to track them."

For the first time, fear for her own safety blossomed in Oku's heart. There had been rumblings of war for years, but everyone had assumed that Father would be the aggressor, taking the battle to other systems to capture resources for the Kingdom. Even when these invaders had come and blockaded the gate, she'd believed all the enemy ships were weeks away from Odin itself.

Casmir's request to have her help his parents, even if he'd retracted it, popped into her mind. Oku would absolutely help them. She would find out where they lived and do what it took to offer them a place in Basilisk Citadel or one of the secure underground bunkers around the city.

Her mother released her shoulder. "Let me know if you want me to send anyone to help you pack. I'll be doing the same. War is coming, I fear."

Oku watched her leave, distress and glumness creeping over her like fog blanketing the city.

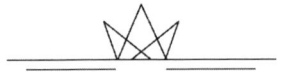

Sweat dripped down the sides of Casmir's face, his aching lungs made his entire chest feel raw, and his left eye blinked in sync with a flickering light in the back of the gym.

A state-of-the-art Kingdom Fleet warship should *not* have lights on the fritz. Maybe he would have a seizure and his taskmaster, who he was currently thinking of as comic-book-super-villain Taurusi the Whipcracker, would take pity on him.

"I'm dying," Casmir announced.

Whipcracker-Kim twitched an eyebrow and glanced over from the treadmill beside him, her black ponytail flopping as she jogged far too quickly and perkily for a sane person. "Dr. Sikou assured me that you're going to live. She cleared you for light exercise."

"I think that means stretching. Or maybe walking from the bed to the bathroom. Not being strapped to a treadmill." Casmir grabbed his towel and dragged it over his face. He reminded himself that he'd almost died a week earlier and that it wasn't embarrassing that he was going half Kim's speed and sweating twice as much.

"You're only strapped to it to simulate Odin's gravity. Your bones and muscles will thank me when we get back home." The thud of her footsteps on the treadmill almost drowned out her added mutter of, "Whenever that will be."

Casmir wished they were heading there now, even if their home system was under siege. He would rather suffer through the fears of war alongside his family than be out here worrying about them, assigned to a warship where he no longer had an official duty. How was a civilian robotics advisor supposed to help Prince Jorg muster an army?

"It's more my lungs that I'm concerned about," Casmir said. "They're aching and burning. Is that normal?"

"Considering the lungs have no pain receptors, no."

"None at all?"

"Few. The lungs don't typically process pain, so any pain you think you feel there is probably originating somewhere else."

"Like from the strap around my hip locking me to this torture device?"

"If you're referring to the treadmill you're walking three miles an hour on—" Kim glanced at some of the burly marines on the nearby weight machines, "—you might not want to say that within hearing of men likely to mock you and stuff you in a gym locker."

"So I should have the treadmill transported to my cabin and only whine to Zee?" Casmir pointed his thumb over his shoulder where his stoic crusher stood guard. Alas, Zee only protected him from projectiles and mauling, not friends with good intentions.

"You don't think he would stuff you in a locker?"

"Not for any malicious reason. Only to save my life. Right, Zee?"

"I would have to first measure the locker, solve a volume equation, and determine if you could fit inside," his looming guardian said blandly.

"Unfortunately, thanks to my teenage years, I know that I fit in most of them."

"I will remember this should the need arise," Zee said.

"I'm not sure my days are any better now that I'm out of bed."

"Truly?" Kim asked.

"No. They're much better. I'm *very* glad to be alive. And grateful to you and Zee for your assistance in keeping me that way. I'll stop complaining as soon as you let me off this treadmill. Aren't we making the gate jump to System Stymphalia soon?"

An alert popped up on Casmir's contact, and he missed Kim's response. Incoming messages to his chip. A courier ship must have run the blockade and escaped with news and mail from System Lion.

He immediately hoped for new messages from Oku. What he got instead was…

URGENT: APPOINTMENT REQUIRED.

Six times.

The messages were from his doctor's office back home. Casmir's first thought was that Dr. Rothberger had somehow heard about his encounter with the Great Plague, but as soon as he opened one and saw a scan highlighting a colorful snarl of brain waves, he realized what had happened. His chip automatically sent reports of seizures or other abnormal brain activity back to his doctor. The weeks of space travel and jumping to another system must have delayed reporting. Had Dr. Rothberger received the data on all of his seizures at once? There hadn't been that many… Three? Four? But that was admittedly atypical. Back home, his medicine had controlled everything. It hadn't been until his space adventures began, along with running into enemies that liked to trigger his seizures by flashing lights, that they'd become more frequent.

Casmir grimaced as he skimmed through the concerned messages requesting he come to the office immediately for testing and a full exam.

"What's wrong?" Kim asked. "Your face is even more distressed now than it was before. If you're truly in pain, you should rest."

"Thank you for that, but it's not the walking. My doctor back home wants to see me."

"He found out about the Plague?"

"No, I'm overdue for a colonoscopy."

She gave him a flat look. "While I believe that is *exactly* the kind of message that couriers would risk their lives running a blockade to deliver, you're too young to be due for that. Unless you've been having more difficulties than your observable bathroom habits suggest."

Casmir snorted, wondering if she enjoyed having her own bathroom here on the ship. "The data from my chip made it to his office, so he knows about my recent seizures. They look kind of bad."

"You need data to tell you that? You were there."

"My body was. My brain was busy… seizing." Casmir pushed his hand through his damp hair. He hoped Dr. Rothberger hadn't commed his parents and shared this data with them, but he probably had. Casmir had them listed as his emergency contacts, and Rothberger was also a longtime friend of the family. Casmir had been seeing him since he was a kid. He grimaced again, distressed that his parents would now worry—*more*—about him, in addition to worrying about the war.

A speaker chimed, and a woman said, "The *Osprey* will jump in fifteen minutes. Find a pod or otherwise secure area for the journey."

Casmir stopped the treadmill, relieved for the excuse to do so. He wiped his face again—as much as he kvetched, he hoped he would gain back a little stamina soon—and unfastened the strap. He wobbled a bit when his foot hit the unmoving deck, and a twinge of dizziness unsettled him.

A solid hand gripped his shoulder, steadying him.

"Thank you, Zee," Casmir said.

"You are welcome."

"You're a fine crusher."

"Yes."

Casmir waited for the spell to pass. He really *did* need to visit his doctor as soon as it was possible. Dr. Sikou was capable, but she didn't have Casmir's records or a basis for comparison. It wasn't as if he was in the same cohort as the sturdy military men filling the ship.

Kim had stopped jogging, but she was gripping the treadmill bar and staring at the panel instead of unclipping and stepping off.

"I don't think that counts as a secure location," Casmir said.

"No. I know." Kim unfastened the strap. "I was reading something that came in."

"Is your doctor also concerned for your welfare?"

"No, it was…" She glanced around the gym. The occupants were filing out, none looking their way, but she lowered her voice. "Someone."

"Someone who is wooing you from afar?" Casmir tried to smile at the notion, but Rache still disturbed him. He was *especially* disturbed that he owed Rache his life. Of course, Casmir was thankful that Rache had shared his blood and sent that vial of immune-system-boosting goo, but he now felt indebted to his clone brother. What if Rache asked for a favor someday? Something that put him at odds—*more* at odds—with the king?

"He's not wooing me. He sent intel." As Kim stepped off the treadmill, she switched to chip-to-chip contact. *Intel that I'm debating whether or not I should share with the captain or intelligence officers here. They would ask where I got it.*

Yes, they would.

Casmir already worried that someone from Royal Intelligence or Military Intelligence here on the ship would realize Kim and Rache weren't quite the enemies they should be. For that matter, *Casmir* and Rache weren't quite the enemies they should be. But he was already in trouble with the king. Kim still seemed to be respected and trusted by the government higher-ups. Casmir would hate for that to change because of Rache. Or because of *anything*.

What's the intel? Casmir messaged. *You can tell me, and I won't ask where you got it.*

You already know.

I can't help my sublime percipience.

She gave him that flat look again, the one she did so well. *I hope I'm there when Zee stuffs you in a locker.*

I hope you're not, since it'll mean someone is shooting at us. Casmir waved toward the exit, and they headed into the corridor and toward the guest cabins.

They only made it halfway before an officer jogging past directed them into a lounge full of pods, with numerous crewmen and women already secured in them, cushioned for the gravitational anomalies of a wormhole jump.

Rache says, Kim messaged as she and Casmir settled in, *Prince Dubashi has put the word out that he's hiring more mercenaries, so merc ships are flocking to System Stymphalia.*

Uh, that's where we're *going.* Dubashi was the Miners' Union leader who'd been trying to have Casmir assassinated. He was also reputedly one of the people responsible for the fleet of warships invading System Lion.

In less than five minutes. I know.

Is Rache going there? To hire on with him?

Kim's lips thinned as they pressed together. *He's going.*

To make war on the Kingdom? Doesn't he need to go off to some secret nebula for a while and caress whatever gate pieces his men acquired?

Would Rache truly join forces with a bunch of grubby mercenaries to flood in after the ships that had already invaded System Lion? His adoptive family lived on Odin. Didn't he have any feelings for the people who'd raised him?

I think I'm going to be sick, Casmir added.

He didn't tell me he's going to hire on. He just said he's going to a big recruiting meeting that Dubashi is hosting on his moon base in a couple of weeks.

He probably didn't say he's going to attack the Kingdom because he doesn't want you to be mad at him. Again.

Kim hesitated. *Maybe, but I think he's trying to do a favor or maybe make amends by sharing this intelligence with me. About the meeting, not about his plans to attend.*

How much of a favor? It's not like we can tell Jorg or even Captain Ishii without explaining how we know. Casmir couldn't imagine even being invited to speak to Prince Jorg. Nor could he imagine that Rache wanted him or Kim to give the prince any tips. What had motivated his sharing? Maybe he hoped to ask Kim on a date since they were both heading into the same system.

Kim turned her palm toward the ceiling. *He also gave me a message to give to you. Or maybe Asger.*

He's contacted me before. Why can't he message me himself? Does he think I've revoked his access to my chip?

It was just a letter, Casmir. I can't ask it questions.

Did he already leave the system?

I think so.

That man is always ahead of us. Casmir leaned his head back, and the pod's walls snuggled him in tight as the computer announced that there were two minutes to jump.

He said he's irked with Asger for killing two of his men and injuring others.

Casmir frowned, remembering those chaotic moments in the astroshaman base as the ceiling of ice had been coming down. Someone had fired first, or maybe by accident, and the Kingdom troops and mercenaries had attacked each other, despite Casmir's earlier efforts to create a truce between them.

I'm not sure if he was serious or just venting, Kim continued, *but he said he'll shoot Asger the next time he sees him. Which could be soon if we're all going to the same place… and he joins up with the other side.*

Am I nuts for wishing we were going to another system?

You want to hide while Odin is threatened?

Not hide, exactly, but I don't want to join Jorg's army, especially if all that happens is they end up fighting mercenaries in System Stymphalia instead of the ships that have already invaded our home system.

I don't think we have any choice. Nobody gave us the option to walk off the Osprey *with Bonita and Qin, and we don't know anybody else with a ship.*

Maybe not a ship, but Casmir had made a friend in President Nguyen, and she had, in a manner of speaking, all of Tiamat Station. She'd invited him to visit and help with her talks with other government leaders from System Hydra. If he could have found a way there, maybe he could have tried to recruit some of them to help battle the Kingdom's invaders.

A moot point now.

"One minute until jump," a computer voice announced.

Kim leaned out of her pod and peered into his. "Casmir? I…" She bit her lip.

Casmir raised his eyebrows at the pause.

"I don't know why it's hard for me to say some things, but I'm glad you survived. I was worried you wouldn't for a while."

"Me too." He smiled. "Thank you."

She patted his arm, then leaned back out of view. The lights dimmed, and the ship glided into the gate. Strange colors pulsed behind his eyelids as conscious thoughts disappeared, the state almost reminding him of a seizure. Eventually, his mind entered a fuzzy stillness similar to but not the same as sleep.

Casmir had only jumped once before, but his exit from the dream-like state was nothing like the first time. The ship lurched hard as his senses groped their way back to reality. His first thought was that they had run into the side of the gate. Was that possible?

An alarm wailed, and men sprang from their pods and raced to the door. Their boots threatened to leave the deck as gravity fluctuated, then settled, then disappeared completely when a shudder racked the *Osprey*.

Casmir stayed where he was, certain his pod was safer than roaming free right now. What was—

"Battle stations," Captain Ishii's voice came over the comm. "All personnel to battle stations."

Casmir groaned. Why didn't anything out here in space ever go according to plan?

CHAPTER 2

"THAT'S RIGHT, YOU HULKING BEHEMOTH," BONITA GROWLED TO the massive warship trying to edge her out of place in the queue for the wormhole gate heading out of System Hydra. "You better make room for me."

A hesitant knock sounded on the hatch, and Qin poked her head into navigation. "Is it all right to come in?"

"Of course. Why wouldn't it be?" Bonita waved to the co-pilot's pod.

"I wasn't sure if you were having a private conversation with Bjarke."

"I'm positive it's only in his own mind that he's a behemoth." Bonita pointed at the *Eagle*, the first of three Kingdom warships, and a freighter from one of the local planets waiting in line. The *Osprey*, with Sir Bjarke Asger—and his son—aboard, had just departed, leaving glittering whorls on the event horizon of the gate.

"I won't ask if you can verify that."

Bonita couldn't verify much about Bjarke, except that he was almost as good of a kisser as he thought he was, which she'd discovered when trying to talk him into taking Qin and Scholar Kelsey-Sato down to the moon. She still felt a little smug about her ability to entice a younger man. She might not be as limber as she used to be, but she had experience on her side.

"Good," Bonita said. "A bounty hunter doesn't kiss and tell."

"That hasn't been my experience with bounty hunters." Qin walked in, magnetic boots keeping her on the deck in the negligible gravity, and slid her tall, athletic frame into the co-pilot's pod. Like Bonita, she wore her galaxy suit instead of combat armor. They weren't anticipating any trouble delivering the cargo Viggo had picked up at Tiamat Station—Bonita didn't have any major enemies in System Stymphalia, and their destination, Sultan Shayban's asteroid palace and station, was known to be a fair and friendly place to do business.

"Maybe I should have specified that a *lady* bounty hunter doesn't kiss and tell."

"That also hasn't been my experience." Qin smiled.

Bonita nudged the thrusters, placing herself solidly in front of the *Eagle.*

"I do hope you know," Viggo's voice came from the speakers, "that I'm not a fan of hulking behemoth warships breathing all over my thrusters."

"Nobody's breathing in space," Bonita said. "Your thrusters will be fine."

"That vessel isn't leaving a sufficient following distance. It could plow into us."

"That's not going to happen. I've flown the Baldur Asteroid Gauntlet fifty times. I can avoid being run over by a warship if need be. If you hadn't set such an ambitious delivery schedule, we could have gotten into the back of the line."

"I didn't know we would be delayed at Xolas Moon for two days while you warmed your lover's many toes."

"He's not my lover. I was visiting El Mago and delivering your gift to him in sickbay."

But before leaving the ship, Bonita had spent a couple of hours with Bjarke in the *Osprey*'s mess hall over a bland version of a mocha, but lovemaking hadn't been involved. He'd been interrupted frequently by passing officers and comm calls from that obnoxious Ambassador Romano. She'd barely gotten a chance to ask him what happened down on the moon.

Maybe it was for the best. She'd been more intrigued by him when he'd been a smartass pirate accountant. She knew how to deal with pirates, bounty hunters, smugglers, and the like. What kind of relationship was she supposed to have with some noble knight from a backward planet?

"Did he like my vacuum?" Viggo asked. "M-784 is one of my favorites."

"I didn't ask. I left it on the table next to his bed."

"*Bonita.* Surely you know when you deliver a gift on behalf of a sentient ship without a body of his own that he'll want to know how well it was received."

"Casmir was unconscious at the time. I'm sure he loved it."

"I do hope he recovers fully from his illness. Human bodies are so dreadfully fragile."

"He's doing better." Qin waved to her lightly furred temple and the chip embedded there. "I got updates from him and Asger today."

"That's good," Bonita said.

Viggo harrumphed. "Casmir hasn't sent *me* any updates."

"You better send him a card to make sure he hasn't taken up with another sentient ship on the side."

"Funny."

The whorls cleared, and an alert on the control panel informed them that they could transmit their destination to the gate. Bonita tapped in the code for System Stymphalia, wishing these Kingdom ships weren't going to the same place she was. After seeing news of the war in their home system and the blockade at their wormhole gate, she understood why they couldn't go home, but what were they planning to do in Stymphalia? Start trouble, she suspected. She hoped the *Stellar Dragon* could deliver its cargo and slip away before anything ricocheted off the Kingdom ships and hit them.

"Are *you* doing all right?" Bonita looked over at Qin as the ship glided toward the gate. "I haven't seen much of you these last few days. You've been in your cabin a lot."

"I'm fine. Good. I've just been thinking about… things." Her cheeks, which lacked the fur of other body parts, showed a pink flush. "Asger," she admitted.

"Which one?"

"Mine. Yours is rude and a jerk to his son."

Bonita hadn't seen Bjarke interacting much with his son, so she couldn't comment on that, but she'd always found the younger Asger stuffy and arrogant, so maybe he needed someone knocking him down a couple of notches. Not that Bjarke didn't have an arrogant streak. He just seemed more… fun.

"He kissed me," Qin admitted so quietly Bonita almost missed it.

The words surprised Bonita. She knew Asger had given Qin that calendar, but she'd assumed it had more to do with arrogance over how beautiful his body was than an interest in anything romantic. Qin was a loyal friend and sweet and pretty, despite the fur, but it was hard to imagine some hunky noble knight who could have any woman he wanted developing feelings for her. For a *freak*, as Kingdom people called anyone who'd been genetically modified.

Bonita hoped Asger didn't have some notion of having sex with Qin just to see what it was like to sleep with a furry cat woman. If he did, she would kick his *cojones* so hard they would fly out his mouth.

"Didn't he try to kill you?" Bonita felt she should quell any chance of a relationship that might hurt Qin.

"Not recently."

"Hm."

Qin frowned at her. "*Your* Asger kidnapped us and locked us in a disgusting sex room."

"It was a regular hostel room."

"That's rented by the hour and cleaned by the decade. Be glad your nostrils aren't as sensitive as mine." Qin wrinkled her nose.

"I'm bemused that you find that a greater sin than trying to kill someone."

"It was a case of mistaken identity."

"Guess you better keep Asger from running into any of your sisters back on the Drucker ship. Assuming you like them."

"I do. I miss them sometimes. Not enough to want to go back… but I've occasionally dreamed of making enough money as a bounty hunter—bounty hunter's assistant—to buy them from the Druckers and set them free. I guess that's silly since I couldn't even afford to legally buy myself from them."

"A commando raid with anti-tank guns and bombs seems more within your reach. Especially since bounty hunters' assistants don't make much less than bounty hunters."

Bonita *had* made more than she expected from carting Bjarke across the galaxy, and Viggo had negotiated a surprisingly good price for the cargo they were taking to Stardust Palace—she assumed the crates were full of weapons and that the person paying them believed the war might seep out of System Lion and encroach elsewhere. Bonita wasn't at risk of becoming wealthy any time soon, but maybe it wasn't crazy to dream of the day when she would own the *Dragon* outright. Would she ever be able to retire? Or would she have to keep working until her reflexes slowed too much and some criminal's DEW-Tek bolt caught her unprepared?

"Maybe you could get in touch with them and they could help from the inside," Bonita suggested into the silence.

The event horizon appeared again, whorls and sparkles brightening the space inside the gate, and she nudged the *Dragon* toward it.

"We were indoctrinated in such a way that it's hard for us to fight against them—the Druckers." Qin sighed. "And we were punished whenever we turned our claws on one of the pirates. Even though my cohort sisters are all capable fighters, we all learned to fear the consequences of anything but loyalty."

If they were like Qin, they were far more than *capable fighters*. It seemed a waste to leave such talent in the hands of a bunch of pirates. But should she truly suggest breaking them out to Qin? To what end? Would she hire them all? Start a mercenary outfit? Bonita was too old to change careers now. Besides, the last thing she needed was the Druckers, with their five warships full of pirates, to come after her.

It would have to be enough that she'd helped Qin get free. Though she didn't know if the Druckers would leave her alone forever. When they'd made their escape from Death Knell Station, they'd left two pirates behind who knew Qin was alive. Bonita hadn't checked to see if there was still a bounty out for her return, but there probably was. She glanced sadly at her friend, reluctantly accepting that their trip to System Cerberus had likely been for nothing.

"We're heading in," Bonita said. "Brace yourself."

"I'm braced."

Somehow, Bonita doubted Qin referred only to the gate jump. Maybe her thoughts were swimming in similar pools right now.

The familiar loss of full consciousness washed over Bonita, and then she was unaware of time passing as the gate's technology defied known physics to take them to a star system a hundred light years away.

As soon as her awareness returned, a beam of crimson light streaked across the forward display.

"We've entered a battle zone," Viggo announced.

"*Hijo de puta!*" Bonita pushed the groggy dream state away, made sure the navigation arm was connected to her chip, and veered them away from the gate. "We didn't accidentally fly to Cerberus, did we?"

"We have arrived in System Stymphalia. Four mercenary ships are firing upon the *Osprey*."

Even as Viggo spoke, the big Kingdom warship flew past, maneuvering with far more agility than she would have expected from such a large vessel. It returned fire as it sailed past the gate, its huge rail guns pounding rounds into a decked-out cruiser on its tail. The mercenary vessel's engineering section exploded, starting a chain reaction that tore the entire ship to pieces.

"Three mercenary ships are firing upon the *Osprey*," Viggo amended blandly. "Two more are heading in this direction."

"I'm getting us out of here while they're distracted," Bonita muttered.

Qin glanced over. "Shouldn't we help? Asger and Casmir and Kim are on there."

"I'll remind you that we don't have the firepower to take on even one mercenary vessel, and the *Osprey's* fellow warships are on the way. They'll be fine."

Qin bit her lip, eyeing the Kingdom warship as a missile blasted into its side, pieces of the hull flying off into space.

"They'll be fine," Bonita repeated, trying not to feel like a dog slinking away with its tail between its legs.

Just because she had friends aboard the *Osprey* didn't mean she was allied with the Kingdom, and whatever fight they were involved in had nothing to do with her. If their king wasn't such an ambitious ass, maybe they wouldn't be attacked in whatever system they traveled to.

"What if the other ships don't get here in time?" Qin asked.

Bjarke's face flashed in Bonita's mind, followed by Casmir's affable smile, and her stomach twisted. "There's nothing we can do to change the outcome."

Qin gazed over at her. Maybe Bonita was imagining the disappointment in her eyes—it was probably just concern for her friends—but that didn't make her feel better.

"Whose ships are those, Viggo? Can you tell who's in charge? Rache isn't out there, is he?" Bonita would be furious with the notorious mercenary if he was attacking the Kingdom, because he'd gotten a new contract, after he'd worked with Casmir and Kim back on that moon. Admittedly, the story she'd heard was that he had *kidnapped* them, not allied with them, but still.

"Two are from the Comet Slammers and three are from Debra's Dire Deathdealers."

Bonita snorted. She'd heard of the alliteration-loving Captain Debra before—there weren't that many female mercenary commanders, so she took note when she encountered them—but couldn't call her a friend. In fact, Bonita had captured and turned in one of her officers. The deadbeat had bought a star yacht and then never made any payments, and a debt collector had put a nice bounty on him. If Debra remembered, she wouldn't be pleased with Bonita.

"I'm an idiot," Bonita announced, and then commed what appeared to be the lead ship. "Captain Debra, this is Captain Laser Lopez. I have a friendly warning for you from one woman navigating the stars to another."

"Her ship has taken some damage," Viggo said when seconds passed without a response.

"Then she should be especially amenable to a warning," Bonita said.

The comm spat static, and then a woman with a husky voice spoke. "Stay out of the way, Lopez, or we'll blow you back through the gate."

"Oh, I intend to." And Bonita did. She had already set a course for Stardust Palace Station, picking a route that took them well underneath the flying energy bolts and missiles. "But since I came from the same place as that ugly warship there, I thought I'd offer you some intel that could save your life. I'll be magnanimous and only charge five hundred Union dollars."

Qin's eyebrows rose.

Bonita muted the comm. "She'll be more likely to believe me that way."

Something between a grunt and a cat hacking up a hairball came over the comm. "I'm not paying you the value of my spit, Lopez. You screwed Lieutenant Gomez, remember?"

Bonita un-muted the comm. "I believe he screwed himself by making off with a million-dollar yacht he had no intention of making payments on."

"Give me your intel, and maybe I'll let you get out of here without accidentally shooting your dilapidated freighter into a thousand pieces."

"*Dilapidated?*" Viggo cried. "I insist that we fly into battle and pummel her immediately."

"What are you going to do? Hurl your vacuums at her? All right, Debra. I'll give you a freebie this time. I squeaked into the queue at the

Hydra gate, and there were seven more Kingdom warships right behind me. I expect them to start popping into the system any second."

"*Seven!* We were told there were only two total."

"They're all coming here because they can't go home. Something about their prince being in this system and raising an army. That sound right?"

"Their prince couldn't be bothered to raise his finger for a manicure. Seven! Are you shitting me, Lopez?"

"Nope. Hope you've got more reinforcements coming."

Bonita cut the comm before Debra could question her further, then shrugged over at Qin. "Maybe it'll help."

"The gate is activating again," Viggo said. "Let us hope, for the sake of your ruse, that the second warship comes through, and not another pushy freighter who cut in line."

"I didn't cut. We were there first." Bonita waved a hand, pretending she wasn't worried for her friends aboard the *Osprey* as they sailed away from the confrontation, but she kept an eye on the rear scanner display.

A second Kingdom warship did indeed come through the gate. Debra's mercenary ships broke off and fled toward the inner system. The *Osprey*, now bolstered by the *Eagle*, turned its focus on the remaining two mercenaries—their captains were probably wondering why Debra had taken off when they'd expected two Kingdom ships.

Bonita spotted two more mercenary vessels speeding toward the gate, but Debra must have commed them a warning, for they veered off in another direction. As the *Osprey* and the *Eagle* obliterated the two that had stuck around, a third Kingdom ship appeared in the system. That ought to lend credence to Bonita's words, even if only four appeared instead of eight.

"That was good, Captain," Qin said. "Thanks."

Bonita nodded, feeling she'd done her good deed for the week. Now, with luck, she wouldn't run into any trouble as a result of it.

Once again, she hoped the Kingdom wasn't heading to the same place as the *Dragon.* It was clear that anywhere their fleet went, trouble would follow. Or be lying in wait to ambush.

Sir William Asger walked onto the bridge of the *Osprey,* bracing himself as the momentum of the ship's maneuvers threatened to overpower the artificial spin gravity and hurl him into a console. One of the damaged mercenary ships flew ahead of them, the big warship accelerating toward it.

"Fire at will," Ishii commanded from his raised seat. "Lieutenant Bombay, open a comm to that ship."

"You're on, sir," the officer replied.

"Mercenary ship," Ishii said, "this is the captain of the *Osprey*, the warship you attacked without provocation. Who hired you to ambush us?"

"Sit on it, Kingdom Captain," came the sneering response. "If *it's* big enough for the job."

"Tell us who hired you, and we'll spare your lives."

During a still moment, Asger moved to Ishii's seat, gripping the back for support.

"Screw you," the mercenary said. "And if you bring a boarding party over, we'll blow up our ship and them with it."

The comm closed.

"Disable them without destroying them, Lieutenant Dag. I want to question one of them under truth drugs."

"You don't think they'll follow through with their threat if you send over a party, sir?"

Ishii grunted. "They won't self-destruct. They're mercenaries fighting for money, not duty-bound warriors fighting for their nation. I expect them to roll over and play dead any minute."

Asger caught the doors to the briefing room opening and his father walking out.

"Do you want me to lead the boarding party, Captain?" Asger had come up to offer his services, assuming a boarding party, or several, might be put together, but now he felt the need to show himself particularly willing to help, to walk into danger for the good of the Kingdom.

"I'll handle that," his father said, stepping up to the other side of Ishii's seat.

Asger glared at him. With his garish tattoos finally removed, he looked more like the disapproving knight Asger remembered from his youth.

His father glared back. Did he not trust that Asger could handle the simple task? Or did he simply not trust *Asger*?

Asger regretted that his father had caught him walking out of that tunnel in the ice base with Rache's mercenaries, but he'd fought with the Kingdom troops against them after that. His father *must* know Asger wouldn't willingly side with criminals.

"I have marines for that," Ishii said.

"The value of knights far surpasses that of run-of-the-mill combat troops," his father said.

Ishii glanced at him. "The pomposity of knights certainly surpasses theirs."

"We know our worth."

"And aren't afraid to tell others about it." Ishii flicked his fingers. "Go ahead, Bjarke. I'll have some of the marines meet you at the airlock on Deck D. As soon as we clean up the rest of this trash, we'll link up and send you over."

Asger bristled. He knew it was petty to care that Ishii was choosing to send his father over him, but he'd volunteered first, damn it. And he thought that he and Ishii had developed a good working relationship these last few weeks. Sir Bjarke had just dropped in out of nowhere, like an asteroid defacing a moon.

"Excellent." His father walked past Asger without offering him a spot on his team, though he paused, as if waiting to see if Asger would ask.

Asger clenched his teeth and held his tongue. His father left the bridge.

"A message came in from your command right before we left Hydra." Ishii waved to the briefing room that Asger's father had come out of. Had he received a message too? "I think they have another mission in mind for you."

"Will I like it?"

Ishii only shrugged.

As Asger walked into the briefing room, he wondered why the message had come to the ship instead of directly to his chip. Because such transmissions could be encrypted to a higher degree? Dare he hope that meant he was being offered something good? Another chance to prove himself? Or was it too late for that?

He was well aware that he hadn't accomplished what his commander had wanted on Xolas Moon. The Kingdom warships had managed to retrieve a few of the gate pieces, but so had every other ship that had been in that crazy scramble at the end. Including Rache's, he suspected. And the astroshaman leader had gotten away with more than half of the gate. Even with the blockade, word must have gotten back to Prester Court by now. Jager couldn't be happy with the outcome.

Baron Farley's broad face came up on the comm display in the briefing room. Asger was alone, the doors shut, so whatever dressing down he was about to receive would be in private.

"Sir Asger," Farley said coolly, "you've once again failed in your mission. Not only that, but you allowed yourself to be *captured* by that devil-damned criminal, Rache."

Asger wanted to argue that he'd only gone along to protect Kim and Casmir, that he'd had no choice, but this message had been recorded days earlier. Arguing would do nothing. Neither would putting his fist through the display.

"I will assign your father to interface with Prince Jorg and the Fleet warship captains on our behalf," Farley continued. "I am assigning you a *minor* task. If you can't handle this one…" Farley's gray eyes lifted heavenward.

Asger's hands clenched the edge of the briefing room table hard enough that his fingers ached. He forced himself to let go, though those fingers only snapped into frustrated fists.

"Take one of Captain Ishii's shuttles to Stardust Palace," Farley said. "You're to fetch the pertundo of an ex-knight, Tristan Tremayne. Prince Jorg wants Tristan executed, but we are tactfully going to fail to fulfill that order. You won't be faulted for that. You'll only be faulted if you can't bring the weapon back. Since he's no longer a knight, he cannot keep it. After you get it, reunite with the Fleet, help Prince Jorg make sure the mercenaries gathering in that system won't be a problem, come help drive out the intruders here, and then bring the pertundo with you to Odin. When this is all over, we'll discuss in person whether you'll be permitted to keep *your* pertundo."

Asger rocked back on his heels, once again tempted to put a fist through the display. Only envisioning his humiliation at having to explain to Ishii what had happened to it stayed his arm.

The only good thing was that Farley wanted to talk to him in person before dismissing him. Maybe Asger would finally get a chance to plead his case and explain that he'd fought hard and done some good while he'd been out here.

He would have to be convincing, because it was a foregone conclusion that his own father wouldn't stand up for him.

With his cheeks hot and his jaw aching, Asger left to gather his gear for a duty that could more easily be achieved by a self-addressed and postage-paid parcel box.

CHAPTER 3

CASMIR TRIED TO CALM HIS NERVES AS HE waved at the door chime sensor for the briefing room on the bridge. Zee was with him, but Casmir wasn't as comforted as he usually was by his sturdy presence. Zee could protect him in battle but not from this.

Ishii had commed him, demanding the presence of his *civilian advisor* for a meeting with Jorg. They were still four days from the planet that the prince's ship orbited—he was trying to recruit reinforcements from one of the larger population centers in the system—but that was close enough for near real-time communications.

Behind Casmir, the forward display on the bridge showed the charred and battered mercenary ship they were attached to and the three other Fleet warships looming beyond it. Casmir had heard a boarding party had gone over to question the mercenaries and find out why they'd attacked.

"If he doesn't answer, we can leave, right?" Casmir asked Zee.

"Do you wish to engage in another treadmill workout?" Zee had been suggesting that all morning. He was as determined as Kim that Casmir regain his health.

"Certainly not, but I could find something to do. Hiding under my bed from the notice of Jager's male children, perhaps." Before this, Casmir had been completing his robot bee schematics and sending them to Kim to include with whatever bee-bacteria suggestions she made to Princess Oku. Even if that project would be delayed by the war, he didn't want to be tardy on his end. He'd also been scouring the news feeds, trying to figure out not just what was happening in System Lion but what was going on in the rest of the systems. The reports were fuzzy on who the commander of the joint fleet was, but more than half the ships belonged to Prince Dubashi.

The lift doors opened and Kim walked out, turning toward the briefing room before she spotted Casmir.

"You were also called to a meeting?" she asked.

"Yes, but Sora isn't answering the door, so maybe he changed his mind and we can leave."

"Casmir Dabrowski wishes to resume his training in the gymnasium to improve his weakened state of health," Zee announced.

Casmir swatted Zee on the solid chest, banging his knuckles and promptly regretting it. "You know that's not true. Did I program you to lie?"

"Crushers are programmed to achieve desired results for their missions. This sometimes involves subterfuge."

"My health is your mission?"

"It will be easier for me to protect you and keep you alive if you are hearty." Zee patted him on the head.

Kim opened her mouth, but Casmir lifted a finger to cut her off.

"Don't say it."

"That your crusher has developed even more personality, and that it's possibly a bug, not a feature?"

"Yes."

"As you wish."

Zee patted Kim on the head.

"Definitely a bug," she muttered.

The door to the briefing room finally opened. Casmir expected to walk into a large meeting with all of Ishii's senior officers, but the only people physically present were Ishii, the marine Colonel Jeppesen, and Ambassador Romano, a man Casmir had been doing his best to avoid since returning to the *Osprey*. It wasn't that hard, since Romano looked through him instead of at him whenever their paths crossed—he probably had no idea that Rache had shared that video of Romano trying to barter Casmir's life for information. Today, Romano was sitting in a chair at the conference table and cleaning his nails, so it was fairly easy to pretend he wasn't in the room, especially when someone more prominent was gazing back from one of the comm displays on the wall.

Technically, *four* people were gazing into the briefing room from displays, but Casmir doubted the captains of the three other warships cared about him or wanted anything from him. The fourth man was another matter.

Casmir had never met Jorg, but he recognized the prince from the media. His angular face was a mask, the long nose hawkish, the blue eyes cool. He looked far more like Jager than his sister Oku, who took after her mother. Thankfully. She was *much* prettier than this man.

Prince Jorg never gave speeches nor made public appearances unless it was at his father's side, so Casmir had no idea what he was like. The media usually said favorable things, that he had passed his knight's training and was working with his father to learn to rule the Kingdom, but Casmir didn't much trust the media, since it had always portrayed Oku as a flake. She apparently didn't mind that, and had even cultivated the image, but didn't that mean Jorg could be cultivating *his* image?

As Casmir stepped up to the table, he vowed to reserve judgment. Maybe he would get lucky and Jorg would be a reasonable man.

Casmir caught Kim giving him a sidelong look as they walked in, Zee clomping behind. She had to wonder why she had been called to this meeting. Casmir wondered why *he* had been called.

It was only bad luck that he and Kim were still here on the *Osprey*. They'd completed the mission they'd been brought along to advise on, even if it might not have been a satisfactory completion in the eyes of the king. Casmir was secretly pleased with how things had turned out, at least when it came to the splitting up of the gate. It disturbed him that so many people had died in that ice base to gain a result that he thought should have been logical to everyone from the beginning.

"Both civilian advisors are here now, Your Highness." Captain Ishii bowed to Jorg's face on the display.

"Step forward, Scholars Dabrowski and Sato." Jorg had a haughty imperious tone, even more so than Asger and the various knights Casmir had met, but at least he didn't call them twerps or common scum.

Casmir stepped into Jorg's view and bowed, with Kim hesitating only a second before replicating the gesture. Zee stepped up behind them and crossed his arms over his chest. Casmir hadn't programmed the crusher on royal etiquette, not imagining that they would be called into court that often, and he hoped Jorg wouldn't choose to take offense.

"That's your crusher, Professor?" Jorg sounded more intrigued or assessing than offended.

"I am a Z-6000, programmed to protect Kim Sato and Casmir Dabrowski."

"We call him Zee," Casmir offered.

"Is it larger than the other ones?"

When had Jorg had an opportunity to see the other ones? Had it been in person? And where *were* those other ones these days? Casmir had heard only a few scattered reports of the military using them to take small stations on other systems. He wondered if those actions were what had prompted Dubashi and his allies to preemptively launch a war in System Lion. Had some of their holdings been impacted?

"About a half a foot taller, yes, Your Highness. When I made him, I was hoping he could best the ones that were hunting me." Casmir's left eye blinked. He hoped Jorg didn't know or wouldn't point out that Casmir had signed an agreement with the military, stating that he wouldn't share any of the work he'd done in their research facility. He was fairly certain the fine print had forbidden him to make more crushers for his private use.

"What would you need to make more of them?" Jorg asked. "Here in this system?"

Casmir let his lips part, even though they weren't ready to utter words. He should have guessed this was the reason Jorg had wanted to see him. But he already regretted having helped to create the original crushers, since they weren't being used as the friendly golem protectors he'd envisioned.

"Time," Casmir said, "a high-quality manufacturing facility that I could rejigger, and a lot of metal and a few medical resources."

"Medical?"

"Yes. For the original project, we had a nanite-manufacturing facility on base, but for Zee, I reprogrammed existing medical nanites. I could send a list of everything I would need, Your Highness."

A list of materials that he hoped would be next to impossible for the prince to acquire here in this system. Casmir didn't think the Kingdom had many trading partners here. Or anywhere.

"What facility in System Stymphalia could meet your manufacturing needs?"

Casmir accessed his chip and scanned the local offerings. A couple of planets had numerous sophisticated manufacturing facilities, but they were both on the far side of the sun from the gate in their current orbits, so it would take weeks to reach them. "The two closest are on Shiva Habitat and Stardust Palace."

The heretofore silent Ishii, who was standing to the side in a stiff parade rest, spoke up. "You may already know, Your Highness, but Sir William Asger just received orders from his superiors to take one of my shuttles to Stardust Palace on some errand."

Some dark emotion narrowed Jorg's eyes at the name of the station, but he quickly masked his thoughts.

"I suppose that would work best. Stardust Palace Station has stockpiles of metals that its many mining ships bring in. Professor Dabrowski, you will go there and negotiate with Sultan Shayban for the right to work on his station and make no fewer than a hundred crushers like that one."

A *hundred*?

Casmir opened his mouth to ask how long Jorg planned to stay in the system, because this task would take some time, but someone on Jorg's ship spoke off to his side, distracting him.

"I am well aware of that," Jorg replied, then focused on Casmir again. "The Kingdom may currently be unwelcome on Stardust Palace, but I trust you can gain access." His voice cooled a few degrees. "I understand you have the ability to win over the leaders of small nations."

"Only one leader, Your Highness." Casmir doubted he could count Kyla Moonrazor. Even if she had kissed him. "And President Nguyen was technically only the Secretary of Education at the time."

"So I understand. Find a way to convince Shayban to help you."

"Do I have access to any funds to pay him? The proprietary alloy we use to build crushers is fashioned from expensive materials."

"I'm not giving that man a single crown." That anger flashed in Jorg's eyes again. "You can ask his wealthy daughter for money if you need it. Maybe that sniveling ex-knight can get it for you."

Casmir couldn't keep from throwing a bewildered look at Kim. Not only did he have no idea what Jorg was talking about, but it didn't even sound rational.

She lifted her shoulders but didn't say anything. She looked like she was trying not to be noticed. Understandable. What impossible thing would Jorg ask *her* to make?

"Find a way to get the crushers made, Dabrowski," Jorg said. "I don't care if you have to steal materials from the bastard."

Steal? How was he supposed to steal tons of metal from the station he then needed to stay on and use for manufacturing? Even if he were so inclined to try, he found the idea so morally unappealing that he would have a panic attack in front of the vault door. Or a seizure.

"After the colossal waste of time Shayban put me through, I'm disinclined to play fair with him. Do this for your king, Professor, and perhaps your past transgressions will be forgotten. I wish to return with an army of crushers as well as a fleet of spaceships from all the allies we can muster."

And how many allies would that be? So far, the only ships the *Osprey* had encountered in the system had tried to kill them. Was Jorg having better luck?

"I will try to find a solution to the problem you've given me, Your Highness." Casmir couldn't bring himself to promise that he would steal the resources to build a hundred crushers, but maybe he could think of… something.

Ishii gave him a sharp look, perhaps catching the nuance of his vague answer.

Fortunately, Jorg didn't catch it—or didn't care.

"Scholar Sato," he moved on.

A grimace crossed Kim's face, but she smoothed her expression before stepping closer to face the display. "Yes, Your Highness?"

"You'll remain with Captain Ishii and rendezvous with my ship, the *Chivalrous*. Then you'll transfer over with any equipment and materials you brought along related to your work."

Kim grew still, as if she already knew what Jorg would ask her to do. An inkling also formed in Casmir's mind.

"To what use will I be putting them?" she asked when Jorg didn't explain.

"Royal Intelligence has uncovered a rumor that Prince Dubashi is having a deadly bioweapon made to unleash on the Kingdom. Perhaps even our home world of Odin. I want you to make something even better that we can use against him first. He's reputedly cowering in this system while his forces risk themselves on our gate. He and his underlings should be an easy target."

"Bioweapon," Kim breathed, the word barely audible.

Casmir read the horror on her face, and the implications dawned on him. She was being asked to make something that could murder people far more widely and effectively than his crushers. It could be genocide, not just murder.

She raised her voice to say, "That isn't my area of expertise, Your Highness. Sayona Station in System Cerberus would be the natural place to shop for such a thing."

"We don't have time to traipse all over the Twelve Systems collecting vials," Jorg said. "We have to recruit *ships* and return as soon as possible. You will come to the *Chivalrous* and put your skills into making something *useful*, Scholar Sato." His portion of the display winked out, the channel closing.

Casmir glowered at the dark screen, resenting the insinuation that Kim's current work wasn't useful. Half of the soldiers in the Kingdom Space Fleet had some of her radiation-absorbing bacteria swimming around in their systems, and the other half *wished* they did. Or—his heart almost stopped—was it possible Jorg had been insinuating the bee project? He couldn't know about that, could he? Would Oku have told him? It was hard to imagine the pompous prince as Oku's confidant, even if he was her brother.

"I guess the meeting has concluded," one of the captains said dryly.

The other faces disappeared one after the other.

"Pack your gear, Dabrowski," Ishii said. "I'll delay Asger until you can get to the shuttle bay. He's probably already prepared to go."

Casmir sighed. He'd been given an impossible task, but he knew Ishii didn't have the power to override it.

"Wait until Asger finds out we get to steal tons of metal and then somehow spend weeks in a manufacturing facility two levels down," Casmir said, though he hadn't pulled up a map of the station yet and didn't know the layout. Maybe the manufacturing facility would be *three* levels down.

"We?" Ishii said. "I think that's *your* task."

"What's his task?"

"Picking up an axe and taking it back to Odin."

Casmir couldn't keep from making a face. "Is it just me, or is my task slightly more onerous?"

"Maybe slightly. Scholar Sato, it'll be a few days before we rendezvous with the *Chivalrous.* We don't have the facilities here for your new… project." The pause was the only hint that Ishii might also not approve of the bioweapon scheme. "But feel free to consult with Dr. Sikou or any of my staff when you're brainstorming. They've had training on reacting to and nullifying such threats. Just no tinkering while you're on my ship." Ishii grimaced, probably imagining some horrific bacteria escaping and eating his entire crew from the inside out.

Kim shook her head and walked out without a word.

Casmir hurried to catch up, hopping in the lift with her and holding open the doors for Zee.

"I am going to have a mate," he announced.

"A hundred of them, if Jorg has his way. Have you ever aspired to have your own harem?"

"Crushers have no sexual function. I merely wish to converse with sapient beings while you sleep and are unavailable for discourse."

Kim leaned forward, gripping her knees.

"Are you all right?" Casmir reached for her shoulder but caught himself, remembering her no-touching preference.

"This is a nightmare, Casmir."

"The thought of Zee with a harem?"

She was too distressed to shoot him the glare the comment deserved.

"Sorry," Casmir said. "I know. The idea of a bioweapon is even more horrific than that of an army of crushers in Jorg's hands."

"*I* can't make something like that. I can punch or kick someone who's trying to hurt a friend, but I can't make some killer weapon that could be used to mass slay people just because some noble idiot who inherited his position ordered me to. He probably doesn't even understand what he's requesting."

"I know this will rankle you, but I suggest feigning incompetence and making him a nice intestinal bacteria to increase motility. Exponentially."

This time, he got the scathing look.

They reached their deck, but Casmir hit the button to keep the doors from opening.

"Are *you* going to feign incompetence?" Kim asked. "Or are you going to make him evil murdering robots?"

"A crusher is not evil," Zee pointed out. "He obeys the commands of those he was programmed to obey. A crusher can be a noble construct, working to combat evil in the universe."

"Which is why, if I am somehow capable of completing this impossible task that Jorg has given me…" Casmir glanced at the walls, aware that some monitoring device might be built into the lift. *I'll program them to obey me,* he finished, silently sending the message to Kim's chip. *Not Jorg.*

Yeah, but you *have to obey Jorg,* Kim replied promptly. *All you're doing is creating a chain of command.*

Not necessarily. You've seen how faithfully I obey Jager. Casmir smiled.

Which is probably going to get you killed and your family locked up.

Casmir lost his smile. *I'm hoping that mitigating circumstances will allow me to wiggle out of that fate. Somehow.*

I doubt the planet being at war is going to make him forget that he has four gate pieces instead of five hundred. And that he's not in control of Tiamat Station with a foothold in System Hydra.

We'll see. I'm hoping to think of something inspired. Such as a way that he could single-handedly save the Kingdom from its attackers and return home a triumphant hero?

His mouth twisted. Even if he were Rache, with all of his money, resources, and enhanced genes, Casmir doubted he could manage that. In the comic books, triumphant heroes never collapsed from medical conditions while deploying their masterful plans.

I don't know if I can feign that much ineptitude, Casmir. It's not hard to make a biological weapon capable of killing people. Killing people is depressingly easy. An untrained thug with a gun can blow away lives like this— Kim snapped her fingers, the harsh sound filling the small lift car.

What if you just tell him no?

A buzz sounded, someone trying to order the lift to another level. Casmir kept his finger mashed against the override.

I don't know. I'm afraid I'll put my father and brothers in danger. Shit, Casmir. I never thought I'd have to worry about our government threatening our families to gain compliance. Is my imagination being overactive? Would Jager really do that?

Casmir thought of his one meeting with the king, his meeting in the castle dungeon. *I… don't know. I'd like to think our government isn't that vile, but the Senate is the only thing to hold the king in check, and I wouldn't be surprised if he could do a lot without them knowing about it. Starting a war would need approval, but making people disappear…* He spread his hand.

Kim's face grew wan, and he wished he'd reassured her that Jager wouldn't harm her family. But he doubted it would have worked. Kim was as smart as he was and much better at thinking rationally. She couldn't be soothed if she knew something was false.

The door buzzed again.

Kim sighed. "Open it."

"What are you going to do?"

She shook her head and walked out. "I don't know."

Come with me to Stardust Palace, Casmir sent silently after her.

She glanced back.

Don't ask for permission. Just get some of your equipment and your gear and meet me at Asger's shuttle. We'll act first and ask for forgiveness later. When they realize where you went, we'll say you saw that the laboratory facilities on the station would be far superior to anything Jorg has on his ship—that's probably even true. Naturally, you assumed that Jorg would want you to work in the best place possible…

Casmir and Zee stepped out of the lift, letting it zip away to another deck.

Kim studied the wall. *I think all that will do is make him suspicious of me for not asking permission first. At best, it'll only buy a little time.*

Time is the most valuable commodity of all.

CHAPTER 4

DR. YAS PESHLAKAI APPROACHED THE PRIVATE DINING ROOM, which he'd never been invited to or even seen before, with trepidation tap-dancing in his stomach. Officially, this was the captain's mess, located off the back of the *Fedallah's* mess hall, but Rache always dined in his quarters. Yas had never seen anyone enter the usually locked door. It was dinnertime, but he struggled to imagine he'd received a genuine meal invitation.

More likely, Rache had finally found the time to deal with Yas's insubordination on that submarine he and Kim Sato had been waiting in on Xolas Moon. As he well knew, the pilot and corporal who had been left behind with them had reported Yas's mutiny. No, not *mutiny* exactly. Yas wasn't subordinate to either of them—as the ship's chief doctor, he was outside of the chain of command and reported directly to Rache—but he highly doubted the captain wanted his doctor helping prisoners to knock out his men.

Rache likely didn't see Kim Sato as a prisoner exactly, but… given that Rache had only managed to snag a few pieces of the gate and not the whole thing, he might be in a dour mood and not inclined to overlook transgressions. He'd definitely been brusque with everyone all week as the *Fedallah* fled the Kingdom warships, made repairs, and flew through the gate to System Stymphalia. He'd been demanding all manner of training drills on top of the repair work and ordering many men to pull double shifts. Yas didn't know if it was because Rache was irritated with everyone's performance on the moon, or if he was about to lead them into something more dangerous than usual.

Yas took a deep breath before waving at the sensor. To his surprise, the door opened to laughter.

Chief Jess Khonsari, Rache's first officer Commander Mendoza, and the intelligence officer Lieutenant Amergin sat around a big slate table with place settings for five. Two bottles of wine rested in the center with glasses already filled. Amergin was leaning back in his chair, already enjoying his, his broad-brimmed hat tipped back on his head, his cybernetic upgrades and half-metal face not affecting his taste buds. Mendoza, who ran the ship during the night shift, was a squat tank of a man with swarthy skin, a bald head, and a black waxed mustache grown far out to the sides with the ends arranged in artful curls.

"You look surprised to see us, Doc," Jess observed, lifting her wine glass, though she didn't appear to have consumed any yet.

Yas resisted the urge to remark on potential adverse reactions with alcohol and her steady painkiller trylochanix. He wanted to *date* her, not lecture her like a father—or a doctor. "I was expecting to be reprimanded. Possibly tortured."

"I don't think the captain does that in the dining room." Amergin slid a hand along the table. "People *eat* here, after all."

"Right," Yas murmured and looked at the remaining seating options. He avoided the place setting at the head of the table, where Rache would presumably sit, and took the empty spot next to Jess. "What's this about?"

"The captain invited us to dine," Jess said.

"And discuss things, I reckon." Amergin tilted his head back to drain his glass, the hat somehow staying in place.

Mendoza nodded once. Yas had only spoken to the man a few times and always found him succinct. Apparently, he was smart and had a knack for space maneuvers and battle tactics, but he was another mercenary who avoided visits to sickbay unless it was to have a bullet removed or a limb reattached.

"I admit I wasn't expecting you, Doc," Jess said. "Rache usually pulls in Commander Brick for meetings, but he's from the Kingdom, and I think this might have to do with the little war the Kingdom is having—and whether we're going to play a part."

She smiled at him, and Yas barely registered her words, instead admiring the curve of her lips. Ah, but the familiar pain lines at the corners of her mouth and eyes seemed deeper than ever. If the *Fedallah* docked anywhere with reputable medical facilities, Yas would suggest, as Kim had recommended, that Jess see a civilian doctor for an exam.

"The question is *which* part," came Rache's voice from the doorway.

He strode in wearing a black galaxy suit and his usual mask and hood. One of the ship's two dedicated cooks came in after him, pushing a large hover tray full of cloche-covered plates. A few promising meaty smells wafted from them.

Rache sat at the head of the table while the cook set cloches in front of everyone.

Yas eyed his a little warily. Even after months of working with Rache, during which Yas had endured no terrible threats to his life or displays of overt sadism, he couldn't help but think of his captain's reputation and envision the roasted heads of Kingdom soldiers under the cloches, perhaps with apples stuffed in their mouths.

Amergin rubbed his hands together and lifted his cloche without hesitation. "Pork chops and cinnamon apples? Now that's a meal. And is that a *bone*? You got us real meat, boss? Not vat protein?"

Half of the plate was filled with greens under some kind of nut and toasted bread crumble, but Amergin ignored those.

"Real meat." Rache leaned back in his chair, not touching his cloche yet.

He would have had to take his mask off to eat, and even though Yas had seen under it, he didn't know if anyone else here had.

"What's the occasion?" Amergin asked.

"We're going to have a discussion," Rache said. "I thought I'd get you drunk first so I can get honest opinions."

Mendoza blinked slowly.

Amergin only snorted and refilled his glass. "I'm amenable to that."

Jess plucked a green sprout off her plate and chewed on it.

"As you know," Rache said, "someone has engineered a war with the Kingdom, someone who put together the first round of an invasion and blockade fleet largely from his own resources but who is now hiring mercenaries for a second round."

"Someone, sir?" Amergin asked. "Are you being intentionally vague for a reason? It's Prince Dubashi. Oh, he's got a few other heads of Miners' Union families helping out, but he's the one that bought eighty percent of those shiny new ships harassing the Kingdom wormhole gate."

"It appears to be Prince Dubashi," Rache said.

Amergin's brows rose. "Do you know more than I do? If so, I need to spend more time plugged into the network."

"Just that a single prince spearheading a war with a Kingdom that controls an entire system—the only government in the Twelve Systems that can make that claim—seems unlikely. As wealthy as the vaunted Miners' Union leaders are, it's hard to imagine even one of them having the resources for all that. I do wonder if someone else is backing him."

"Who else would have even more money than Dubashi?" Amergin asked.

Rache spread a hand. "That's the question. I did encounter astroshamans working with the terrorists on Odin, who may or may not have had a link to Dubashi, and there are astroshamans in this system now."

"I don't know if they have those kinds of funds, Captain. They always portray themselves as above such human vices as hoarding money."

"What they portray and what is reality may be different things. They're as far-flung as the Miners' Union and far more secretive. According to one of their leaders, they control the gate we just flew through."

Mendoza looked at Rache and spoke for the first time. "Didn't see sign of anything other than the typical joint-governments patrol ship when we flew through, sir."

"It's possible she—Moonrazor—gave us false intelligence, but I'm inclined to think she spoke the truth, since she wasn't speaking it to *me*."

"To Casmir?" Yas guessed.

"Yes. It's possible that the true mastermind here is irrelevant, other than that it's wise to know who one is working for before accepting a contract, but what we have here is an opportunity to be a part of an attack force that can destroy King Jager. I don't usually care to work with other mercenaries, but it may be worth it. The question is whether Dubashi and his allies truly have the power to take down the Kingdom military. And if that matters to us, so long as *we* don't get taken down. Should we join in against the Kingdom if we're getting paid—some upfront, obviously—regardless?"

"Surprised you're even asking, sir," Mendoza said. "You hate the Kingdom. Everybody knows that."

Yas didn't countermand the comment, but he immediately thought of Kim, who Rache clearly did not hate, and that she was from the Kingdom. Did she have family there? Yas only knew of Kim's loaded-droid mother, but he assumed she had friends and relatives on Odin. And would object to Rache helping to destroy her world.

But it was possible Rache wouldn't let that sway him. After all, he kept kidnapping Kim against her wishes. Yas wondered if he'd asked for forgiveness for those offenses after the fact. And if he would do the same if he participated in destroying her home.

"I hate Jager," Rache clarified. "I don't necessarily want to see the Kingdom subjects bombed, but in a planetary-scale invasion force, such as is underway, Dubashi will find it difficult to select pinpoint targets. He will inflict mass destruction in an attempt to win by attrition. If that is his goal. I don't know. I'm curious about his plans. That's why we're heading to his moon base for his meeting."

"Were we invited?" Amergin asked.

"Not specifically. He put out a blanket invitation to all mercenaries in the Twelve Systems. He said he needs a lot of men and ships and that he'll pay well."

"You thinking we might be the ideal force for a pinpoint attack?" Mendoza asked.

"I know we would be. We've fielded assassinations before."

The blood in Yas's veins chilled. Even though he'd known what Rache was when he agreed to join—and even more so when he'd agreed to stay—the idea of abetting murder—he couldn't call it anything else—disturbed him.

"Shouldn't be hard to find someone to pay us to assassinate that king," Mendoza said. "If Dubashi won't, someone else will, I bet."

"Yes," Rache said, almost a whisper. He rested his elbow on the table and slowly curled his fingers into a fist.

Even with the mask hiding his features, it was easy to see that he wouldn't shy away from the task, that he relished it. Maybe he'd been waiting a long time for it.

"You look like an evil tyrant plotting despotism, Captain," Jess said.

Rache lowered his fist and looked at her.

"You did ask for honesty."

"About the war," Rache said, "not about my tyrannical attributes."

"If you ply your officers with wine, you can't be surprised if you get general unbridled feedback."

"So far, all you've consumed is three sprouts and a mushroom."

"Veggies make me candid. Ask the doc. It's a known trait of the food group."

Both Rache and Jess looked at Yas. "Uh, you're thinking of their ability to make you regular. Fiber, you know."

"Oh, is that it?" Jess asked. "Huh."

"*Do* you have opinions?" Rache looked around the table. "I'm wary about getting into bed with Dubashi, but with so many other ships attacking the Kingdom, it would be easier than ever to slip in for an assassination."

"We can slip in and get back out before trouble catches us," Mendoza said. "We've proven that. I'm not afraid to take the ship to System Lion if the pay is right. A king won't be an easy target, but it sounds like you're going to do it yourself, so…" He twitched a broad shoulder.

"So the danger is largely mine, yes."

Yas eyed Jess sidelong, wondering how she felt about working for an assassin. How often before had Rache taken missions like this? Yas wasn't sure why, but he found the jump from mercenary to assassin a distressing one. Being hired to fight a war was one thing, but sneaking into a man's bedroom in the dark of the night and slitting his throat was vile.

"Just let me know if you need me to paint a fresh shuttle for you to sneak down to the planet in," Jess said to Rache, not noticing Yas's glance. She didn't sound disturbed by the open talk of assassination.

"No concerns from engineering," Rache said. "Noted. Amergin?"

"Seems you've got more intelligence than I do right now, sir, but I'll see what I can uncover as far as Dubashi's allies—or masters?—go. And if the astroshamans truly do control the gate in this system, it would be good to know. Right now, they're not stopping anyone from coming or going."

"We just put a wrench in Moonrazor's machinery. If nothing else, they might want to stop *us* from going. I confess, when I took us to System Hydra to get the gate, it was *Jager* whose plans I wanted to thwart." He sounded wry.

Yas wondered if there would be future ramifications for making enemies of the astroshamans.

"Doctor?" Rache prompted. "Concerns? Objections?"

"To you assassinating a king?"

"To any of it."

"I have concerns about and objections to assassinations in general, but I'm not your oracle. I do wonder, if we care—" Yas gestured to include everyone at the table and the ship in general, "—who ends up in charge of the Kingdom if you kill the king."

"Prince Jorg, but since he's here in the middle of this system full of mercenaries, I wouldn't be surprised if he didn't make it back home."

"So, who ends up in charge if we kill the king *and* his heir?"

"Princess Oku is the next oldest and would be the next heir by birthright, but it's unlikely the Senate would accept her, since she hasn't been trained as a potential ruler or involved herself in politics whatsoever. Prince Finn is another spoiled brat and four years younger than she, but they would probably back him. Unless other strong leaders step up and encourage the Senate to elect a ruler from within their ranks. A lot of nobles have blood ties to the ruling family. It would be civil war at that point." Rache waved his hand again. "It wouldn't be our problem."

"No, we're just creating the problem and handing it off to them."

"The problem already exists," Rache said, his tone cooling. Maybe he didn't want all this honesty, after all. "Jager."

"Is he a problem because he's king or because he's your personal enemy?" Yas asked.

Jess kicked him under the table and shook her head slightly.

"Both reasons," Rache said.

Mendoza watched their exchange but said nothing. Amergin gnawed on the bone of his pork chop, also watching.

"I'll just say one more thing, then," Yas said. "What if we stayed out of all this and let others figure it out? I know you're a mercenary and war is how you pay the men, but you have a personal stake in this. Maybe it would be wiser to find work elsewhere."

"My entire career has been personal, Doctor." Rache rose to his feet. "Nothing has changed. We're going to Dubashi's meeting."

After he walked out, Amergin pointed at Rache's plate. The cloche had never been lifted. "Give me his pork chop, will you, Mendoza?"

Jess shook her head and stuck her fork into her own meal. Yas wished they were alone, especially since he couldn't help but wonder if Rache, out of his need for revenge, was going to take them into a situation that the *Fedallah* and its crew might not be able to escape from.

Kim felt like an escaping felon, skulking down to the shuttle bay with her luggage and two of her cases of medical equipment on a hover sled trailing behind her. She kept her chin up and tried to look like she wasn't doing anything wrong, but she hoped she wouldn't pass Captain Ishii, Ambassador Romano, or anyone else who knew she was supposed to transfer to Jorg's ship in three days. Not flee the *Osprey* ahead of time.

The warship was still attached to the mercenary vessel they'd captured, with a boarding party rounding up their enemies, so maybe that would keep the command staff distracted.

An inkling of relief trickled through her when she spotted the door to the shuttle bay. She hurried inside with her equipment, then halted. Asger and Casmir were talking outside a shuttle to her left, but Captain Ishii was to the right in the large bay, talking to Bjarke and monitoring as troops dragged unconscious or bound mercenaries out of another shuttle.

Ishii was sure to notice her.

Can you distract them? she quickly messaged Casmir, but it was too late. Ishii glanced at her, and then turned for a longer look.

Kim strode toward Casmir with some notion of throwing all her belongings through the open hatch, leaping inside after them, and ordering Casmir to override whatever attempts Ishii made to keep the shuttle from leaving. He could do that, couldn't he? After all, he'd hacked into a brilliant astroshaman's private network.

She felt Ishii's gaze upon her but didn't meet his eyes, instead pretending not to notice him. Maybe she could say she'd brought this equipment for Casmir. As if medical tools and vials of refrigerated specimens were exactly what would help him create a crusher army. What if she said it was for some doctor on Stardust Palace?

Ishii waved to Bjarke and walked toward Asger's shuttle. Casmir looked at Kim, flicked a finger toward the open hatch, then trotted toward Ishii to head him off.

"Sora," he said with more ebullience than usual. "What did Sir Bjarke learn about the mercenaries? Who hired them? Do you think we'll be in danger flying all the way to Stardust Palace in this little shuttle?" He pointed at it, putting his back to Kim. "Asger is a fine warrior, but there aren't many weapons or much shielding on that thing. This system looks to be a lot more dangerous than we thought."

Ishii looked at Kim—she'd almost reached the shuttle, but it wasn't as if she would be safe once she was inside. Even if they escaped the bay by some miracle, if Ishii's comm officer ordered Asger to turn back, he would. *He* didn't play as loose with his career and his future in the Kingdom as Casmir did.

Ishii allowed himself to be intercepted. "We're going to question the mercenary captain under eslevoamytal, but he claims to have been hired by Prince Dubashi."

"What are you doing?" Asger whispered as Kim approached.

She brushed past him and navigated the hover sled into the shuttle. "Coming along. You don't mind, do you? I don't eat much."

"I just found out *Casmir* is coming along," Asger said.

"Then you can't be surprised to see me. We do everything together." Kim could still hear Ishii and Casmir talking, but the shuttle now blocked them from view.

"Even making armies of crushers?"

"Yes, I'll be holding the glue gun for him." As Kim pushed her luggage inside and climbed in after it, she spotted Zee already aboard.

He took her equipment and started securing it without question. Maybe he was a touch buggy, but she was starting to appreciate him.

"Kim…" Asger stood in the hatchway, watching her. "I was told you're going to be transferred to Jorg's ship."

"An error. Stardust Palace Station has far superior facilities for creating the bioweapon that Jorg wants." A statement she did not know to be true. She'd been too busy rushing to pack to do any research. For all she knew, the station had a closet of a sickbay with nothing but bandages and Skinfill. "I'll be working there while the prince gathers his allies."

Her entire body seemed to flush star hot with the lie. She was bad at deceit to start with, and lying to a friend was even worse.

Kim rushed to the two front seats, both to avoid Asger's dubious frown and to see if Ishii was coming or if Casmir was keeping him delayed.

The forward display was powered up, showing Ishii and Casmir standing in front of the shuttle. She flicked on the comm pickup so she could hear what they were saying, even as she sent Casmir a message.

I'm in.

Good, came his prompt reply even though he was gesturing and speaking to Ishii at the same time. "Prince Dubashi is the guy who's been trying to have me killed."

"I'm aware of that." Ishii was looking at Casmir instead of the shuttle. Good. "That ought to be incentive for you to work on Jorg's request for an army. The idea of someone like that invading System Lion should make you furious."

"Oh, I'm definitely upset over that. Will the crushers be used for boarding parties when we break through the blockade and return to our system? Or to attack Dubashi here? I heard he's still in this system instead of leading his army. That's odd, don't you think?"

"I doubt he has any military experience, so no, I don't find that odd. And I'm not privy to Prince Jorg's plans for your crushers. But listen, Casmir." Ishii gripped his shoulder. "Don't do anything to irk him. Make him the crushers he asked for. Maybe he'll be pleased with you then and speak on your behalf to the king."

Casmir raised his eyebrows. "Do you think he would? I've never met him, but I've never gotten the impression that he's the type to stand up for the common man."

"You're not a common man. In any sense of the word."

"Well, this is true."

Ishii dropped his hand. "Find a way to get what he wants done, Casmir. Don't screw this up." He didn't add *again*, but it seemed to hang in the air unspoken.

Casmir must have heard it, too, for he grimaced, but only briefly. Then he nodded firmly. "I'll do my best to come up with something that will help end the threat to our people."

"*Come up with something* is not what he asked. He gave you a specific thing to do. Do it, Casmir."

Casmir saluted vaguely without reassuring Ishii of anything. Ugh, did he already have some ridiculous alternative scheme in mind?

Ishii scowled as Casmir trotted away. He must have been asking himself the same question.

As Casmir rounded the shuttle and entered through the hatchway, Ishii looked right at the camera that fed the forward display. Kim braced herself, expecting him to come in and drag her out. She wanted to shout at Asger, who'd come up behind her and was standing by the pilot's pod, to hurry up and shut the hatch and take them out, but it wasn't as if they could leave while people were walking around out in the bay. It had to be emptied of personnel and depressurized first.

What would Ishii do after he pulled her off the shuttle? Throw her in the brig? Tell Jorg she'd tried to escape?

"If he stays there, we're going to run him over when we take off," Asger said.

Ishii looked toward the other shuttle, or maybe toward Bjarke. Kim wasn't sure if their newest knight had noticed her walk across the bay—or thought anything of it, if he did. He hadn't been in the briefing room when Jorg had told them about the bioweapon. Now, Bjarke was busy forcing a mercenary who was putting up a fight toward the door.

Ishii looked back toward Asger's shuttle for a long moment, then turned and walked out of the shuttle bay.

"Huh." Casmir had come up behind her to peer at the same display.

"Either you distracted him," Kim said, "or he's pretending he didn't see me."

"My allure distracts men *all* the time." Casmir patted his hair. "I just wish it distracted more women."

Asger squinted at Kim. "I knew you were lying."

"I'm abysmal at it," she admitted. Her face was still flushed.

The comm beeped, and she jumped.

"Shuttle A-3, you have permission to depart."

Bjarke and the last of the crew and prisoners had departed. Lights flashed in the bay outside, warning of imminent depressurization.

Asger slid into the pilot's seat. "I only packed enough food and water for two people."

"I don't eat much," Casmir said. "And there are emergency rations, I'm sure."

"You two are determined to make sure I stay in trouble with my superiors, aren't you?"

"Not me." Casmir touched his chest. "I'm *supposed* to be here."

Kim sank down into one of the other pods. "I hope there's so much else going on that Prince Jorg forgets about me and his desire for a bioweapon."

"Bioweapon?" Asger asked.

"That's what he wants me to make. And why I'm doing my best not to rendezvous with him."

"The use of such weapons is against the Intersystem War Treaty," Asger said.

"I think invading someone else's system is against the treaty too," Casmir said.

"War is allowed. You just have to do it fairly." Asger's fingers danced across the control panel, and he pulled the navigation arm out.

"What a strange treaty," Casmir said. "I'd amend it if I got the opportunity."

"Let's get out of here before someone changes their mind about our stowaway." Asger activated the thrusters, and the bay doors opened.

Casmir slid into the pod next to Kim. "What are you going to do when we get to the station?"

Kim had no idea. Hide out and hope Jorg forgot about her?

"I told Asger I'd hold your glue gun while you make crushers."

"Well, no wonder he knew you were lying."

CHAPTER 5

THE FIRST DAY OF THEIR SHUTTLE TRIP PASSED uneventfully, and Casmir stopped worrying about the *Osprey* or one of the other Kingdom warships chasing them down to fetch Kim. He did not, however, stop worrying about how they would gain access to Stardust Palace Station when they arrived in two days. If anything, he worried *more* about that now.

He'd been going over the previous month's local news in the system—there had been a great deal about events at Stardust Palace. As he'd learned, Prince Jorg had come to announce a betrothal to Sultan Shayban's daughter, Princess Nalini, but there had been an attack during the betrothal ball, an assassination attempt on Jorg's life, and some incident where Jorg offended the princess deeply. The reports were missing some details, but it was clear that Nalini's father had also been offended. Sultan Shayban had issued a statement right after Jorg left that people from the Kingdom were no longer welcome on his station. Indefinitely.

"Asger?" Casmir sat tucked into the pod next to his in navigation while Kim practiced combat moves on Zee in the back, answering his questions about robots in literature in between trading punches. The shuttle was flying at a constant speed, so any sense of gravity was negligible, but she didn't seem to mind—maybe she *wanted* to practice combat in zero-g. Casmir was just glad that he hadn't yet been queasy on the trip. "Sora said you were being sent to the station to retrieve an axe. What's that about?"

Asger had been frowning over the news feeds as Casmir ran them on one of the displays. "Not an axe, a pertundo. There's a knight—an ex-knight—on the station, and Baron Farley wants his weapon back. Farley said Jorg wants him dead, but he's not asking me to assassinate him." Asger shuddered. "Thankfully. I know Tristan. He's a good guy. He's a commoner, but he managed to get a knight to take him on as a squire, and he worked really hard to be made a knight himself. I'm not sure what happened or why he's in this system. I haven't talked to him in about a year."

"Something to do with people getting shot at that ball and Jorg almost being assassinated, I'll wager." Casmir waved at the display.

"Seems likely."

"What's his last name?"

"Tremayne."

Casmir flipped through more feeds, this time running a search on the ex-knight. "Uh, he's recently been named a business partner to Princess Nalini, who is a real-estate developer of note in this system."

"*Business* partner? What a strange career to switch into."

Casmir pulled up a recent picture of Nalini with Tristan standing next to her. They were gazing at each other and exchanging secret smiles. "I think I can guess why Jorg hates him. He got the girl."

Asger lifted a finger, as if to object, but it was hard to misinterpret the look those two were sharing.

"You're being ordered to storm onto the station and take the weapon of a man who is now in good with the sultan's favorite daughter." Casmir pointed to text in the article that described Nalini as exactly that. "And I'm being ordered to steal resources from the family, sneak into their manufacturing facilities, and somehow make crushers. Asger, is it just me, or are we the bad guys in this scenario?"

Asger's expression grew pensive. "We don't know the full story—" he waved at the picture, "—or what Tristan did. I am simply following orders to reclaim something that doesn't belong to him if he's no longer a knight." Asger arched an eyebrow. "But if you're sneaking into a space station to steal materials to make super weapons, you're *definitely* a bad guy."

Casmir nodded glumly. "I was afraid of that."

"I meant it as a joke."

"But it's not a joke. That's exactly what Jorg asked me to do."

"Oh. Sorry." Asger tilted his head. "*Really?* He didn't give you money to buy materials?"

"I'm not even getting paid for my time as a civilian advisor." Casmir gazed at the vast starry blanket on the forward display. "Which isn't important, unless I want to buy souvenirs at the palace. Stopping the war and protecting our people is. But not at the expense of others who aren't involved."

"What are you planning to do?" Asger asked warily.

"Talk to the sultan and try to make a deal with him. I am concerned, however, that we're heading toward their station in a blatantly Kingdom shuttle, and they hate the Kingdom this week."

"I saw that. I'm worried they won't let us dock."

"Me too." Casmir leaned forward in his pod as much as the insulating walls snuggled up to his shoulders would allow. "Where's Bonita and the *Stellar Dragon*? They came to this system, too, didn't they?"

"To deliver a cargo, yes."

"Do you know where?"

Asger shook his head. "I haven't been in touch with them since… er, I'm trying to figure something out. With Qin. I may have inadvertently given her the wrong idea about… things."

Casmir made a note to ask him about that later, but he wanted to get their future resolved first. "I don't need to figure anything out with Qin. Or Bonita. I'll send them a message. See if you can locate the *Dragon* in this system, will you?" Casmir pointed at the scanner panel.

"Who's in command of this shuttle, me or you?"

"You are in absolute command of everything inside this hull. But scan the system, please."

Asger snorted but did as asked.

When Casmir sent a cheerful *Hello, Laser* to Bonita, he got an answer more quickly than he expected. Wherever they were, it wasn't far enough for a lag in communications.

El Mago, how are you? Do you know anything about the Kingdom shuttle stalking us? That's from one of your warships, isn't it?

Stalking you?

"They're on a similar course as we are," Asger reported. "A few hours ahead."

Oh, Casmir added. *That may be us.*

You've taken up stalking?

Breaking and entering and theft, actually. Per my orders.

Those sound like screwy orders.

Tell me about it. Ah, Laser, are you by chance going to Stardust Palace?

To drop off a cargo of weapons that are probably intended to annihilate the Kingdom if its troops come anywhere near the sultan's turf, yes.

I see you've been catching up on the local news, Casmir sent.

It's the stuff of theater. Your Prince Jorg sounds like a real charmer.

Is there any chance you'd be willing to deliver a few passengers along with your cargo?

Kingdom passengers? I don't think the sultan will sign off on that.

He needn't know we arrived with you. It's just Asger, Kim, me, and Zee, of course.

What's wrong with your shuttle?

Aside from the giant gold and purple crown on the side?

Ah, they won't let you dock?

We haven't asked yet. I thought it would be better to come in unannounced as opposed to being forbidden to dock and then coming anyway.

Casmir... are you trying to get me in trouble?

No, we just want a ride. If your ship is searched, we'll happily say we stowed away and you had no knowledge of it.

So I'll merely appear to be incompetent rather than a smuggler of Kingdom spies?

That sounds like one of those questions a man should never be manipulated into answering.

Which Asger do you have?

Uh, the one we all know. Casmir hadn't spoken to Sir Bjarke Asger, unless gaping at his tattoos and un-knightly demeanor counted. William Asger had come to visit him in sickbay. Bjarke was probably among those who were irritated that Casmir had let Moonrazor get away with most of the gate pieces.

I suppose Qin will be pleased about that. Did Bonita seem disappointed?

Casmir would have to get the full story from them of what they had been up to and how they'd come across Bjarke. All Casmir had heard was that Kim's mother, the other android professor, and Bjarke had been transported to Xolas Moon by the *Dragon.* One missed out on so much while being sick and trying not to die.

I also have Viggo's vacuum with me, Casmir messaged. *I didn't want to risk leaving it behind where it might be tossed into a recycle bin.*

He'll be pleased about that.

You're the only one left that I need to please, it seems. What can I offer? To repair your robots? Instruct you on how to repair robots yourself? Purchase you flowers on Stardust Palace with my nonexistent pay? Arrange a massage?

Who's giving the massage? Your hands look kind of puny.

They're fantastic hands for the intricacies of wiring robots and attaching components to circuit boards.

I'm not an astroshaman. I don't have those things.

I can program Zee to massage you.

Ugh, just bring the vacuum. We'll wait for you.

Excellent. Thank you.

I'm going to regret this, aren't I?

Have you regretted the other times you've brought me aboard?

Deeply and daily.

"I've talked Bonita into taking us aboard," Casmir said, "and letting us stow away until we reach the station."

"How'd you manage that?" Asger asked.

"I believe I promised *not* to give her a massage."

"You have a way with women."

Casmir studied his hands. They were perhaps smaller than those of someone like Asger, but he had long fingers and thought they looked artistic and capable. Certainly not puny. But maybe he would get some of those hand-squeezing gizmos to increase their strength. In case he ever had the opportunity to massage a woman. His father occasionally gave his mother foot rubs, which she said she enjoyed greatly, since she had to work on other people all day at work. Maybe he could download some schematics—diagrams of muscles—with instructional tips.

"They're going to wait for us," Casmir said. "Can you program the autopilot of the shuttle to return it to the *Osprey*?"

"Yes, but Ishii will be irked with me for abandoning it and leaving it to find its own way home."

"Better than being blown up for approaching a hostile space station uninvited, don't you think?"

"I'll let you explain that logic to him when he comms us."

"That should work. I'm practically his favorite person."

"Yes, I'm sure you're in his will."

The comm panel beeped. At first, Casmir thought it would be Bonita, wanting to finalize arrangements, but it was the *Osprey*.

He grimaced. "It's too early for them to know we've made arrangements to deviate from the plan, right?"

"It's not too early for them to have noticed their microbiologist is gone," Asger said.

"I'm a bacteriologist," Kim said, coming up behind them, her braid floating in the weightless environment.

"What's the difference?"

"Instead of studying vague small things, I study specific small things."

Casmir smiled, though Asger didn't seem to know if that was a joke or a serious correction.

He reached for the comm. "I better answer it."

Casmir lunged and caught his wrist. "Unfortunately, you're enjoying your sleep cycle right now and didn't hear the comm."

Asger eyed him sidelong. "They'll leave a message that I will be expected to check when I *wake up*."

"A message is fine. With a message, we'll have time to come up with a reasonable response without nervous tics giving away that we're scrambling to make up something."

"I don't have nervous tics," Asger said.

"Must you rub in your genetic superiority at every chance?"

"I'm not sure your genes explain your eye," Kim observed, sounding calmer than Casmir at the idea of lying to Ishii. No, wait. It wouldn't be Ishii. Ishii had looked the other way when Kim had left.

Casmir groaned as he realized who it likely was.

"They left a message," Asger said.

"I'm sure he did."

"You know who it is already?"

"Yes." Casmir tapped the panel to play it.

He wasn't surprised when Ambassador Romano's cranky face popped up.

"Sir Asger," Romano snapped, "is Scholar Sato on your shuttle? We're two days from rendezvousing with the *Chivalrous*, and the computer can't locate her aboard. Dr. Sikou hasn't seen her since yesterday. No other shuttles have left in that time. She may be stowing away. I trust you wouldn't have *knowingly* taken an unauthorized passenger along with you." Romano's eyebrows crashed together in a V. "I command you to respond to this message as soon as you receive it. We will not show up to the prince's ship without the person he's most eager to see."

The message ended.

"I'm the person he's most eager to see?" Kim asked dubiously.

"He must have big plans for your bioweapon," Casmir said. "Or he's seriously lacking for female companionship. According to the news, what was supposed to be his betrothal didn't go well."

"I'm not sure which of those things sounds worse."

Asger grunted. "I can't blow off an ambassador. I have to comm him back. I'll... say I haven't seen you."

From the distasteful way Asger's lips curled, Casmir knew he didn't want to lie. He might not have nervous tics, but he would want to be honest and honorable, as a knight should be.

"Wait." Casmir held up a finger, then loosened his pod and scrambled under the console. He opened a panel, turned onto his back, and attempted to place his boots so that his legs wouldn't float away. "Zee, hold me down, please, will you?"

"Yes."

Zee, who could also magnetize his soles, squeezed his massive form between the pods and clamped Casmir's legs to the deck.

Casmir pulled up a schematic for the shuttle, glad network access was good in this system, even in the empty space between destinations. He poked around until he located the bottom of the comm unit. "Can someone get me my tool satchel, please?"

Kim had anticipated the request and promptly handed him a few tools, wedging the rest of the satchel under his back.

"Excellent." He opened up the housing.

"What are you doing, Casmir?" Asger peered under the console.

"Making sure your return comm call goes well."

"You're not going to knock out the system, are you?"

"Not *completely*." He tinkered for a minute and said, "Go ahead. Report in."

As Asger commed the *Osprey,* Casmir considered what else he could do from the navigation console that might give them a legitimate reason to abandon the shuttle and board the *Dragon.* Whatever it was, he would have to make sure the craft could still autopilot itself back to the warship. Ishii would be more than irked if they caused him to lose one of his shuttles.

"Environmental systems?" he murmured. "That would affect us without affecting the shuttle itself. But I'd have to make it look like a believable maintenance problem, not something that one of us sabotaged…"

A spatter of static came from above.

"Casmir," Asger said dryly. "What happened to Romano's message?"

"It's a mystery. Unfortunate that it was scrambled before you were able to review it."

Kim crouched down, gripping the edge of the console to anchor herself. "You do know you're on the path to becoming a not-so-juvenile delinquent, right?"

"I like to regularly partake in the kinds of mischief my students might employ, thus to remain savvy to potential shenanigans that could affect testing and grading."

"Ambassador Romano?" Asger's voice floated down. "I saw that you commed, but we're having some trouble recovering the message. What can I do for you?"

A fresh spatter of static filled the shuttle.

"I'm sorry, sir," Asger said, "but this transmission is broken up for some reason. Are you able to read me?"

More static. A few clipped words made it through, but the message was incomprehensible.

"Sir? I still can't understand you. Is it possible that some mercenary ship is blocking our transmission? I heard Rache was coming to this system."

Kim glanced at Asger, then frowned down at Casmir. "Did you tell him?" she mouthed.

Casmir shook his head, clunking it against a heat sink.

Even angrier static came through, then stopped abruptly.

"He ended the call." Asger sounded faintly offended.

"Darn." Casmir finished tinkering. "I regret to inform you, Sir Asger, that a wiring error is going to cause our environmental systems to go out in about four hours. We'll have to arrange passage on another ship, since we won't have enough reserves to make it to Stardust Palace."

“Four hours?” Asger asked. “Is that how long it’ll take us to catch up to the *Dragon*?”

“Precisely so. How convenient for us.”

“You *are* a delinquent.”

“I’m just watching out for my friends,” Casmir said.

“In a delinquently manner.”

“Is that a word?” Casmir asked Kim.

“An adverb dating back to the fifteenth century on Old Earth, yes.”

“Ah, good. Someone must have foreseen that I would be born. Like a prophet.”

“A prophet of delinquency?”

Casmir smiled and patted Zee on the arm. “You can let me up now.”

“Should delinquents not be restrained for the good of those around them?” Zee asked.

Kim raised her eyebrows.

“Is your crusher making a joke?” Asger asked.

“It’s a possibility,” Casmir said. “Zee, in the Kingdom, we rehabilitate minor delinquents. Only heinous and dangerous criminals are dumped in the asteroid mines.”

“I don’t know,” Asger said. “I kind of like the idea of you being restrained. We’d all be less likely to get in trouble.”

“Funny, Bonita said something similar.”

“Funny.”

“They’re linking up to our airlock.” There was impressive excitement evident in Viggo’s voice, considering he had no vocal cords. “Casmir will be aboard in minutes.”

“Do you have a row of equipment lined up for him to repair?” Bonita asked from her pod in navigation.

“I always have equipment in need of fine-tuning, but I am mostly eager to discuss some new articles that have been published on robotic zero-g ship-repair facilities.”

"He's been busy—and sick. It's possible he won't have had time to read them." Or a desire to read them, Bonita added silently.

"He's always read everything related to robotics. We had a wonderful discussion when he was last on board about the self-repairing, modular, reconfigurable rover robots currently studying the volcano moon of Chantico."

"Fascinating."

"Isn't it? Even Zee was interested and chimed in."

Bonita resolved to record the three of them discussing volcano-studying robots so she could listen to it the next time she had insomnia. That discussion would put her to sleep far more quickly than that herbal stuff she had.

The comm beeped. Expecting a message from Asger or Casmir, Bonita answered without hesitation. Viggo usually closed his virtual mouth when someone commed.

But the familiar face that popped up on the display didn't belong to either of them.

Bonita folded her arms over her chest and quirked an eyebrow. "Sir Toes. Were you lonely with nobody but stodgy marines to talk to?"

Why did she have a feeling this had to do with Asger, Casmir, and Kim? Had they gotten *permission* to leave that warship?

"Exceedingly lonely, dear Laser. I also wished to show you my new face and find out if you found it more desirable than the last." Bjarke gestured to his cheeks like a robot vendor pushing cheap knickknacks in a space station concourse.

Though he did not look cheap. He'd finally removed the tattoos, he'd shaved off his beard, and he'd also trimmed his hair. The gray mixed with the blond didn't detract from the fact that he was handsome—even with the garish tattoos, he'd been handsome.

But, expecting an interrogation or accusation, Bonita merely waved a hand. "Enh. Your face isn't what fuels my fantasies."

"Oh, that's right. It's my toes you dream of."

"Yes, they keep me up nights."

"Rubbing yourself in sensitive places, I hope." He grinned and wriggled his eyebrows.

Damn it, it was an alluring grin, and she caught herself remembering the kiss they'd shared. It had been the first she'd engaged in since her ex-husband left her, unless one counted the prostitute she'd briefly considered spending the night with—until he'd called her "grandmother" and said he gave discounts to senior citizens. Bastard. *Bjarke* had never hinted that he believed her old.

Bonita shook her head, reminded of her vow to avoid entanglements with men. They always had an agenda. Just because Bjarke had turned out to be a knight didn't change anything. A knight wouldn't be interested in a bounty hunter who could barely afford to keep her ship flying. If he was flirting with her, it was because he wanted something. Again.

"More likely rubbing alcohol over myself to remove contaminants from our last meeting," she growled. "What do you want, Toes?"

He blinked, and his smug arrogance faded. "Did I offend you, Bonita? You know I enjoy our verbal repartee, and I thought you did too."

"I assumed we were done exchanging it, now that you don't need a ride anywhere, and you're off doing knightly things." Bonita caught voices floating up through the ladder well, and she leaned back and closed the hatch to navigation. If Bjarke was looking for Kim and Casmir and Asger, she didn't want to help him. She wasn't sure yet if she would risk the Kingdom's ire by trying to hide that she had them, but she wouldn't volunteer the information.

"The knightly things *have* kept me busy, I admit. I regret that I didn't get a chance to comm you before leaving System Hydra. I was thinking of composing a letter or a video recording when your plucky freighter pushed its way into the queue behind us at the gate. Imagine my surprise when it appeared in the same system that we were traveling to. My first assumption was that you were stalking me because you ached to continue what we started back in your guest quarters on the *Eagle*..." There was that eyebrow wriggle again—the man didn't stay contrite or un-smug for long. "But then you took off without a word. Am I less stalkable than I thought?"

"The only people likely to be stalking you are the Druckers for spying on them."

"That's disappointing. Especially after our dalliance. At the time, I was positive you enjoyed it, since you had such a firm grip." His eyelids drooped to half mast, and she imagined him naked in her bed, the blankets covering... very little.

She frowned and smacked the image out of her mind. Wasn't she too old to be manipulated by her hormones? Age ought to be good for *something*.

"If you're talking about the kiss-and-grope we did in the lavatory, I'm not sure I'd call that a dalliance."

"No? You dallied nicely as you were pressed up against my hard chest."

"I was pressed up against the hard toilet too. It's not comming me for a date."

"Well, no wonder you're grumpy." Bjarke grinned again. "A date is an excellent idea. Perhaps if I finish my knightly duties, as you call them, and help stop this war some megalomaniacal prince has started with my people—" the grin disappeared, his eyes growing hard and determined, "—then I can catch up with you. I would like to see you again, perhaps without military men walking up every five minutes to interrupt. Where did you say you're going?"

"I didn't."

He glanced down at some display. "You're on course for Stardust Palace, I see."

"*Now* who's the stalker?"

"I just need to know where to send gifts."

"You can keep your gifts."

"Are you sure? I wanted to thank you for comming those mercenaries and getting them to leave us alone."

He'd found out about that? Despite her determination to remain aloof, that warmed her. She hadn't expected anything—it wasn't as if she'd been that much help or risked herself—but it pleased her that he knew about it. Even if she doubted that was the reason he'd commed her. Bjarke wanted something. She was sure of it.

She shrugged. "They would have left you alone anyway when your other ships showed up. They were only expecting two, you know. Someone lied to them."

"Lies abound in space. I've grown used to them. What's unusual out here is to find someone willing to fight at your side and watch your back, especially when that someone has no reason to love the Kingdom—or its knights. I confess to being touched." He rested a hand on his chest, and his eyes seemed sincere, at least for a moment. Then a teasing smile curved his lips and he added, "Only by my own hand, alas. But often. In my bunk in the dark of night."

"Is rubbing alcohol involved?"

"Something less astringent and more lubricating."

"I'll bet."

"I hope to see you again soon, Laser. Very soon." He smiled again and ended the call.

She stared as the display went dark. She'd expected him to ask about her new passengers. Had he only wanted to confirm that she was going to Stardust Palace? To what end? It was unlikely he would be able to get away from his duties for a quickie across the system.

Which was, she told herself firmly, absolutely fine. If he showed up at the station, it would only lead to trouble.

CHAPTER 6

QIN WAITED IN THE CARGO HOLD FOR ASGER to finish remotely programming his shuttle to detach from the *Dragon*'s airlock and fly off—presumably back to the warship it had come from. Kim and Casmir had already headed up to the guest cabins, with more than a dozen of Viggo's robots swirling in and out of their path, accompanying them as Viggo's opera played on the speakers. Fortunately, it had faded—the volume had made Qin's ears want to furl up like flowers in a hailstorm—with Viggo now chatting enthusiastically to Casmir about rover robots.

Though her keen hearing caught the words, she didn't pay much attention to them as she watched Asger, studying his profile.

Unfortunately, after a quick smile, he hadn't been studying her back. Or looking at her at all.

Granted, it had only been a few minutes, and he was busy with a task, but she sensed his discomfort. Qin had a feeling he would tell her that their kiss had been a mistake, that knights did not have relationships with strange furry women who'd been hatched in a scientist's lab.

She couldn't be surprised, but even though the rejection was only in her head at this point, she felt preemptively disappointed. She vowed not to bring it up unless he did. If he wanted to forget or pretend it hadn't happened… well, she was used to that.

Asger stepped back, watching the shuttle fly away on the display. "I guess we're committed," he muttered.

"Are you in trouble?" Qin asked.

"There's a war going on back home, I'm on a menial mission I don't want to undertake, I'm not trusted by my superiors, and I may get kicked out of the knighthood when I get back home. It hasn't been the best month." He smiled sadly at her.

"Because of the gate?"

"Because we only got a few pieces of it, yes. And because I lost it in the first place. Also, I failed to find President Chronos and keep him alive… even if he was already dead by the time we got there." Asger spread his arms, looking oddly helpless for such a strong capable fighter, but then he shrugged and waved a hand, as if to dismiss his concerns.

Did that mean he didn't want to talk about them?

"If you don't continue to be a knight, I'm sure the captain would give you a job." Qin smiled, intending it as a joke to lighten his mood, though there was a wistful part of her that wouldn't mind having him here and going on adventures together. She liked fighting with him. He was very dependable and good about watching her back, but he also trusted her to be competent and defend herself.

"Don't take this the wrong way, but that would be quite a demotion."

"It was a promotion for me." Her smile flagged. She didn't feel insulted, but she was sadly reminded about the vastly different worlds they came from.

"Sorry. I'd just feel… I spent years training to become a knight, and I always believed I'd help defend my entire world—system—and do great things. It's disappointing to be relegated to running errands."

"I understand. Is that what Casmir and Kim are doing too? Running errands?"

"No. Casmir is supposed to build an army of crushers, and Kim is supposed to make a bioweapon. For Prince Jorg and the war effort."

Qin digested that. "On Stardust Palace?"

Asger nodded. "And I'm picking up a parcel to take home." Asger shook his head. "I want another chance to prove myself to my father and my superiors, but I'm not sure how I can do that from some sultan's palace on the sidelines."

Qin wanted to step forward and rest a hand on his arm—or even hug him. He always looked so anguished when he spoke of Bjarke. It made her wonder if she'd lost less than she always thought by not having parents. Were all family relationships so fraught?

Asger looked down, and she realized she *had* stepped forward and rested her clawed fingers on his arm. She hadn't meant to, and she blushed as he stared at those claws. They were painted purple with bright yellow starbursts this week, but that didn't make them any less animal.

Not human. Freak. The words she'd heard so often echoed in her mind.

He lifted his gaze, meeting hers, and she wasn't sure what he was thinking, but he didn't move for a long moment. She remembered their kiss and how different it had been from the plundering mouths of the Drucker pirates—the few that had even bothered with kissing. Most of *them* hadn't wanted anything so intimate, simply to sate themselves.

She was sure Asger wouldn't be like that—if he *wanted* to be with her. But did he? And would he find it too embarrassing to admit and act on if he did?

Asger stepped back, and she let go of his arm.

He cleared his throat. "Is it all right to use the same cabin as last time?"

"Yes."

"Good. Thanks."

His pace was quick as he hurried away.

He hadn't openly rejected her or called her a freak, but… it was hard not to feel rejected anyway.

Yas was looking up civilian doctors on Stardust Palace and a few other stations that were near their path, on the off chance that the *Fedallah* might divert and he could convince Jess to see someone. She had seemed to be herself at that dinner the other night, but he remembered her wincing in pain from an intense headache while preparing the submarines back in System Hydra.

Rache walked into sickbay, and unease hollowed Yas's stomach. He'd hoped that being invited to his dinner meant Rache wasn't irked with him, but Yas kept expecting him to bring up the submarine incident. Or maybe he had come to let Yas know he hadn't appreciated his condemnation of assassinations.

Rache leaned his hip against one of the exam tables, his arms folded across his chest.

"I don't suppose you're finally here for your exam?" Yas asked.

"No. And I don't think Lieutenant Tanken or Corporal Meatpaw will be coming in any time soon." Those were the names of the two men Yas had drugged. "They've assured me that they don't trust you and want to know what I'll do to punish you, assuming I don't punt you out an airlock and replace you with another surgeon."

"Surgeons willing to work for no vacation and little pay are hard to come by."

"As I told them. What happened down there? What was Kim trying to accomplish? I assume she was the mastermind and that you didn't get a random urge to take an aquatic tour of the moon."

Yas licked his lips, reluctant to put the blame on Kim, even if it had been her idea. He'd gone along with it. So far, Rache sounded calm rather than dangerous. Yas had a feeling his tone would be different if he'd helped anyone other than Kim.

"She wanted to comm her ship so she could call down medical help for Casmir. She was worried he wouldn't make it."

"And you prepared drugs to knock out two of my men."

"I assumed they weren't interested in helping Casmir." Yas twitched a shoulder. "And I felt I owed her for the help on Skadi Moon and with the pseudo radiation. She didn't have to save us back there on that research ship."

"I understand that, but if one of the Kingdom ships had shown up to drill a hole in the ice after detecting your noise—what did you do, fire torpedoes at the ice?—it could have been disastrous for us. It *was* disastrous for the men we lost inside the base."

Yas lifted his chin. "That had nothing to do with what Kim and I did on that submarine. You chose to invade an astroshaman base. You had to expect casualties."

Rache stared at him through his mask. Yas made himself stare back, hoping he was right to believe that Rache would appreciate his frankness rather than meekness or a plea for forgiveness.

"Next time we go on a dangerous mission," Rache said, "you will *not* betray any of my men or sidestep my orders. Nobody's a paragon here, but we have to know everybody on board has our backs, including our doctor."

"It shouldn't be a problem if you don't kidnap any more people I consider friends."

Rache kept staring at him, not moving from his spot. Yas had meant it as a light comment and hoped it wouldn't get him in trouble. He didn't know if he truly considered Kim a friend yet—or if she would consider him one—but she was at the least an acquaintance in the field that he respected and would help if possible.

"I'll keep that in mind." Rache pushed away from the table and headed for the door.

Yas glanced at the list of doctors he'd been researching. "Is there any chance that we'll be stopping at any stations in this system, Captain?"

Rache paused. "You need supplies?"

"I want to set up an exam for someone if possible, someone I may not be able to help myself."

"Why can't you help this crew member?"

"It's a special case. When's the meeting with the Miners' Union prince? Any chance of a stop before that?" Yas assumed they would have a new contract after that meeting and would head straight to System Lion to help batter the Kingdom's forces.

"We are on track to be early for the meeting," Rache said, "but I was thinking of harassing Prince Jorg's ship along the way. Or utterly destroying it."

"Wouldn't the proper mercenary thing be to wait until someone's paying you to do that?"

"Yes, but some missions are worth taking on simply because the opportunity exists." Rache was looking at the wall rather than Yas, his voice hard, almost zealous.

By all the stars, did he want to kill Jager's son too?

"Like getting that gate?" Yas didn't remind Rache that the deadly mission had been self-appointed with little to gain, but he doubted he had to when Rache had just brought it up.

Rache looked over his shoulder. "You've grown frank of late, Doctor."

"Because you haven't flogged me for previous bouts of frankness."

"Ah, my mistake. Though I've heard it's unwise to flog someone who might one day hold your life in his hands."

"Very much so. You could fire me."

"Don't sound so hopeful when you say that."

"Well, if you want my opinion, you should set your personal grievances aside and only take work that pays—and isn't likely to get many of your men killed."

Yas would certainly prefer to survive his five-year obligation to Rache.

"Mercenaries get killed, Doctor. It's the nature of the business. Unless you're suggesting we take up hauling freight."

"Is that an option?"

"Not if I want to be able to afford the salary of a surgeon. Or crew." Rache resumed his walk to the door, pausing only long enough to add, "Don't knock out any more of my men, Yas. If you foster ill will with more of them, I may have difficulty intervening in time to prevent consequences."

A chill went through Yas. "Consequences?"

"The croaking raven doth bellow for revenge." Rache disappeared into the corridor.

CHAPTER 7

OKU WAS IN THE PROCESS OF PACKING UP the greenhouse, making sure all of her valuable seeds and plant specimens would be stored in one of the vaults under the castle, when the ground shook. An alarm wailed in the city, and Chasca yowled a complaint.

"Don't worry, girl." Oku eyed the dark roof of the greenhouse, struggling to keep her tone calm and soothing. "I'm sure it's nothing."

She remembered the faint shaking of the earth when that temple had been bombed. This had been more vigorous. An earthquake? Or could it be an attack?

The vroom of nearby shuttles taking off filled the air, and Oku's two bodyguards ran into the greenhouse.

"Your Highness," one said, "we must get you to one of the safe rooms."

Oku was reluctant to leave her packing, out of fear that she wouldn't be allowed to return, but the big men would not likely give her a choice. Besides, she was curious to find out what was going on. Outside, twilight had faded into full night, and the city had been quiet until this.

Another alarm started up. Oku recognized the distinct undulating noise even though she'd only heard it a couple of times in her life, both for drills. The air-raid siren.

Chasca sprinted past the bodyguards and out the door, racing between the landscaping lights and out onto the dark lawn. Oku winced, hoping she wouldn't disappear under a hedge somewhere. That noise had to be pounding her sensitive ears.

"Are we being bombed?" she asked, knowing the bodyguards would be on the security comm channel.

"Some stealthed ships slipped past our planetary defenses and are dropping bombs on the city, yes. Our local fighters are scrambling into the air to attack back, and the orbital defenders are descending. There's nothing to worry about, as long as we get you to safety." The bodyguard gripped her arm.

Though she hated being manhandled, she knew they were doing their jobs, and she let them escort her through the courtyard and to the stairs in the back of the castle that led to an underground safe room. Her mother had tried to get her to move to Basilisk Citadel that morning, but she'd wanted to make sure all her experiments were set up so they wouldn't die if she was gone for a week or more. Oku had been certain they would have plenty of time—and advance warning—before something happened. Now she regretted that certainty. She hadn't yet contacted Casmir's parents or asked her father for permission to bring them to the Citadel.

Two ships fired at each other out over the ocean, one barely visible because of fog rolling in. Oku stared, mesmerized by the crimson and orange DEW-Tek bolts they spat at each other, brilliant against the dark cloudy sky. She'd never expected war to come this close.

"Your Highness." Her bodyguard tugged on her arm, and from his exasperated tone, she feared he would toss her over his shoulder.

"I'm coming," Oku promised but didn't move. "Chasca!" She didn't see the dog anywhere. She couldn't leave her to spend the night up here, in danger and cowering in fear. With enemy spacecraft so close, it was inevitable that they would target the castle, this ancient symbol of what all the Kingdom stood for.

"Hurry," the second bodyguard called, holding the door to the castle open. "Bring her!"

"I'm trying."

"I just need to find my dog. She's probably under the hedges over there. I'll—"

Her fear came true, and her bodyguard hoisted her off the ground.

"Damn it, Jordan," she growled, barely resisting the urge to jam her knee into his groin or pound at his shoulders. These were her protectors, and they were doing their job. She knew that. It was only her fear for Chasca that made her resist.

"I'll come back and look for her, Your Highness." Jordan ran for the door.

Oku slumped, no longer fighting, though she strained her neck, hoping to spot her furry gray companion so she could direct Jordan where to look.

A boom sounded, and the ground shook again as he stepped across the threshold and into the well-lit interior.

"I suppose that's one way to make sure she obeys," a familiar voice said from the stairs. Her brother Finn. As he trotted down the steps ahead of the bodyguards, he kept speaking over his shoulder. "But if they'd left you outside, and you'd been bombed, there'd be fewer siblings between me and inheriting the crown."

Oku rolled her eyes. "You'd hate running the Kingdom. You'd actually have to do work. I know how allergic you are to that."

"I'd just have people do the work for me."

"That's not how it goes. With great power comes great amounts of paperwork."

"Oh? Disappointing."

Jordan must have decided that Oku wouldn't fight him further, for he set her down. She let the guards lead her down the stairs—other castle staff were heading the same way, so it would have been a fight to run back up—but she couldn't help glancing back and hoping Chasca would find her way inside and be safe. She also worried for Casmir's parents and hoped the planetary defenders would soon fight back the bombers. She would feel horrible if something happened to them when she could have helped them.

"Your Highness," a woman's deep voice said, and Oku's closest bodyguard of more than twenty years stepped out of the masses. Maddie was six feet tall with the shoulders and thick neck of a wrestler, despite being in her fifties now. "You made it. Good. I checked your rooms, where you should have been at this late hour."

"It's not that late." Oku touched Maddie's arm fondly. "And I'm allowed to stay out past dark these days, you know."

"Nobody should be staying out late now." Maddie's weathered face was glum, but it usually was. Oku could only remember a few times when she'd gotten the stoic woman laughing. "Was Prince Finn bothering you?" Her eyes narrowed.

Oku smiled, remembering the time that eight-year-old Finn had stolen a chart she'd been making for a science presentation, and Maddie had caught him dumping it in a fountain in the courtyard. She had proceeded to dump *him* in the water. Finn, despite being twenty-two with a decent showing of a beard now, still avoided Maddie. Their parents hadn't obeyed his wishes to "punish the wayward servant," not after Oku had shown them her soggy presentation.

"No more than usual."

Her older brother, Jorg, was the real ass. Oku was glad he was stuck in another system, even if that meant there was no chance of a bomb dropping on his head.

"We'll be taking the secret tunnels to the Citadel shortly," came an authoritative voice. It sounded like Senator Andrin, a cousin of the family who worked in the castle. "We hope the bombing will end soon, but King Jager has deemed the castle unsafe. He and Queen Iku are already at the Citadel."

The rumbles of dozens of conversations echoed through the large chamber, servants and staff and senators and knights with offices in the compound. Oku looked toward the stairs she'd come down, a last few people dribbling into the safe room.

It would be harder to slip out once she was in the modern and well-fortified Citadel. If she was going to find Chasca—and Casmir's parents—she needed to do so now. She could *order* her bodyguards to let her go, but she feared she would come up against the limits of her power—any order her father had given in regard to his family would supersede anything she said.

"Maddie." Oku drew her bodyguard into a corner and lowered her voice. "I need to get out of the castle and into the city to collect a couple of friends and bring them with us to the Citadel. I also need to find Chasca. Will you help me slip out?"

Maddie frowned. "Friends from the university?"

"Not this time." Oku thought her research compatriots from the botany and biology departments would be safe on their own, since the university had its own underground safe rooms, and most of them lived on or near campus. "These friends live in the Brodskiburg District."

"You will get me in grave trouble with the king and queen if we don't show up at the Citadel tonight."

"You say this as if it hasn't happened before." Oku smiled. She'd always taken the blame, telling her parents she'd ordered Maddie to assist her with whatever plot had later forced them into a mandatory visit to her father's throne room.

Maddie sighed. "Less often in recent years. I'd thought you'd matured."

"This is important. It's not about getting unadulterated native soil from the forests beyond the city limits or trapping wild pollinating insects to study."

Another sigh. "I will help. What do you want me to do?"

Senator Andrin walked past with another senator that Oku had seen in meetings with her father, but they were deep in conversation and didn't glance her way.

"…can't believe this is happening," Andrin said.

"We should have let him start his war," the other said. "It would have been taking place on someone else's home turf then."

"Maybe. Or our forces would have been spread thin—thinner—when this happened."

The two men tramped up the stairs. Going to look for someone who was missing?

"We'll follow them," Oku whispered, "and pretend we need to help them do… whatever they're doing."

"Very well, Your Highness."

"You needn't look so glum when you trail after me."

"Trust me, it's warranted." But Maddie managed a quick smile.

Oku hugged her, then lifted her chin and strode after the senators, as if she had every right to do so. Finn noticed and frowned but didn't try to stop her. Maybe he still hoped for a bomb to drop on her head. Jordan also noticed, and he took a step in her direction, but he saw Maddie and must have decided she could handle Oku.

Good. Oku pulled up a database from the network so she could look up Casmir's parents' address, frowning at how slow the connection was. Had one of the server centers been hit?

As they climbed, the rumble of thunder and booms of explosives grew audible again, and Oku shivered with fear, with the knowledge that she could get killed out there tonight. She kept going anyway.

Asger knew alcohol wasn't a proper post-workout beverage, but Bonita had left it out after putting it in the chicken meal she'd made for dinner, and after eyeing it from the treadmill for an hour, he'd decided to indulge. And maybe take the edge off the knowledge that he was getting himself deeper into trouble. Again.

He couldn't blame Kim for not wanting to make a weapon capable of killing thousands—if not millions—but why couldn't she have stowed away on someone else's shuttle? What would he do if he was ordered to leave the knighthood?

Occasionally, the thought surfaced that maybe being kicked out would be for the best if he was serving the kinds of people who ordered the development of bioweapons, but it would feel like such a failure. And it would mean giving up everything he'd worked for, and maybe having to walk away from the beauty of Odin forever. The idea made him feel like his throat was closing up and suffocating him.

He remembered Ishii lamenting that this wasn't the best time to be a soldier in service to the king. Asger wondered what it would have been like in the old days, serving under Admiral Mikita. But he had knowledge that Ishii lacked, and it was hard for him to imagine Admiral Mikita without seeing Casmir, smiling up from under the console he'd sabotaged, with dusty cobwebs draping his shaggy bangs.

From the beginning, Asger hadn't had any trouble being Casmir's protector—even before he'd gotten so sick, he'd looked like someone who needed protecting—but following him into war was another story. Whatever he was, he wasn't some great leader.

The hatch opened, and Asger looked back, hoping for Qin. He knew he shouldn't—he'd told himself that their kiss had been a mistake, that he shouldn't lead her on when he couldn't stay here and be a part of her life—but he couldn't help it that his heart wished for her company. He felt bad that he'd pulled away from her touch in the cargo hold. But he was more worried about what would happen if he *didn't* pull away.

Maybe it was for the best that it was Casmir who walked in. He carried a towel and headed straight for the two treadmills pulled out, but he paused when he spotted Asger sitting on the front of one, tequila bottle in hand.

Casmir waved. "I don't think you're putting that to its proper use."

"The treadmill or the tequila?"

"The treadmill. Kim assures me they're designed for self-torture, not sitting on, standing on, or hanging clothes from."

"I'm sure the words she used involved getting in shape. Or possibly growing *cojones*."

Casmir grinned. "Those were *Bonita's* words."

He draped his towel over the bar, stepped on, and grabbed the waist strap. "Sorry to interrupt your drinking session, but I am attempting to regain my health, and I'm told laboring on gym equipment is the way to do it."

"Labor away. I'm just…" What was he doing? Feeling sorry for himself? Yes. Did he want to admit that? No. "Pondering how I'm going to walk up to a man I respect and ask for his pertundo. We're arriving tomorrow."

"Since I've already been accused of being a delinquent this week, I won't feel naughty suggesting that you sneak into his cabin while he's not there and take it."

"I can't do that."

"Oh, is there a security code on his door? I could come along to help if you like."

Asger gave him a dark look, though he knew Casmir was joking. Probably. "You've got a theft of your own to plan. You'll be busy."

"This is true. I've been researching Sultan Shayban, the ruler of Stardust Palace and millions of people who have flocked to his nebulous nation in the last few decades. He controls Stardust Palace Station, three habitats, and has exclusive mining claims on two of the three asteroid belts in this system. Guess who has the other asteroid belt, as well as six belts in other systems? Yes, the nemesis I did not want but seem to have, Prince Dubashi. It seems he's got a lot of nemeses. Did you know that the reason Sultan Shayban was willing to betroth his daughter to Prince Jorg was that he wanted an alliance with the Kingdom, because Dubashi has been encroaching on his mining territory and trying to steal some of his big contracts?"

"I did not."

"I'm hoping I can use that. The enemy of my enemy and all that. I plan to talk to him and try to make a deal rather than stealing anything."

"You *are* going to make crushers for Jorg then?" Asger sipped from the bottle as Casmir started up the treadmill at a brisk walk.

"I'll try to make crushers. It's one of the few things I can do that could potentially help with the war. Obviously they'd have to get close enough to enemy ships to board them in order to be useful, but that'll probably happen. I'm not convinced *Jorg* is the proper commander for them, but I can at least make them, and then… we'll see."

Asger squinted at him. "We'll see?"

"I'm mulling over possibilities. I'm worried about my family back home."

"Me too. Though *my* closest family is here in System Stymphalia."

"The way you said that makes me feel like I should pat you on the shoulder and say comforting words."

Asger snorted. "You'd fall off the treadmill if you tried."

"Yes, but that could happen regardless."

Asger scraped at the corner of the label on the bottle. "You know he's never said he's proud of me?"

As soon as the admission came out, he grimaced and acknowledged that he was soundly on his way to getting drunk.

"Your father?"

"Yeah. He wasn't around much, and we didn't have that many conversations, so I'd remember if something like that had slipped out. But what I remember are a lot of stern lectures about how I wasn't measuring up to expectations."

"That had to be rough on you."

Asger shrugged.

"It's hard to feel like you're enough," Casmir said, "when someone you respect is looming over you telling you that you aren't."

"I'm pretty sure he regards me as a disappointment, if not an outright mistake. Definitely an obligation. If you're noble, you're supposed to have an heir. I wonder if he ever really wanted a kid." Asger decided he might regret all of this honesty later and attempted to shift the focus. "You ever have any problems with your father, Casmir?"

"No. When I was growing up, he was—both of my parents were—always very supportive and accepting. My problems were generally at school with my peers, whom my parents couldn't protect me from. I got teased and pushed around and made to feel inferior, mostly by large angry kids who probably felt they weren't living up to their fathers' expectations."

Asger snorted. "The circle of life."

"The circle of feeling ashamed and belittled and worthless. It's something we should work on collectively as human beings. Maybe then, we wouldn't all be driven to prove ourselves by beating on our chests and starting wars."

"I'm buzzed enough that I'm not going to feel awkward because we're talking about this."

"Ah. I'll pretend I *do* feel awkward, since manly men don't talk about feelings, right? And I'm manly, not damselly, despite what Rache says."

"You're… special." Asger wondered how much Casmir remembered of being carried through that compound by his crusher. Even if Asger had been sick, he doubted his ego would have allowed him to be placed in a position that connoted such weakness. Why it mattered, he wasn't sure. Casmir was the only reason any of them had made it out of there. Maybe it was unfair of Asger to say that he wasn't a leader. He just wasn't the kind of leader that Asger was accustomed to—or that the Kingdom would recognize.

"*Evolved*, a woman once told me."

"Was it your mother?"

"My grandmother, actually. She's wise, witty, and makes the best *sufganiyot*. You should always listen to her."

Asger took another drink. "You shouldn't admit to others that your best compliments from the fairer sex came from your grandmother. We'll pretend this conversation didn't happen."

Casmir cocked his head as he plodded along. "Do you need for it not to have happened?"

"Maybe. Knights don't talk about—" Asger waved vaguely, as if his thoughts and emotions floated in the air around them, "—insecurities. We're strong. We're bricks. Bricks aren't vulnerable."

"Unless you drop them from a moderate height, and then they shatter all over the place."

Casmir said it lightly, jokingly, but Asger stared glumly at the deck. Lately, he had sometimes felt like he was on the verge of shattering.

"I'm sure you'll be fine," Casmir said apologetically.

"I'll figure it out. I'm just tired of being on the wrong side of what my superiors want. I'm *trying* to do the right thing, but it never turns out right in their eyes, even when it *feels* like we had a victory. I can't catch a break. I feel more like a felon than a noble."

"I'm sorry. I'm not helping that. It's your bad luck that you keep getting stuck with me."

Asger shook his head. Maybe it *was* bad luck, but he didn't believe that Casmir was truly a delinquent. Jorg, Romano, and maybe even Jager were the problem. They were asking for things that went against Asger's upbringing, against the morality that had been drilled into him as a boy and a squire and finally as a knight.

"I'm beginning to think *they're* wrong, Casmir. Not us. But I don't know how that helps me."

"You've read the great philosophers. Sometimes, governments need to change. We act like they're these monolithic immutable things, but in the end, they're just people, and people are fallible."

"You're talking about rebellion. I can't be a part of something like that." Asger shied away from the idea. "I swore my loyalty to the Kingdom. I gave an oath."

"Oaths should be given to people, not governments, not systems. And don't you think you should get to *know* the people before swearing fidelity?"

"Even if I wanted to, it's too late to take it back. Oaths are forever."

"Well, *I* never swore an oath. I hope you'll forgive me if I fail to follow orders to the letter to make robots to kill people. And I hope you'll forgive Kim if she refuses to make some horrible bacteria to kill people on an even grander scale. I can't blindly follow rulers who order such things. I'm only sad that it's taken this upheaval in my life for me to look beyond my simple existence to realize people like that were in charge of us all."

"You're making me nervous." Asger eyed Casmir, sweat already starting to bead on his forehead. "You're not going to turn into an anarchist, are you?"

"Rache already has that job. I do think I need to be an agent for change."

"What are you going to do?"

If anyone else had been talking this way, Asger wouldn't have thought much of it, but Casmir had already proven he had a knack for making things happen on a large scale. Asger wasn't sure whether to admire that or be afraid of it.

“I don’t know yet, but don’t you think we should live in a nation where people aren’t trying to kill other people, and where good and honorable men and women are rewarded instead of punished?”

“I think… if I agree with you, I’m going to lose a lot more than my pertundo.”

Casmir lifted a shoulder. “Maybe you’ll get something greater in return.”

More likely, he would get killed.

Disturbed by the conversation and wanting to end it, Asger rose and turned on a wall display. Maybe they should check the local news before they arrived at Stardust Palace.

He found a report, an android anchor showing footage and reading news, but it wasn’t for Stardust Palace or even System Stymphalia. Asger recognized the skyline of Zamek City. Spaceships he *didn’t* recognize—they were definitely not Kingdom models—were flying down from the clouds and dropping bombs.

Dread and helplessness filled his heavy limbs, and he heard Casmir stopping his treadmill.

“I thought we’d have more time,” Asger whispered.

Casmir stared at the display, equal parts fear and determination on his face. “Now more than ever, we have to do something that can make a difference.”

“We will.” Maybe it was the tequila talking, but Asger needed to believe that.

CHAPTER 8

STARDUST PALACE STATION WAS INSIDE AN ASTEROID, MAKING it look, at least from the outside, undeserving of such a lofty name. Casmir hoped there were a few spires, towers, and turrets on the inside. Even drab gray Drachen Castle back home had impressive towers and turrets. Though he supposed such things were impractical in space, where the omnipresent threat of radiation was more likely to kill the residents than a roving horde of bandits or an army with siege equipment.

"I've been here before," Bonita said from the pilot's pod where she was guiding the *Dragon* into one of the large entrance tunnels toward what was probably a large cylindrical can spinning inside, providing gravity for its residents. "There were bowls of mints in the spacers' lounge."

"Thus meriting a rave review?" Casmir sat in the co-pilot's seat since Qin wasn't around, his stomach surprisingly calm as they swerved left and right, up and down, to navigate a tunnel that must have been designed with defense in mind. They passed more than one missile platform along the way. Almost as good as an old-fashioned turret with arrow slits.

"When you've been the places I've been, little luxuries like that make an impression."

Casmir braced himself as Bonita took a turn like a teenage boy racing an air bike. The grin that stole across her face promised she still knew how to enjoy herself at the helm. But as they flew into a straight portion of the tunnel, she must have remembered Casmir's tendencies, for she squinted over at him.

"You're not going to throw up, are you?"

"I don't think so." He glanced back, noticing Kim using the various holds and jambs to pull herself into navigation. "My stomach has been surprisingly calm since I recovered from the Plague. Maybe I wore it out with the countless times I emptied its contents on Xolas Moon. Much to the chagrin of my companions."

"The immune booster might have some lingering effects," Kim suggested.

"Oh?"

"If memory serves, one of its actions is to help your liver, kidneys, and lymphatic system in detoxifying, metabolizing, and clearing endogenous and exogenous substances from the body. Histamine—we've discussed its role in motion sickness before—should be included."

"Are you saying I'm less likely to vomit *and* to sneeze at grass and pollen?"

"I'm not sure how long it will last, but yes."

"I hope this palace has a park. I want to walk shirtless through a flower garden and rub pollen all over myself."

Bonita gave him a weird look.

"Because I usually can't do that," Casmir explained. "Sniffles and hives."

"You made me wonder if you and Qin share a common ancestor," Bonita said.

"Because she likes to go shirtless in gardens?"

"She likes *gardens*. And grass and nature and climbing trees. I'm not sure how much of her clothing she removes during the experience."

The comm beeped, saving Casmir from speculating on cats in his ancestry. "Is that the station? Should we hide under the console?"

Kim arched her eyebrows.

Bonita frowned at the comm panel. "Actually, it's the *Osprey*."

"Ugh," Casmir said. "We should definitely hide under the console."

"Just lean out of the video pickup." Bonita waved for Kim to scoot to the side, then reached for the comm. "It may be Bjarke again. Though it may not, I suppose. Are you here if they ask?"

"Asger and I are here, due to comm troubles and a failure in the environmental system of the shuttle we were riding in. It was kind of you to rescue us."

"You want me to lie to your captain?" Bonita's concern seemed feigned.

Casmir doubted she had his difficulties with deceit, especially to some communications officer she didn't know, but he felt compelled to set her mind at ease. "They're not lies. The shuttle truly has those problems."

"*Now*," Kim murmured, squeezing behind Casmir's pod.

Bonita answered the comm. "This is Captain Lopez."

"Captain Lopez, this is Captain Ishii. If Sir Asger is aboard your ship, I need to speak with him at once."

Bonita surprised Casmir by not adding a *please* to what seemed like an unfinished sentence from Ishii—Kim would have. Bonita only smiled at Ishii's face on the display as she tapped the ship's internal comm. "Asger, a jilted lover you left behind needs you."

"A jilted shuttle owner, maybe," Ishii grumbled, only mildly apoplectic at Bonita's irreverence.

Asger stepped into navigation, the addition of a fourth large person making it claustrophobic. Kim eyed the space under the console, maybe wishing she'd chosen that spot.

"Asger here, Captain."

"Care to explain why the expensive shuttle I lent you just docked in my bay without anyone in it?" Ishii asked.

"We thought it might be easier to gain access to Stardust Palace in a civilian vessel. It seems Prince Jorg irritated the sultan, and Kingdom subjects are not welcome there."

Ishii's brow wrinkled in confusion. Had nobody reported the local news to him? "That doesn't mean you get to ditch my shuttle and send it back empty through mercenary-infested waters. If some thug with a railgun had taken pot shots at it, I would have made sure the Fleet billed *you*."

"My apologies, Captain, but it developed some malfunctions, and we weren't able to comm you for permission." Asger didn't look at Casmir, but his jaw tightened, and Casmir guessed he was annoyed at having to bend the truth.

"Sorry," Casmir whispered to him, wishing he'd taken the comm, even if Ishii had specifically requested Asger.

"Yes, my mechanics saw the malfunctions," Ishii said. "It looks like someone let a *rat* loose under the console."

"A *rat*?" Casmir mouthed in indignation. He'd been careful to make all of the malfunctions appear to be plausible signs of wear and tear. Admittedly, he'd replaced a shiny new cable with a frayed one, but there hadn't been teeth marks in it.

"Perhaps you should have all of your shuttles fumigated before they see further use. We'll continue the mission as planned. Asger out." He reached for the comm, but Ishii snapped at him to wait.

"You don't get to hang up on me, Asger. I want to talk to Scholar Sato."

Asger hesitated, glancing at Casmir and Kim for the first time.

"I *know* she's there," Ishii said. "And Romano has figured it out too."

Kim closed her eyes. Casmir wanted to give her a hug. He was used to being in trouble by now, but Kim had been the perfect student all through school and the perfect law-abiding Kingdom subject back home. She wouldn't even consider littering—he'd seen her run a block to pick up an escaped wrapper caught in the wind. And now, she was defying Prince Jorg.

"I'm here," Kim said.

Asger stepped out into the corridor to make room for her in front of the camera. He bumped into Zee, who'd also come up to navigation at some point. If anyone else came up here, the ship might tip over.

"Prince Jorg's people commed," Ishii said, "to ask if you need any special equipment or accommodations. What do you want me to tell them? Are you going to work on his bioweapon on Stardust Palace?"

Kim stared at the display just above Ishii's head. Casmir couldn't tell if she was contemplating her answer or didn't intend to answer. Her face was always hard to read, and it was as opaque as Rache's mask now.

"If I can honestly tell him that," Ishii said, "*I* might not be in shit too deep to swim in over misplacing you."

Kim blew out a slow breath. "I've contacted a Scholar Sunflyer there who runs a laboratory full of sophisticated research computers and equipment. It's… similar to what I have at work and definitely better than anything on a military vessel."

Similar to? Casmir asked her via his chip.

She's a mycologist. It's a mushroom lab.

Casmir tried to imagine weaponized mushrooms, which resulted in his mind's eye visualizing a rocket exploding in the atmosphere over a planet and spewing out shiitakes.

"I'll work on… something there," Kim finished aloud.

Ishii rolled his eyes. "Wonderful. Is Dabrowski still going to build crushers, or is he also choosing to screw up his future? *Further*."

Casmir leaned into view—there was little point in pretending he wasn't present. "If I can figure out how to get permission and the materials to do so, I will definitely work on crushers. Even if I can't get permission, I'm sure I can find a way to build at least one."

After all, he'd built Zee during a long night-shift on Forseti Station.

"*One?* Jorg wants an army."

"I understand that, but building an army would require lengthy access to a dedicated manufacturing facility and millions of crowns' worth of resources. Not to mention weeks if not months to complete."

"Casmir, if the prince says to make an army, you make an army. Not excuses."

"I am a veritable army of one," Zee said from the hatchway.

Ishii squinted over Casmir's shoulder at him. "Does your crusher have more personality than it used to?"

"Zee has the ability to learn from those around him."

"Casmir assures me it's a feature, not a bug," Kim said.

Ishii didn't look amused. "Look, you two. You're not in my chain of command, and I'm not going to order you not to fuck up, but this may be your last chance to make up for past transgressions and improve your standing in the king's eyes. If we can come sailing back into System Lion as heroes, with powerful weapons to deploy to drive out the invaders, I'm sure much will be forgiven. *Casmir.*"

"Why'd you say my name specifically?"

"You puked in the combat armor I lent you after promising you wouldn't."

"I had the Great Plague."

"And you have a lot more that needs forgiving than Scholar Sato." Ishii cut the channel.

"Up until I made this choice, what had I done that needs forgiveness?" Kim asked.

"You talk to Rache and spend time in enclosed places with him," Casmir said.

Bonita raised her eyebrows, but she'd remained silent for the comm call and seemed inclined to stay that way.

"You're the one who gave him underwear," Kim said.

"It was more of a re-gifting than a giving." Casmir smiled, but it didn't last. "Do you think Royal Intelligence knows about that gift? And dinner?"

"They probably know about everything."

"I'm screwed."

"Are you really going to build crushers for Jorg?"

"I'm still waiting for the invoice to catch up with me for the materials I used on Forseti Station to build Zee."

Kim didn't smile.

Casmir sighed. "As I was telling Asger last night, there's no way I can sneak into the manufacturing facility here and make use of it for months without permission. I'm going to have to get an audience with the sultan."

"The ruler of the station and owner of legions of mining ships and entire asteroid belts?" Bonita asked. "You think he'll take a meeting with you?"

"Why wouldn't he? I'm delightful."

"As am I," Zee said.

"I wonder *where* Zee is getting his personality," Bonita said.

"It's a mystery," Kim grumbled.

It was the most colorful shuttle bay Casmir had ever seen. Technically, it was a bay for entire ships, since there were yachts and freighters even larger than the *Dragon* docked inside under warm yellow lighting that shone on artistically arranged silks draped on the walls and wrapping columns and arches. Cheerful glowing orbs in pale greens, blues, and purples floated above the ships, and illusionary coconut palms and tamarind trees rose up in the rear of the cavernous bay. Or maybe they were real. They appeared to be protected behind a Glasnax wall. Maybe Casmir would get that chance to rub pollen on himself here.

Robot loaders rolled up as soon as Bonita opened her cargo hatch.

"Do you want help doing… whatever it is you're doing?" Qin asked as Casmir, Kim, and Asger prepared to slip out of the hold.

"No," Kim said.

Casmir shook his head. "You'll be better off if you pretend you don't know us Kingdom types."

"That's a given." Bonita leaned against the hatchway behind them. "Comm soon if you're going to need a ride out of here. We're not staying to see the sights."

"Are you sure?" Casmir pointed to the palms, their leaves being rustled by some breeze blowing from who knew where. "They have trees. And you mentioned those mints."

"We're only staying long enough to line up the next cargo. Unless there's an appealing bounty to hunt down."

"Probably just mine." Casmir grimaced. "I'd forgotten I'll have to worry about that."

"I am here to protect you, Casmir Dabrowski." Zee strode out onto the ramp.

One of the robot loaders had been rolling up, but it stopped when he stepped in its way. "Move aside, traveler," a computerized voice said from its speaker box. The robot didn't have a head or anything close.

Zee gave it a baleful look.

"Thank you, Zee," Casmir said. "And thank you for the ride, Laser. If you get a cargo, we'd appreciate it if you let us know where you're going next." He looked at Kim. "Just in case things don't work out here."

Kim's expression was bleak.

Asger had already descended the ramp and was eyeing their surroundings. Before Casmir, Kim, and Zee caught up with him, he strode toward an exit with an interactive directory next to it. Casmir had already downloaded the publicly available map of Stardust Palace, which showed a public half of the station, and a private half reserved for the royal family and its staff and friends. But he hurried after Asger, also wanting a look, specifically at the levels containing the manufacturing facilities.

Numerous robots and androids passed in and out of the bay, loading and unloading cargo, but there were few people in the area now. Bonita had pre-paid her docking fee, and nobody had come out to search or inspect her ship. Casmir had worried about being caught and questioned, so he was relieved it hadn't come to pass.

Asger touched a box deep within the blued-out section of the directory labeled *private*. "That's Princess Nalini's suite."

"Are you sure you don't want help getting in?" Casmir patted his tool satchel. "Or maybe we could use one of the doors those robots are taking freight through and sneak around. Ah, wait. Never mind." He touched his chip where he'd downloaded the map. "This is the only corridor that leads toward the palace half of the station without going up and through numerous secured areas."

Even though he had his own mission, Casmir felt compelled to go along and assist Asger if he wished, if only to keep him from using his pertundo to hew down doors that a little electronic hacking could open. Currently, that pertundo was crammed into a large rucksack on his back, along with, Casmir guessed from the bag's lumpy bulk, his telltale liquid armor and purple cloak. Clad in brown trousers, a beige tunic, and a long brown duster he might have found in a guest closet in the *Dragon*, Asger was trying to go incognito.

"We better split up." Asger looked at Kim and Casmir, both of whom wore nondescript galaxy suits. Casmir didn't think anything about them would stand out… until they spoke and revealed their Kingdom accents. It was also possible someone would recognize Zee as looking like one of the Kingdom crushers that had been in the news a couple of months earlier. "Then if one of us gets caught, it won't impinge on the others' missions."

Asger waved at a sensor next to the directory, but the door didn't open. Ah, maybe there *would* be an inspection, after all, before anyone was allowed to leave the bay.

I have a thought, Kim, Casmir messaged her chip as he slipped his hand into his tool satchel and eyed the door's control panel.

I'm afraid to ask.

Don't worry. I'll tell you. Friends share.

Wonderful.

First, have you confirmed if Rache is in the system?

I haven't sent him a message since we arrived.

Ah. You should.

Kim squinted warily at him. *Why?*

It occurred to me that you couldn't be expected to build a bioweapon if you were locked up in a criminal's brig.

What?

Why don't you see if he'd be willing to come kidnap you from that mycology lab? The lab where you'll obediently be starting to work on Jorg's weapon. But alas, the nefarious Tenebris Rache, having heard of your project, might want the weapon for himself and kidnap you. Again.

You're a loon.

Why? He's proven that he likes *kidnapping you. Nobody should doubt that he would do it again. And it could save you from having to choose between doing something loathsome that you'll regret and openly defying Prince Jorg. Oh!* Casmir had pulled out his lock-picking device and was about to apply it to the door's control panel, but he paused to share the gleam in his eyes with Kim. *And while you're his prisoner, and taking a break from discussing literature, maybe you can talk him into helping the Kingdom drive off the invaders instead of helping the invaders put everyone we love in danger.*

Your mind must be an interesting place to spend time.

If that's your way of saying my plan is brilliant, I concur.

"Take your time, Casmir," Asger muttered, shifting from foot to foot.

"Sorry, I was distracted by an idea."

"You decoded the entire wormhole gate security system in less time than this."

"I stand properly chastised." Casmir pressed the magnetic fob on his lock picker to the control panel as he poked around on the station's wireless networks.

Before his device thwarted the lock, a different door opened farther down the wall. Whirs and clinks sounded as two Excelsus defender robots on treads rolled out, with an android in a purple and blue uniform with silver piping walking between them.

Casmir cursed, stuffed his picking device back in his satchel, and held his hands wide. Innocently wide.

All three mechanical beings walked toward his group. That android wore the most colorful security uniform Casmir had ever seen, but he had no doubt that was what it was. A stunner and a pistol hung from the android's belt.

"I'm going to try not to be caught," Asger said, giving Casmir and Kim quick pats on the back.

Instead of yanking out his pertundo to hack down the locked door, he sprinted off across the bay. The android shifted from walking to running and veered after him. Even without his strength-enhancing armor, Asger was a natural athlete. He half-sprang and half-climbed twenty feet up the side of a shuttle, ran across it, leaped to another ship, and disappeared from sight. Instead of duplicating the maneuvers, the android ran around the parked spacecraft, trying to head him off.

Meanwhile, the two blocky robots continued toward Casmir and Kim, shock cannons and projectile weapons built into their frames.

Casmir raised his hands.

"Should *we* try not to be caught?" Kim asked.

"Just because I'm puking less these days doesn't mean I can replicate Asger's athleticism." Casmir eyed the approaching defenders and the cannons pointed toward him.

Zee shifted to block Casmir and Kim from the robots. "Shall I destroy them?"

"No," Casmir said. "We're peaceful civilians coming to visit the station. It'll be hard to make friends if we obliterate the security robots. But, uh, *do* keep them from shooting us, please."

Kim glanced in the direction Asger had gone, as if she was still contemplating running. *She* could probably replicate Asger's route. The door that had denied their exit earlier unlocked itself, and a man and a woman in security uniforms stepped out with stunners.

Zee shifted to watch them while he continued to block Casmir and Kim from the robots.

The woman eyed Casmir coolly. "I'm the new assistant chief of security, Gokhale. Kingdom subjects aren't welcome at Stardust Palace at this time."

"Thank goodness," Casmir said. "We're fleeing a bunch of Kingdom subjects. Humorless sorts. You know the type. We're seeking refuge here, and we have some intelligence that may be useful to the sultan. We'll happily trade it if you make sure that knight doesn't drag us back to his fleet." Casmir waved in the direction Asger had gone.

He could feel Kim's gaze on the back of his head. Maybe he should have run his story by her before spouting it out.

Assistant Chief Gokhale exchanged a long look with her comrade before turning a skeptical expression back on Casmir. "You're fleeing the knight that we observed you chatting amiably with and offering to help?"

She pointed at the wall above the door. Casmir couldn't see the security camera, but he trusted it was there.

"I'm an amiable fellow," Casmir said, "and a teacher. I'm willing to help many people, even my captors. How hard is it to get an appointment with the sultan? Is there a form you can fill out? Do you know if he has any interest in robotics? I'm a professor in the field. Do you want to look me up? I would also be happy to do some consulting while I'm here. Does he have any automated mining equipment that could use a tune-up? I'm very versatile."

"Very hard," the man said.

"Pardon?" Casmir asked.

"It's very hard to get an appointment with the sultan from within one of our jail cells."

"In that case, perhaps I could comm from a library or coffee shop?"

The man stepped forward, flex-cuffs in hand, but Zee shifted to block him.

"You may not touch Casmir Dabrowski," Zee announced.

"Professor," the assistant chief said. "If that's truly what you are, I suggest you have your bodyguard step aside, and come with us without a fight. If your story checks out, maybe we'll let you leave. Soon."

"Ah, but I'm not looking to leave soon. Would you tell the sultan that a refugee from the Kingdom is here and wants to talk to him? I've traveled widely of late, and I have quite a lot of intelligence that he may find useful." Casmir didn't know if he could truly tell the sultan anything that he didn't already know, but he would do his best to scrape up useful information if he got the chance. He smiled his most charming smile at Gokhale. "I'd really appreciate you letting him know. And *he* might appreciate it if he finds my intel useful. Surely, you want to make the sultan appreciative. Maybe he'll promote you from assistant chief to *chief*."

"That job is taken. Come with us." Gokhale reached for Casmir's arm, noticed Zee shifting menacingly toward her, and let her fingers stray toward her pistol.

Casmir had no doubt that Zee could disarm both of them before they could fire, and then deal with the Excelsus defenders for dessert, but he also knew that could get him punted out the nearest airlock—if not shot by some backup security system built into the bay.

"We'll come peacefully." Casmir patted Zee on the back. "We're not here to cause you trouble."

"Somehow I doubt that," Gokhale muttered.

She waved for her comrade to lead the way and for Casmir, Kim, and Zee to follow, with her and the security robots trailing after them.

What intelligence do you have to share? Kim asked chip-to-chip.

I have so much *intelligence, Kim. My memory is amazing, my brain a sponge for all I encounter.*

So, you've got nothing?

Not... nothing. I know secrets to network games, everything about the robotics industry, and I even know who's behind the pen name of Sir Remington the Third, the famous creator of the Royal Riders series of comic books.

I should have just stayed and built the bioweapon.

You don't mean that.

Kim sighed. *No.*

I'll get us out of this. Trust me.

Casmir hoped he was telling the truth. After seeing the news from back home, a new urgency filled him, a need to get back to Odin and make sure his family was all right. The last thing he wanted was to spend the next year moldering in a jail cell.

CHAPTER 9

"CASMIR AND KIM HAVE BEEN ARRESTED," VIGGO SAID, his voice coming from the speakers in the cargo hold.

Bonita frowned and lowered the tablet she'd been using to search for her next freight job. "*Already?*"

Qin, who'd been helping the cargo robots load and remove the crates and barrels secured in the hold, paused. "What happened? Did Asger get arrested too?"

"Asger ran away from an android, leaped over two ships, and disappeared from my camera range," Viggo said. "I do not know if he was ultimately captured."

Bonita wasn't surprised when Qin turned to her and said, "I should help him."

"You should stay right here," Bonita said. "I may need you soon. If those three were arrested, someone will probably figure out which ship they came in with, and we could get a passel of security officers visiting *us*."

Qin's fingers clenched and she looked toward the open hatch, but she didn't move toward it.

"At least wait until after the cargo has been fully unloaded and we've received the last quarter of our payment," Bonita added. "I'm sure Asger can handle himself."

"It is likely Casmir and Kim are already in a cell," Viggo said. "Lamentable. Perhaps I could use my cadre of robot vacuums to stage a rescue."

Bonita thought people would pay money to witness such a thing, but she felt compelled to quash the idea. "What would you do if they were all blown up, and dust started collecting everywhere and coated all your wires and sensitive parts?"

Viggo paused in what might have been mute horror. “My human crew would have to clean,” he said finally. “A distressing notion, considering you don’t even make your bed, Bonita.”

“I make it before I go to sleep.”

“Which is odd. You’re supposed to make it when you get up in the morning, so that your cabin is properly tidy throughout the day.”

“You must have been a riot of fun to fly with when you were human.”

Bonita walked to the cargo hatch, navigating around the robot loaders—the conversation hadn’t caused their work to falter—and gazed into the large bay. She hoped to spot their contact coming to sign off and transfer the last of the payment—she wouldn’t let the robots off-load everything until that happened. Unfortunately, she spotted a female android in a security uniform heading their way.

“Is that the one that chased Asger?” she asked quietly.

“No,” Viggo said. “A male android chased him.”

Bonita braced herself to deal with questions. Maybe when Casmir had originally messaged her, she should have pretended that her chip was on the fritz.

“Captain Lopez?” the android asked, walking up the ramp.

Qin came to stand behind Bonita. She wasn’t wearing her combat armor, but she would still be a formidable foe, even for an android. But if a fight broke out, and Bonita had to try to take off without permission… nothing good would come of that.

“That’s me.”

“Three Kingdom subjects arrived with your freighter. At this time, Kingdom subjects are not permitted on Stardust Palace.”

Bonita shrugged. “They were stowaways who didn’t pay for their passage. I didn’t even know about them until a couple of days ago. If you catch up with them, tell them they owe me four hundred Union dollars, would you?”

Qin frowned.

Maybe it wasn’t a good idea to paint Casmir, Kim, and Asger as criminals, but it sounded like station security had already decided that everyone from the Kingdom fell into that camp.

“My security chief has deemed that you are a possible threat,” the android said.

“Yes, seventy-year-old women are terrifying. Maybe your chief heard about my knee surgery and that I can walk without limping now. Unhampered locomotion does make me formidable.”

"You will not be permitted to enter the rest of the station. If you need to purchase supplies, you may do so online and have them delivered. As soon as you've restocked your ship, you will leave."

Bonita grunted, amused that they were letting her shop instead of punting her out immediately, but this station *was* run by a successful capitalist. Such a man wouldn't turn away potential sales.

"I need time to see if I can find another cargo," Bonita said.

"As an ally of the Kingdom, you are not welcome on this station. You must leave within three days."

"I'm not an ally of the Kingdom. I told you. Those were stowaways."

"Captain, I am programmed to detect sarcasm and deceit in humans. You have three days before you will be forced to leave the station." The android walked away.

"I wonder if she's programmed to dodge bullets," Bonita muttered.

"I could get my Brockinger," Qin offered.

"Bonita," Viggo said, "you have a comm call."

"Oh, wonderful. What fresh joy is the universe bringing me?"

"I would answer, but I'm not certain how to interpret your relationship with Sir Bjarke at this time."

"Yeah, neither am I."

Bonita climbed up to navigation, leaving Qin to watch the robots and hold back the last chunk of the cargo until the payment came through. She found Bjarke's face waiting for her on the display and slid into her pod.

"Good morning, Laser," he said, "I've transferred to Prince Jorg's ship the *Chivalrous*."

"Thanks for the update. Are you going to read from your diary and tell me about your breakfast menu too?"

He smirked. "I fear you'd find my diary too scandalous for your wholesome ears."

"Wholesome, right. That's me. What do you want today?"

"It seems that Scholar Kim Sato was supposed to transfer over to the prince's ship with me. Imagine my surprise when Captain Ishii told me she was no longer aboard the *Osprey*."

"Weird. But it's not really your problem, is it?"

"Actually, it's been made my problem."

Bonita kept her face neutral, but she had a feeling it was about to become her problem too. She should have known better than to take those three aboard. Friendship was a burden, at times. Why had she let herself start considering them friends?

"Huh," was all she said aloud.

"A camera caught Scholar Sato in the shuttle bay with Professor Dabrowski, climbing into William's shuttle." All trace of humor vanished from Bjarke's eyes, and he paused to let his jaw clench and a muscle in the side of his cheek twitch.

What was between father and son that they couldn't get along with each other? Shouldn't Bjarke be comming *Asger* about this?

"I understand the shuttle had some convenient malfunctions, and they needed to transfer to your ship," Bjarke continued.

"So?" Since Ishii had already spoken to Kim, Casmir, and Asger, there was no point in lying.

"Are they on the station now?"

"Being arrested, last I heard."

Bjarke blinked. Whatever answer he'd expected, that must not have been it.

"Haven't you people been watching the news?" Bonita asked. "Prince Jorg created a fluff, and Sultan Shayban forbade people from the Kingdom to come to his station. *Any* people from the Kingdom."

"I'm sure the prince was only trying to recruit people to help with the fleet he's raising to take back home."

"That's not what it sounded like. Not that I care, but maybe you should read up on him before leaping to follow his orders."

"It is my duty to follow the orders of the crown."

"I suppose if you can obey pirates, you can obey anyone."

A grimace flashed across his face, making her wonder what he'd done in his year undercover, but he masked the expression quickly. "I've been instructed to recover Scholar Sato, bring her to the prince, and give her the opportunity to do as she was originally asked. As a Kingdom subject, she, too, is bound to obey the crown."

"Lucky her. Is there a reason you're telling me about all this? They're off my ship, and I didn't know when I took them aboard that they were fleeing the Kingdom instead of on an errand for it. I guess they're smarter than I thought."

Bjarke's jaw tightened again. Maybe she shouldn't be goading him. He didn't seem to mind personal teasing, maybe deeming it as flirting, but digs at his royal employers appeared to be less welcome.

"I commed you to see if they were still aboard and if you'd be willing to recover Sato for me and deliver her to the prince's ship."

"They're not, and I wouldn't."

"I'm authorized to pay a reasonable rate. You *are* a trained bounty hunter, I understand."

Now, Bonita was the one to clench her jaw. As if she would betray friends or even acquaintances that were trusting her. Yes, she'd turned Casmir and Kim over to Rache shortly after they met, but she'd barely known them then. This was different, and she didn't bother hiding her glare. Maybe Bjarke didn't know that she considered Kim a friend, but even so, this was insulting.

"If you want them," she said coolly, "you'll have to come here to get them."

"I see."

Should she warn Kim that he might come? Or try to delay him? She didn't know how far away the *Chivalrous* was—the more she learned of Jorg, the more ridiculous she found that name—but maybe only a couple of days, going by the length of the lags in their conversation.

At the least, Bonita shouldn't make it obvious that she would impede Bjarke—or make an enemy out of him. She lightened her tone and said, "Maybe I'll let you squeeze my butt again if you stop by."

She cut the comm before he could answer and nibbled on her knuckle. Then she hit the internal comm. "Qin? Maybe you should go help Asger, after all. And see if you can get Casmir and Kim out of jail. The Kingdom is coming looking for them."

Kim considered Casmir's crazy plan as the security officers led them through the corridors of the station, up a lift, and to a detention center. Unlike the public areas, the walls inside lacked colorful silks and banners. However, a single potted palm tree in a corner continued the theme of copious foliage.

She thought someone might question them—the assistant chief had implied they might be allowed to leave if their stories checked out—but apparently that would be later. Gokhale and the male officer marched them into a room full of computer consoles and displays showing feeds from cameras all over the station. They removed their galaxy suits, Casmir's tool satchel, and Kim's stunner, then marched them down a corridor of cells.

A few grimy criminals lurked behind the bars they passed, their faces and knuckles bruised. One man leered at Kim, making her wish she'd worn more than underwear and a sleeveless shirt underneath her galaxy suit, but the temperature-modulating SmartWeave fabric was meant to be worn against the skin.

One woman with as many bruises as the men leered at Casmir. At least this system had equality of a sort.

The officers tapped a key fob, and bars went up, inviting them into a cell. Zee planted himself outside of it.

"It would be against my programming to allow you to be incarcerated, Casmir Dabrowski."

"What if you're incarcerated with me and can continue to protect me?" Casmir asked.

"You must let me remove the weapons from these humans so that we can escape."

"We don't want to escape. We want to talk to the sultan." Casmir stepped into the cell and waved for Zee to come inside.

Kim stepped into the cell, trusting that Zee could break them out if need be. The bars were sturdy, but Zee was sturdier.

"That is unlikely to be done from within a jail cell." Zee lifted his large head. "Unless you allow me to find this sultan and bring him here. I am certain I can accomplish this, and it would speed along your mission." Zee nodded firmly. "Yes. I like this plan."

"He schemes as much as you do," Kim muttered to Casmir.

"Have you arranged your kidnapping yet?" he muttered back.

"No. I'm debating if it's ludicrous or clever."

"I'm stung that my cleverness wasn't immediately apparent."

The security officers were fingering their weapons, shifting their weight, and exchanging frowns with each other. Kim and Casmir had stepped into the cell, so they couldn't shoot *them*, but Zee hadn't budged.

"What do we do with this thing?" the male officer whispered.

"Shoot it?"

"It looks like it's made out of solid metal."

"Metal melts."

Zee turned his head toward them. "My melting point is over four thousand degrees Celsius."

The male officer looked dubiously down at his pistol.

"If you have a sun nearby that you can throw him in, that might be effective." Casmir smiled. "But listen. We don't want trouble. I already told you. All I seek is a meeting with Sultan Shayban. I'm positive I can help him with his concerns about the Kingdom and maybe even his foe Prince Dubashi."

For the first time, the officers reacted to Casmir's babbling, sharing sharp glances with each other at the prince's name.

"If I can get Zee here to join us in our cell, will you promise to send a message to the sultan, letting him know a visiting professor wants to talk to him and has much to offer?"

"We don't make deals with prisoners," Gokhale snapped. "Mehta, get that thing in there."

"Er." The male officer eyed Zee, who managed to convey excellent balefulness, given that his facial features were amorphous at best. He tried firing his stunner at Zee. It did nothing. Gokhale lifted her gaze toward the ceiling. The male officer considered his pistol again but must have decided it would be unwise to fire a bolt that might bounce off in a confined space. Finally, he stepped forward and tried to push Zee into the cell.

Zee did not budge, other than to give Casmir a do-I-really-have-to-put-up-with-this look.

Kim was half-tempted to suggest they let Zee do what he wanted, find the sultan and bring him here, but she doubted it could be accomplished without seriously hurting people, and she'd seen how Zee carried prisoners—dangling over his shoulder. Shayban might be less inclined to negotiate—or whatever it was Casmir planned to do with him—if he was delivered thusly.

"Maybe a robo-tractor?" the officer suggested.

"My offer stands," Casmir said magnanimously. "Or you could just leave him there. Maybe his forbidding presence will prompt good behavior from the other prisoners."

"He's blocking the fire aisle," Gokhale muttered, then pinned Casmir with an exasperated glare.

Kim couldn't tell if she was contemplating his offer or contemplating shooting him, but Zee was watching her and would prevent the latter.

"Fine, I'll pass along your message," Gokhale said. "I can't promise the sultan will heed it or even read it. He's a busy man."

"Just don't leave out the part about how we can help him with Dubashi, who has made himself my enemy too. I'm positive we can assist each other." Casmir stepped forward and gripped Zee's arm. "Come inside, please, Zee."

Kim half expected the crusher to continue to be recalcitrant, but Zee allowed Casmir to tug him into the cell. The bars clanged down behind them with zeal, and the officers stomped away. Kim wondered if they would deliver any messages other than to warn their colleagues to stay away from this cell.

"Thank you, Zee," Casmir said.

"You are welcome."

"Kim." Casmir turned to her. "You may want to try sending that message to your sick grandmother now, in case they have a signal blocker built into the detention area and turn it on."

With a flash of alarm, Kim realized that was a possibility. She quickly checked for network access, afraid she might have missed her opportunity. Ah, but the signal wasn't blocked, at least not yet. There was a public network that she could access.

The relief that flooded her surprised her, and she snorted in disgust, realizing she *wanted* to send a message to Rache—wanted to see him again. She would, however, make Zee break them out of here himself, rather than begging for Rache to rescue her from a jail cell. Asking him for a favor was bad enough; she refused to appear helpless in front of him.

"You're getting better at deceit," she observed.

"Who, me?" Casmir touched his chest.

If I send it, promise me we won't be in this cell when he arrives, she messaged Casmir. *I want to be kidnapped, not rescued.*

Assuming Rache would take the time to come. If he was already halfway to Dubashi's meeting for mercenaries, it might be too late.

If it's clear that we're not going to gain the sultan's attention, I'll have Zee break the bars late in the night shift, and we'll take a more direct route to getting a meeting with him.

Like breaking into his suite and standing next to his bed while he's sleeping?

I said more direct, not creepy stalker-ish. We'll stand by his kitchen table.

That's a relief. All right, let me see if Rache is awake and close enough to this part of the system for real-time communication.

Casmir bowed and stepped back, as if to give her privacy. There wasn't much privacy to be had in the six-by-six-foot cell. There wasn't a bunk or any furniture at all. Hinges on a square panel on one wall suggested a foldout toilet. How delightful it would be to use it with an audience. Even though Kim and Casmir shared a bathroom back home, it was never at the same *time*.

Rache,

Casmir and I are in a bit of a... situation. Prince Jorg wants us to use our skills to create unpleasant things that could harm a great number of people. I would rather not create something that could be used to great human devastation in the war. I know you don't owe me any favors, but I thought... Is there any chance you could meet me on Stardust Palace and pretend to kidnap me? If I'm your prisoner...

Kim shook her head as she wrote the words, hardly able to believe she was making this request instead of telling Jorg straight out that she wouldn't build a bioweapon. But... she couldn't help but fear that Jorg and Jager were the kinds of people who would threaten her family to get what they wanted. Her mother had stayed behind in System Hydra to work with the archeology ship from Tiamat Station that had managed to snag a piece of the gate, but her brothers and father were in Zamek City. Close and convenient targets for anyone in the castle.

If the Kingdom—Jager and Jorg—believe I'm your prisoner, I'm hoping I won't be blamed for not being able to serve them, and that my family won't be in danger. That's the crux of it. I wouldn't worry overmuch about myself, but... Well, you know how it is.

Did he? The Lichtenbergs, who had raised him, were presumably back on Odin. Did it worry him that they might become casualties in a war?

I don't know if it's possible or where you are in the system now, she finished, *but if you're able to come "kidnap" me, I'd be more appreciative than I was the last two times you kidnapped me.*

Kim hit send before she realized that being more appreciative might be construed as an innuendo. She hoped she hadn't just promised to have sex with him.

"Are you curling your lip because it's not going well?" Casmir asked. "Or because you just noticed our lavatory facilities?"

"He hasn't answered yet. I just hit send. But I didn't phrase things well."

"I don't think you have to be diplomatic. He likes you."

She grimaced. "That's the problem."

Casmir snorted and smiled, though it was a bemused smile. "You must be a challenge to woo."

"I have no doubt."

I'll bet ten thousand Kingdom crowns, came Rache's response after a delay of about twenty seconds, *that this is Casmir's plan and not yours.*

He did come up with it. My enthusiasm is a little grudging.

You don't wish to see me again? I'm distressed. The twenty-second pauses appeared to be a result of the time lag rather than how long it took him to answer. That meant his ship wasn't on the other side of the system, but it wasn't close.

Kim was almost relieved. She wasn't convinced this was a good idea, and if she met Rache again, she would prefer it to be on even footing, not with her in his debt.

I don't want to ask for a favor, she admitted. *I don't like to inconvenience people.*

Or is it that you don't want to appear needy or be indebted to them?

That may be part of it. Since she'd been thinking exactly that, she saw little point in denying it.

"He's not close, is he?" Casmir whispered. He'd sat down with his back to the wall.

"Not very."

"Hm." Casmir tapped his chin, probably already scheming up an alternative plan.

How soon would you need to be kidnapped? The Fedallah *is three days past Stardust Palace Station.*

Are you on the way to the meeting with the prince?

I'm going to the meeting, yes.

Why did that sound somewhat evasive? Was there something *else* that he was doing first?

You're not really contemplating joining in with a bunch of mercenaries to attack the Kingdom, are you? Kim suspected her disapproval came through with her words—maybe she shouldn't lecture and ask for a favor at the same time, but she couldn't help herself.

It looks like it'll be a fun shindig. It would be a shame to miss out.

She couldn't tell if he was joking or not. *If you help blow up my father's dojo, I'll never speak to you again.*

That would be dreadful. I will consider your objection while I listen to Dubashi's proposal.

Kim wanted to convince him not to go to that meeting at all, but that would be easier done in person. And maybe Dubashi wasn't hiring people to attack Odin itself. Maybe he wanted more refineries blown up. Rache excelled at that. She felt bitter bile rise in her throat at the idea of him helping to demolish her people's resources. Even if she was irked with Jorg right now, the Kingdom was home.

We are currently on track to be early for that meeting, Rache added. *Dubashi put out the call to mercenaries in Cerberus and other systems, as well as locally, and he's expecting more arrivals, I gather. I was thinking of doing something unwise in the meantime, like harassing Prince Jorg's ship, but he's gathered those four Kingdom warships around him, along with a couple of suck-up dreadnoughts from the Moonrise Free Stations government, so it would be dicey. My doctor advises against it.*

Do you consult him often regarding missions and tactical matters?

Rarely, but he's started offering opinions, regardless. I've decided not to flog him. If I were to bring a shuttle to Stardust Palace, would you be able to meet me in one of their ship bays, or would I have to break you out of a secure detention area, thus to add verisimilitude to this ploy?

Kim eyed the cell bars. She had no intention of staying here for three days, nor, as she had been thinking before, did she want to need rescuing by Rache. *If you need me to meet you in a bay, I could, but I was thinking of the station's mycology lab, where I'll be pretending to go along with Jorg's request.*

She felt silly admitting she would *pretend* to do as Jorg had bid—would Rache think her a coward for not standing up to the prince? She was certain *he* would.

Or would he? He'd worn that mask for all these years so he could act freely against the Kingdom without, she was guessing, ramifications to those who'd raised him, to those he might still care about. Maybe he would understand perfectly.

Will I also be kidnapping Casmir? Rache asked.

I'm not sure. I think he may plan to do as Jorg asks, if he can, but I'm positive he's not going to program his new minions to obey the man. It occurred to her that she was committing treason by sharing the prince's plans with a criminal, and she resolved to be as vague as possible. Especially if he might end up fighting on the other side.

Very well. I will come. This will give me a chance to properly apologize for kidnapping you last time.

You're going to apologize for kidnapping me by kidnapping me again?

At your request. Have you finished The Sun Never Sets in Space *yet? A man must have stimulating conversations with the woman he kidnaps.*

I have finished it. I'll compose discussion points while Casmir and I are—Kim caught herself before finishing that with *in jail* and admitting to being in more trouble than she'd implied—*waiting on the station.*

Perfect. But do me a favor once I've collected you, please, and don't talk my doctor into any shenanigans that involve him acting against the crew. He already has trouble enough getting people to show up for exams.

So I've heard. Thank you. How does it work when you hire mercenaries to kidnap you? Do we need to scrape together a payment?

Mercenaries do typically expect to be paid, but this mission is without precedent. His customary dryness came across even in the purely text message. *Perhaps I'll tell the men they're there for shore leave and nothing more, then come alone to retrieve you.*

Kim knew she shouldn't like the idea of spending time alone with him, but they'd had so few opportunities. A few minutes here and there on a balcony or in an airlock chamber or the navigation cabin of a submarine. What would it be like to escape from all these horrible adventures and spend an afternoon or even a day together on a warm, sandy beach somewhere, discussing literature? Would she confess to the books she'd written? The books he'd *read* but didn't know were by her?

"He's not sending virtual kisses or something is he?" Casmir wrinkled his nose.

Kim blinked. "What?"

"You're wearing a dreamy, wistful expression."

"For your information, I was thinking of sandy beaches and escaping from war and killing. Don't you have some schematics to tinker with?"

"I can still *see* when I'm looking at something on my contact." He squinted at her. "Are you on these imaginary sandy beaches alone or with company?"

"That's none of your business."

Thank you, she sent a final message off to Rache. *Let me know if I owe you anything.*

She winced as soon as the words sped away, realizing she might again be setting him up to expect some kind of reciprocation. But she couldn't ask him to fly his entire ship three days out of the way and not offer *something*. She worried about that because she wasn't sure that what he might want was something she was willing to give. The idea of setting up expectations and not being able to meet them concerned her.

And it became an even greater concern when more than the typical twenty seconds passed without a response. He was thinking about his answer.

You will not owe me anything, he finally replied. *If I have to kidnap Casmir, tell him I expect him to build* me *a crusher.*

So much for being vague about what their assignments were.

Rache wouldn't want a crusher if he knew how much space they took up in a jail cell.

I'll mention it, she sent.

Good. I'll let you know when I'm close.

Kim looked at Casmir, who arched his eyebrows, still paying attention to her despite whatever else he was doing.

He's coming, she messaged him. *He's three days away.*

Oh, good. His face crinkled up. *You're not going to owe him any odious favors, are you?* Casmir was far too good at reading her. *While you were messaging him, I realized he might ask for* things *in return if he agreed to help. Before, I was just thinking of getting you out of Jorg's sights, and maybe delaying Rache so he didn't make that meeting in time and jump on the mercenaries-against-the-Kingdom train, but I realized... Uhm, I don't want to be responsible for you owing him...* things.

Actually, all he said was that if you also need kidnapping, he expects you to build him a crusher.

Oh. Casmir looked up at the towering Zee. "You may soon have your choice of mates, Zee. Many, many mates."

"You do not sound pleased by this, Casmir Dabrowski."

"I'm concerned that so many people want crushers to aid them in battle."

"We do excel in this."

"Yeah." Casmir smiled sadly.

I told Rache that we wouldn't be in a detention cell when he arrived, Kim added. *I don't think he wants to commit a great deal of his forces to breaking us out, and I'd also prefer that mercenaries not shoot the locals.*

Yes, me too. Three days is plenty of time to get out of here and find a way to have a chat with the sultan.

Kim hoped so. She wasn't convinced those security officers would get a message to the sultan, no matter what they'd told Casmir.

CHAPTER 10

THE BOMBING HAD STOPPED, BUT ALARMS WAILED IN the city, and more air ambulances than Oku had thought existed flew through the rainy sky, landing on rooftops and in intersections, teams rushing in to carry out the injured. Or dead. Oku, on foot and wrapped in a long jacket with the hood up, paused to stare at one such scene—and the great pit where a building had been and now only rubble remained.

Anger welled up inside of her, pushing aside the fear that had been a constant companion that night, first while sneaking out of the castle and then while navigating the wet smoky streets. What right did these invaders have to come to their system and bomb innocent civilians? Any grievances the rest of the systems might have from once being conquered by the Kingdom were over three hundred years old. She was certain these invaders were only here because they thought they could get away with it and claim Odin for themselves. Maybe her father and some of his expansionist talk had annoyed a few people, but it couldn't warrant this.

An alarm flashed on her contact, letting her know that her blood sugar was climbing. She snorted. Of course it was. But it hadn't been that long since her last beta-cell infusion, so her pancreas ought to be able to handle the necessary insulin release to stabilize it.

Maddie set a hand on her shoulder. "We should continue, Your Highness. Complete this errand before your parents send troops out to hunt you down and I'm accused of kidnapping you."

"Nobody will accuse you of that after all this time, Maddie. And anyway, I wouldn't let them."

A wet nose pressed against Oku's hand. Chasca, who'd found them when they'd been crossing the courtyard, was sticking close now, her long gray tail clenched between her legs. Oku wished she'd dared take her dog back down into the underground passages and to the Citadel, but she might not have been able to slip out again.

"But yes, we're going." Oku tore her gaze from the scene, from the charred and unmoving bodies lined up on the street, and followed the map laid out on her contact. They were almost to Casmir's parents' building. Would they be home? Hunkering together on the sixth floor of their apartment building? Or would they have fled to one of the schools that had been designated as shelters?

Oku thought of comming them, since they had a public code listed, but she didn't know what she would say. She felt oddly nervous about introducing herself to them. She also had a perhaps illogical fear that they might flee if they knew someone from the castle was coming, that Casmir might have warned them of… well, she wasn't sure what. But from what her mother had said, the mission Casmir had been taken on hadn't been going to plan, and he might be held responsible for some of that. His parents *shouldn't* have anything to fear, but when Oku's father lost his temper, he was almost as apt to lash out as Jorg.

"That's the building," she said, relieved to find the hundred-year-old brick structure standing.

Searching for the entrance, she turned down a narrow side street crammed full of air bikes, bicycles in racks, and personal vehicles. A stone sign over the entrance read *Gideon's Court* along with the frieze of some ancient warrior or soldier leading a battle. Had Casmir grown up here? She didn't see any outdoor space for children to play, not even any trees planted on the sidewalks. Chasca sniffed a lamppost.

The door was locked, but Oku waved her signet ring with its electronic transmitter under the gold band, and it opened. The inside was clean and well maintained, but the lights were out. Conservation or had a transformer been hit nearby?

Aircraft zoomed past overhead, flying low, and the floor shuddered. Oku bypassed an elevator, questioning if it would work, and climbed stairs in the back.

"Ah, good. The princess is determined to help me stay in shape," Maddie said as Chasca bounded past both of them, perhaps believing the upper levels would be safer from threats than the lower.

Alas, Oku didn't think it worked that way. "I care about your health, Maddie. What if you keeled over and I had to get a new bodyguard?"

"You'd fail to find one as lenient and yet efficient as I."

"There's no doubt about that."

Most of the doors were shut tight on the hall of the sixth floor, but a couple of children had their noses pressed against a window at the end. When Oku and Maddie walked off the stairs, the kids glanced back, then scurried into a nearby apartment.

Oku found F-11 and knocked. There wasn't a security panel or camera or anything electronic, as far as she could see. She'd thought the building a hundred years old but wondered if it was much older. This part of the city dated back almost as far as the castle itself.

A tall thin man with a dark beard, thinning hair, and glasses opened the door, still clothed despite the late hour. There was just enough light for Oku to identify him as Casmir's father, Aleksy Dabrowski. She'd met them briefly at the clinic where she'd caught up with Casmir weeks earlier.

"Scholar Dabrowski?" Oku started to offer her hand, but Chasca bumped her hip, sniffing inside the apartment.

"Yes. Ah." Aleksy looked down at the dog. "We have a cat."

"Sorry." Oku dropped a hand and grabbed Chasca's collar, wishing she'd thought to bring a leash. The dog had free run of the castle grounds and usually stayed out of trouble, so she hadn't had it with her in the greenhouse. "You can bring him with you. Or her."

Aleksy squinted at her, as if he were trying to place her. There were candles and emergency lanterns glowing inside the apartment, but the hall was dark, and she was in shadows.

"I'm Oku," she said. "We met at the Pierce Clinic last month. And this is my bodyguard, Maddie—Madison. And that's Chasca. We came to invite you and your wife to Basilisk Citadel. It's a lot more protected than this old building, and if the bombers come back, you'll be safe there."

Aleksy had the look of an academic trying to puzzle out a particularly challenging problem. Oku knew this must be surprising—usually, she would have four bodyguards with her if she traveled outside of the castle, and she would be on the way to one of the research facilities or the university, or some big venue for a dreaded public appearance. This was… unorthodox.

"Who is it, love?" Irena Dabrowski asked, coming up behind Aleksy as he seemed to realize *which* Oku she was and stepped back to bow.

He almost bumped his wife out of the way. A fit woman of about sixty, she dropped a hand on his back and frowned curiously at Oku. He swatted at her and whispered, "Princess Oku. Bow."

"Women curtsy, love."

"That's not necessary," Oku said, though Irena had been scrutinizing her in that same puzzle-solving manner before committing to such an action. Oku repeated her offer.

"I don't understand. Does someone have need of a physical therapist?" Irena touched her chest. "Or, uhm." She looked at her husband. "Math?"

"The world *always* has a need for math." Aleksy straightened. "But it rarely knows it. Unfortunately."

"I like math," Oku said, "but I came because of Casmir."

"Oh." Their eyes brightened.

"Is he home?" Aleksy asked.

"Is he safe?" Irena reached toward Oku but kept herself from grabbing her.

The naked display of concern touched Oku, and it was a moment before she could answer, as she tried to remember if her parents had ever been so worried about *her*. Her mother cared for her, she knew, but she was a reserved woman who seemed more at ease doing charity work for people from other parts of the planet than loving her own daughter, and her father… Though he was occasionally indulgent and smiled fondly at Oku, he always seemed like he would have preferred more male heirs. The fact that he'd had Jorg and Finn gene-cleaned and hadn't bothered to fix her issues had never ceased to distress her after she'd learned about it. When she had asked why, he'd said that it didn't matter to the public if girls were perfect, and he'd pointed out that gene-cleaning was illegal in the Kingdom, so she mustn't ever mention that Jorg and Finn had been granted it.

"The last I heard from him, he was fine." Oku didn't know how much Casmir had messaged back to his parents, but she wouldn't mention the Plague in case he hadn't shared that with them.

"Fine? Did you hear from him recently?" Irena frowned. "With the blockade… and those messages we've gotten from Dr. Rothberger about the alerts *he's* gotten. Do you know Casmir has had several *seizures* while he's been out in space?" Irena looked like she would grip Oku's arm but grabbed her husband's instead.

Seizures? Casmir hadn't mentioned those to Oku. In fact, he hadn't mentioned the Plague either. She'd gotten that information from her mother.

Maybe he hadn't wanted to worry her—or his family. She thought about offering to show them the last video Casmir had sent, but it was a couple of weeks old now, and might not alleviate their concerns. Besides, what would they think if they saw it? She'd have to explain the bees and maybe more that she wasn't prepared to explain.

Aleksy patted Irena's hand. "Now, now, of course she wouldn't know. And is not to blame for anything that's going on out there. Your Highness, do you want to come in? I—are there just two of you?" He peered into the dark hallway.

Chasca wagged her tail and butted her head against his hand.

"Three," Oku said. "I don't want to disturb your cat."

"She'll survive a visitor. She can't be any more disturbed than she already is." Aleksy glanced toward the ceiling.

"If you want to pack up, I can escort you to the Citadel tonight. Just in case there's more trouble before dawn."

The wail of alarms was muffled but still audible through the old walls and real glass windows.

"The Citadel is the safe place for the nobility." Irena's brow creased. "I don't understand why we…"

"Because Casmir asked me to check on you and see that you were safe."

Aleksy mouthed a silent, "Oh."

"I didn't realize he knew you, er, you knew him that well," Irena said.

"We've met a couple of times and exchanged messages. He's working on a project for me, or was. And now he's in danger because of the work my father assigned him, so it's the least I can do to come offer you this."

"Oh, that's very kind," Irena said. "But we have to go to work in the morning, and we can't leave when none of our neighbors get to go."

"It might be worth considering." Aleksy eyed her, turning his concern toward his wife. He would want her to be safe, surely. "Did you see the news? The Meadows Building was completely destroyed. It's only a few blocks away. The center of the old city must be an appealing target."

"I don't think anybody will have work for a few days," Oku offered.

"But the Abelmans are sick, and the Vidals have a new baby." Irena frowned. "It wouldn't be right for us to receive special treatment. Rabbi Tzadak can't even see anymore. I've been checking on him in the evenings when his children can't come visit."

Oku stared at her, though Aleksy was also nodding. It hadn't occurred to her that Casmir's parents might not *come*.

She looked at Maddie, wondering how she was supposed to rectify this. It wasn't as if she could invite the whole building to the Citadel. She was reasonably sure she could get the Dabrowskis in, but how many hundreds of people lived here?

"Why don't you go, Aleksy?" Irena asked. "There won't be school for several days, so you won't be missed. I can stay here and—"

"Absolutely not," Aleksy said.

"Do you want me to pick them up and carry them?" Maddie asked.

Oku knew she wasn't serious, but she asked, "Could you?"

Maddie eyed them. "Only one, I think."

"Too bad Casmir's crusher isn't here," Oku said.

"His what?" Aleksy asked.

"He hasn't told you about that project? I suppose it was top secret until recently. I mean, it still must be, but now that he's wandering around with one…"

"Oh, the black robot?" Aleksy asked. "Is that what they're called? He introduced it as Zee when it came to dinner. The cat was terrified of it and wouldn't come out from the back of the closet until the next day."

Oku glanced at Chasca, wondering how the dog would feel about Casmir's loyal companion. She'd been around androids and automated cleaners all her life, and other than occasionally barking at the floor-mopping robot that cruised through Oku's rooms in the morning…

"Is there any chance more than the two of us can come?" Irena asked.

"Sh." Aleksy gripped her hand in warning. "We can't presume."

"Rabbi Tzadak, at least," Irena said, having less trouble with presuming.

Oku took a deep breath, hoping her parents would allow this. Her mother would understand, she thought, but if she wasn't around, and Father was the one gaping at her when she showed up at the Citadel with the residents of an entire building…

"Go ahead and invite your close acquaintances," Oku said. "But there are limited resources in the Citadel, so we can't take everybody in the building. As it is, we'll probably have to punt out a few nobles."

She expected a snide comment about what a negligible loss that would be, but if either of them thought it, they were too circumspect to voice the words.

"Thank you," Irena said, hustling back into the apartment. "I'll get on the comm. Aleksy, pack some clothes, please. And the cat. I'll get her food."

Aleksy waved for Oku and Maddie to come in and then hustled off.

Oku resisted the urge to poke around, though her heart pinged with a strange mixture of longing and interest when she saw family photographs, some of Aleksy, Irena, and Casmir, and some of them with what had to be their extended family. There were a couple of young Casmir holding up robot-shaped trophies and grinning with teeth that had been crooked at the time.

She bit her lip, amused, able to see the man in the boy, his eyes gleaming as if with some scheme. She had to remind herself that Casmir had been adopted—her mother's doing—and these weren't his blood parents. They seemed such a good fit that it was easy to imagine that his real parents—his three-hundred-and-thirty-odd-year-old parents—would have been similar.

She thought of the Lichtenbergs and David, who'd had access to everything growing up in a well-to-do noble family, but the times she'd visited, she'd had the impression of the baron and baroness being somewhat distant figures, even though they'd expected much from David. *Jager* had expected much. They'd always seemed to treat David more like a ward than a son. Maybe that explained the aloofness he'd developed. She'd thought it arrogance when she was younger. Now, she wasn't so certain.

Oku shook her head, not sure why she was thinking of David, since he'd been gone for ten years. Maybe if he'd had the opportunity, he would have grown out of some of his haughtiness, though maybe not. David and Jorg had seemed cut from similar patterns, and it wasn't as if age had improved Jorg.

"Ah." Aleksy paused on his way past with a valise to look at the photograph. "He was very proud of that trophy. I believe he slept with it for most of the summer. We had his teeth straightened the following year. He wasn't willing to do it until someone told him he'd have a better shot with girls if his smile wasn't crooked. He has an aversion to doctors and dentists and all things medical, really."

"I understand." And she did. She might not have to deal with *seizures*—was that a chronic issue for him?—but she well remembered her own fears, somewhat assuaged these days, and her father sternly telling her that princesses did not cry and hide under the bed to avoid blood draws. He'd always been stern when explaining that her behaviors or achievements were substandard. "Did it work?"

"Hm?"

"The teeth straightening. Did it work on the girls?"

"Mm, perhaps not as well as hoped. Maybe if the trophies had featured a disc hurler or a footballer, but we were always afraid to let him play, and when he did play, he didn't have much natural aptitude." Aleksy smirked wryly. "It was as if we shared blood after all. Did you know he was adopted?"

Oku realized she knew more about Casmir's origins than his parents did. Why, she wondered, had her mother kept it a secret from them for all those years? And even from Casmir? It hadn't been until those terrorists had appeared and started hunting him down that she'd felt compelled to warn him, however belatedly. Maybe she'd never intended for Casmir to find out where he'd come from. Had she worried he would try to wriggle his way into the nobility? Or that he would believe he was owed something? Oku had a hard time imagining either scenario from Casmir.

"You're supposed to talk him up to girls, love," Irena said from the kitchen, where she'd finished her comm calls and was packing a cooler with frozen casseroles and who knew what else.

Should Oku tell Irena that the Citadel would have provisions? Though depending on how many friends of the family showed up, maybe packing some food wasn't a bad idea.

"Ah?" Aleksy asked. "In that case, Your Highness, he was lovely at hurling discs and balls and winning the admiration of girls."

"I said talk him up, not *lie*," Irena said. "He had several girlfriends. Remember that sweet little Anya who became a space-habitat architect? Too bad she was transferred to the lunar base. Oh, and Kagami in school. She became an animal cyberneticist and moved to the southern continent, I believe. And Hannah became a xeno-seismologist and left the system completely."

"So what you're saying is he attracted intellectual girls with substance," Oku suggested, though she supposed careers in the sciences didn't automatically convey substance to a person. She identified with that type and was inclined to think favorable thoughts toward them.

"Yes." Aleksy nodded, pleased to go along with this. "But they all kept moving to pursue their careers."

"Love, I think the problem may be Zamek City rather than Casmir."

"Either that, or he drives them to flee the continent, if not the planet, with his antics," Aleksy said fondly.

"I'm sure that's not it," Oku said.

"I do wish he'd meet a nice Jewish girl and have some babies," Irena said, dragging the cooler out of the kitchen. Maddie rushed forward to help her with it. "Though right now, I'd be pleased if he came home safe. Or maybe I should wish that he stay in another system until all this is resolved." Irena lifted her gaze heavenward.

Oku barely heard her. Her mind had hiccupped and stopped processing at the words *Jewish girl*. Thanks to her mixed-race parents, Oku had two religions she could draw on, but neither of them was Judaism. Not that she wanted to marry Casmir or settle down and make babies with him—she definitely wasn't ready for *that*—but a twinge of alarm flashed through her at the thought of his parents not approving of her because she wasn't the right religion. Would that truly matter? After all the knights and nobles who'd tried to win her as some trophy or to solidify a relationship with the royal family, Oku almost laughed at the notion of not being acceptable as a mate.

But it wasn't that funny. It was a little distressing.

Aleksy pulled a cat carrier out of a closet and visibly braced himself. "This will be difficult. She's already upset due to the bombing and sirens."

"Understandably so," Irena said.

Chasca, who had recovered from her earlier alarm at the storm, was pawing at something under the couch. As Oku moved to pull her away, she succeeded in swatting out a mouse toy on tiny hidden wheels. It flashed a green light and tipped over, righted itself, then rolled in a circle. Chasca dropped into a bow with her forelegs stretched out, and her tail swished back and forth.

"That's not for you," Oku murmured, pulling her back to the doorway.

Hisses and meows sounded from a bedroom. Oku imagined the looks the other people in the Citadel would give the newcomers as they arrived with a cat carrier. A *noisy* cat carrier. Maybe it wouldn't matter. Oku imagined others from the castle had brought their pets.

"I believe we're ready," Aleksy said, appearing with the now-full cat carrier, from which protesting sounds continued to issue. He peered into the hallway. "Ah, and the others are showing up too. Perhaps we should check on the Satos? Kim is stuck off on that mission with Casmir, isn't she? Her family doesn't live that far away. They're very capable, but nobody can survive a bomb landing on their head."

"No," Oku murmured, trying not to panic at what her father's reception would be when she showed up, after sneaking out herself, with a bunch of strangers.

Maybe she would get lucky and he wouldn't be around. If he was, she would get more than a stern lecture about inappropriate behavior. He might turn these people away.

Asger crouched atop one of the many stacks of shipping containers in a massive dimly lit hold several doors down from the bay where the *Dragon* was docked. And where he hoped that android was still looking for him.

After racing over and around ships, Asger had lucked out, having a nearby door open as robot loaders exited with cargo. He'd leaped over the back of one and made it into a corridor before the door shut. He was positive there were cameras in those corridors and someone would track his passage soon, but for now, he seemed to be alone in the quiet hold, save for a couple of security drones flying around. He'd already mapped their routes so he could avoid them and noticed that they were zipping past below the level of his shipping containers. With luck, that meant whatever cameras they possessed were focused on the floor.

"Should have sent Tristan a message and asked him to come to the ship," Asger muttered.

But he didn't have Tristan's chip ident. They'd crossed paths often in the halls of Prester Court, and chatted a number of times, but Asger had been a couple of years ahead of him in his own training, and they hadn't had occasion to work together since becoming knights. Had Asger been back in System Lion, he could have looked up any knight's contact information on the network, but System Stymphalia's databases didn't have that classified information, nor had he found a comm code for Tristan here on this station. The announcement that Princess Nalini had made him a business partner was only a week old, so Tristan might not have lived here long.

Even if Asger had been able to contact him, there was no guarantee Tristan would want to see him, especially once Asger explained why he was here. If he'd been kicked out of the knighthood, he had to be bitter about it, and he might ignore requests for meetings with old comrades.

Asger dug into his rucksack, ignoring his telltale knight's gear for now, and pulled out a dusty hat with a wide brim that he'd found in his guest quarters on the freighter. Maybe it would help hide his face from the cameras. He tugged his thick hair back into a bun and stuffed it under the hat, then pulled a stunner out of his pack and stuck it in the large pocket of his similarly borrowed duster. Taking advantage of his quiet moment, he'd pulled up the station map and planned a route that should get him to Princess Nalini's suite. Where he hoped Tristan would be.

Asger thought about checking on Kim and Casmir—the main reason he'd sprinted off had been in the hope of luring security after him so his friends could move about freely—but he doubted he had much time before someone tracked him down.

A faint hiss reached his ears. A door opening.

The security android? Asger couldn't see the entrance from his spot, but he assumed this was someone looking for him. He dropped down behind the shipping containers, wincing when he landed more loudly than he'd planned, his gear clinking in his pack. He took a circuitous route around more stacks of containers, careful to avoid the drones, and made his way toward the door, hoping to slip out behind whoever had come in.

A clang sounded, and he halted. Something clattered to the floor. He definitely was not alone in here.

As he continued toward the exit, he pulled the stunner out again. He spotted the door and eased toward it, hoping to sneak out, but ready for a fight. Though he would prefer not to hurt anyone or damage any robots or equipment, he was on a mission and wouldn't be deterred. Even if it was a mission he wouldn't have chosen for himself.

He'd almost reached the door when a thud sounded, something landing behind him. He whirled, pointing the stunner. His first thought was to curse because the person was armored. Then he realized she wasn't wearing a helmet… and that he knew her.

"Qin?" Asger stared at her—not only was she wearing her full combat armor, save for the helmet, but she was also toting a stunner and her big anti-tank gun on a sling. "What are you doing here?"

He was so startled to see her that he forgot about the drones. One zipped into view and sped toward them.

Qin casually slung her Brockinger off her shoulder and fired. When the round hit the drone and exploded, pieces flew in a thousand directions as the hold flared briefly with fiery light.

“I came to help you.” Just as casually, Qin returned the weapon to her shoulder.

Asger didn’t know whether to be pleased to see her or embarrassed that she thought he needed help. “How did you find me?”

“Your scent.”

He glanced at his armpit before remembering she had cat genes… and probably a cat’s nose.

“It’s not bad,” she said dryly. “It’s just uniquely yours. Everyone’s scent is.”

“I’m glad nobody gave the security androids super noses. Did they go after Casmir and Kim?”

“They’ve been arrested, yes.”

Asger swore. “I was afraid of that.” He touched her arm. “We better get out of here. Someone may have heard that.” He waved toward the lingering smoke and pieces of drone all over the floor. “And let’s try not to blow anything else up, eh? I’ll accept your help—thank you—but my job isn’t to give these people more reason to hate the Kingdom.”

“I understand. I didn’t think my stunner would do any good on a drone. I crunched the other one between my hands.”

“Impressive hands.” He flashed a smile and caught a warm blush on her cheeks. He nodded toward the door. “I’ve got a map downloaded. We may have to force open a few doors along the way.”

Qin flexed her gauntleted hands. “I’m ready. After you finish your assignment, we should help Kim and Casmir.”

Asger nodded.

He wouldn’t have argued, regardless, but then she added, “Bjarke is on his way to retrieve Kim. Jorg wants her.”

“We’ll get her first.” Asger gritted his teeth with determination, even though his insides twisted as he imagined confronting his father, who also happened to be a senior knight and his putative commander in this system. He thought of Casmir’s words about the need for change. Maybe it had already begun.

“We’ll get her,” he repeated and meant it.

CHAPTER 11

AFTER TWO HOURS OF LYING ON THE COLD floor in their jail cell, Casmir had hacked into all of the secured networks on the station, located the sultan's chip and ergo the sultan, determined he was on a conference call with four other leaders of thc Miners' Union located in the system, and spied unnoticed on the virtual meeting. In a short time, he'd learned far more about the state of the Miners' Union than he had from days of reading articles and news reports on the public network.

Someone poked his shoulder.

"I'm fine, Zee," he said.

"It's me," Kim said dryly from his side.

"Oh." Casmir opened his eyes.

Zee still loomed protectively at the gate to their cell, staring into the empty corridor. Kim knelt beside Casmir.

"I assumed it was him, because you're not very touchy-feely."

"And Zee is?"

"He ruffles my hair sometimes, and I'm positive he wouldn't mind a hug."

"I'm not going to contemplate what it says about me as a human being that your robot is better at touching than I am."

"That you're unique, quirky, and unlikely to transmit diseases through hand-to-hand contact."

"I'd request you put that on my grave, if you outlive me, but we don't do epitaphs."

"No room on the family gravestone?" Casmir had gone with Kim to her grandfather's funeral a couple of years earlier, and he remembered the monument with all of her dead ancestors' names engraved on the front.

"Alas, no." Kim waved at him. "I wanted to make sure you're all right. That floor is hard and cold, you're in nothing but your underwear and socks, and you were deathly ill less than two weeks ago. Maybe you could get Zee to transform into a couch."

"I can't imagine it would be a very soft couch."

"He's not programmed to take on cushiness?"

"The military didn't want cush."

"I can form into any shape," Zee announced, "but I would only pattern myself after furniture if it helped protect Casmir Dabrowski or Kim Sato or served some mission-essential purpose."

"Meaning, he'd be willing to turn into a couch to be pushed out a skyscraper window to land on an enemy." Casmir patted Kim's arm. "Thank you for checking on me, but I'm fine. I've actually been feeling unusually invigorated of late. Do you think that's another side effect of Rache's potion?"

"I think that's the desired *main* effect."

"Ah. I didn't know having a boosted immune system would impart vigor."

"Having less than optimal health is draining."

"Tell me about it." Casmir sat up, his back aching a little after hours on the cold floor—apparently, the potion could only do so much. "I wonder how long the effects last. Do you know how much it costs to buy the immune booster?"

"The one he gave you is about fifty thousand Union dollars from Jotunheim Station."

"Fifty *thousand*?" He gaped at her. "Kim, I don't make that much in a year."

"Apparently, being a mercenary captain is more lucrative than being a teacher."

"That *can't* be right. I mean, I believe he makes more than I do, but he must be investing in businesses on the side or something. Have you seen his bank books?"

"Of course not."

"I thought he might want to show off his net worth to you. To impress you."

"You know that wouldn't work."

"But does *he* know it? Men aren't the best at sussing out what women want, I've been told."

"Have you shown Oku your bank books?"

"Dear God, no. That wouldn't impress her." Casmir switched to chip-to-chip messaging for his next comment—he probably should have done that *before* discussing Rache, however vaguely, but he doubted anybody was monitoring them. Nobody had brought food or water or even checked on them. *I've been watching the sultan's meeting with some other Miners' Union leaders.*

Has it been illuminating?

What I've gathered is that Shayban has a loose alliance with a couple dozen princes, sultans, presidents, and whatever else these people choose to call themselves when they're wealthy enough for admission into the Union. Four of them are in this system and can speak close to real time with him. He's the most powerful of the bunch—wealthiest—but he's still far enough down the ladder to be threatened by Dubashi. They're not talking about their history, but I gather that the original leaders of the Union banded together a few generations ago to fix prices and do the other delightful things that are good for the owner of a company and bad for the consumer.

So we're dealing with selfless heroes.

Casmir shrugged. *Whatever the original intent was, it was done before most of the current leaders were alive. I say most because there was a mention of Dubashi and someone else being over two hundred years old and fans of anti-aging treatments. What matters and may be useful to us is that Shayban is, as I'd gathered from my earlier research, vehemently displeased with Dubashi, who's not only been encroaching on his territory but also tried to kidnap his daughter to stop the wedding to Jorg and what would have been an alliance with the Kingdom. I think if I could talk to him, I might be able to convince him to work with me.*

Were you able to tell if the security officers delivered a message about us?

No. They might have sent one off, but Shayban has been in his meeting for hours. Casmir eyed the bars. *I'm contemplating letting us out and seeing if we can slip into the palace and crash the sultan's meeting. Politely.*

Polite crashing sounds difficult.

You just say please and thank you a lot as you're breaking down the doors—or hacking the locks, in my case.

They took your tool satchel.

It's on a table in the security control center we passed through. I saw it on a camera.

Kim raised her eyebrows. *Have you become more adept at hacking into systems of late, or is network security here particularly lax?*

I have *had more practice than I typically got during my days as a robotics instructor, but yes, the network here is unsophisticated compared to what the astroshamans had.* Casmir pushed himself to his feet. *Are you ready?*

To break out?

Yes.

I'm ready. This cell lacks an espresso machine, and I haven't even caught a whiff of brewing coffee since we stepped onto this station.

It is the night shift, you know.

She gave him the scathing look this comment apparently deserved. *There had better be some decent coffee somewhere that we can find.* Kim stood up and shook out her arms, anticipating that they would have to fight a couple of guards. Zee could handle that, but she might get a chance to help.

Yes, finding coffee should be our priority.

I think so. I'm starting to miss my cabin on the Osprey.

I'm surprised you didn't pack up your espresso machine to bring with you.

I should have. I wasn't sure how stealthy I'd have to be to sneak aboard the shuttle with you and Asger. Shot glasses clink. I'm ready.

"Zee?" Casmir murmured. "We're going to break out now."

"Do you wish me to bend the bars?" Zee asked.

A clank sounded, and the bars rose of their own accord.

"Not necessary." Casmir tapped his temple where his chip was located. "But be prepared for a—"

Zee jerked a hand up, finger to the vague orifice that served as his mouth. "A threat has arrived," he whispered.

Casmir craned his ears. Snoring came from one of the other cells, but he couldn't hear anything else over it. Even though Zee's auditory receptors were built into his molecular matrix and he didn't have dedicated ears, he could hear better than a human.

"I detect the sounds of a scuffle in the security control center we passed through," Zee added.

Casmir tapped into one of the cameras on the network and pulled up the room on his contact display. It gave him a view from above the entrance door, showing six men in rumpled ill-fitting uniforms poking at the computer consoles or standing guard with weapons. Two men—he couldn't tell if either of them was one of the officers who'd arrested them—were stuffed under one of those consoles in nothing but their underwear, with flex-cuffs around their ankles and wrists.

"Who breaks into a detention center?" Casmir whispered, though he'd learned that the computers in that room controlled security, including cameras and defense robots, all over the station.

"People wanting to break out someone detained within?" Kim murmured.

"Or *kill* someone detained within." Casmir didn't recognize any of the people in what appeared to be stolen uniforms, but after having assassins come at him more than once, he was quick to consider the possibility that these fell into that category.

Kim looked sharply at him.

"If they're *not* here for me," Casmir said, "this could be our opportunity to walk out without a fight or even being noticed. The guards are tied up. We could let those people do whatever it is they're doing and slip out after they're done."

His mouth twisted with distaste at the idea of doing nothing. What if these people were a threat to the entire station? Could they access environmental controls from that room?

"That's what I would advise." Kim twitched an eyebrow. "Odds are poor that you'll do that."

Casmir issued a lopsided smile. "Yeah." He patted Zee on the back. "Go subdue those people, please. Don't kill anyone. Just disarm them and… er, how can we keep six people from escaping?"

"Zee could turn into a couch and block the door," Kim suggested.

Zee looked at them. "I will use my initiative."

He strode out.

"I don't think he's willing to turn himself into furniture under any circumstances," Kim said.

"Possibly true." Casmir started to step out of the cell, but Kim grabbed his shoulder.

"Let him take care of them. We'll come after, find our galaxy suits, and sneak out."

"There are six of them, and they're armed. Even Zee may find that challenging if they have explosives."

"And how would you help?" She waved up and down his underwear-clad form. She wasn't much more clothed than he.

"I could call in some robots."

"You can do that from here."

Casmir hated sending Zee into danger while he cowered in the background, but he nodded acknowledgment. "True."

"Someone's coming from the cells," a man barked.

"Get the gas!"

Gas? What kind of gas?

Casmir hoped they would realize Zee wasn't human and couldn't be affected. But he, Kim, and the other people locked up could be.

Clanks sounded, at least two items hitting the floor further up the corridor, and a cacophony of chaos erupted. Bangs, thumps, yells, and cries of pain. Then the weapons fire started.

Casmir leaned out into the corridor. Through the exit doorway, he could see bodies flying across the control room, along with the orange and red of DEW-Tek bolts streaking about. But closer, between two cells in the corridor, a pair of canisters spewed out visible smoke. The door to the control room closed, ensuring it would be confined to the cells.

"Yellow-green gas," he whispered, the first hints of a sweet cloying scent reaching his nose. "Any idea what it is?"

"Nothing we want to inhale. Hold your breath, run past, and hope we can get out."

Before Casmir could warn her that the door was closed, Kim sprinted past him, toward the canisters. He took a deep breath of what he hoped was still clean air at the back of the cell and ran after her. Kim kicked the canisters farther down the corridor and sprang for the door.

As Casmir scurried to join her, jumping over one of the canisters skidding past, hands reached through bars, and one man almost caught him.

"Let us out too," someone implored.

"What is that stuff?" someone else asked, someone who'd been close to where the canisters first landed. The words were followed by a pained retching sound.

Kim batted at a wall sensor, but the door didn't open. There weren't controls on this side.

With his lungs already starting to ache from holding his breath, Casmir accessed the wireless security network and searched for controls that would release them. Kim banged on the door.

Casmir found the controls. Before he could override the lock, a black fist slammed through the door like a pile driver. Zee grabbed the warped metal, tore the door from its mount, and hurled it across the room at a man firing at him.

An alarm flashed across Casmir's contact. *Door inoperable.*

No kidding. And now they wouldn't be able to close it again to cut off the smoke—the sickly stuff oozed into the control room.

Kim sprinted through the haze to the door on the other side. It opened without hesitation. Casmir, lungs burning, raced after Kim, springing over an unconscious man—or a body?—on the floor.

Tears streaked down his cheeks, and snot tumbled from his nose. Whatever that gas was, it was more than a sedative.

He made himself wait until hc was in the outer corridor before gasping in a breath of air. But he must have caught too much of the smoke. His stomach spasmed, and he bent over, heaving its contents on the floor.

Just when he'd thought he might be cured of throwing up in space…

Next to him, Kim also bent over and threw up. More retching came from within the control room, though the sounds of fighting were dying out.

"What's going on?" demanded a male voice from a few meters down the corridor.

"I'm not sure, Sultan," a woman said.

Casmir dragged his bare arm across his eyes, aware that he was still in his underwear, and stared blearily into the muzzle of a rifle. It was one of four pointed at him. Four firearms held by four grim-faced guards. Behind them stood Assistant Chief Gokhale and a man Casmir recognized only because he'd spied on his conference call.

"Oh, good," Casmir said, forcing himself to look past the weapons to the assistant chief. He wiped his mouth and smiled. "You've arranged my meeting."

Nobody smiled back. Casmir hoped station policy was to not shoot people in their underwear.

Next to him, Kim recovered enough to straighten and raise her hands. Casmir slowly did the same, realizing he had no way to explain any of this. What if he and Kim were mistaken for allies of the men who'd broken in to do… whatever they'd been doing? If Zee had knocked them all out, the security officers might not be able to tell. Or question anyone except Casmir and Kim.

Qin's nose wrinkled as she followed Asger through carpeted and silk-lined corridors, most of them dimmed for the night cycle. Far more artificial odors than usual for a space station lingered in the air, stirred about but not largely diminished by the ventilation system. She identified more scents of perfumes, incense, and aromatic oils in burners than she'd known existed, nearly drowning out more pleasant smells from potted hibiscus and bougainvillea growing along trellises mounted to the walls.

She resisted the urge to pause and sniff a few of the flowers as a palate cleanser—nostril cleanser—to all the incense. Mostly because Asger might find it silly if his fearsome cat-woman ally stopped to smell the plants.

"This way, ma'am," Asger said, waving to Qin when a servant in a uniform identical to one he'd purloined as soon as they made it into the palace passed down their corridor. "We're almost to your meeting."

The servant frowned at him, then gawked at Qin, but he continued past without trying to stop them. He was fifteen or sixteen, perhaps too young to worry about intruders even if he identified them as such.

So far, the ruse had worked on a couple of servants, but Asger and Qin had been forced to stun three others, who were now locked in rooms and closets, gagged and tied.

Asger continued to wear a determined face, not showing his worries, but he had to be concerned about getting caught before they could complete his task, free Casmir and Kim, *and* return to the *Dragon* to get away from the station before Bjarke arrived. It was a daunting to-do list.

Qin thought it inevitable that one of those people would free themselves or that a security camera would catch them and some monitoring officer would identify them as the intruders they were. She could hardly believe they'd not only made it into the palace end of the station but were approaching one of the lifts that led to the royal suites.

But when they turned into the hallway that held it, two alert guards stood in front of the lift, wearing scimitars, batons, and stunners. And, unlike everyone else they'd encountered, they were clad in combat armor.

Asger's uniform didn't keep them from recognizing that he didn't belong. They lifted the stunners.

Qin snapped her helmet on and charged past him—she was wearing her armor and he wasn't—and sprang at them. They fired the stunners. Their blue nimbuses flashed before her faceplate but did nothing to stop her. One grabbed his baton, but the second man leaped at her, roaring like a lion.

She blocked a combination of punches that he launched at her chest and face, then smashed a punch of her own into his torso. He half-blocked it, but she was too strong, and his defense failed. He stumbled backward as his comrade lunged at her with the metal baton in hand.

He never reached her. Asger had raced up beside her, and he managed to bowl the man over, despite his lack of armor. They tumbled to the carpet, grappling on top of the blue shag.

"Security alert," Qin's foe started. "We've got intruders in—"

She grabbed him and smashed him into a wall. Silks tumbled down, metal dented, and his words turned into a grunt. But it might be too late.

Qin threw him against another wall. She didn't want to hurt people, but when they were armored and couldn't be stunned, there was little choice. Protected, the man wasn't seriously wounded by the hard blows, and he jumped to his feet. She lunged at him again, this time latching onto his helmet. She twisted it hard, her claws trying to extend inside her gauntlets, and a snap echoed in the corridor. The seal broke.

Even as he punched her in her unguarded chest—she barely felt it through her armor—she ripped his helmet off. Now, she could use her stunner. But she'd dropped it in the scramble. She cracked her faceplate against his forehead, trying not to use so much force that it would break his skull, then jumped back. As she whirled to look for her stunner, someone else fired.

Asger. His stunner nimbus struck the man squarely in the now-unprotected head, and he crumpled.

At first, Qin wondered how Asger had defeated an armored foe when he was in the servant's costume, but then she spotted the man lunging at his back. Asger sprang to the side, barely missing a punch that could have knocked his head off.

Qin snarled and rammed into the man, throwing a palm strike that smashed into his faceplate. She ripped his helmet off as she'd done with the other man, and Asger's stunner fire landed an instant later.

"Good work." He rushed to the lift. "Remind me to put my armor back on when we get a chance."

"Maybe you can change in the lift."

Asger tapped at the controls, but the doors did not open. They required a retina scan.

He eyed the unconscious men. Qin planted her hands on the doors and pushed and pulled. Metal squealed as she forced them apart.

Asger stuck his head inside, looking for the car. Wherever it was, it wasn't on their floor.

"Maybe not." He took his pack off, pulled out his armor, and started changing on the spot.

Qin waved at doors along the corridor until she found one that wasn't secured. She dragged the unconscious men into someone's empty quarters. There probably wasn't any point—she assumed that security had been alerted and reinforcements were on the way. But Asger needed time to change. By the time she had them stashed away, he wore his silver liquid armor, his pertundo on his belt. No more pretenses. He led the way into the dark lift shaft, finding narrow rails that they could climb up.

"I recently did this with your father," Qin said as she followed him up, trusting he knew which level they wanted.

"Beat people up and climb a lift shaft?"

"Yes."

"I suppose he did it more nobly and bravely and effectively than I."

"Actually, he complained a lot."

"Really?" Asger sounded startled.

"Really."

A wrenching sound came from above, and light slashed into the shaft. With his armor on, Asger could also force open doors. He jumped out, landing softly on another carpet.

When Qin pulled herself out after him, she was surprised there weren't guards waiting. Asger had landed in a fighting crouch, so he must have expected that too.

"Maybe the security chief is in bed." Asger ran off down the empty corridor.

The doors were spaced farther apart here, set back in alcoves with pillars draped with colorful banners marking them as special. Sophisticated lock panels and cameras were set into the walls of the alcoves. Were these the royal suites?

Vining flowers also wrapped some of the pillars, soil-filled planters built into their bases, and Qin couldn't help but pause to touch a particularly fragrant purple trumpet. What kind of flower was it? More than once, she'd thought about planting a few flowers in her cabin on the *Dragon*, but she feared they wouldn't do well in the gravity shifts, including occasional zero-g time. She inhaled deeply, then rushed to catch up with Asger.

He was looking over his shoulder, and she blushed, hoping he hadn't caught her sniffing. What a silly time to admire the flowers. It wasn't as if it was *real* nature.

"We're almost there," Asger said.

"Good."

Qin continued to be surprised that she and Asger had gotten this far. Where was the rest of the station's security?

Asger turned into an alcove and faced a sturdy door with some winged mythological creature engraved in it. Qin squeezed in next to him.

"Are we ripping this one open too?" she asked.

The engraving was beautiful. It would be a shame to destroy something that appeared handmade, but they couldn't have much time.

"I don't want to startle another man with knight's training." Asger touched his pertundo on his belt, hesitated, then grabbed his stunner and rang the door chime.

Qin stared at him, incredulous. They'd sneaked and fought their way up here, and he rang the doorbell?

Several seconds passed before Qin heard voices on the opposite side of the door. They were barely audible, even to her keen ears, and she couldn't make out what they were saying, but it sounded like a man and woman.

Qin assumed they wouldn't answer—what crazy person would look at the camera display, see two warriors in combat armor, and open the door?—and was about to warn Asger that they might be calling for security. Then the door opened.

A handsome, well-built man with a short beard stood inside, holding a towel around his waist with one hand and gripping a pertundo with the other.

Asger stared for a few seconds, then waved at the bare chest. "I see body-guarding works differently here than in the Kingdom."

The man looked at Asger's stunner. "If you shoot me, my towel will fall off." His voice was deadpan and unconcerned.

"I'd rather not see that." Asger lowered the stunner.

"I thought not."

A beautiful, dark-haired, bronze-skinned woman in a robe came up behind the man and peered around his shoulder. "I wouldn't mind seeing it."

The man raised his eyebrows. "Even if I'm unconscious and flaccid?"

"Flaccid?" she asked. "That would be disappointing."

"Are my services needed?" another woman spoke from somewhere to the side of what looked like a grand foyer. Or did that flat voice belong to an android?

"I don't think so, Devi," the dark-haired woman said, resting a hand on the man's shoulder. "I believe this is… an acquaintance of Tristan's."

"Like Prince Jorg was an acquaintance of Tristan's?" Devi asked.

Asger and Tristan both shook their heads.

Qin found everyone's calmness surreal. It was as if they had been invited up here rather than fighting their way.

"I need to talk to you, Tristan. And, ah—" Asger glanced at the woman next to him, "—if you have sway and can halt the security alert that is no doubt in progress, we would appreciate that. We had to fight a couple of guards to get here. We tried not to hurt anyone badly."

Tristan raised his eyebrows, and the woman frowned.

"Why didn't you comm me?" Tristan asked.

"I don't have your contact information."

"So you beat up the palace guards?" the woman asked.

Asger spread his hands. "That wasn't my first choice, but as soon as I stepped foot off our ship, your security android tried to arrest me. It seems the Kingdom isn't welcome here right now."

"That is true." Tristan turned toward the woman. "Asger is a peer, Nalini. Would you mind calling off security?" He glanced toward the corridor. "Even though it doesn't sound like anyone is on the way."

The woman's eyes grew unfocused as she accessed her chip. Then she shook her head. "There isn't an alert. I don't see anything about anyone coming."

Asger frowned. “How is that possible?” He looked at Qin. “I heard that guard sending a message.”

Qin shrugged. This was the most bewildering infiltration she’d been on.

“Maybe they’re busy with something else.” Tristan’s expression grew grim. “Come in.” He waved to them. “What brings you here, Asger and… friend?” He squinted at Qin.

She braced herself, surprised the word *friend* hadn’t been *freak* since this was someone from the Kingdom.

“This *is* my friend, Qin,” Asger said.

She was glad to be acknowledged as a friend but couldn’t help but wonder what it would be like to be introduced as something more intimate.

“And I have orders to collect your pertundo.”

CHAPTER 12

"WHICH ONE OF YOU IS PROFESSOR DABROWSKI?" THE only man in civilian clothes asked. He looked to be in his sixties or seventies and wore flowing golden robes, matching slippers, and a white turban.

"The shifty one, Your Highness," Assistant Chief Gokhale said.

Casmir blinked innocently and pointed an inquiring finger at his own chest.

It slowly dawned on Kim that this was the sultan. Should she let Casmir do the talking—he'd been the one angling for a meeting—or try to explain what had happened?

Since all of the rifles and glowers were pointing at Casmir's chest—why was it that people always assumed a man was a greater threat than a woman?—Kim decided to speak first.

"This is Professor Dabrowski, and I'm Scholar Sato. We were arrested when we arrived on your station—for no reason, as far as I can tell, except that we are Kingdom subjects. Something was going on in your control center, and some idiot threw gas into the detention cells—" Kim made a point of sniffing loudly and wiping her eyes, "—so we ran out."

"How did you run out of a locked cell?" Gokhale demanded.

Kim frowned, as if confused by the question, though she worried her acting abilities wouldn't be up to snuff. "The bars came up. Is there a security measure in place to release prisoners in the event of a fire, air leak, or other danger?"

Casmir clasped his hands behind his back. He looked wan and like he might have inhaled more of that gas than Kim had, but her stomach was still writhing too.

"Sultan Shayban?" Casmir asked. "I was hoping to speak with you. I have a proposition. But, ah, maybe you want to let your people deal with the… intruders first."

"Leave a couple of men out here with them," the sultan told Gokhale, "and figure out what's going on inside. My comm chief alerted me to two ship-transport freighters waiting outside of our asteroid, loitering suspiciously."

Gokhale and two of the riflemen stepped warily into the control room. Four more men had appeared behind the sultan, all armed and in a vibrant teal and dark blue uniform. His bodyguards?

A vent started up in the control room almost immediately. Kim waited for a complaint or cry of alarm in regard to Zee. She was surprised Casmir hadn't shouted a warning for him to cooperate and not hurt anyone.

"A proposition?" The sultan looked Casmir up and down. "You don't seem to be in a position to propose much of anything, boy."

"I'm an academic, sir. The things I offer are stored up here." Casmir touched the side of his head. "Not in my pockets." He looked down at his bare legs and chest. "Fortunately."

Kim sighed, doubting this would go well.

A curse came from the control room. They must have found Zee.

"Mehta and Kudla are stunned and tied up," someone called. "And who *are* these people? They're in stolen uniforms. And they're unconscious. What the hell. Did those nudies do that?"

Where's Zee? Kim messaged Casmir, her arms starting to ache from holding them up. But the humorless riflemen continued to point deadly weapons in their direction.

You wouldn't believe me if I told you. Casmir smiled at her, not looking as daunted as he should, given the situation. Maybe he had collected a cadre of security robots that were ready to wheel in under his command.

"Sultan Shayban," Casmir said, "I know this isn't the best time, but I believe I can help you. Do you have time for that meeting? Uhm, I can put on my galaxy suit, if I can find it, so you don't have to be concerned about my… lack of pockets."

Shayban opened his mouth, but Gokhale stepped out, her dark eyes wide and her skin much paler than it had been a moment before.

"You better see this, Your Highness," she said.

Footsteps came from behind the sultan's bodyguards. They glanced back but didn't otherwise react when another man jogged into view.

He also wore a security uniform but had more braided tassels on his shoulders than the assistant chief.

"Sorry I'm late, Your Highness. The Excelsus robots weren't at their posts."

Shayban raised his eyebrows. Fortunately, he appeared calmer and almost amused by all this, rather than angry. "Where were they?"

"Uh, they're around the corner back there. Poised for… I don't know what. Someone appears to have overridden their programming and given them new commands."

Kim refrained from looking at Casmir.

"It's Dubashi's men, Your Highness," Gokhale said. "I ran their chips, but I hardly needed to. I recognize one from past criminal trespass on our station." She stepped back into the control room, waving for everyone to follow.

Kim hadn't figured out what was happening yet, but it sounded like Casmir wasn't getting blamed for the robots or the cell bars going up.

"We'll all step inside," Shayban said. "Come Professor, Scholar. We'll get to your story next."

Wouldn't that be fun.

Kim let Casmir go first, and he stepped into the mess of smashed stations, broken office chairs, and downed people, then turned to the right and sat on a tarry black sofa resting against a wall. Kim almost fell over. Zee.

Casmir patted to the seat next to him. The "couch" was as hard as Kim had suspected it would be, and she felt odd about sitting on their bodyguard.

"I see my tool satchel." Casmir pointed.

He didn't try to get it. Security officers filled the room, several pulling up camera recordings, and one trying to question a groggy man they'd managed to rouse. The tied-up guards were pulled out from under the console and released, though they were still unconscious.

"I'm more interested in finding my galaxy suit right now." Kim rested a hand on her bare legs, cold and a little self-conscious.

You don't suppose Dubashi sent these people to kill me, do you? Casmir was eyeing the unconscious intruders, now identified as Dubashi's men.

I don't see how he could have known you would end up here. But it is quite a coincidence that they happened to show up here while we were detained.

Casmir shook his head bleakly. *It's so bizarre to be wanted dead by a man I've never met. What does he truly believe I can do to help the Kingdom in its war? And why does Dubashi hate the Kingdom so much?*

You can't think Rache is the only one Jager has angered.

Did he ever tell you his story?

Rache? Yes.

Will you tell it to me?

No.

Casmir lifted his brows. *No? Really? But you tell me everything.*

It's not my story to tell. You'll have to ask him yourself. And possibly rub his head. That makes him chattier.

Casmir's look of curious inquiry turned to one of mild horror. *I'm not rubbing anything of his. That's illegal in the Kingdom.*

Probably not in System Stymphalia.

Kim rubbed her arms, tempted to hunt for her temperature-modulating suit. Her undergarments lacked SmartWeave fabric.

Maybe she could. Nobody was paying much attention to them. With the owner of the station looking on, the officers were working hard to quickly figure out what had happened. A woman reviewing the camera feed looked around the room, and her brow furrowed as her gaze lingered on the couch. She opened her mouth, no doubt to reveal Zee's identity, but Shayban came and sat with a weary sigh next to Casmir. The woman gaped but opted not to say anything.

"Long day, Your Highness?" Casmir asked.

"Many meetings," Shayban said. "I enjoy the spoils of my wealth and appreciate that my family is well cared for, but I do occasionally miss the days when I captained an exploratory mining ship and my only meetings were with my first officer and the ore."

"Ore is delightful."

"*I* certainly appreciate it."

"It can be transformed into so many things." Casmir patted the couch fondly. "I'm not aware of anything that meetings can be transformed into."

"Headaches."

"True."

The frazzled assistant chief reported to Shayban, standing painfully erect. Kim might have felt bad for her predicament, if Gokhale hadn't been one of the ones to arrest her.

"We'll be here all night trying to figure out everything, Your Highness, but after a preliminary investigation, it looks like Dubashi sent a team to try to take over the controls for Ship Bay Three—we've received a report that our officer on duty there was also knocked out. We'll have to question his people thoroughly, but as you know, all of our fighters and combat vessels are housed there. It's likely they wanted to render them inoperable or perhaps even steal them. The ship-transport freighters waiting outside of our asteroid just fired up their engines and are leaving."

"Why is Dubashi picking a fight with me while he's got his hands full picking a fight with the Kingdom?" Shayban mused.

"No idea, sir, except that if he's short on ships and were to steal some of ours… We have quite a bit of firepower here."

Do you think this has something to do with us? Casmir messaged Kim while Gokhale's report continued. *Or is it a coincidence?*

We may have to wait until Dubashi's men are questioned to find out. Assuming station security tells us what they find. As far as they know, we're suspicious interlopers too.

Not me. I'm bonding with the sultan.

By letting him sit on your crusher and agreeing that meetings are odious?

Precisely. We'll be having breakfast together in the morning.

You're rather optimistic for someone sitting here in his underwear with puke drying on his chest.

I'm hoping he'll take me up to his suite for a shower before breakfast.

You're an intruder, not his date for the night.

We'll see. I saw the wistful look in his eyes when he longed for his ore-exploring days. This is a man who loves metal, and I am a man who also loves metal, and the things it can be made into. We're kindred spirits.

You got all that from your two-sentence exchange, huh?

Absolutely.

"There's one more thing, Your Highness." Gokhale eyed the couch uncertainly. "After reviewing the camera footage, I'm reasonably certain that you're sitting on one of the Kingdom's killer crusher robots."

Shayban's eyes bulged, and he surged to his feet. "What?"

"Zee was single-handedly responsible for defeating the intruders, Your Highness." Casmir rose to his feet, waving for Kim to do the same.

He didn't react to the weapons that shifted over to focus on the "couch." "Zee, you can show yourself now, if you wish."

Zee morphed before their eyes, returning to his hulking six-and-a-half-feet of intimidating killing power.

"Oh, magnificent," the sultan breathed, looking him up and down. "What alloy is he made from? Are there no wires and circuit boards? Or are all of his operating instructions and sensors and everything integrated into… what? Some kind of liquid matrix?"

"I'll be happy to tell you all about him." Casmir patted Zee's arm. "I'm one of the original creators. Zee, this is Sultan Shayban. I believe he's deeply grateful for your assistance in subduing the intruders."

"Oh, yes," Shayban said. "I wish I'd seen it. You say there's a video, Gokhale?"

"Yes, Your Highness."

"Do have it sent to me. I want to know all about this—what did you call it?"

Casmir opened his mouth, but Zee spoke first.

"I am a Z-6000, programmed to protect Kim Sato and Casmir Dabrowski. I am the most superior crusher constructed to date."

"His mantra developed an addition," Kim muttered to Casmir.

"He's pleased with himself for passing as a couch."

"I am highly adaptable and capable of learning from the humans—and the furnishings—around me," Zee added.

"Fascinating." Shayban reached out and touched Zee's solid chest.

"Yes," Zee said.

Shayban's eyebrows rose.

"I forgot to program him with modesty," Casmir said.

"I've always found modesty to be either a sign of low self-worth or a fabrication used to improve people's opinions about a person. I don't care for it." Shayban faced Casmir. "How much would you charge to make me a crusher like this?"

"How interesting that you would bring that up…"

Kim watched in bemusement as Casmir schmoozed the sultan. Maybe he would find an effective solution for his problem after all. If only she could find a better solution for hers than arranging her own kidnapping.

Asger sat on the edge of a beige suede couch in the living room of a spacious suite decorated with dozens of maps of cities, continents, space stations, and habitats. There were also numerous blueprints of sprawling structures, often alongside a photograph of the completed complex. It wasn't the decorating scheme he would have expected from a princess, but he remembered from his research that Nalini was a real-estate developer.

The couch looked expensive, and he felt uneasy putting his armored butt on it. What if he creased the suede? Or scratched it with his pertundo handle?

Qin, either with similar concerns or no interest in sitting, stood behind the couch like his bodyguard. Nalini was in the kitchen, talking on the comm, and Asger felt tense for more reasons than the furniture. Would security come up soon to collect them? Tristan had invited them inside to talk, but that didn't mean someone wouldn't be by to arrest Asger afterward.

Tristan returned from a back room, now wearing dark blue pants and a tunic with light blue trim. They made Asger think of pajamas but seemed typical of the station attire he'd seen. Tristan, it seemed, had gone native.

He carried his pertundo, the telescoping shaft in its most compact form, and he offered it hilt-first to Asger.

Asger blinked and accepted it. He hadn't expected Tristan to give it up easily.

"I assumed someone would send a message ordering me to mail it back." Tristan headed into the kitchen, returned with a tray of miniature sandwiches cut into triangles and stuffed with pâté, set it on the low table, and sat in a chair that matched the suede couch. "I didn't expect a personal visit," he added with a shrug. "I would have given it to Jorg when he told me he'd make sure I was kicked out of the knighthood, but he was being such a smug ass that all I wanted to do was shove it up his—" he glanced toward the kitchen where Nalini was visible and also at Qin, "—poop hole."

"Is that the kind of language you're required to use around princesses?" Asger asked.

"I try to be a gentleman around ladies." Tristan rested his elbows on his knees and clasped his hands. "Is it true that Jorg is still in the system and trying to raise an army? That's what the reports I've seen have said, but it's difficult to tell for sure what he's doing."

"It's true." Asger didn't know how much he should say to someone who'd switched to what the Kingdom would probably consider the enemy side. At the least, *Jorg* would.

"And it's also true that invaders have blockaded the gate back home?"

"Yes."

"We saw the footage of Odin being bombed." Tristan stared at his hands. "I don't regret the choices I made, but I regret that they mean I can't return to help. Even if my family is gone or… incarcerated—" he said that last quickly and quietly, "—I have friends there, and it's where I grew up. As hard a time as I had in Zamek City sometimes, I think it's always what my mind will conjure up when I think of home."

"There was some bombing going on in the capital itself, the last I saw." Asger grimaced, also wishing he were there to help.

"I'm surprised they sent you for my pertundo with all that happening."

Asger's grimace deepened. "I'm not the most trusted knight right now. I think this mission is my punishment."

Tristan matched his grimace. "From Jorg?"

"From Baron Farley. I don't think I'm on Jorg's radar. Jager's maybe."

"That's so much better."

"The king is stuck in System Lion, so I'm not that concerned about him for the moment."

"Is it just me, Asger, or is it odd that our forces couldn't swiftly repel an invasion fleet? We have, what, a hundred warships spread throughout System Lion? How many did the enemy bring? I heard Dubashi is at least partially behind it. Is that true?"

"I think so. I've been out of the loop on another mission, so this came as a shock to me. We were—I mean, Jager was—trying to make inroads in other systems. I hadn't heard of any threat on the horizon at all. Jorg's orders are to raise an army to bring home to help break the blockade."

"I want Odin and all of our habitats and stations to be safe," Tristan said, "but I'm terrified of Jorg having the authority to lead his prick to the toilet, much less men into battle."

"I thought you were using polite language for the ladies present," Nalini said, coming in from the kitchen, where she'd likely heard much of the conversation.

"I am." Tristan smiled at her. "I said prick instead of penis or cock."

"Ah, I see. Yes, my sensitive ears are much less maligned, now that I think about it."

Asger glanced back in time to see one of Qin's sensitive and pointed ears swivel slightly. She hadn't been speaking, merely watching the door and a female android that had been introduced as Nalini's bodyguard, Devi.

Asger wondered if he should invite Qin to sit on the couch beside him. Would she? She was clearly on edge. He also kept expecting trouble to find them. They'd destroyed security drones and stunned and tied up several people. To believe that there wouldn't be consequences, and that they could sit here and munch on finger sandwiches, was silly.

"I've heard much worse," Qin said, and Asger realized his gaze had prompted the others to look at her. "I'm not a lady."

"All women should be treated like ladies," Tristan said.

Qin focused on him and tilted her head curiously. "Are you really from the Kingdom?"

Asger's cheeks heated as he remembered *his* initial reaction to Qin. He was amazed that Tristan didn't seem fazed by her… *catness*. He hadn't been out of System Lion for *that* long, had he?

"I was." Tristan's face grew glum until Nalini sat down next to him in his chair, a chair that wasn't designed for two people. They seemed amenable to sharing.

Asger looked away and pretended he wasn't made uncomfortable by them gazing adoringly at each other.

"I will be sad to see my—the—pertundo go," Tristan said. "I suppose it's naive to hope that something will change and one day I could…" He looked at Nalini. "I wouldn't leave you, of course, but it would be nice to be welcome back on Odin."

She smiled. "From what you've said, there would be plenty of real-estate opportunities we could explore."

Asger felt his mouth drop open. "Tristan was talking to you about real-estate opportunities?"

"I've been learning about rent-to-value ratios and determining a multi-family property's capitalization rate," Tristan said.

"Is that what you were doing when I got here? In the towel?"

"Something like that."

Asger tapped the extra pertundo, knowing it would feel like a greater burden than it was as he carried it back to the ship. "I'll let you know if anything changes back home. You were a good knight, Tristan. You worked harder than anybody and deserved the position. I don't know what all happened with Jorg…"

"I punched him." Tristan twitched a shoulder. "And fell in love with a woman he was a jerk to." He looked at Nalini, who nodded firmly.

"He doesn't rule the Kingdom yet," Asger said. "If I ever manage to prove myself worthy of *my* position, and gain the king's favor, I'll ask him about you. Or if…" Not for the first time, Asger found himself thinking about the conversation he'd had with Casmir. "Or if the Kingdom itself ever changes. I have a friend who thinks it should."

"Is it one of the friends who's in jail here?" Qin murmured. "Maybe we should see if these people here can get them out."

Nalini opened her mouth, but the door chime rang. "Devi, will you get that?" she asked instead of whatever she'd planned to say.

"I will, so long as you remember that I am first and foremost your bodyguard. There's a robot in the closet that's supposed to open the door and clean the floors."

"We'll have to see about getting it fixed now that we're home for a week or two."

"Did another knight come with you?" Tristan asked Asger.

"Not a knight, no. Someone who could probably fix any broken robots around here though."

"*Probably?*" Qin asked.

"Definitely," Asger said. "The robots might fall in love with him afterward and follow him around while playing operas."

"Technically, Viggo plays the operas. Always the same one. He's got the robot vacuums choreographed to it."

Tristan looked like he didn't know what to say.

A throat cleared in the foyer, and a man in a security uniform peered into the living room. Asger braced himself. Qin rested her hand on her stunner.

"Your Highness?" the security officer asked diffidently even as he frowned fiercely at Asger and Qin. "Those… *people* attacked a number of staff and security officers. I don't believe you're safe, even with Tristan."

"I'll be all right," Nalini said. "I've got Tristan *and* Devi to protect me."

"That is correct," Devi said, "and one of us is a more capable protector than the other. Tristan is a little on the dim side, you know."

The officer shook his head. "Your Highness, there's footage of them destroying drones and beating up two men. They should be taken to the detention center. Or deported. If you don't agree, I will have to speak with your father."

"I'll speak with him myself," Nalini said. "I understand the detention center is in a state of disrepair."

Asger raised his eyebrows, wondering what she'd learned from her comm calls. He hoped Casmir and Kim—and Zee—hadn't made things worse.

"Er, that's temporary."

"Perhaps you should deal with Dubashi's men and not worry about these two people," Nalini said. "I'm questioning them and will have them kicked off the station if they don't give me the right information."

"Oh." The officer digested that. "This is an interrogation?"

He looked at the tiny sandwiches on the tray.

"It is. Princesses feed their captured prisoners before they interrogate them. The etiquette books require that we be regal and polite."

"I think you're teasing me, Your Highness."

Nalini picked up a few sandwiches, stacked them, and walked them to the officer. "Please enjoy these and go back to your station. Trust that I'm capable enough to deal with these minor threats to the palace's safety."

The man looked glummer than a pallbearer at a funeral, but he accepted the food and allowed Devi to walk him out.

Asger allowed himself to relax an iota once he was gone and it appeared that he and Qin were safe, as long as they stayed in Nalini's good graces.

"Tristan," Asger said, "is there any chance you could get our friends out of the detention center? They didn't do anything. Their only crime is being from the Kingdom."

"What are their names?" Nalini asked, returning to the living area.

She must not have learned *everything*. Strange that she'd mentioned Prince Dubashi.

"Scholar Sato and Professor Dabrowski," Asger said.

"Professor Dabrowski, the roboticist?" Tristan asked. "He's here?"

"You know him?"

"Not personally, but I watched a number of his free lectures on the network. I couldn't afford— Uhm, there wasn't time in my training for a formal university education, but I was looking for instruction that went beyond the rudimentary mathematics courses I had, and he has lectures up on calculus, linear algebra, kinematics, and the like. And he used robots to demonstrate a lot of the concepts. They were enjoyable lectures."

"Kine-what?" Asger hadn't known Tristan had academic inclinations. He couldn't remember ever seeing his fellow knight toting a book around.

"The geometry of motion, it's called. In mechanical engineering, it's used to predict the movements of systems composed of joined parts like engines or a robotic arm." Tristan grinned. "Or a human arm holding a pertundo. For one of my final presentations, I applied mathematics to hand-to-hand combat to explain why some attacks and defenses that are thousands of years old have changed little over time. They've proven their effectiveness."

Tristan glanced at Nalini, and she smiled back fondly.

"This is why I've put him to work in my business," she said. "Not so much for math related to combat, but he's getting quite good at calculating returns on investment on the fly."

"And here I would have guessed it had to do with what he looks like in a towel," Asger said.

Qin nodded agreement. Asger tamped down a twinge of jealousy that arose.

"That doesn't hurt either," Nalini said.

Tristan's cheeks turned pink.

Nalini held up a finger. "I'll check on your friends, but I don't think they're in the detention center. I *hope* they aren't. There was an incident there with some of Dubashi's men being caught infiltrating our security center and… I'm not sure yet. They're being questioned."

Qin stirred. "I hope someone wasn't after Casmir. He's still got that bounty on his head, doesn't he? Issued by Dubashi."

Asger stood, wanting to go check on their friends himself. But he waited for Nalini, who had the abstract gaze of someone checking the network or reading messages on her contacts.

"Ah." She snorted softly. "They're with my father."

"Your father the sultan?" Asger asked. "Are they being questioned?"

"You could say that. My father wants your professor to build him something called a crusher."

CHAPTER 13

CASMIR DIDN'T EXPECT TO RECEIVE ANY MESSAGES WHILE he was in System Stymphalia, since he didn't know anyone here besides Ishii—and that dreadful Ambassador Romano—but a text came in while he and Kim and Zee were following Sultan Shayban and his bodyguards to Stardust Palace's manufacturing facility. It was from the last person he thought would voluntarily talk to him again.

Greetings, my roboticist nemesis, Kyla Moonrazor's words popped up on his contact. *I did not expect you to follow me to this system. Are you stalking me? Did my kiss stimulate you so?*

I didn't know you were here, Casmir replied.

A likely story. I told you we can take control of this gate when we're ready to make use of it.

I assumed that wouldn't be for a few decades since you only got part of the gate.

Don't remind me. It was rude of you to call down all those scavengers to steal pieces. We should have worked together. We could even now be preparing to leave the Twelve Systems.

That's not my goal.

I'm distressed that my kiss didn't sway you to follow me across the stars.

Casmir decided mentioning that she was old enough to be his mother—and then some—wouldn't be a flattering observation. *Given my sweaty, puking, plague-ridden state during that kiss, I assumed it was only to throw off Rache and keep him from shooting you.*

That is possibly true. The mercenary is vexing. He almost got me three times, and he collapsed half of my base and killed one of my fellow high shamans. I will shoot him as soon as I get a chance. Or perhaps strangle him.

An alarm gong rang in Casmir's mind. Was Moonrazor on the station? The station Rache was on his way to visit?

There wasn't a lag delay between their exchanges. She had to be here or somewhere close.

What are you doing now that your plan has been delayed? Casmir wouldn't mention that Rache was on the way.

Regrouping. Contacting other high shamans in this system. What are you doing on Stardust Palace Station?

Casmir definitely wasn't the stalker in this pairing. Why was she keeping tabs on him? He had never given her permission to contact him through his chip, nor should she have been able to track him through it, but he wasn't surprised that she could. If she was here, it was also possible she'd seen him in person or on a camera.

He caught himself glancing over his shoulder. There was nobody trailing after them, and Zee walked solidly and protectively behind him.

Kim raised her eyebrows. Casmir waved a finger; he would explain after he figured out what Moonrazor wanted.

I'm a civilian advisor commanded to do work for the Kingdom Fleet, he replied, figuring she could guess as much and that he wasn't giving away secret intelligence.

Working for the military? What a waste. You should come work for me.

Your offer still stands?

Certainly. I contacted you to thank you for removing the security system on the gate. It will be much easier to study it and replicate it now.

Somehow, Casmir doubted that was the real reason she'd sought him out, but he said, *You're welcome.* Then, since she appeared to feel grateful toward him, he added, *May I ask a question I've been wondering about?*

Go ahead.

What were your people doing on Odin this past year? I was assigned to stop some terrorists who were bombing our cities, and the leader, the former chief superintendent of Royal Intelligence, was wearing some cybernetic upgrades and had what looked like astroshamans defending his base.

Shayban slowed down as they entered a refining area full of ore being processed, the warm air heavy with the scent of molten metal. They stepped onto a flat automated cart that rolled up to their group, and it whizzed them through the massive facility.

Shayban gestured to stockpiles of materials and spoke proudly of all that he'd built on his station. It occurred to Casmir that this place would be large enough to build and house gate pieces. He wondered if Moonrazor was here investigating the possibility.

Casmir nodded and made suitably enthusiastic noises as he read Moonrazor's reply.

Those weren't my *people. Your former chief superintendent Bernard was one of Dubashi's new followers, seeking to prove himself worthy in the new order Dubashi wants to create and setting up a base in a remote location for... certain reasons. So many seek to curry Dubashi's favor, simply because he is rich. He barely qualifies as a high shaman, but he's as old as dirt, so it would be difficult to evict him from the fold. Besides, once my people and I leave the Twelve Systems, we'll care nothing for what he does here or on Odin. Let him have his world.*

His world? Odin? Casmir frowned at the implications.

But what he asked was, *Prince Dubashi of the Miners' Union is an astroshaman? A high shaman? One of your leaders?* That surprised him more than anything else she'd revealed.

Of course.

That's not in his public record. I've been reading about him. He doesn't have any obvious cybernetic upgrades in his photos.

He opts for subtle human-like upgrades. There are many high shamans who do not advertise their association with the order to outsiders. But I'm sure one of your Royal Intelligence officers could have ferreted it out. I do not know if Dubashi offered anything to Bernard for stirring up trouble on Odin, but it is likely Dubashi did want reports back and may have subverted the chief with some offer. Everybody knows Dubashi has had his eye on Odin for years.

Not everybody. Casmir hadn't known anything about the prince, or even heard about him in the news, until he'd learned about the bounty on his head.

When you say he wants Odin, Casmir replied, *do you mean he wants control of the planet?*

I mean that he wants the *planet. Odin is the crown jewel in the Twelve Systems. Breathable air, the perfect blend of earth and sea, millions of species of animals and birds and fish that can survive there. The most Earth-like planet in the systems. Everybody covets it, even if they say they don't. Even those of us born in space feel the call of grasses and forests and lakes under a yellow sun. It's in our genes. I suppose Dubashi is still human enough to long for those things.*

The cart took them from the refinery into an area filled with giant robotic tools, manufacturing equipment, and conveyor belts. Shayban pointed toward a glassed-in work area at the back.

Casmir, suspecting he would soon need his full attention to negotiate with the sultan, attempted to finish his conversation with Moonrazor. *Thank you for answering my questions.*

You can consider my debt to you repaid.

Casmir hadn't believed Moonrazor in debt to him—if anything, he'd expected her to resent him for working against her in her base—but if she wanted to give him information, he would cheerfully take it.

And know that I wouldn't object, she added, *if you killed Dubashi. He is not a true believer who is fully committed to transcending our flesh forms and fully embracing the next evolution. It was only his money that bought him his position in the order, long before I was influential enough to object, and there are many who resent that he has used us to further his ambitions.*

I'm not a killer.

Send your pet mercenary after him then.

Casmir choked on the idea of Rache being his minion—or even working with him toward the same goal.

The cart whirred to a stop, the group stepping off in front of an assembly line with the housings for robotic floor moppers flowing past on a conveyor belt. Casmir recorded a short video clip to share with Viggo, in case he would be interested in adding to his collection of robot cleaners, or simply wanted to see the manufacturing process.

"Mining is the primary way my family and our people earn our livelihoods," Shayban said, "but we do manufacture a few consumer goods that are popular in the system. We also build security drones and robots, so I believe you'll find that we have everything you need to make a crusher."

Shayban looked Zee up and down again, admiring his lines as if he were a treasured lover.

"This is far more than I could have asked for, Sultan," Casmir said. "And I'm quite willing to make you a crusher if you supply the materials, but…" He glanced at Kim. This would be the challenging part. "I was actually sent to make an army of them to serve the Kingdom."

Shayban's bushy eyebrows drew together.

"That's what I was *ordered* to do," Casmir hurried on to explain. "Mind you, I'm not in the military, and even though I'm a Kingdom subject, I prefer to do things my way. I've learned that my crushers can be used to hurt—to kill—innocent people, so I'm not eager to hand them over to a military leader or even a prince."

"*Especially* a prince, I should think," Shayban said with a distasteful snarl.

Casmir spread a hand, not wanting to argue. "I've been debating how I can help my people get Dubashi's forces out of our system without burdening my conscience with more guilt than it already carries. I believe that if I personally command the crushers I make, I can ensure they aren't used for evil."

Shayban frowned at him. Right, he didn't know Casmir well enough to know he wasn't evil. Or maybe he was wondering where Casmir planned to get the materials to build this army.

"I understand we have a common enemy in Prince Dubashi," Casmir said.

"Yes… I was willing to work with the Kingdom because of that common enemy, but then your king sent me a spoiled prince who's not fit to touch my daughter."

"Now he's sent you a polite roboticist who only wants to touch your ore." Casmir offered his most affable smile.

"How much do these crushers cost to make, and what exactly will you do with them once you build them?"

"They're not inexpensive. I can send you a raw materials list and approximately how much time I'll need in your workshop. If I can retool some of your manufacturing equipment, the process will go much more quickly. As for what I'll do with them, I hope to take them back to System Lion to help break the blockade and protect my people on Odin."

Casmir shivered as Moonrazor's words came to mind. He didn't know if he could trust that anything she'd told him was true, but if it was, and if Dubashi truly wanted his entire planet…

"How does that help me with my Dubashi problem?" Shayban asked. "Once his mercenaries and military forces are cleared out of your system, will you lead your Kingdom fleet back here to deal with him?" Shayban's eyes narrowed with speculation. "And once Dubashi has been ousted, will you leave the asteroid belts and territories he controls in *my* hands?"

"Ah." Casmir wished he could say yes, because Shayban looked like he might trust him to do it, if he gave his word, but the Kingdom fleet was far from being under his command. "I'm only an advisor, so I couldn't guarantee that the captains would be willing to come back here to help you afterward."

Worse, Casmir highly doubted that Jorg would consider that—especially if Shayban had recently refused his marriage proposal to his daughter. Jorg might even argue that Stardust Palace should be the first station to be usurped by the Kingdom if it was able to expand again. Though Casmir hoped that once his people succeeded in driving off the invaders, they would settle down and learn to be happy with what they had. Was that wishful thinking?

Shayban's lips pressed together in disapproval.

"I understand that I'm asking for a great deal," Casmir said, "and it would be unwise for you to give resources to a random stranger who wandered onto your station."

"And out of my detention center."

"Yes. What could I do for you in exchange for the time and resources?"

"Am I correct in assuming that you don't have access to a bank account that can transfer cost plus ten percent to me?"

"I do not have access to a bank account with money sufficient to buy more than a twelve-pack of fizzop and a pizza. A small pizza."

"If that's true, your government doesn't pay its civilian advisors sufficiently."

"Tell me about it. For reasons I haven't figured out, Kim gets paid, and I don't." Casmir extended a hand toward her. She was watching this exchange without commenting.

"She's prettier than you," Shayban observed.

"Is that the reason? Huh."

"It could be that I haven't made a habit of irking my superiors or the king." Kim sighed. "Until recently."

Shayban rubbed his chin. "I confess that my eagerness to have a robot like yours makes me *want* to work with you, Professor, but my business acumen points out that I would be foolish to give away what I'm going to guess is the equivalent of millions of dollars in the highest-grade metals and materials. Especially when I will receive only one robot worth a fraction of the cost of all of those materials."

"I am worth far more than my constituent parts," Zee said.

"Even so…" Shayban looked from Casmir to Zee and back.

He looked thoughtful and shrewd, not flummoxed, and Casmir suspected he'd already come up with a solution he would find acceptable. Casmir didn't know if *he* could find it acceptable. What if, out of some spite from the father of a wronged daughter, he ordered Casmir to build his army and then deploy it against Jorg?

"I will agree to give you the space, time, and resources you need to build one hundred and one crushers," Shayban said, "if you agree to take this army to Prince Dubashi's moon base and use it to take it over and kill him."

Kill? Why did everybody want Casmir to kill people?

"I'm not a murderer, Sultan. Nor can I build crushers that will murder people for me." Casmir was already haunted by the knowledge that the crushers he'd helped create for the military were being used to invade stations in other systems—or had been. He had no idea where they were now. Had they been brought back to System Lion in time to help? Or did Jager have them holding some random station in a system that wasn't in position to help the Kingdom?

"Then promise to capture Dubashi and bring him back to me, where I can arrange to have a piano fall on him." Shayban glanced at Zee. "Or perhaps a very heavy couch."

Casmir grimaced. His stomach writhed at the idea of kidnapping someone, knowing the end result would be his death, but this Prince Dubashi, whom he'd never met, had been trying to kill *him* for months. All because he had been cloned from Admiral Mikita and, Casmir assumed, Dubashi feared he would turn into some brilliant military tactician who would serve Jager and stop the prince from achieving his goal of taking over System Lion. How Dubashi had even learned about him, Casmir didn't know. Had former chief superintendent Bernard been the one to blab? How had it even come up?

"Stopping Dubashi could stop the war," Kim observed quietly from his side.

Yes, there was that too. Stopping the war mattered a lot more than the bounty the prince had put on Casmir's head.

"Can we just imprison him without dropping anything death-manufacturing on his head? Or without shooting him outright?" Casmir smiled hopefully at Shayban. "I understand that he's made himself an enemy of the Kingdom and of you, Sultan, but I'm more a fan of rehabilitating people than arranging their murders."

"Dubashi is more than two hundred years old, thanks to all the age-reversing technology in the galaxy," Shayban said. "I doubt his senescent brain would be pliable to rehabilitation, even if he wished it. However, if you want me to say I'll put him in a cell instead of killing him, I'd be willing to let you believe that."

Casmir snorted. Given how easy it was to break out of the sultan's cells, maybe it was best that Casmir *didn't* believe Shayban would stick Dubashi in one.

"May I have a moment to discuss your proposition with my friend?" Casmir gestured at Kim. "Even if I agree to making a kidnapping attempt, I need to think about how we could get to his base and get in."

Shayban blinked. "Do you not have the use of Jorg's ships?"

"Uh, probably not. We're really more… independent operatives."

Kim's eyebrows twitched, but she didn't point out that she was independently fleeing from Jorg currently.

"I see." Shayban waved toward an empty corner behind an assembly line. "Do consult, but don't take too long. It's getting late." He yawned for emphasis and walked up to Zee and asked him what his core mission was and how he felt about being someone's bodyguard.

Casmir was tempted to wait to hear the answer, but he didn't want to irritate Shayban and lose his opportunity by dawdling.

"What do you think?" Casmir asked Kim when they were alone.

"You don't already have a scheme worked out?"

"Well, I thought after Rache kidnapped you, I would stay here for a few weeks to work on this, but it sounds like I'll also need a ride to this moon base as soon as I can get some crushers made. I could ask Bonita, but she may have already arranged a new cargo, and the *Stellar Dragon* isn't a warship, nor does it have a slydar hull for sneaking into enemy territory. Rache's *Fedallah* would be ideal. Do you think he would kidnap both of us? And take us along to his meeting? How willing are you to rub his head again to warm him up to the idea?"

Kim rolled her eyes. "I knew you had a scheme. And I'm not."

"Not what? Willing to rub his head? Are you sure? He probably likes it. I'd like it if…" Casmir trailed off, reminding himself that he hadn't yet asked Oku for that coffee date—or seen her for weeks—so he shouldn't voice confessions regarding shared rubbing.

"I'm not willing to rub his head to get what *you* want."

"I said what *we* want. We're a team, Kim. Didn't you know? I thought that was implied when you agreed to share a bathroom with me."

Kim lifted a hand. "I'm willing to concede that capturing this Dubashi could be integral in stopping the war at home and keeping him from sending more assassins after you, and both would be good things, but I'm not using my body or anything else to manipulate Rache. If *you* can talk him into helping, fine, but are you really contemplating taking on Dubashi and his entire base by yourself?"

"Zee would be with me, and whatever other crushers I have time to build." Which might not be many, Casmir admitted. How far away was Rache now? "Asger might help, too, but… I'd be reluctant to pull him in on my scheme, as you call it. Thus far, knowing me hasn't been good for his career."

"Shocking."

Casmir opened his mouth for an indignant reply, but Kim lifted her palm and continued on.

"Even if Rache was willing to take you, I doubt he'd help you with Dubashi. He wants to get a contract with the man." Kim curled a lip. "You'd have to convince Rache that you're not working against him."

"That would be challenging. It would be easier if he was a little duller."

"Would it? Then you'd be duller too."

"I don't think intelligence is entirely genetic."

"Well, he's not dull. And you're not qualified to infiltrate enemy bases."

"And yet, it's been my new part-time job of late. Maybe it's the kind of thing where on-the-job training is sufficient."

"I'm afraid you'll get yourself killed. I can help you, but it's not as if I have any great abilities that qualify me for taking over bases either. I'm not… I'm not even sure why I'm still out here." Kim bent forward and gripped her knees, staring bleakly at nuts and bits of wire on the floor—or maybe not seeing any of it.

"Are you all right? Do you need coffee?" Casmir patted her on the shoulder, though only briefly, since he didn't know if she would appreciate the physical offer of comfort.

"Dear cosmos, yes."

"You should stay with Rache. I'll handle Dubashi. It's not like I would put on combat armor and confront him with my physical might. I haven't met a network yet that I couldn't get into. Dubashi's may be challenging since he's an astroshaman, but I'm sure I can do it."

Kim stared up at him. "He's a what?"

"Oh, I'll decant that all for you later. I had a chat with Kyla Moonrazor. She might give me more information if I tell her I'm planning to kidnap Dubashi. Or have couches fall on him. She says she doesn't like him."

"You *talk* to her?"

"Not willingly. She thanked me for turning off the security defenses on the gate pieces."

Kim kept staring at him. Casmir rubbed his nose, half-worried he had boogers dangling.

"Casmir," Kim finally said. "Why is it that you're capable of winning over our enemies, but all you've done is irk the royals and ambassadors who have the power to have your family incarcerated and you hanged?"

"Technically, it's only one ambassador. And one royal. Jorg hasn't met me in person yet. He may find me delightful."

"I doubt it."

"I find your lack of faith… possibly justified. If I do better with enemies, maybe I should try to woo Dubashi. How do two-hundred-year-old princes feel about gifts of underwear? For that matter, I'm still looking for a gift for Rache. What says thank-you-for-the-immune-system-booster and wouldn't-you-prefer-to-infiltrate-Dubashi's-base-with-me-instead-of-working-for-him?"

"I don't think it's been invented yet."

"No? The gift industry is failing to meet demand. Disappointing."

Kim straightened. "Can you send the crushers you make in without going in yourself? Rache isn't going to give up his vengeance quest for you, and I think even if you get Asger's help, you'll be in over your head."

"I suppose that's possible."

Casmir couldn't imagine sending in robots without being there himself, but Kim was right to worry, and he wouldn't worry her further by insisting he would go along, not yet. First, he had to build his army. And make sure he could get a ride with Rache. He also felt compelled to try talking Rache out of working against the Kingdom.

"We'll figure it out." Casmir nodded at Kim. "I'll tell Shayban we agree to his terms. And that you need access to that mushroom lab so you can pretend to be working on Jorg's project when you're kidnapped." He pointed at her. "I haven't forgotten about your scheme. Don't worry."

"I'm so heartened."

Oku sat in the front seat of the auto-bus she'd called for, using her royal security code to override citywide orders for all transportation services to be deactivated until the bombing ended. Rain pounded on the roof, and she glanced out the dark windows often, worried she would spot enemy spacecraft in the dark night sky.

"Almost there," she murmured, not expecting anyone to hear her over the conversations filling the back of the bus. Casmir's parents' closest forty friends and family were back there.

Chasca, who was sitting between her legs, swished her tail across the floor.

"You sound worried, Your Highness," Maddie said from the seat next to her.

"The news is sporadic and not as revealing as you would hope." Oku waved at her chip. She'd been watching news updates as they drove. "I'm worried we'll be caught unaware when a bomb drops on our heads. And I'm worried they won't open the doors of the Citadel for us."

"Which one is more of a fear?"

"The latter." Oku also worried that they *would* open the doors, and she would have to face her father. But she imagined Casmir, whenever he was able to return to Odin, being grateful to learn his family had been safe during the bombings, and decided it would be worth the lecture. She'd also stopped and picked up Kim Sato's surprised relatives. Their home had been damaged, and they'd been taking refuge in the family dojo. Fortunately, a neighbor had directed Oku to the right spot, so it hadn't taken long to gather them up.

With no other traffic, they made quick time to Basilisk Citadel, though they had to take a few alternative routes, since intersections and streets had been turned into craters. Oku still couldn't believe this was happening here in her home city. With the rainy darkness pressing against them and fog creeping in from the ocean, it all felt surreal.

An android in a Kingdom Guard uniform strode out of the small gate station and toward the bus. Oku hopped out so he could identify her.

Soft rain dampened her cheeks as she waited for him to study her, scan her chip, and look at the passengers inside the bus. Would he allow everyone in or check them against the list of those who had been invited to the Citadel?

A spaceship rumbled through the sky overhead. One of theirs? Or one belonging to the enemy?

The android glanced up at its passage, then issued a command to open the doors. "You are expected, Princess Oku."

A forcefield winked out. The android waved for her to get back into the bus and continue inside.

Relieved, Oku rode inside with the others, trying to keep her chin up and display a calm facade so none of her guests would worry. But that facade threatened to crumble when, as soon as they parked among some other vehicles inside, her father appeared, striding toward the bus with Finn and two inky black crushers.

Oku gaped at them.

Casmir had mentioned that he'd worked with the military more than a year earlier to make the first crushers, but she'd never seen any of them except for his, and only on a video. Zee hadn't been with him the two times they'd met in person.

Though she wanted to hide under one of the bus seats, Oku knew she had to fight for these people's right to stay here. She'd invited them. If her father turned them away, what would they think of her? For some reason, the idea of Casmir's parents being disappointed in her, or believing her some powerless pawn who couldn't make decisions for herself, stung.

Something thwapped her leg. Chasca's tail. She looked up at Oku with hopeful brown eyes. She wanted to go out and explore.

"Stay here for a minute." Oku held up an open palm for her stay command. "I'll see if there are any bushes out there for you."

The tail drooped in disappointment at the delay. Oku made sure to close the door of the auto-bus when she got out.

"Father," she greeted, the lights along the rampart in her eyes as she faced him, rain pattering onto the bubble of the forcefield far overhead. That same forcefield would prevent bombs from reaching the Citadel.

Oku glanced at Finn—he wore a smug smirk rather than a concerned where-have-you-been expression, and she wondered if he'd let Father know she'd sneaked out of the castle. The crushers remained a few steps back. Were they her father's new bodyguards?

"What is that?" Father pointed at the bus.

The occupants hadn't yet tried to get off. Several faces old and young were pressed against the windows, watching the exchange.

"I brought some people here for safety," Oku said. "There's plenty of room. I know there is."

"*Some people?* What people? There's a list of those who are invited to come during emergencies. Random citizens off the street are not on the list. It's the senators, our family and staff, and the best and brightest in the city, those who are too valuable of resources to lose to chance."

Was that how he saw people? That only the best and brightest had value? Oku shouldn't have been surprised. It wasn't as if she hadn't grown up in the castle and seen her father frequently. But he was usually subtler with his prejudices, less likely to show them. The fact that he was being so blunt was a testament to his anger and maybe the lateness of the hour. Was he angry because she'd sneaked out and he'd been worried? Or simply that she'd presumed to disobey orders?

"These are the family and friends of some of those best and brightest," Oku said. "I went and got them as a favor."

"To whom?" Her father crossed his arms over his chest.

Her mother's warning popped into her mind, that she shouldn't indicate she had any link to or interest in Casmir. But it was too late. If Oku didn't answer and find a way to get her father to accept this, these people would be turned away.

"Casmir Dabrowski and Kim Sato."

Oku expected exasperation or for her father not to remember who they were and to be puzzled. But he stared at her without reacting at all. Finn was the one who looked puzzled.

A couple of servants showed up, perhaps thinking they would be asked to lead the newcomers to rooms, but they waited, watching her father.

"You've met them?" Father finally asked.

"Yes. Casmir, I've met twice in person. Kim once, just for a minute. But I knew they wanted to make sure their families were safe, since they aren't here themselves to help."

"What do you mean *in person*?" His eyes narrowed, and Oku sensed the disapproval her mother had predicted. "You've spent time with him aside from exchanging messages?"

Ah, he knew about the videos and text exchanges?

Barking came from behind Oku, and she jumped, her response forgotten. Chasca had nosed the door open and slipped out of the autobus. She was staring at the crushers, the short gray fur on her back bristling as she barked uproariously.

Oku lunged and caught her by the collar before she decided to attack. Horrific images flashed in her mind as she imagined the killer robots knocking Chasca into a wall.

Annoyance flashed across her father's face. He didn't come forward to help. As he'd always said, her pets were her responsibility.

Fortunately, as Chasca strained against her grip and kept barking, letting everyone know the spawns of evil were standing a few feet away, one of the servants jogged forward with a leash. Maddie also came out of the bus.

"I'll take her, Your Highness."

Between the three of them, they managed to clasp the leash to Chasca's collar, and Maddie pulled her toward one of the interior buildings. Oku called a thank-you after them as Chasca struggled to get free and rush back to protect her. Oku hoped there weren't any more crushers lurking around the compound.

When her dog was inside, the barking fading, Oku faced her father again. Finn was smirking, probably whispering to their father about how *he* wasn't the troublemaker in the family.

"Dog versus crusher," Finn said. "There's a match that wouldn't go well for one of the combatants."

Their father waved him to silence. "Why have you been corresponding with Dabrowski, Oku?"

She gathered a steadying breath, her nerves frayed. "He had an idea for one of my biology projects, and then he roped in Kim, and they're both working on it. I hope they'll be able to return home soon, and this will all end." She waved toward the sky. "Is there any hope of that, Father?"

Maybe if she directed his attention to the war, he would forget whatever he was thinking about her and Casmir.

"Do you have feelings for him?" he asked bluntly.

Finn's mouth dropped. Why was he even here? Oku wanted to shoo him away.

"Not really." Was that a lie? Oku didn't know. They'd only met face-to-face twice. She would call Casmir a friend after all of their messages back and forth, but she could tell her father meant more than friendship. "I know you expect me to marry some prince or emperor or king. I've avoided developing romantic feelings for people."

"Good. Does he have feelings for *you*?"

Something in his expression made her think that was the question he'd meant to ask first. As if it didn't matter if *she* had feelings for a man, but if Casmir reciprocated them, then that was a problem.

"I'm not sure." And she wasn't. But then she remembered that recent video, the BEE MINE? spelled out in flowers.

Casmir had been goofing around, but the joke had seemed to hint of more than feelings of friendship. Which was surprising, considering how little actual time they'd spent together, but she'd been propositioned by knights who'd only known her from afar, claiming they had fallen in love with her radiant beauty. A turn of phrase that made her want to gag, not return their supposed love.

"Maybe," she amended quietly, hoping she wasn't betraying Casmir by admitting that. But she didn't want his family to be turned away, and maybe now, her father would understand why she had to help them. "Isn't he working for you? Wouldn't it be a good thing to ensure his family is safe while he's off with the Fleet?"

"He's not *with* the Fleet right now. It's questionable whether he's helping us at all or if he's working toward his own ends."

Fear curled through her veins. What was Casmir doing out there? He wouldn't work against the Kingdom, would he?

"He doesn't seem ambitious," she said, careful not to defend him too strongly, lest her father believe she was besotted or something silly. That would make it easy for him to dismiss her arguments on this subject. "What ends would he be working toward?"

"Anything that isn't obeying the crown is treasonous."

Oku didn't know what to say to that. Casmir was a civilian, not a soldier or a knight. Surely, he'd never sworn to obey the crown. Kingdom subjects had gained their freedom long ago—nobody was a serf without rights, without freedom and independence. If her father didn't know that, he hadn't studied the history and social sciences books that her tutors had given her when she'd been a student.

"He has proven himself valuable though," her father said, stroking his chin thoughtfully now. His eyes were narrowed again, this time in speculation rather than suspicion, she thought.

Oku had been less worried when he'd simply been angry.

"It would be better to get him back, if he has indeed gone astray, and turn him steadfastly loyal to the crown, as Admiral Mikita was to King Ansel all those years ago."

Finn continued to look puzzled. And maybe a little disappointed that Oku wasn't being yelled at.

"That loyalty was won because of Mikita's love for Princess Sophia, his desire to prove himself to her." Father looked Oku up and down, as if seeing her for the first time. Or, more accurately, as if debating for the first time if Oku could be used as some prize to win a man's loyalty.

Oku couldn't make herself smile. The idea nauseated her.

"These people may stay." Father gestured magnanimously to the auto-bus. "If you come with me to record a message once things settle down. And after you've rested and cleaned yourself up." He waved at her rain-dampened hair and whatever grime plastered her face after traveling through the debris in the city. "Do you agree?"

Did she?

Two spaceships flew past overhead, the fiery orange of their thrusters visible against the gray clouds. One ship fired at the other before they disappeared from sight beyond the Citadel walls.

Her father kept watching her, as if he wasn't worried at all about the chaos that had descended on Odin. Soon, another boom came from the city, another bomb dropping.

Oku couldn't send Casmir's family back out there. It galled her that her father would do so if she didn't play this game with him. But what else could she do?

"I agree," she said quietly.

CHAPTER 14

YAS WOKE UP IN HIS CABIN ON THE *Fedallah*, red lights coming on and a speaker announcing, "We are engaging in combat. Report to battle stations and prepare for high-speed maneuvers."

He tossed his blankets aside as the warship spun and veered off in a new direction, his stomach objecting as acceleration fought with the ship's regular spin gravity. What was going on? The last he'd heard, they were detouring to Stardust Palace to pick up someone—Rache hadn't told him who.

He scrambled to tug on his galaxy suit as the promised high-speed maneuvers continued, then wobbled to the door. Yas headed toward sickbay but paused when he came to the intersection that branched off toward the bridge.

"Computer, are there any injured waiting for me in sickbay?" Yas asked.

The ship's AI answered. "Sickbay is currently empty."

Curiosity spurring his decision, Yas trotted to the bridge, pausing to grip handholds on the walls when the maneuvers grew intense. A faint shudder emanated from the deck. Were they firing? Or was someone firing at them? Or both?

He knew he should report to sickbay, but if nobody was waiting for him, a couple of minutes shouldn't hurt…

When Yas entered the bridge, he found Rache standing behind his seat, gripping the back with one hand and his other balled into a fist that his chin rested on as he watched the forward display. Yas looked in time to catch a missile striking the hull of a ship and burrowing in before it exploded. Violently.

Pieces of the vessel—it looked to have been a freighter—flew in a thousand directions. An alarm flashed as one piece streaked straight toward their bridge—or whatever camera was transmitting to the forward display. Yas jumped as it hit. But it didn't damage the camera. The display continued to show bits of the lifeless ship, the larger remains of the wreck dark and deprived of power.

And the crew dead?

"We were attacked?" Yas couldn't remember experiencing any surprise attacks for as long as he'd been on board. The *Fedallah*'s slydar hull usually kept enemies from locating them.

Rache's black mask turned toward him. "Not exactly, Doctor." His tone was dry.

The helmsman whooped. "That's one Kingdom bastard that won't be going home."

"Oh," Yas muttered with realization.

Had Rache veered off from his destination to blow up a Kingdom ship for no reason? Was he being paid?

"What about the shuttle?" Rache asked.

"It's accelerating away from us, still on course for Stardust Palace, sir."

"Can we catch it before it gets there?"

"I don't think so, sir. It's fast, and it didn't slow down to help with the fight."

"It was ordered not to," Lieutenant Amergin reported from the comm station. "I just decrypted their transmissions back to the *Chivalrous*. The prince's people said for the shuttle—there's a knight aboard—to make it to the station and find the bacteriologist."

The bacteriologist? Could that be Kim Sato? Yas couldn't imagine who else might be working with the Kingdom fleet.

Rache looked sharply at Amergin. "The knight is on the shuttle? He wasn't on the freighter?"

"Yes." Amergin checked a readout. "Confirmed. Sorry, sir. Looks like I got it wrong before."

Yas was confused about everything except the long stare that Rache gave Amergin. The mask hid his eyes, but there was no doubt to the ice in them. Amergin had made a mistake.

"I don't think we could have caught the shuttle, anyway," the helmsman offered into the chilly silence that had descended over the bridge. "It had too much of a lead. What heading, sir?"

Rache, still staring at Amergin, said, "Continue to Stardust Palace."

"We going to hunt down the knight there, sir?" The bloodthirsty assassin Chaplain was on the bridge, fondling one of his knives.

"Very likely." Rache looked away from Amergin and toward the display. "We'll find him."

Amergin sagged with relief, as if he'd dodged a blow.

"I can do that, sir," Chaplain said.

"We'll see," Rache murmured, shifting around to sit in his seat as the helmsmen altered their course.

The *Fedallah* regained its usual smooth flight.

"Are we already on Dubashi's payroll and taking out Kingdom ships?" Yas asked quietly.

He kept any judgement out of his tone, since he didn't know what was going on. If that reference to the bacteriologist had been about Kim, Yas didn't have to ask why Rache would get involved. But why would a knight be sent to *find* her? Wasn't she already on the Kingdom's side? Working as an advisor?

"No, Doctor. Not yet." Rache looked at him. "But thanks to a transmission we intercepted earlier, I know that knight is trying to pick up the same person *we're* going to pick up. A person who doesn't *want* to be picked up by the Kingdom."

"And she wants to be picked up by us?" Yas asked dubiously.

Kim hadn't been delighted by either of Rache's previous kidnappings of her. And he was still confused as to why she would be avoiding the Kingdom.

"She requested it," Rache murmured, the words for Yas's ears only.

"Kim?" Yas would feel like an idiot if they weren't thinking of the same person.

"Yes."

Yas groped for a way to ask his other questions, knowing Rache might not want to talk about it—about her—in front of the bridge crew.

"Your station during combat is not on the bridge," Rache said before he could speak.

"Nobody's injured and in sickbay yet," Yas replied, though he knew he was in the wrong and it was a dismissal. His curiosity would have to wait until later to be sated.

As he started for the exit, the comm pinged. Yas paused.

"Incoming message, sir. It's coming from a moon halfway across the system. Prince Dubashi's base."

"Oh?" Rache asked. "He hasn't contacted us directly before. Put it on."

The face that came on belonged to a gray-haired woman, not Dubashi, but she wore a black uniform with a lot of silver trim, numerous medals, and tiny braids dangling from epaulets, so Yas guessed she was a high commander for the prince. The two Miners' Union families in Yas's system had their own militias, and with all that Dubashi was trying to accomplish, it wasn't surprising that he also did.

"Captain Rache," the woman spoke formally. "I am General Kalb. His Greatness, Prince Dubashi, has noticed that your ship is in the system but isn't on course for our base, as most of the mercenaries who received our invitation are."

"They spot us because of the fight?" someone whispered. "Or they got something that can see through the slydar?"

Rache held up a finger for silence on the bridge.

Kalb glanced to the side at some readout. "You appear to be on course for Stardust Palace. Is this correct?"

A few of the bridge officers exchanged worried looks. She *could* detect them somehow.

"I am not in the practice of announcing my destination to the galaxy," Rache stated, his voice cool.

There was a delay as the transmission crossed the distance to the base.

"Nonetheless, we've been watching the larger mercenary ships in our system and are aware of their movements. If you *are* going to Stardust Palace before coming to our meeting, please confirm. We have a mission we would pay you to carry out."

"What's the mission?" Rache asked.

"Our agents report that a Star Kingdom microbiologist is harbored there. His Greatness wants her brought here alive and will pay fifty thousand Union dollars. He also wants the Kingdom roboticist Casmir Dabrowski, who is also there, dead, and will pay the same. We require the body as proof of his demise. Accomplish these small tasks, and we will pay you well before we offer even more through a contract for your entire ship. We want to give you the opportunity and honor to serve us in our war against the vile Kingdom."

Yas held his breath for Rache's reaction. That Dubashi wanted Casmir dead was old news, but why would he want Kim?

Rache didn't react at all. "If I encounter these people on the station, I will keep your offers in mind. Rache, out."

He made a cutting motion to Amergin, and Kalb's face disappeared, replaced by the remains of the ship they were flying through.

"How're they tracking us, sir?" someone asked.

"Amergin will find out," Rache said.

"I'm on it, sir," Amergin said.

"Let me know if that shuttle slows or changes course and we have a chance to catch it." Rache headed for the bridge doors.

"Yes, sir."

Yas followed Rache out. As soon as the doors shut behind them, he whispered, "Why would a Miners' Union prince want Kim?"

Could Dubashi have some need for custom bacteria to be developed?

"I don't know," Rache said.

"Do you know why he wants Casmir dead?" Yas knew about the bounty, but he didn't think anyone had ever told him why it existed.

"I assume because of his genes and what Dubashi thinks Casmir might become to Jager."

The genes that Rache shared. Could Dubashi know about that half of the equation? What if Dubashi was trying to lure Rache to his base because he also wanted *him* dead?

Or maybe Dubashi didn't care about Rache's cloned genes. It wasn't as if Rache would ever become an ally to King Jager. But was Casmir an ally of his? And if so, would it truly make a difference in a war? Having met Casmir, Yas had a hard time envisioning him following in the footsteps of the legendary war hero Admiral Mikita.

"I'm going to my quarters to do some research," Rache said when the lift doors opened, "into why Dubashi might be in the market for a bacteriologist."

Yas couldn't think of anything good.

"I think this is the place, though it's not… what I expected." Kim stopped in front of a Glasnax door etched with a human-sized toadstool.

Throughout the station, potted trees and flowering bushes were typical decorations, but here, to either side of the door, half-decomposed logs stretched, elevated above the floor on stands. A variety of colorful mushrooms grew out of tidy holes drilled in the wood, their earthy aroma mingling with the scent of decaying wood.

"I had no expectations," Asger said. "This lives up to them."

"You don't have to come in." Or follow me around, Kim did not add.

It would be a while before the *Fedallah* reached the station, but she didn't want Asger lurking around her when Rache made his incursion to rescue her. Correction: rescue *them*. Kim hoped Rache would give her an hour's warning, so she could tell Casmir to grab his things and meet her up here. She also hoped they could slip out without Asger knowing. Given that Rache had threatened to kill their friend if they crossed paths again, Kim wanted to keep them far away from each other.

Asger shrugged. "I've completed my mission, so I don't have much to do until my ride gets here. Since I sent back my shuttle, I gave up my autonomy. Unfortunately. Prince Jorg is sending a shuttle." He looked at her, hesitated, then shook his head. "Until then, I'm assuming that my mission is to wander around looking decorative on a hostile space station." Asger lifted his purple cloak.

He was wearing his full armor and armed with his pertundo and a stunner. Since Casmir had made friends with the sultan, nobody had objected to Asger, Kim, or Casmir wandering around.

"Maybe it won't be hostile to the Kingdom for long," Kim said. "Casmir seems to be charming the sultan."

"You think his charm is powerful enough to repair the damage Jorg did by offending the princess?"

"His charm plus a crusher might. For a robotics lover, it's a winning combination. Let's hope it's enough. Our fleet needs allies to take back to System Lion for the fight, and it sounds like Shayban has a lot of ships." Kim didn't see a door chime, but a small plaque on the wall proclaimed that the laboratory hours had begun, so she stepped up close enough to trigger any sensors. The door slid open.

Asger stuck close behind her as she entered, reminding her of Zee looming protectively. She wondered again why he was with her. If he had nothing to do, he could be doing it with Qin and Bonita on the *Dragon*. The last Kim had heard, they were still looking for work, another cargo to haul or a criminal with a bounty on his head.

"Are those mushrooms growing on the walls?" Asger whispered.

"They appear to be." Kim gazed around the large clean entry area, the familiar scent of disinfectant reminding her of her own lab back home, though a faint mealy, farinaceous odor lingered under it. "I assume those are decorative or for hobby purposes and that more controlled grow rooms exist elsewhere. The laboratory synthesizes mycological drugs and supplements for numerous consumers in System Stymphalia. I saw a mention of a gift shop where you can purchase lion's mane and reishi teas."

"They're on the ceiling too." Asger gazed upward.

Kim walked toward a wide door-filled corridor leading away from the entry area they had entered. A sign did indeed promise numerous growing chambers, spawn rooms, and laboratories in that direction. She didn't see a sign mentioning offices or her contact Scholar Natasha Sunflyer.

"I'm now suspicious of the *protein burgers* Tristan and I had for dinner last night." Asger lowered his gaze from the ceiling and prodded one of the wall mushrooms. "They didn't taste like real meat or vat meat or anything meatish."

"Mushrooms have been a food staple since Old Earth days, but if it makes you feel better, I think those burgers were made from insects. Crickets have proven adaptable to space station living, so they can easily be bred for food." Kim had actually referenced some of the work done to increase their viability in space for her bee project. She didn't care for foods that crunched and squished oddly in her mouth, though she found insects less unappealing than so much of the rubbery seafood her father had tried to foist on her as a kid, but she acknowledged them as practical for others.

"I do not feel better, no." In fact, he looked a tad green.

"You've never had inago or hachinoko in the capital? There are a lot of tsukudani vendors that serve them as street food. I seem to remember a vending machine at the university."

"I don't know what those are, but no. I'd have to be extremely drunk to buy insects out of a vending machine."

"Scholar Sunflyer?" Kim called uncertainly down the corridor. "Are you here? I messaged you a few days ago about visiting when I arrive. Can you use a helper?" She looked at Asger. "Or two?"

Kim thought it would be politic to offer her services instead of coming straight out and asking for lab space and use of the equipment here. Besides, it wasn't as if she truly wanted to make progress on Jorg's bioweapon assignment.

"I'm here more in the capacity of bodyguard," Asger said.

"Oh?" Kim asked warily. She and Casmir had deliberately not told him about their Rache-kidnapping plan. Asger couldn't have found out through some other channel that Rache was coming, could he? "Is there some reason you believe I need a bodyguard here?"

Asger hesitated. "My father is the one piloting the shuttle that's coming."

"Coming to pick you up?"

"Yes," Asger said, "but that's a secondary task. When the *Osprey* rendezvoused with Jorg's ship, the prince noticed that you weren't there to transfer over. He sent my father in a shuttle to retrieve you."

Damn, she had *two* would-be kidnappers? What if Bjarke got here first?

"There's more," Asger said. "The fleet sent a Kingdom freighter to Stardust Palace for a provisions run. It left shortly after my father's shuttle. Rache's *Fedallah* popped out of nowhere and attacked the freighter. It put up a fight and maneuvered as well as it could, and that bought my father time to get away, but he thinks Rache might be right behind him and headed this way too. With his stealthed ship, there's no way to know. It depends on if there's something here that he wants, or if he wants to stay back by our fleet and harry it."

No, Rache was coming here for Kim. Did that mean it was her fault that he'd blown up that ship? Or had he seen an appealing target on the way and gone for it?

"Did the crew of the freighter survive?" she asked quietly.

"No. He blew up the entire ship."

Kim bent over and rested her forehead on a cool counter. Rache wouldn't have crossed paths with that freighter if she hadn't asked him to come here. This had been a mistake. She should have told Jorg to screw off and accepted that her life on Odin was over.

"Rache wouldn't be after Casmir again, would he?" Asger sounded puzzled. "Because of however many gate pieces he got away with? I assume, if he was going to kidnap anyone again, it would be your mother and that other loaded droid professor."

"I..."

Footsteps sounded, saving Kim from answering. At least for now. But it wouldn't save her from worrying. Where could she hide that Bjarke wouldn't find her? And that Rache would? And should she even go with him after this?

"Hello. I'm Scholar Natasha Sunflyer, Scholar Sato. Please forgive my slowness—I was in the middle of an experiment."

The woman walking toward them in a white lab coat had atypically long fingers and a brainpan that appeared one and a half times its normal size, though she was of average height and build. Kim had seen genetically engineered humans on Tiamat Station and here on Stardust Palace, but she hadn't gotten used to it yet. Most of them had either been wildly different, like Qin, or exactly like humans, if perfect-looking specimens. Natasha, who appeared to be in her early twenties, didn't fall into either category.

She nodded politely at Kim, then smiled curiously at Asger.

"I understand completely," Kim said, hoping she caught herself before she gaped too long at the woman's large, broad forehead. "As I said in my message, I'm a bacteriologist from the Kingdom, and I'm visiting for a few days."

Or at least, she had *expected* to be here for a few days. If Rache and Bjarke were both on their way here and would soon be on the station searching for her, there was little point in getting involved with anything in the lab. Other than being able to say she'd visited the research facilities here, should her plan go awry and Bjarke succeeded in dragging her back to Jorg.

"Oh, wonderful." Natasha smiled. "It's been so quiet here since my father disappeared. Do you want a tour? We develop custom fungi strains to create new antibiotics to combat resistance to old antibiotics and send them to hospitals and medical centers throughout the system. I don't know why I said we. It's mostly just me and a few android helpers."

"Your father disappeared?" Asger frowned. "From the station?"

"Yes. Three months ago. He's a virologist."

Kim rummaged through her mind, trying to think if she'd read publications by a Scholar Sunflyer. She wouldn't have likely come across Natasha's work, since her lab back on Odin didn't handle mycology, but they did have virologists on the staff.

Natasha guided them into the complex on the tour she had offered. "It's too bad he's not here. He would have liked to meet you." She smiled back at them.

"I assume she doesn't mean me," Asger murmured.

"Scholar Sato," Sunflyer said. "I've read some of your papers and about your work. We've brought in some of the transgenic bacteria your corporation makes for producing enzymes that break down antibiotics in the wastewater treatment plants in the Kingdom. Such a wonderful idea. And you've proven that it helps reduce antibiotic resistance in general, haven't you?"

"Proven is a strong word, but numerous studies have lent evidence toward that," Kim said. "Enough that the government has employed them on a wide scale. Who is your father?"

"Scholar Serg Sunflyer. He had us created twenty-four years ago." Natasha waved to her head and wiggled her long fingers. "My three sisters and I. He's a music lover and wanted us to be superior players of the nebula piano, but he also gave us enhanced intelligence in the hope that we would go into research. I'm the only one who did. One of my sisters fixes auto-cabs, one teaches poetry, and one is traveling the system and finding herself. Genius doesn't always impart ambition."

"Did your father have a lab here too?" Kim asked.

"Yes. He was working on methods to keep DNA from mutating under the effects of certain common viruses. He prefers work that helps people now. Years ago, he worked in System Cerberus at Sayona Station and created virologic weapons." She shuddered. "He'd been recruited, and the pay was very high, but he's such a warm-hearted man that it was hard to imagine him engaging in that."

Kim eyed Asger, though she didn't know if he'd twigged to the ramifications. He hadn't been in the room when Jorg had said Royal Intelligence believed Dubashi had a bioweapon. Was it possible that Dubashi had kidnapped this expert and forced him to build one?

"I do hope that some old enemy or competitor from System Cerberus hasn't come back to haunt him," Natasha continued. "There was no sign of a fight or damage to belongings in his quarters. And the cameras didn't catch anything. He simply disappeared from Stardust Palace. I've heard nothing from him, and I'm worried."

"We have a friend who finds people," Asger said.

Kim grimaced. If Dubashi was responsible, the last thing they should do was send Bonita in that direction. But Asger didn't seem to have made the connection yet. Admittedly, Kim had no proof. Just a hunch based on the sudden interest in bioweapons in this system.

"Oh, really?" Sunflyer laid one of her long hands on his arm, and there was a hint of the adoration Kim had often seen in young women's eyes when meeting knights. Or maybe that was *desperation*. Did Sunflyer think a knight had special enough powers to easily find a missing person?

Asger's eyes widened in what might have been incipient panic at this closeness from a strange woman, but he covered the expression and didn't pull away. "Yes."

"A Kingdom knight, like you? I was thinking of hiring a private investigator to look for my father, but knights go undercover and have all manner of combat skills, don't they?"

"They sometimes go undercover for the king, yes, if they have the knack for it." Asger's lips flattened, and Kim wondered if he was thinking of his father's undercover stints. "But I meant Captain Bonita Lopez. She has a freighter called the *Stellar Dragon*, and it's docked here now. Technically, Bonita is a bounty hunter, but she might have the resources to locate missing individuals."

"Oh." Natasha's lips rippled. Perhaps bounty hunters were less appealing than knights. "Are you sure I couldn't hire you to look for my father?"

"I'm not a mercenary, ma'am. Uhm, Scholar. I can't hire out my services. Maybe Tristan could. He's not a knight anymore."

"No, but he is a real-estate developer now, and that keeps him busy. I've met him. He's a nice boy. Polite. Nice ass." She nodded firmly at her assessment.

Asger's eyes flew open. Apparently, he hadn't expected the comment from an erudite scholar.

Asger turned to Kim. To hand the conversation off to her? For verification on the ass?

"I hadn't noticed," Kim said.

Asger shook his head in mute horror. Maybe that hadn't been what he'd silently been asking.

"Scholar Sunflyer," Asger said sturdily. "I highly suggest you contact Captain Lopez. This is her line of expertise."

Natasha released his arm. "Ah, I understand. Forgive me. I was excited at the idea of having a knight work with me. Yes, I'll look into her."

Kim thought about mentioning her burgeoning hypothesis that Dubashi had been involved, but that might unnecessarily alarm Natasha. And she had no evidence yet, nothing but a passing remark by Prince Jorg, who was a dubious resource at best.

"If you recommend her, I will contact her." Natasha nodded. "Thank you."

Asger looked relieved to have her attention focused elsewhere.

Kim hoped that whoever had taken Scholar Serg Sunflyer, it wasn't Prince Dubashi. She feared Bonita and Qin would be in over their heads if they tried to extract someone from a base that had to be well-guarded by people and technology. And… a bioweapon? Kim shuddered at the idea.

If Dubashi had poor Scholar Serg Sunflyer locked up in his base creating something horrific, it might be a suicide mission for any of her friends to go there. And yet Casmir was planning right now to infiltrate it. His crushers might not be affected by a biological weapon, but they also wouldn't know how to disarm it safely. The only one in their group who realistically could…

Kim dropped her face into her hand and, with dread and certainty, sent a message to Casmir. *I think I need to go along with you to Dubashi's base.*

She would figure out how to tell Rache that later. She hadn't even told him that Casmir was coming along with her.

"One problem at a time," she murmured.

CHAPTER 15

CASMIR CARRIED A BAR OF DIURANIUM TO THE cart in the refinery he'd claimed for transporting his raw materials, positive the hunk of metal would weigh more than sixty pounds on Odin and telling himself that meant it only weighed thirty pounds here in the lesser gravity. That should mean he wouldn't break out in a sweat or start panting. Definitely not.

"It's fine," Casmir muttered to himself as he most definitely panted. "You're still recovering from being deathly ill. A little sweat is normal."

He eyed a robot loader parked against a wall and thought about putting it to work, but he already had an assistant.

Zee trotted past, his arms morphed into something akin to shelves, shelves stacked high with a dozen bars identical to the one Casmir carried. He slid them onto the cart and passed Casmir on his way back to retrieve more.

"Show off," Casmir said.

"It is unnecessary for you to assist me in this task, Casmir Dabrowski." Zee loaded up his arms with more bars.

"I know, but I feel guilty when I ask someone else to do work while I'm sipping lemon fizzop while sitting in the shade under a palm tree." He hadn't been doing that, but he could have, since several types of trees were potted along a long side wall of the manufacturing facility. A robot vacuum trundled under their branches, sucking up leaves that had fallen during the night.

There was sun, too, in a manner of speaking. A dangling spherical light fixture on the ceiling radiated something similar to noon sunlight back home. The wall behind and above the trees had been painted a pale blue imitation of a sky. The wall opposite featured a darker blue ocean at the bottom. The gritty metal floor had been given the color of a sandy beach. The riotous color in the palace and the visitor areas hadn't surprised Casmir, but he hadn't expected anything other than utilitarian gray in the manufacturing area.

"You were not sipping or sitting," Zee said. "You were retooling Assembly and Manufacturing Area Number Three for production. Perhaps you should be sitting. You have been ill, and humans need to rest and recover from illnesses."

"Yes, thank you, but Kim assures me I'm ready for work. Also, I finished the retooling and am waiting for that android to return with the nanites and nanite-programming machine from the medical laboratories."

Casmir wondered if Kim was in one of those labs. This was his second day on the job, and he hadn't seen her since the day before. They had exchanged a few messages, but he didn't know where she was staying.

He'd slept in this facility, in a little office he'd discovered with a sofa—one made from softer materials than a crusher—and a beat-up coffee machine. It also had a wall display that ran the financial news, where System Lion's war was being mentioned frequently in relation to how it was affecting the markets everywhere else. There had been few details about what was going on, but Casmir's stomach knotted with fresh worry every time he walked past the display. He couldn't bring himself to turn it off in case… In case something important happened.

Would he and a little army of crushers be able to make a difference? Was there some better use of his time and his brain that he could be employed in? He had to believe that going to Dubashi's base in this system and capturing the prince could turn the tide of the war. That made this project seem worthwhile and not something wasteful that he was doing while his family and friends back home were in danger.

After surreptitiously wiping moisture from his brow, Casmir picked up another bar. Not that Zee would mock him if he noticed the sweat. And nobody else working in the area was close enough to observe him. Most of the employees here were automated, robotic, and indifferent to his presence.

A grinding noise sounded across the bay, and orange sparks flew, highlighted against the dark background of ocean waves painted on the wall. Casmir's vision blurred, and a faint buzzing came from the back of his mind. He closed his eyes, grimacing and willing his brain to straighten itself out. He'd taken his seizure medication that morning, damn it. And faithfully since he'd wakened from his Plague-induced stupor.

His sensory awareness intensified, and he grew highly aware of the faint fumes of molten ore, the drone of ventilation fans, and the grinding of machinery.

As he was thinking that he should set aside the bar and sit down before he fell down, a hand gripped his shoulder, as if to hold him upright.

"Are you having a seizure, Casmir Dabrowski?"

"Maybe a little one." The uncomfortable sensation passed slowly, though a pulsing behind his eyes suggested he would have a headache for the rest of the day. So long as he didn't collapse and lose precious work time recovering. He risked opening his eyes, but he kept his back toward the corner where the grinding was going on. "I'll be all right."

"I will assist you." Zee wrapped an arm around his waist and carried Casmir and the bar he still held to the cart and set him on it. "We have now loaded the two hundred bars you asked for."

"Very efficient. Thank you for the help." Casmir set his single bar down and rested his hands on the forward console. "You're almost as good as the therapy dogs back home on Odin. One of Dr. Rothberger's patients has one that can tell when a seizure is coming on before she can."

"*Almost?* I will search for a protocol that will teach me how to recognize and anticipate better than an inferior canine."

Casmir smiled. "Hopefully, when I get back home, I'll get a chance to see my doctor and get my medication adjusted. Or maybe, once my brain returns to normal gravity, the medication I'm on will start working better."

He turned on the cart, hoping he could drive it over to the manufacturing bay without trouble. Even without seizures fuddling with his senses, his strabismus made his depth perception weak. It was a foregone conclusion that he would lose his right to drive his air bike back home for a while, once Dr. Rothberger analyzed the data his chip had sent and marked on his record that he wasn't currently in remission with his seizures. Kim got around without a vehicle, and Casmir knew he could, too, but it saddened him to lose some of his independence. Driving, he reminded himself, should be the least of his concerns revolving around going home. After seeing those videos of bombs being dropped in the capital, he worried about the kind of home he would find when he returned to Odin.

Casmir navigated the cart toward the large doorway between the bays, confident that he could gauge the width without trouble. Even so, he let out a sigh when the cart cleared the sides. With so few human workers about, he wasn't worried about injuring anyone if he misjudged a doorway and knocked heavy metal bars off his cart, but he would prefer not to make a mess. Or *be* a mess.

When he reached the conveyor belts and robot arms of Area Number Three, a red warning light flashed, and a barrier rose up out of the floor, startling him. He reached for the brakes on the cart, but under the heavy load, it did not slow quickly. He tried to turn it to avoid the barrier, clearly some automatic protection for the equipment that deployed when it sensed something large approaching, but he misjudged the distance—or was simply too slow to react. A cacophonous scrape echoed through the bay as the cart struck it.

Metal dented, and paint chips flaked to the floor as Casmir wobbled for his balance. Zee gripped his shoulders to help keep him upright. Fortunately, the bars were heavy enough that they didn't slide off.

The barrier retracted into the floor, dented and scraping loudly as it sank into its housing. Casmir clambered off the cart, wincing at the damage. It could have been worse, but he anticipated the sultan sending him a bill when he found out. Or requiring a second crusher as payment.

"The android approaches with nanite equipment," Zee said, indifferent to the banged up side of the cart. "Soon I will have a mate."

Casmir spread his hands, groping for his equilibrium—and to slow his hammering heart. "Yes, Zee. You will."

"How long did it take you to make me?"

"I built you in one night, but you were a one-off made with a lot of hand tools and gumption. This is taking longer to set up, since we're going to do a run of a hundred, but once the process gets going, it'll be faster overall."

Casmir turned to face the approaching android and struggled not to grimace. It wasn't alone. Sultan Shayban strolled along at its side, a cup of tea in one hand and an unreadable expression on his face. Another big man, perhaps a bodyguard, walked behind him, but Casmir barely noticed him. Shayban had seen the crash. He couldn't have missed it. Casmir, cheeks flaming with embarrassment, wanted to hide behind Zee.

"Good morning, sir." Casmir smiled and hoped to convey good cheer, good cheer that would rub off, to Shayban. "Sorry about that mishap. I hadn't noticed that retractable barrier there."

"It's fine." Shayban waved dismissively, and Casmir relaxed a bit. "But maybe your crusher should drive. Can he?"

"I can do many things," Zee said. "If I was not originally programmed with an ability, I can research and learn how to do it, but I am moderately flummoxed by canine seizure detection. The article I am reading says it is *unknown* how dogs detect seizures and alert their owners fifteen minutes to twelve hours prior to the event. It is speculated that the canines notice changes to human behavior or scent, but I cannot self-program based on speculation."

Casmir rubbed his face as Shayban raised his eyebrows and asked, "Seizures?"

"Never mind, Your Highness. Yes, I will have Zee handle the driving if we need more metal."

"Very good. I was hoping for a demonstration of his talents as a bodyguard. I have seen his talents as a couch, and I also saw the video from the detention center where he defeated six intruders. That was excellent. But can he come out ahead in a battle against a superior fighter? The crusher you will make me will be identical to him, yes?"

"Yes," Casmir said. "I suppose it depends on *how* superior the fighter is—how cybernetically enhanced and well trained—but the original crushers, from which I borrowed heavily to create Zee, were designed to be great warriors and protect my planet." Casmir hesitated to admit how much of a role *he'd* played in their design. He'd been so naive then, believing he was building protectors, as the military had told him, and not aggressors that would be unleashed on unsuspecting enemies of the Kingdom. He wondered if Jager's incursions into other systems had resulted in the war that was now being fought in their home star system.

"What do you think, Tristan?" Shayban turned to the bodyguard, or what Casmir had assumed was a bodyguard, behind him.

The man wore combat armor, but Casmir now wondered if that was to test Zee rather than because threats were typical here on the station.

"I'm happy to test him for you, Your Highness. I don't have my pertundo anymore, but we can punch and grapple."

Tristan? Pertundo? Was this the man Asger had come to see? He did have a Kingdom accent and the brawny build of a warrior who kept himself fit.

Asger had sent a note the day before, letting Casmir know he was fine, that he'd located Tristan, and that he'd returned to the *Dragon* with Qin, but he hadn't mentioned if he'd parted on amiable terms with the ex-knight.

Tristan bowed like a *current* knight, then stuck out a hand to Casmir. "It's an honor to meet you in person, Professor. I've watched some of your lectures."

"Oh? Which ones?" Casmir knew knights received schooling equivalent to a basic degree, but most of the courses he'd recorded and published on the public network were geared toward advanced university students.

"Linear algebra, calculus, kinematics, and a few others."

"Really?" Casmir asked. "Were you planning a second career in engineering?"

"Not exactly. I needed my math scores to bring up my essay scores on the knight exam, so I tried to learn as much as I could."

"Tristan is helping my daughter now with investments for the family," Shayban explained. "We are fortunate to have him here. Your prince is an idiot for driving him out of the Kingdom's service, but we shall not complain, not about *him* at least."

Casmir smiled bleakly, worried that Jorg was also in the process of driving Kim out of the Kingdom's service—or the Kingdom altogether. When Casmir had suggested that Rache kidnap her, he'd only been trying to be helpful, but what if she felt she couldn't go home and ended up staying aboard the *Fedallah*? Flying into battle and being put at risk day after day on the mercenary ship? Casmir had barely spoken to Jorg, but he already disliked the prince.

"Zee, can you unload these for me, please?" Casmir waved at the bars and pointed to where they needed to go. "Before you test your combat prowess against a knight?"

"A former knight," Tristan said quietly, sadness hooding his eyes even though he had won a position of status here.

"Am I to refrain from hurting him?" Zee again altered his arms into something akin to forklift prongs to lever piles of bars off the cart.

"I think so. Just defend yourself, please."

Casmir took his new nanite equipment from the android and started to work as Tristan drew Zee into an open area. He wasn't worried about Zee being able to sufficiently prove his worth, especially against someone without weapons. It would take explosives to blow Zee to bits, and even then, he was good at sucking his bits back together and recovering. It was a little distracting working while crusher and knight were flinging themselves around nearby—at one point, Tristan sailed into a wall hard enough to dent it, and Casmir felt less bad about denting the cart. Shayban watched with avid appreciation as he sipped his tea.

Eventually, Casmir grew so absorbed in his programming work that he forgot about the fight and tuned out the clanks and thuds of combat. He didn't know how much time had passed when Shayban tugged at his sleeve and drew his attention from the project.

"When you program my crusher," Shayban said, "will it follow my orders and my orders only?"

"Is that what you wish?" Casmir would have assigned the sultan as the primary person to protect, but he'd been planning to give himself the ultimate power when it came to commanding the crushers he made. As strong as Zee was, Casmir worried about other crushers being used against him—or against innocent people—so he wanted the ability to reclaim them if need be. But there was no need to mention that to Shayban, was there? "Zee is programmed to protect and obey myself and Kim Sato. I could do the same for you with yours."

"Very good. I would like my crusher to obey only me but to protect all the members of the royal family. I do not feel safe even in my own palace with Dubashi trying to steal my ships and stir up all manner of trouble."

"That's understandable. Did you ever find out for certain if that was why those people broke in?"

"It was. I don't know why Dubashi feels the need to steal my ships when he has so many of his own, but I'm relieved he failed." Shayban nodded at Casmir, and also Zee, as if to acknowledge their role. "Professor, after you create my crusher and the crushers that you'll take with you to defeat Dubashi, will I be able to have more made?" Shayban waved at the manufacturing equipment, and his tone turned dry as he added, "I assume you will go back to the Kingdom with my millions of Union dollars' worth of materials after you deal with Dubashi."

"I need to go back and help stop the war, yes." Casmir's eye blinked as he debated a political way to say that he couldn't allow what Shayban was asking. "I think the Kingdom would send assassins after me if I left the schematics with you. I signed a contract and a non-disclosure agreement, you see."

No need to mention that it was sketchy that Casmir had used the schematics stored on his chip, information that *shouldn't* have been stored, to make Zee. But since Jorg had ordered him to make more crushers, maybe that would be forgiven. He hoped.

"Oh? Did you work on the original development?"

"I led the team," Casmir admitted. He'd been so proud of that once.

"*You* invented them?" Shayban watched as Tristan, who was either a glutton for punishment or enjoyed working out against a challenging opponent, sailed into a wall again. "You must be *very* good."

"I had a whole team. It wasn't only me. I just came up with the technology for integrating nanites into the molecular matrix of the alloy itself and creating a hive mind of a sort so that the brains are spread across the entire malleable structure."

"So you basically came up with the whole thing." Shayban smirked at him.

"I… had help." Casmir had been trying *not* to take credit.

"We have some decent programmers and roboticists here. If you find that your work in the Kingdom isn't as appreciated as it should be, I invite you to move here and head up a research and development lab."

So he could make something similar to crushers but that wouldn't violate the contracts he'd signed on Odin? Casmir made himself smile—better to have a job offer than be thrown back into a cell—but he could see the gears spinning in Shayban's eyes. The sultan didn't seem a bad sort, but he had an enemy in this system and was probably worried about galactic politics as a whole and protecting his mining empire.

"Thank you, Your Highness. That is tempting, but my family and community are back on Odin, and I teach at the university there and already have a position running a lab. It's very fulfilling." Or it *had* been. Would his job still be there by the time he finally made it home? Would King Jager allow him to return to it? Maybe Casmir should tell Shayban he would think about it, in case he had to leave System Lion.

The idea of leaving his family and never getting to ask Oku on that coffee date made the notion particularly glum.

"I'll double your salary," Shayban said. "And we've been contemplating for years starting up a university here to include robotics, manufacturing, and medical research facilities. We've been drilling deeper into the asteroid and expanding our station in anticipation of offering more hotels and housing for such. You could be on the board and have a say in the opening of the institution. I imagine you would find it quite freeing after living under the stifling rules of the Kingdom."

"I… That's very interesting, Your Highness. I will think about your offer."

"Good. And if you succeed in bringing me Dubashi tied up and slung over your crusher's shoulder, I'll make it *quadruple* your pay in the Kingdom." Shayban thumped him on the shoulder. "I do believe in rewarding talented people and enticing them to stay."

"A good philosophy," Casmir murmured.

So this was what it was like to leave academia and work in the civilian sector. He could see why so many good people were tempted. But the thought of abandoning the Kingdom bothered him for more reasons than his family. If all the good people left, what would remain? The Kingdom needed to be fixed, not left to fall into greater disrepair.

Bonita woke up in her cabin to a soft chime.

"You have a message, Bonita," Viggo said over the speaker.

"Important enough to wake me from my rejuvenating sleep?"

She wished her sleep were rejuvenating. Usually, it was sporadic and interrupted by hours of staring at the ceiling. One thing she missed about being younger was how much better her sleep had been back then. At least her knees no longer woke her up with stabbing pain when she shifted her legs the wrong way under the covers.

"You were grinding your teeth and clenching your fingers in your pillow. It didn't look that rejuvenating."

"Have I mentioned how wonderful it is that you spy on me in my sleep?"

Bonita pushed her covers back and checked the time. It had been three days since Casmir and Kim had left to do whatever it was they were doing on the station. The *Dragon*'s cargo had all been picked up, Bonita had been paid, had paid Qin in turn, and she was still trying to line up a new cargo. So far, she'd only found jobs that would require her to fly halfway across the system for the initial pickup. That was a waste of fuel. She would much rather grab something close.

In truth, she kept expecting Asger, Kim, or Casmir to ask her for a ride. Maybe that was why she'd been half-hearted in her search for a new cargo. A part of her knew that she should get on with her life and have nothing more to do with those Kingdom troublemakers, but a part of her had come to find the ship quiet and empty when they weren't around.

"I don't think it can be considered spying," Viggo said, "when you are sleeping in a cabin that is within my small but not inconsequential dominion. I keep track of everything that happens on board this ship."

"Who sent the message?" Since it was morning station-time, Bonita grabbed her boots. She might as well get up.

"Your strong, sexy bear."

"Bjarke? I didn't know you were attracted to him."

"I'm not, but I've observed that your heart speeds up when he talks to you."

"Dominion my ass. You're *definitely* spying on me."

"I have few hobbies. Don't deny me the joy of prying into your personal life."

"You're strange, Viggo."

Bonita headed for navigation, expecting to find a recorded message, but Bjarke was live and on hold.

She smoothed her hair and checked herself in a mirror to make sure there weren't massive dark bags under her eyes, then snorted at her vanity and answered.

"My lovely Captain Laser." Bjarke appeared far perkier than she, though a couple days' worth of beard growth scruffed his chin, and his hair was tousled, as if he'd been pushing his hands through it again and again. "Were you sleeping? Or perhaps being held captive by enemies? I cannot otherwise understand why you would delay so in answering me."

It seemed he was back to lighthearted flirting with her instead of requesting that she collect Kim for him—and being irked when she said no.

"I was sleeping, in fact. I'm sure Viggo could send you videos."

"I don't *record* you," Viggo murmured.

"Viggo?" Bjarke asked. "Ah, yes your sentient ship."

"Sort of. He used to be the owner of the ship, but when his death was imminent, he had his consciousness uploaded into the *Dragon*."

"So… essentially, he's a man."

"I am quite male," Viggo said. "When I had a body, it was virile and attractive."

"I'm fairly certain it was scrawny, and he got beaten up frequently," Bonita said.

"Lies," Viggo said.

Bjarke scratched his jaw. "I was trying to figure out if I should threaten to beat him up for peeping at you in your sleep, but I don't know how that would work."

"You could kick one of the bulkheads next time you visit," Bonita said.

"He can try," Viggo said. "I have deadly weapons at my disposal."

"A cadre of robot vacuums?" she asked.

"I was thinking of the railgun."

"He would have to be outside for that to be effective."

"He has to be outside before he can come inside."

Bjarke cleared his throat. "If you don't mind, Bonita, I did comm for a reason, not to hear you snipe at your ship."

"I still don't know where Kim Sato is if that's what you're going to ask." Bonita wouldn't mention that she'd warned both Asger and Kim that Bjarke was coming to get her. "She hasn't been back to my ship."

Never mind that Qin and Asger had seen her the day before, taking a break from her work in a local laboratory to order espresso from one of the station's coffee stands. Just because that had been true yesterday didn't mean Bonita knew where she was *now*.

"Would you tell me if you *had* seen her?" Bjarke asked.

No. "I don't know. Would you offer something in exchange for the information?"

"A foot rub?"

A little tingle went through her at the idea. It had been a long time since anything besides the sonic foot massager in the sauna had rubbed her feet.

"Tempting. I'd consider it. How far away are you?" Bonita was certain Asger and Kim would both like to know.

"Close. Only a few hours from the station. But I thought I should warn you, as I intend to warn the palace itself, that the insidious mercenary Rache is after me."

"*After* you? Does that mean that he's flying behind you in the same direction or that he's trying to get you?"

"Both. I was given a shuttle to fly to Stardust Palace to retrieve Sato, since you so rudely refused to collect her for me. A freighter that launched shortly after I did was sent to purchase fuel and supplies from the station. Rache and his big warship came out of nowhere and attacked. The freighter had no chance. I was tempted to turn and help, but the captain ordered me to escape while he bought time for me, and there is unfortunately little this shuttle could do against a warship, regardless. The eight-man crew of the freighter was destroyed."

Bonita leaned back in her seat. She hadn't had as many encounters with Rache as Kim and Casmir, but after that awkward dinner in Zamek City, she had stopped thinking of him as an enemy. It wasn't as if she would consider him an ally, but she hadn't been considering him a threat, at least not to her, a non-Kingdom subject. It was, however, chilling to think that he'd killed eight men for no reason. Or had there been a reason?

"Why did he attack the freighter?" Bonita wondered.

"Because we are from the Kingdom, and the bastard hates the Kingdom," Bjarke growled.

"Hm."

"I wanted to warn you to be careful if you're leaving the station any time soon," Bjarke added. "Especially if you get hired to take a cargo to the Kingdom ships. He may target you to keep them from getting supplies." He raised his eyebrows. "*Are* you leaving soon? Or will you be there a little longer?"

"Are you inquiring because you want to take me to dinner?"

"Yes. Will Viggo be jealous?"

"No, he'll only remind me of my failed marriages and bad luck with men."

"But you'll ignore him and have dinner with me, anyway, right?"

Bonita wondered if she could convince Bjarke to spend his visit with her and forget about hunting down Kim. "Of course. I always ignore him."

"Really, Bonita," Viggo murmured.

"Excellent news," Bjarke said.

"*Really*." Viggo played a haughty sniff—it sounded like someone inhaling their own nostrils hard enough to shoot them out the other end.

"I'll give you a time after I've taken care of my business."

His business? Capturing Kim?

"You should come see me first. What are you going to do? Tie her up in your shuttle while we go to dinner?"

Bjarke squinted at her. "I must suspect your motives, dear Laser. Are you *sure* you haven't seen her?"

"I haven't seen her, but look, you're going to get yourself killed if you try to go after her alone. You know Casmir's crusher is programmed to protect her as surely as it is him, right? And what's with the kidnapping scheme, anyway? It's obvious she doesn't want to do whatever your prince wants. She left for a reason. If you drag her back over your shoulder like some primate…"

"I will take her back in flex-cuffs like a civilized law enforcer," Bjarke said coolly. "Prince Jorg has ordered it, and as a knight of the Kingdom, I am bound to obey."

"Your prince is succeeding in turning you into something even the Druckers didn't manage. A villain."

Bjarke cut the comm.

"I don't think I'm getting a dinner date or a foot rub, Viggo," Bonita said.

"Are you going to warn Kim that he's almost here?"

"Yes. She probably needs time to make sure Zee is standing at her back when Bjarke shows up."

"Do you think even Zee can defeat a trained knight?" Viggo asked.

"I don't know."

CHAPTER 16

QIN WAS IN THE SHIP BAY, MONITORING THE loading of provisions onto the *Dragon,* when Princess Nalini walked into view. She was a beautiful woman with alert brown eyes, flawless skin, and straight, silky black hair clipped back from her temples. Qin rubbed the furry back of her hand self-consciously.

Assuming the princess was off to a ship of her own, Qin didn't think of greeting her until she realized Nalini was heading straight toward her. She bit her lip. What was the protocol for addressing princesses? Qin hadn't bowed or even spoken to her the other night. Since their meeting had started with Tristan answering the door in a towel, Qin had assumed that formalities weren't in order.

She settled on a bow, almost clunking her head on a squat robot loader whirring up the ramp with a food crate, then wondered if a curtsy would have been more correct. In the fairy tales she'd read, girls always curtsied, but learning the motion hadn't been a part of her combat training.

Nalini lifted a hand, two gold rings gleaming on her fingers, and stopped in front of her. "Hello, Qin, wasn't it?"

"Yes, uhm, Your Highness."

Qin was glad Nalini hadn't given her fur and fangs a second look, neither now nor when they'd met. Now that she was largely away from the Kingdom and its influence, she shouldn't encounter as many people who thought genetically engineered people were odd.

"You can call me Nalini. I'm looking for Tristan—he's not answering the comm, and he has his chip off. I thought he might have come down here to visit Sir Asger."

"They're not here. I think Asger is guarding Kim." Qin wished Asger *were* down here. She'd thought it would be nice if they could spend some time together, but he hadn't been back to the ship often. She hoped it wasn't because he was avoiding her. He had, however, specifically mentioned that he believed Kim might be in danger. From whom, he hadn't mentioned.

"Oh, hm." Nalini gazed around the bay, where six other ships of various sizes were docked, none of their crews in sight.

She smelled of jasmine flowers and a hint of the sandalwood incense that Qin had noticed burning throughout the palace side of the station. Scents that attracted men, she supposed, wondering if she should get some perfume. She'd always avoided it since scent was a way for enemies to track someone, especially enemies with enhanced olfactory senses such as she had.

"I'm a little concerned," Nalini added, "since he made an enemy of Prince Jorg. I was relieved that all your Sir Asger wanted was his weapon back. I thought the Kingdom might send assassins."

"He's not my Sir Asger," Qin admitted. "And I think the Kingdom is too busy to worry about single ex-knights right now."

"No? I thought you and he exchanged a few warm smiles and looks."

"We're just friends. I've helped him with a few problems, and he's helped me, or offered to, if I need it."

"What would you need help with?" Nalini looked from her boots to the top of her head. "You seem very capable. And tall." She smiled.

"I…" Qin wasn't sure how much she wanted to tell a stranger about her problems. She opted for the short explanation. "I was purchased from a lab and raised by pirates who still think they own me. I have to watch out. They've caught up with me before and tried to take me back."

"Ah. System Cerberus. Yes. Can you buy your freedom?"

"Maybe, but it would take a lot more money than I have."

"You should get the total. Then you'd have a goal to work toward. It seems unfair that a person should have to buy their own freedom, but if it's the best option for a restful life, then it would be worth it."

"I'm sure it would be, but I don't make that much money, and I don't want to leave Bonita." Qin pointed her thumb toward the cargo hold. "She's my captain and employer."

Nalini tilted her head. "Do you have any money left over after paying for expenses?"

"I guess. My expenses are minimal. Bonita provides my food and of course my cabin. And she covers the cost of my armor maintenance and ammunition for my weapons."

Nalini blinked. "Your weapons?"

Qin patted the Brockinger anti-tank gun slung over her shoulder. "When I escaped, I took this girl with me, and a couple of others, but Bonita said it was only fair that she provided funds to make sure I'm well-armed and armored. We've been running freight a lot lately, and some passengers—" Qin thought of Bjarke, "—but we also hunt bounties. I think Bonita wants to do more of it now that her knees are better."

Nalini waved away these details. "My point was going to be that if you have some left over each month, you can put it into investments that will grow over time, until you have enough to pay off whoever thinks they own you."

"I don't have very much left each month. Not that kind of money."

"Small amounts can grow into large amounts in time. Are you familiar with the concept of compound growth?"

Qin shook her head.

"Hm, I can send you some of my lectures and some basics on the markets. If you believe the Kingdom will come out ahead in this war, this wouldn't be a bad time to pick up some of their stocks that are taking a hit right now. Though, as you might guess, I'm a bigger proponent of real-estate investing, since you acquire both property that increases in value over time and rental income that can, in the right markets, cover the mortgage and all the carrying costs in the meantime. It takes more money to get started, but you can invest in one until you've acquired enough for the other."

"I... hadn't thought of investing. I'm not very... mathy." Qin waved, uncertain of the proper term. "My academic education ended at twelve when I became a full-time combat specialist. I mostly read, er, romances. And fairy tales."

"It's never too late to develop an interest and learn. I'll send you my lectures. Tristan assures me they're not that dry." Nalini winked. "There are slides with cartoon characters."

"I'd like that." Qin heard Bonita's footsteps in the ship's cargo hold and faced the hatch before she appeared.

"We have a problem," Bonita announced, then frowned at Nalini. "Who are you?"

"Princess Nalini."

Bonita didn't bow or curtsy. She only said, "Huh," and faced Qin again. "Toes is on the way."

"Toes?" Nalini mouthed.

"He's coming to get Kim." Bonita ignored Nalini.

Qin wished she wouldn't. Nalini was telling her how to make money. Qin wanted to make her a new friend. But she could see why Bjarke was a larger concern.

"The Kingdom sent him?" Qin asked.

"That asshole prince," Bonita said. "I don't even know him, and I'm sure he's an asshole."

"He is," Nalini said shortly.

"I've warned Kim and Casmir," Bonita said. "Kim, oddly, didn't seem that concerned. I thought she might want to hop on our freighter and get smuggled out of here. But she mentioned that she'd be leaving soon, like she already has something lined up." Bonita frowned. Offended that they might get a ride with someone else? "I haven't heard back from Casmir. He's probably engrossed in making little Zees."

"I believe they'll be the same size as the existing one," Qin said.

She caught a familiar scent and rose on her toes, gazing across the bay toward one of the entrances.

"You know what I mean," Bonita said. "Carbon copies. I wonder if they'll all have his personality, such as it is."

Asger entered the bay, and Qin waved at him. She'd painted her claws pink with blue raindrops that morning and caught herself extending them, hoping he would notice them. And think they were pretty.

He lifted a hand in return, but his face was grim. If he noticed the claw paint, he didn't show it as he joined them at the base of the ramp.

"I heard from my father again," he said without preamble, bowing to Nalini and nodding to Bonita. "He's almost here."

"We know," Bonita said.

"How?" Asger asked. "I've known he was coming, but not when. I thought it would take him longer to get here."

"He told me."

"Did he also tell you to stay out of his way while he's kidnapping Kim for Prince Jorg? And to be prepared to leave with him without making any trouble? He treats me like I'm a wayward child instead of a full-fledged knight." Asger must have been angry, because he didn't seem to think anything of admitting this in front of a near-stranger.

"You are wayward," Bonita said. "Has he seen your calendars?"

Asger's face flushed red.

Qin waved and shook her head at Bonita, hoping she wouldn't continue with the joke. A joke that was, Qin knew from her conversations with both Bjarke and Asger, too close to the truth.

"Are you going to leave with him?" Qin asked. "And, uhm, stay out of his way as he tries to get Kim?"

Asger pushed a hand through his blond-brown locks hard enough to dislodge several strands. "I don't know. I need…" He looked at Qin, but then glanced at Bonita and Nalini, as if he'd decided he didn't want to discuss this in front of them after all.

Qin lifted a finger, about to offer to talk about it in private with him, if he wished, but a message from Casmir came in on her chip, and she paused.

Bonita, Qin, Asger, and Kim, could you please come to the manufacturing facility? I can't leave at the moment, but we need to have a quick meeting. I've ordered snacks. And I also have entertainment.

What kind of entertainment can there be in a manufacturing facility? Bonita responded to the group message. *Watching robots stamp out cogs isn't riveting.*

I disagree with that, but I meant the unarmed combat show. Tristan has returned for the third day in a row to test his mettle against Zee.

"Oh," Qin said. "Nalini, I know where your ex-knight is."

Nalini raised her eyebrows.

"Fighting a crusher in your manufacturing facility," Qin said.

Nalini's brows climbed higher. "*Again?*"

"I didn't realize combat with Zee was that engaging," Asger murmured. Then he messaged, *We're on our way, Casmir.*

We won't have much time before Bjarke gets here, Bonita added.

That's why I called for a quick meeting, Casmir replied.

Are you sure you want Kim out in the open?

Oh, she'll be well protected.

"What does that mean?" Asger's face creased into a worried expression. Worried for Kim? Or worried for his father? Or both?

"Maybe that some of his crushers have come off the assembly line?" Qin suggested.

"I don't know if I want to see this or *don't* want to see this," Bonita murmured, but she headed down the ramp.

Qin let her go ahead with Nalini, then walked beside Asger, who waited for her before starting off.

"Are you all right?" she whispered.

"Just disgruntled that it looks like I'm going to have to pick sides. And the side I'm more inclined to pick could seal the coffin on my already dying career in the knighthood." He spotted her painted claws and pointed. "Those are nice."

"*Thank* you." Qin beamed a smile at him, tickled that he'd noticed.

Maybe she responded more enthusiastically than he expected, for he missed a step. Or maybe she'd flashed her fangs at him, and he'd found it alarming? She reined in her lips to form a tighter, non-toothy smile.

A mix of emotions crossed his face, and she struggled to read them. It was as if he was wrestling with something. His hand twitched toward hers but only made it halfway before dropping back to his side.

Had he almost taken her hand? She pretended not to notice the failure to go all the way. At least he wasn't fleeing in the other direction.

Qin waved her fingers and added, "I'm glad you like them."

"I do. And you're welcome."

"Maybe Casmir will have some clever idea to help you avoid having to pick a side."

"*Casmir's* ideas are what have gotten me in trouble in the first place."

Was that true? Qin didn't know what all had happened with them in System Hydra. "Then why are you still talking to him?"

Asger sighed, his shoulders slumping. "Because I like him. And I think he cares more about doing the right thing than my superiors do."

Oku followed her father into the Citadel's command center. It had been two days since she'd arrived, but she hadn't slept much since then. She'd been making sure Casmir's and Kim's family and friends were settled in and being treated well, and then there had been the bombings. The city had undergone three more attacks.

She didn't think anyone had slept during the one the previous night. The Citadel might be bomb-proof, but it wasn't soundproof. Chasca had spent hours in the closet of their small bedroom. Every time Oku had dozed off, she'd woken minutes later with a start, either to bombing or whimpering about the bombing. That morning, Oku had applied more makeup than usual in an attempt to mask her weariness. At least her skin was dark enough that the bags under her eyes weren't that noticeable. Even so, she felt like something Chasca had dragged out from under a bush rather than a radiant princess to be dangled as a prize to a potential suitor.

"Sire?" an older man asked from a set of desks and news displays in the command center.

Oku recognized him as Senator Boehm, one of her father's distant cousins and a retired knight.

"Yes?" Her father stopped.

"The Fleet admirals report that they've driven off the bombers from Odin, our orbital stations, and the lunar base. Enemy ships are still harrying the habitats. Most of them are state-of-the-art with slydar hulls that are difficult to detect. Further, many of the ships we successfully knocked down were automated. We'd wondered why this hodgepodge invasion force full of mercenaries would be willing to make what turned out to be kamikaze runs, but it's because there weren't human pilots or crews. We've knocked down dozens, if not hundreds, of ships by scanning the energy signatures of their weapons fire to estimate their locations. Even if there's no loss of life on their side, Prince Dubashi and his allies must be spending a fortune on this."

Her father smiled tightly. "Yes. No doubt."

"I spoke with Chief Superintendent Van Dijk early this morning. She said Royal Intelligence has learned of something she's calling a slydar detector and that the technology would be a great asset if we could get our hands on it."

Oku lifted her eyebrows. That was wonderful news. Not only would it help with the war, but she knew that the Kingdom Fleet had never been able to catch Rache's mercenary ship because of its slydar hull. It had been terrorizing the Kingdom for years, and every subject in the system wanted the villain killed.

Surprisingly, her father only nodded. Had he already known about the existence of such a thing?

"She's going to report later about the possibility of sending a team through the blockade to try to get one of these detectors," Boehm added. "We've had poor luck getting anyone out except the occasional automated courier ship."

"It would be worth the risk in this case, Sire."

"I'll read her report and think about it."

Boehm hesitated. "Yes, Sire."

Her father continued on, waving for Oku to follow.

They entered his private office, and she almost jumped when she brushed past two crushers guarding the doorway on the inside. Their empty faces, only vaguely human, gazed blankly at her. Why did they seem so much creepier—*scarier*—than Casmir's Zee?

Her father ignored them and pointed for Oku to stand on the rug in front of his desk. He shifted a comm terminal around so that its camera would capture her upper body.

"It'll be a few days before he gets this," her father said, "so we'll assume he has the crusher army built by then."

"Crusher army?" Oku looked at the two dark figures by the door.

"Jorg ordered him to build a hundred new crushers to assist the fleet he's putting together in System Stymphalia to attack the blockade. We've done some tests where we shoot them over to other ships like torpedoes. They force their way inside and take over. A couple of crushers have been destroyed or thrown out airlocks to drift in space, but they often catch the enemy by surprise. It's been effective. We've got a couple hundred crushers already here on Odin and out with ships in the other systems, and we have the facilities to make more, but it will be useful for Jorg's fleet to have some. Dabrowski *appears* to be following orders to make them. I don't, however, think that's Dabrowski's highest and best use. I want him back here, brainstorming ideas for us, and working loyally for me."

"Brainstorming ideas… to end the war?"

"Ideas for the future. I trust our forces will be able to end the war on their own."

If that was true, would Odin be suffering through these bombings? How many people had died last night? How much of the city had been demolished? Oku was afraid to check the news with her chip, afraid to know.

"Are you still thinking of expansion?" she asked. "After all this?"

"Yes. When the time is right. For now, let's see if we can secure his loyalty, eh?" He extended a hand toward her, as if to say, "That's where you come in."

"What do you want me to say?" Oku felt numb.

Maybe she wouldn't have to say anything, and he would handle it all. But was that wise? To let her father do the talking without knowing what *he* would say? What if he promised Casmir her hand in marriage if he was an obedient roboticist? And what if it was a lie? Wouldn't her father still want to use her to cement an alliance with a powerful government in another system? She was his only daughter, his only chance for that.

Not that she wished to be a bargaining chip. When she'd been younger and first told of her destiny, Oku had dreamed of running off, changing her face, and applying for an anonymous position in the science department of a university far, far from here. That dream resurfaced in her mind now.

"Just smile and be encouraging." Her father shifted to stand next to her. "I'll do most of the talking. You speak up when I cue you."

"All right."

Oku couldn't manage any enthusiasm. Unfortunately, she wouldn't later be able to send out a private message to Casmir via her chip to let him know that she'd been manipulated into this. It sounded like Royal Intelligence had snagged her past messages and shown them to her father. If she did something he would consider a betrayal, she didn't know what would happen. At the least, Casmir's family would be evicted from the protection of the Citadel.

After he ordered the comm to record, her father gave one of his not terribly convincing smiles and spoke. "Professor Dabrowski, I hope this message catches up to you before you do something foolish. I'm aware that you invited other governments to come get a piece of the wormhole gate I specifically told you to assist our Fleet in recovering in its entirety for *us*." The smile had disappeared with his first words. "I didn't want a handful of pieces. I wanted the whole thing and for no one else to have it, not until the Kingdom had studied it and determined its best use. I'm also aware that you assisted the secretary of education on Tiamat Station with becoming *president* there. We had a loyal minion in that position, one who would have given the Kingdom a foothold in System Hydra.

I understand he may have been dead when your team arrived—your team that you were not authorized to put together and leave Ishii's ship with—but we wouldn't have chosen that *woman* for the position."

Oku was glad her father didn't have an arm around her shoulders, because his hands were clenched down out of view of the camera. She was sure his grip would have been hard.

"I'm concerned by my most recent report," he said, "which hints that you might not be precisely obeying my son either. I don't know what it is you hope to gain out there by working against us, but if you fancy yourself some future ruler of the Twelve Systems, know that assassins will find your back and you'll never sleep." He took a deep breath and forced another insincere smile. "I am, however, willing to allow that some of your choices may have been naive or even accidental."

Oku, watching her father's face, didn't think he believed that at all.

"I'm offering you one last chance to come back into the fold, to take your place as court roboticist—you requested that position, as I recall—and to work at my side. Should you return to Odin and prove your loyalty, I'm even willing to offer you a prize."

The sick feeling returned to Oku's stomach. There she was. Her father's prize to be given away to a suitor.

"Princess Oku is not yet betrothed, and I gather you have some interest in her. Royal Intelligence has been kind enough to decrypt the videos you two have been sending back and forth and share them with me."

Oku's heart plummeted into her gut. Confirmation. He had seen the videos, not just the text messages. How many people in Royal Intelligence had watched them? Seen her silly recordings of Chasca rolling around on her back? Seen Casmir dressing up his crusher for her? Mortification mingled with anger and indignation in her body until she was shaking.

"Smile, and say something," her father murmured to her, nudging her in the ribs with his elbow.

Say something? She could barely think, barely see. She felt trapped. A prize trapped in a cage.

"Good morning, Casmir," Oku said numbly, tongue almost tripping over the simple words. "I look forward to you returning to Odin and introducing you to Chasca. She isn't, however, a lover of crushers, I've learned, so we may have to wait to introduce her to Zee."

Oku bit her lip, not knowing what else to say. She didn't want to make any promises to Casmir that she couldn't keep—that she wouldn't be *allowed* to keep. This whole setup felt so dishonest. A betrayal to Casmir. But had Casmir betrayed the Kingdom? She wanted his side of the story. She couldn't imagine the affable man she'd been trading videos with having a secret nefarious side.

Her father raised his eyebrows, as if he expected more. What? That she wanted to marry Casmir if he proved himself? The thought of saying that made her want to gag. It was manipulative, and she didn't want to be bound by that any more than Casmir likely did.

"I hope the war will end soon, and that you and Kim have time to help me with my bee project," Oku said. "Oh, and your family—hers too—are in the Citadel now. They're safe. I, uhm, liked the picture of you holding your robotics trophy." Her cheeks flamed, more because her father was watching her than because of any embarrassment she would have felt at confessing that to Casmir.

Her father must have decided she'd served her purpose with her babbling. He faced the camera again.

"I trust you understand clearly what's at stake now, Professor, what prize awaits you if you do the right thing and support the world that gave you the opportunity to become the man you are now. Support the Kingdom, and you'll have a place in it forever. Become its enemy, and you'll regret it."

Oku was still shaking, or shaking again, when he turned off the recording. She couldn't believe he'd threatened Casmir right in front of her. How was *that* supposed to make him want to be loyal?

"Let us hope you are a sufficient enticement," her father said, "and that he fancies the idea of being Prince Consort someday."

"Would you actually *allow* that? Or is this all a lie?"

Her father's nostrils flared. In indignation that he would be anything less than honest and honorable? "It is not what I had planned for you, but if he proves he can be more valuable than an alliance to another royal, I suppose I might. If he doesn't, well, at least we might get some use from him in the meantime."

"Why—" Oku paused to lick her lips. Her mouth had grown so dry. "Why does he matter that much to you? I know he was cloned from Mikita's genes, but… he's just a robotics professor."

Her father's eyes narrowed. "He's demonstrating himself capable of far more versatility than his job title suggests. I wouldn't have guessed—but your mother, it seems, was right. I want him working *for* the Kingdom, not against it. Not for his own gain. I made him. I made *both* of them. I'm not having another one turn against me."

Another one turn against him? What did *that* mean? David Lichtenberg was the only other clone she knew of, and he'd been dead these last ten years.

Her father strode out without explaining, taking the two crushers with him, and leaving her feeling like she'd just betrayed her best friend.

CHAPTER 17

THE CLANGING OF CRUSHER FISTS AGAINST COMBAT ARMOR was giving Casmir a headache, but the whoops and cheers of Sultan Shayban, his son Samar, and two of his more bloodthirsty daughters ensured Casmir couldn't shoo the impromptu arena match to another area. He supposed he should be glad that he'd been introduced to half of the sultan's family and that the man seemed to enjoy spending time here among the crushers.

Completing his mission had been looking promising, though he only had the first batch of twelve crushers done, but depending on when Rache arrived—and, as he'd just learned from Bonita, Bjarke—Casmir might have to leave in a hurry. Still, he'd automated much of the process and with a little more tweaking, the other eighty-eighty crushers could possibly be produced without his supervision.

The din of combat died down, and Casmir spotted Asger, Qin, and Bonita, along with Princess Nalini, heading his direction. Nalini veered over to her father and said something to the sweaty Tristan, who'd been testing himself against four crushers. Casmir was also using Tristan to test his crushers, ensuring they would follow the orders he'd given them to defend themselves while not acting as aggressors.

Kim appeared next, riding an automated cart in through another doorway. She reached Casmir first, hopping off before it came to a full stop. He sighed with longing at the simple display of athleticism and tried not to think about the cart he'd crashed.

"How long until your earnest kidnapper arrives?" Casmir asked quietly.

The others paused to watch Tristan as he started up another round of ex-knight versus crushers. All save Princess Nalini, who'd continued on to her father. She poked him in the shoulder and pointed toward the ceiling, or perhaps some office on a level above where he was supposed to be working. Casmir had been surprised at how often the sultan had come down to check on the project. He reminded himself that one of these first dozen had to stay with Shayban, so he needed to make eighty-nine more, not eighty-eight.

"Which one?" Kim didn't sound amused.

"I don't know Bjarke well enough to know if he's earnest."

"Determined, if nothing else." Kim lowered her voice. "I actually haven't heard from Rache since we initially arranged this, so I'm not sure when he'll arrive, but Asger told me that Rache attacked a Kingdom freighter accompanying Bjarke. And destroyed it utterly."

"Ah." Many more words flooded Casmir's brain, such as that she was crazy to have any kind of romantic relationship with him, but wasn't he himself engaged in a relationship with Rache? He'd come up with this plan, been willing to ask Kim to ask Rache for a favor… To protect her, Casmir could tell himself, but he'd started to think of Rache as something other than an enemy. Not a *brother*... but something. But how could he feel anything toward someone who targeted and killed Kingdom subjects? Or human beings of any kind? "Are you rethinking going with him?"

Kim flattened her lips together. In irritation? Disapproval? Distress? All of the above?

"I know you don't want to make a killer weapon, but maybe it would be better to go back with Bjarke and tell Jorg in person that you won't do it."

"I wish you'd advised that before I asked him to come."

"I know. I'm sorry. I was just worried about you and your family. I like your brothers. They never tried to beat me up with their elite warrior skills."

"I never tried to beat you up either. Any punches were purely to instill proper behavior."

Casmir smiled. "I know. You're good people. All of you. I don't want anything to happen to you, to them, to their dojo, their home. When did I start to fear our government instead of fearing for our government, Kim?"

"Probably when you met some of the people running it." She squinted at him. "You never said exactly what happened in Jager's dungeon. Did he threaten your family?"

"*He* didn't. He only agreed that torturing me seemed reasonable. Van Dijk was the one to mention that my family could be used against me."

"Wonderful. The chief superintendent of Royal Intelligence." Kim rubbed her face. "That's why I'm afraid to go to Jorg now, to defy him openly. But that's not the reason I sent you that message yesterday, the one you failed to acknowledge." Her eyes narrowed.

"Did I?" A number of messages had flown past while he had been engrossed in his work. He'd barely slept the last two nights. He was surprised he wasn't a wreck. For that matter, he was surprised he wasn't sneezing and sniffing incessantly from those trees along the walls. Some of them were flowering. Before Casmir could scroll back to check his messages, Kim reminded him.

"I said I needed to go along with you to Dubashi's base."

"Oh. I did think that was odd. I was going to ponder it before answering. And then I forgot to answer."

A crusher thrown across the floor came to an abrupt stop nearby when the same barrier that had protected the equipment from Casmir's cart popped up.

"I can see where you would be distracted," Kim remarked.

The crusher hopped up, undamaged, and sprinted back to fling himself at Tristan—who was ready. Zee was watching from the sidelines, and Casmir wondered if he was selecting his future mate. And what the mate would think about it.

"Tristan isn't the only one who's been by. The sultan keeps bringing burly warriors to test themselves." Casmir faced Kim again. "Why do you need to come along?"

"I met the scholar running one of the local research facilities, and her virologist father went missing three months ago, possibly kidnapped."

"And would someone want a virologist for the same reason someone might want a bacteriologist?"

"Scholar Serg Sunflyer actually has a background in biological weapons, so he'd be a more logical candidate. I think I'm… someone Jorg feels he can call on because I'm a Kingdom subject located in the system he's gathering forces in. I've been somewhat versatile and far-flung with my research and projects, but there's nothing on my résumé that should have suggested me to him otherwise."

"I do remember Jorg saying he feared Dubashi already had a bioweapon of his own."

"I'm only guessing that his people may have kidnapped Scholar Sunflyer. His daughter, Natasha Sunflyer, said there hadn't been any witnesses. But it does seem that Dubashi has perpetrated quite a few crimes recently on the Shayban family. His people, as I've learned, tried to kidnap Princess Nalini so she couldn't be betrothed to Jorg."

Casmir frowned. He hadn't been that excited by the idea of infiltrating Dubashi's base *before* the possibility of a bioweapon had come up. He'd only agreed because he'd needed the materials for the crushers.

"The crushers would be immune to a biological weapon," he reasoned aloud. "If Dubashi does have something already built, I can send them in first, and they can destroy it."

"One of your lugs bumbling into a biological weapon sounds like a good way to accidentally unleash it and kill everyone in the base."

"I object to you labeling them as lugs, but I concur on the rest. I shall hope that *nobody* has biological weapons."

Kim's lips twisted dubiously, and Casmir wondered if she knew more than she was saying. Did she have more than a hunch? Some evidence?

Bonita started toward Casmir with Qin following her, but Qin paused and looked back. The two daughters, both beautiful women in their twenties, were sashaying up to Asger. He'd started a conversation with Tristan, who was taking a breather, but they zeroed in on him. One laid a hand on his chest. Qin gaped at this audacity.

"Are you another sexy knight?" the handsy daughter asked.

With the fighting paused, Casmir could hear the words, though he didn't *want* to witness beautiful women flirting with Asger. Even though he had high hopes for the future coffee date he hadn't yet asked Oku on, his ego took a battering whenever women passed him by to drape themselves over a friend.

The second daughter sidled up to Asger's other side and slipped an arm around his waist.

"This isn't boding well for my quick meeting," Casmir observed.

He reminded himself that he didn't need Asger for his plans. His main reason for including him in that message had been to find out where he would be so he could keep Rache out of his way. And vice versa.

"It's not boding well for those women to avoid being eviscerated." Kim pointed at Qin.

Qin had gone from gaping to silently fuming, and her claws were indeed extended, her fingers curled, as if ready to slash a few deep gouges in someone.

Casmir didn't know if Asger saw her reaction, but he squirmed out of the women's grip.

"My friend needs me." Asger pointed at Casmir. "He's sexy too, if you're interested. And he's a robotics genius."

Casmir cringed, knowing from firsthand experience that this was not the kind of proclamation that sent women flocking to him. Not that he *wanted* the daughters to flock to him—they appeared more predatory than loving—but it was always hard being rejected. They looked at him, and he forced a polite smile. His left eye blinked a couple of times. Great, maybe he'd have a seizure next.

"He's more our father's type," one woman said with a snicker.

"The geekier the better. His wives don't mind."

Shayban may or may not have heard the words, but he waved to shoo them out. "My break is over. And so is the show. Everyone who has employment here should get back to it." He sent a moderately scathing look to the daughters, patted Nalini on the shoulder, and headed for the exit.

Qin retracted her claws as Asger walked past, and she fell in beside him. She'd smoothed the rage from her face. Casmir wondered if Asger knew he had an admirer—maybe he'd expected it after giving Qin that calendar. It was none of his business, but he hoped Asger didn't hurt her feelings.

"You don't think he's with that cat… *thing*, do you?" one of the daughters whispered loudly.

Casmir had no trouble hearing it, so he was positive the words would reach Qin's ears. She clenched her jaw and didn't look back.

"If true, knights have bizarre tastes. First Nalini, now a freak."

"And here I thought it was only in the Kingdom that people were ignorant and prejudiced enough to call people names," Kim said, not bothering to lower her voice.

"Humanity has a long way to go to find enlightenment as a whole," Casmir said.

Asger put an arm around Qin's shoulders as they walked toward Casmir and Kim.

"Sorry," Qin said quietly. "I didn't mean to growl. I wouldn't have shredded them to pieces."

"Were you thinking about it?" Asger asked.

"Maybe a little, but I know we're not… anything."

"Nothing? Do I need to get you another calendar?"

Casmir looked away, feeling he was intruding on a private conversation.

The two daughters huffed, apparently realizing Asger wasn't coming back to them, and walked out.

"It's a good thing they weren't the Shaybans I had to talk into helping me," Casmir said.

"You do better with chubby white-haired men than hot women?" Bonita asked him.

"Do you really need to ask that?" Casmir raised his eyebrows.

"I guess not."

Casmir drew the group back into a corner where they could talk quietly. He thought about switching to chip-to-chip communications, but he doubted Stardust Palace security would care about their Kingdom politics even if they overheard them on some monitoring camera. They might care if the Kingdom politics made a mess on their station, but Casmir hoped it wouldn't come to that.

"Bonita," he said, "I don't know how much you've caught of our various schemes, but I thank you for warning Kim and me that Bjarke is coming."

This time, Asger's jaw tightened. Casmir was sad that the mere mention of his father angered him.

"Do you want me to fly you out of the station before he arrives?" Bonita asked Kim. "I don't think we have much time, but I just got a job offer, so I'm open to leaving soon."

"Was it from Scholar Natasha Sunflyer?" Kim looked at Asger as she spoke.

"Yes," Bonita said. "I was going to ask if you know her."

Asger cleared his throat. "We may have mentioned that you're a bounty hunter and might take her assignment."

"*You* mentioned that," Kim said. "After touching her mushrooms."

"That sounds kinky," Bonita said.

Asger lifted his hands, either embarrassed or apologetic.

"It's fine. You're not supposed to feel bad about referring people to me." Bonita extended a hand. "If I'd known you would be willing, I would have given you a stack of business cards."

"What she's asking could get you killed," Asger said.

Bonita looked at him as if he were slow. "As opposed to all the assignments I've taken hunting down murderers, rapists, and deadbeats who don't make payments on their spaceships?"

Asger gazed at her, as if he hadn't previously considered that her profession was deadly.

"Which category is most dangerous?" Casmir asked curiously.

"The deadbeats are least predictable."

"How do knights who go undercover as pirates fare?" Casmir asked.

"He went from unpredictable to insufferably predictable when he revealed himself." Bonita squinted at him. "Why do you ask?"

"I was hoping you'd be willing to meet him when his shuttle arrives and help him find Kim."

Bonita's squint narrowed. "Help him find Kim or help him *not* find Kim?"

"Which would you and your honor find least unappealing?" Casmir asked.

"What honor? I just reminded everyone that I'm a bounty hunter. I do what it takes to pay the bills."

"If that were true, you and Qin wouldn't have refused Rache's money and come back for me on that refinery." Casmir smiled to let them know he still appreciated that. He was fairly sure Bonita hadn't even *liked* him at that point. Casmir wasn't positive that had changed, but he believed Viggo would come for him now if he got himself in trouble, and Bonita might have to ride along.

Qin beamed at the acknowledgment.

Bonita wrinkled her nose as if her nostril itched. "I wouldn't want him—and through him, your prince—to get Kim, but I'm not tickled at the thought of manipulating and lying to him either."

"*I* wouldn't mind." Asger smiled sourly.

"I suppose that's an option too," Casmir said, "but I'd hate for my plan to result in further estrangement between you and your father."

Asger grunted. "What plan do you have? Hiding Kim away somewhere while Bonita leads my father around by the nose?"

"His *nose* isn't what I would use for a handle," Bonita murmured.

Asger's brow wrinkled. "I really hope I misinterpreted that."

Bonita's grin was a touch wicked.

"Kim and I will actually be leaving the station," Casmir said. "We just need someone to buy us time so Bjarke doesn't find us first."

"Leaving the station?" Asger stared at him. "You haven't built all your crushers. Where will you go?"

Before Casmir could answer, Zee decided to join the conversation.

"Casmir Dabrowski will fulfill his promise to Sultan Shayban by taking the crushers to infiltrate Dubashi's base and capture him. I will have many days of travel during which I can assess which of these new crushers will be a suitable mate."

"Infiltrate his *base*?" Asger demanded as Casmir tried to hide his face behind his hand.

"That was a secret, Zee," Casmir muttered.

"You did not state that. I am excited to possibly find a suitable mate. I wished to share my plans."

Kim shook her head and mouthed, "*Bug*."

Casmir didn't agree, but he made a note to start explicitly telling Zee when something was a secret.

Asger gripped his shoulder. "You weren't going to tell me? You were just going to leave me here alone with my angry father?"

"How can he be angry? I'm doing what I had to promise to do in order to, as Zee said, fulfill my promise to the sultan. He wants Dubashi. I'm going to get him. That's what he wanted in exchange for all this." Casmir waved to include the crushers, the materials, and the manufacturing equipment. "For the crushers Jorg ordered me to make."

Asger released him. "I get that. But why didn't you ask me to come? You *can't* go alone."

"I'll be with Kim and Zee and all the crushers." No need to mention Rache's role as taxi.

Asger scowled. "I'm coming."

"That's a bad idea," Kim said and mouthed, "Rache," to Casmir.

"I know," he mouthed back.

"You're going to need *real* help if you're trying to get to Dubashi," Asger said.

"I am real help." Zee lifted his chin. "I am programmed to protect Kim Sato and Casmir Dabrowski."

Asger ignored him. "Do you have any idea how heavily guarded his base will be?"

"No," Casmir said, "but I'm hoping to find the blueprints on the way. And that they will reveal a big glowing self-destruct button. Does that ever happen outside of comic books?"

"No," everyone said together.

"Darn."

"Are any more crushers going to be ready before we have to go?" Kim asked.

"I don't think so, but I'm automating the process so the run will self-complete." Casmir hoped he had time for that. "Then I'll have to come back and pick them up after… our valiant and successful kidnapping of Prince Dubashi, which will result in the eradication of the threat to the Kingdom."

"Feeling optimistic today?" Kim asked.

"Why wouldn't I be? I haven't thrown up, had a seizure, or even sneezed at those potted date-palm trees over there, which is a marvel since they're dusting the floor with their odious yellow pollen. You say I also have that potion to thank for my snot-free nose?"

"Ew," Bonita said.

Kim nodded. "It likely had a regulatory effect on your immune system in general. Allergies occur when your immune system overreacts and unnecessarily produces antibodies to what it perceives as foreign invaders."

"Any chance it's permanent?" Casmir asked.

"Probably not. You better start saving up your money for another dose. As soon as someone starts paying you again."

Casmir thought of Sultan Shayban's offer of employment. If he truly paid four times more than Casmir made back at the university, he might be able to afford boosters such as Rache apparently paid for from his petty cash stash.

"Casmir," Asger said sturdily, his continuing scowl making it clear he didn't appreciate the change in topic. "I'm going with you."

"Don't you have orders to go back to Prince Jorg's fleet with your father?" Casmir asked.

Asger's scowl turned mulish.

"We don't have much time." Bonita waved at her chip. "Viggo just informed me that Bjarke's shuttle is approaching the outer asteroid."

And where was Rache's ship? Casmir looked at Kim, but she only shrugged.

"Thank you, Laser," Casmir said. "If you're willing, I need one of you two to go down to the bay and lead him up to the mushroom lab where Kim was last seen working. Because it's obvious that she'll want to go back there as soon as this meeting breaks up. Right, Kim?" Casmir raised his eyebrows.

"Where else would I go?" Kim replied in an unconvincing deadpan voice.

She was an even worse liar than he was.

But Casmir took it in stride, smiling at them.

"Where will she really go?" Asger asked.

"Better that you don't know."

"I'm going with you, Casmir."

Casmir shook his head. As much as he would like Asger's help in this endeavor, it would be better for his career if he stayed here and joined his father. It would be better for his *life* if he avoided Rache.

"You going to do the lying?" Bonita asked Asger.

"I could punch him in the nose, knock him out, and leave him tied up in a closet," Asger said.

"Do you think you could?" Qin asked curiously. "He's had the same training you've had, hasn't he?"

"He's old," Asger said shortly, as if an outcome in his favor were a foregone conclusion.

"And has those extra toes he has to balance on," Bonita said.

Asger stared at her. "What?"

"Never mind."

"Just buy us a couple of hours. And then we'll be gone." Casmir hoped he was right.

"I can't believe you want to leave me here," Asger said. "And won't tell me how you're getting to that base."

"The less you know the better."

"Are you trying to get me in trouble again?"

"You just volunteered to punch your father and superior knight. I don't think I'm the one getting you into all this trouble."

"That may be true," Asger admitted in sad acknowledgment.

Casmir patted him on the shoulder. "You'll find a way to help and show them how worthwhile you are. Starting now. But might I suggest simply luring your father out of the ship bay rather than punching him? Show him the nice mushrooms you were poking earlier."

Asger snorted, but he waved at Bonita and Qin to follow him out.

"If you *do* decide to punch him and knock him out," Qin said as they headed away, "I can hold his arms behind his back for you."

"You'd do that?" Asger asked.

"To help you, yes."

"I'm pretending I'm not hearing any of this," Bonita grumbled, walking away with them.

"You're a good woman, Qin." Asger draped an arm around her shoulders. This time, Shayban's daughters weren't there to witness it and make snide comments.

"I didn't tell Rache he'd also be kidnapping you and however many of these crushers you're bringing," Kim said when she and Casmir were alone.

"All of them. We'll be a delightful surprise."

"You use that word frequently. I don't think it means what you think it means."

"My vocabulary is sublime. You cannot question it. I know at least fifty words appropriate for describing comic book villains. Are you all packed? Rache could be right behind Bjarke. We better head down to the shuttle bay so we can meet him there while Bjarke is being led around the station."

"I'm ready. Are you?" Kim eyed the crushers.

"Yes. They travel light. I just have to let the sultan know that operations will continue without me for a few weeks. I wouldn't have minded having more crushers to take along, but this timing might actually work better to make him more comfortable about this. He'll believe I intend to get the prince and return if I'm leaving the majority of the force behind to come back for later."

"Yes, his comfort is what's most important here."

"He's the one who lent me this space and millions of crowns—dollars—in raw materials."

Casmir waved for the crushers to queue up behind him, not surprised when Zee pushed one aside to take the place right behind him.

Kim shook her head slowly and with obvious concern. Casmir reassured himself that this *would* work and that it would help his people back at home.

They just had to get past Bjarke and off the station first.

CHAPTER 18

THE *STELLAR DRAGON* WAS FULLY SUPPLIED AND READY to take off. Bonita had officially accepted Scholar Natasha Sunflyer's assignment, and the woman had even paid her a deposit up front. That wasn't common in the business. Bonita was determined that she would find Natasha's father—or at least learn without a question of a doubt what had happened to him.

Since Asger had volunteered to steer Bjarke away from Kim, there was no reason for Bonita to linger on the station, but she found herself tidying up and making excuses to check on things in the ship. A part of her wanted to leave and avoid seeing him, but a slightly larger part of her *wanted* to see him, even if he'd turned into an uptight knight obsessed with his mission. She still liked his flirting.

Besides, Qin didn't appear to be in a hurry to leave. Rather, she had positioned herself to watch Bjarke's arrival. She was cleaning her Brockinger at the base of the *Dragon*'s cargo ramp while Asger paced back and forth in front of her. They weren't speaking, but Bonita sensed that Qin was there to lend moral support.

Bjarke's shuttle docked at one of the airlocks rather than asking for permission to fly into the bay, which would have forced the station to clear it while it was depressurized. After a few minutes, Asger halted his pacing, going even more rigid than his combat armor. Bonita didn't have to follow his gaze to know that Bjarke had walked off his shuttle.

Qin was also looking in that direction. She'd probably caught his scent before Asger had caught sight of him.

Bjarke gazed at Asger, took in Qin and Bonita—she was standing in the hatchway, leaning against the jamb as Viggo's vacuums went over the recently loaded supply crates—and then looked toward the other ships in the bay, as well as the visible exits.

Bonita wondered if station security would try to detain him—she'd been hoping he wouldn't be allowed to dock, as that would have solved the Kim problem completely. Bonita didn't know how Kim planned to get off the station, but Casmir had said they both meant to leave. Maybe he'd schmoozed the sultan for a ship they could borrow.

Bjarke's roving gaze paused on an android security guard stationed near an exit, and Bonita thought he might ignore her, Qin, and Asger altogether, and head off to search on his own. But after his perusal of the area, Bjarke strode toward Asger.

He wore a form-fitting galaxy suit rather than a knight's liquid armor, which either meant he didn't think Kim would pose that much of a threat or he didn't want to be obviously associated with the Kingdom when he was roaming the station. The suit accentuated his muscular form nicely. He wasn't quite as tall or broad as Asger, but he had an impressive physique, and Bonita remembered the topless picture he'd sent her early on.

She kept herself from admiring him too thoroughly and too openly, but couldn't help but wish he'd come all this way for *her* rather than on an errand for his prince. What would it be like to be with a man who felt that kind of loyalty toward her?

Bonita shook her head, reminding herself that relationships were trouble. All the men she'd cared for who'd started out feeling, or feigning, such loyalty had turned into dicks in the end. Bjarke was probably the same way.

Still, he looked at her before he reached Asger, his gaze sliding down *her* form-fitting galaxy suit, and warmth flushed her body. Maybe it was her imagination, but his gaze seemed interested rather than dismissive.

Bonita folded her arms over her chest and feigned indifference, but she used the gesture to give her boobs a little boost. As one got older, one had to assist gravity.

Bjarke smiled wryly in her direction, but his face grew grave as he stopped in front of Asger. He glanced at Qin, looking like he wanted to ask her to leave, but she had returned to cleaning her gun and pretended not to notice him. Bonita hoped Asger opted to lead his father astray, not start a fist-fight. Especially since Qin had offered to help. Even though

Bjarke wore his pertundo and a stunner on the utility belt of his galaxy suit, Bonita doubted he could overcome both of them. And being ground into the gritty metal deck by them would be sure to ruin his mood.

"William," Bjarke said. "You said you completed your mission here?"

Asger blinked. Maybe that wasn't the opening he'd expected.

"I have," Asger said.

"Where's Tremayne's pertundo?"

"In the *Dragon*." Asger waved toward Bonita and the open cargo hold behind her. "Ishii's shuttle developed malfunctions, so I had to transfer to this ship."

"I heard." Bjarke's tone was cool, completely lacking in the sardonic edge he used with Bonita. "You will fetch the weapon and return in my shuttle with me."

Asger shrugged. "Fine."

"And you will help me retrieve Scholar Sato."

"No, sir. I won't."

Bjarke clenched his jaw. Asger glared defiantly back at him. Qin hadn't looked up from her Brockinger, but she'd reassembled it, and her hand rested on the barrel. She was poised to leap to aid Asger if needed. Bonita wondered if he realized how loyal a friend—maybe more than a friend—he had in her.

"I am not making this request as your father. Baron Farley sent orders that I could put you to use out here as I see fit."

"Baron Farley has implied on more than one occasion that I'll be kicked out of the knighthood when I get back."

Bjarke's nostrils flared. "Is that what you *want*?"

"No, but—"

"After all the strings I had to pull to get you affirmed into the knighthood to start with?"

"Something you only did because you would have been embarrassed if I didn't make it. It's not like you cared about me or what I wanted."

Their voices were escalating and drawing more gazes than the android security officer's.

"Of course I cared. What are you talking about?"

"You were never there to do anything with me when I was growing up. How could you possibly care? You didn't even know me!"

Asger's fingers balled into fists. Did he see the startled expression flash in Bjarke's eyes?

Bjarke visibly gathered himself. "William, this isn't the place for tantrums. If you won't help me complete my mission, you will wait in the shuttle for me to return."

"With a woman you intend to kidnap against her wishes?" The fists tightened.

This was going to devolve into an ugly brawl soon. Qin must have thought so, too, for she surged to her feet and looked to Asger for a signal.

"She is a Kingdom subject," Bjarke said. "Her duty is to serve the Kingdom in a time of need, and this is definitely—"

"I'll take you to her," Bonita cut in, aware of Asger's fist cocking back. Maybe the two needed to have a down-and-out-brawl, but not when they were carrying deadly weapons and Qin planned to jump in to help. Not only might one of them be seriously injured, but Bonita could see the rift between them growing irreparable if Asger truly did knock his father out and lock him up on the station somewhere.

"*Captain*!" Asger blurted in a betrayed tone.

Bonita couldn't tell if it was feigned or if he believed she would do it. He should have known better, since he'd been at the meeting with Casmir, but maybe he was putting on a show to make Bjarke believe her.

Bonita shrugged. "If you two fight, you're going to get blood all over my cargo ramp, and it'll be annoying to have to clean it."

One of the robot vacuums whirred past the hatchway behind her. She didn't look at it.

"You know where she is?" Bjarke pinned her with a considering gaze. "Before, you implied that you wouldn't help me."

"I don't particularly want to, but I also don't want to see you get pulverized."

Bjarke snorted. "William could not best me."

"*William* isn't alone." Bonita looked at Qin.

Bjarke studied her for the first time. They'd fought together, so he ought to know what Qin was capable of. But then, he'd run over to the other ship shortly after they'd started that ambush aboard the *Machu Picchu.* Depending on what had gone on in that astroshaman base, Bjarke might not have witnessed her full capabilities yet.

Qin lifted her chin under his scrutiny.

"You would battle me, Qin?" Bjarke asked. "After we climbed elevator shafts together? I'm distressed."

"I like Asger—William. More than I like you. And I stand beside those I like."

"I see." Bjarke shifted his focus to Bonita. "You said you know where she is now?"

Bonita shrugged again. "I know where she's staying, and I know where the lab is that she's been working in. We can go check those two places."

Bjarke held her gaze, then looked slowly around the bay again, as if he suspected Kim of being hidden nearby. Which was possible. Numerous ships occupied the landing pads and blocked the view to the far side.

"Very well," Bjarke said. "You may guide me to those locations, the most likely first."

"May I? How magnanimous of you. If I help you, and we find her, I'm going to expect you to buy me dinner and rub my feet."

Asger made a gagging noise. Viggo, who was monitoring everything taking place on his cargo ramp, issued a similar sound. Bonita rolled her eyes.

"Will this foot rubbing occur *at* dinner?" Some of the tension finally ebbed from Bjarke's face as his tone grew lighter. "That doesn't seem sanitary."

"Dinner at a fancy restaurant—your treat—where they don't print the prices on the menu because they're so exorbitant. Foot rubbing back in my cabin." Bonita pointed a thumb toward the cargo hold. "Though I assure you there's nothing unsanitary about my feet. I wash and pumice them regularly."

Judging by the twist of Asger's lips, he was considering another gag.

"Ven acá pendejo." Bonita stalked down the ramp, linked her arm with Bjarke's, and led him away from the ship. To her surprise, he allowed it. "Finish preparing the ship, Qin," she called over her shoulder. "We'll leave in the morning."

"Yes, Captain."

Qin and Asger stared after them.

Bjarke walked closer than she would have expected if he was angry. Maybe he was only angry with Asger and not her. That would change, unfortunately, when he realized she was leading him away from his quarry, not toward it. That made her sad, but she walked resolutely into the rest of the station. It was better than letting father and son pummel each other in front of her cargo ramp.

"*Pendejo?* Does that mean mighty bear?"

"No. You're thinking of *oso pequeño*. Or *osito*." She smiled and patted him on the ass.

"You're insulting me, aren't you?"

"Just correcting your high opinion of yourself."

"I see." His eyelids drooped into a sultry expression. "And what name will you cry out when I'm bringing you to unprecedented heights of pleasure during our lovemaking tonight?"

Damn her for finding his throaty whisper sexy. "That depends wholly on your performance."

Bjarke stopped in the middle of the corridor. Since their arms were still linked, she did too.

There hadn't been much foot traffic going in and out of the ship bay, and they were alone at the moment. He shifted, pushing her gently but firmly against the wall, and he kissed her.

She was so surprised that she stood slack-jawed for a few seconds, but his hand found her hip, then drifted higher, and her body tightened in anticipation of pleasures she'd almost forgotten she could experience. She stirred, running her hands up his back and moving her mouth against his, the kiss far more rousing than it should have been, hungrier and more demanding than the brief one they'd shared on the Kingdom warship. She'd initiated that one, surprising him. This time, he was in control, and fiery heat flushed her body as she thought of making her teasing words from earlier a reality.

She gripped his hard, muscular shoulders and leaned in, thoughts of wrapping her legs around him flashing through her mind. To hell with all the warnings from her past. She wanted him. She twined her fingers into his hair and pulled his head closer, sliding her tongue against his. They danced and wrestled for pleasure and dominance.

Too soon, his lips left hers, but his mouth didn't go far. He ran his tongue along her lower lip, as if savoring her taste. "Don't screw me, Laser," he murmured, his eyes intense, burning into hers.

"That's your job." She heard the breathlessness in her voice, and she could feel the reverberations of her heart thundering against her ribs, her breasts pressed against his chest.

"Help me complete my mission, and I'll show you how good I am at that job." He brushed his stubbled jaw against her cheek as he leaned in to nibble her earlobe.

Bonita, eyes rolling back in her head, was abruptly glad she didn't know where Kim was. He was manipulating her—did this kiss mean anything to him?—and she knew it. How ironic that she had drawn him away to manipulate *him.*

Even knowing he was using her, her body wanted this to turn into far more than kissing and groping in a corridor. The temptation to give in to him was real.

Could she pretend that she *was* giving in? Take him up to some hotel room, say it was where Kim was staying, and then convince him to spend the night with her? That would give Kim and Casmir time to get away, wouldn't it? And Bjarke deserved being deceived when he was trying to use sex to get her to help him, didn't he?

"Is she really in that lab?" He rubbed the back of her neck, fingers as sensuous as his mouth.

"Look, I don't know where she is at this minute. All I can do is show you to the places where she's been these last few days."

The fingers left her neck, and his mouth left her earlobe. Cold disappointment surged through her, but she struggled to keep her face neutral as he assessed her with his gaze. He was trying to tell if she was telling the truth or not. She gave him nothing.

"Show me then." He linked his arm with hers again and guided her back into the middle of the corridor, heading for a lift.

Her legs were rubbery, and it had nothing to do with old knee injuries. "Are you ever *not* undercover and serving your king?"

"Rarely." He eyed her sidelong, then shifted his arm so he could cup *her* ass this time. "But I would enjoy rewarding you for your assistance."

"Rewarding me? Like I'm a good hound that's retrieved some prey for you?"

"Like you're the sexy, snarky, independent woman you are." They stepped into the lift, and his considering gaze locked onto her again.

She'd seen that gaze from men enough times to know what it meant. He wanted her. He knew he shouldn't give in, but he'd crossed a line from playing a role to wanting to cave to carnal pleasure. Earlier, she'd been considering a hotel room, but maybe they didn't need that for her to distract him for a lengthy period of time.

She turned into his arms, planted a hand on his chest, and pushed *him* against the wall. His eyes flared, not with indignation but with fierce satisfaction, as if he'd wanted exactly this. He slammed a hand against the control panel to hold the lift, and pulled her against him, his lips taking hers again.

He would be livid when he realized what she was doing, but it wasn't as if she expected to have a future with some Sir Noble Knight from the Kingdom. Let them have one exciting, memorable encounter. It would all be much less complicated then, anyway.

Kim shifted from foot to foot, anxious to get out of the shuttle bay and off Stardust Palace Station. Bonita had led Bjarke out of the area—thankfully putting an end to the angry conversation between Bjarke and Asger that had floated back through the bay, past the ships that Kim, Casmir, and Casmir's twelve-crusher army were hiding behind. Asger remained in the bay—Casmir's access to the station's security cameras were allowing him to give updates of things beyond Kim's sight. He was speaking with Qin at the base of the *Dragon's* cargo ramp.

"How do we get rid of him?" Kim whispered to Casmir. "*Them*," she added. Qin might be as likely to fight Rache as Asger.

Casmir was leaning against the wall next to her, his gaze unfocused as he concentrated on the network security cameras—or read a comic book. It was hard to tell. "How much time do we have? If they're still there when Rache gets here, we may have to just tell them to stay back."

Kim spread her hands, palms up. She'd sent a message earlier and gotten the vague response of *Today*.

"You were programmed with the Star Kingdom Royal Bodyguard Manual?" Zee asked quietly.

"I was," came several soft replies.

"I have seen you practice defense on the knight, but there are times when we may be asked to be the aggressors. It is Casmir Dabrowski's wish that we not take human lives. Is this understood?"

"Yes. Casmir Dabrowski is the maker. His will must be fulfilled."

Kim raised her eyebrows at Casmir. He only shrugged.

"There are many ways to disable human opponents without killing them," Zee went on. "We will employ those techniques when necessary."

"What about rendering other crushers, robots, and androids inoperable?" one of his new buddies asked.

"If it is determined that they are the enemies of Casmir Dabrowski, and a threat to our mission, we will need to remove them from the fight. It is not necessary to do so much damage that they will be forever inoperable."

"When I first met you," Kim murmured to Casmir, "I wouldn't have guessed that you would end up building a loyal robot army."

His eye blinked. "Are you sure? I think my parents could have predicted this when I was four and making *vroom vroom* noises as I drove my first robot cab around the kitchen floor."

"It wasn't so much that I thought you lacked interest as… initiative."

"Or megalomania?"

"That too."

"That's one of my fifty words for describing comic book villains, you know. Which I hope I'm not in danger of becoming." Concern wrinkled his brow. "I just didn't want to program them to obey Jorg. Or Jager. Or anyone with an inordinate amount of control over the lives of my friends and family."

"Understandable." Kim refrained from adding *if a bit creepy*. She found the robots quietly discussing their battle tactics—with Zee setting himself up as general—discomfiting, but she wouldn't add to Casmir's concerns by saying so. She hoped they truly were all willing to obey him and didn't develop a recalcitrant independence. So far, Zee's personality was quirky rather than dangerous, but what if they didn't all come out that way?

"Maybe we should have waited somewhere else. We're not going to be able to avoid attracting notice for long. I'm on the network and have convinced that security android in the doorway over there not to look this way, but some captain or crewman is bound to come get something from his or her ship soon—" Casmir waved at the two closest yachts parked near them, "—and report us. We're conspicuous."

Kim eyed the crushers, all made from the same black tarry material. "They would be invisible if you turned out the lights."

"I think turning out the lights would also be conspicuous."

"I suppose. I'll message Rache. He sent me a succinct note this morning and said he was getting close, but nothing since then."

"Succinct?"

"Yes, it's the opposite of what you are. Is that not one of your words for describing villains?"

"It's not. A good villain gets chatty before revealing all to the hapless hero. That's right before the tables are turned, the legions of mindless sycophants are defeated, and the hero gains the upper hand." Casmir glanced at the crushers. "Maybe I *am* the villain. This is distressing, Kim. I may need some time to reflect. Fortunately, it'll take close to a week to get to this moon base."

Kim did not point out that he was demonstrating his anti-succinctness. "Don't you have that holiday coming up where you fast and don't talk? I like that one. I get a lot of reading done when it's so quiet around the house."

"Yom Kippur? Yes. I suppose I won't be home or anywhere with a synagogue. I hope I'll have an opportunity to observe it wherever I am. I could use some quiet time for praying for repentance and contemplating ways to achieve atonement." Casmir's face twisted into a bleak expression.

Kim had only meant to joke about his chattiness, not fill him with regrets and sadness, and she mentally kicked herself for the words. "Maybe we won't make it back home in time," she said, groping for something comforting to say, "but we'll find a way back soon."

"I hope so."

"Who could stop you?" Kim waved to the murmuring crushers.

"Enough warships to blockade a wormhole?"

"Rache's ship has that slydar hull. Maybe if you kidnap Dubashi before he can hire Rache to attack the Kingdom, Rache will be forced to continue his taxi gig and cart us home."

Casmir's eyes grew wistful. "That would be nice. Do you think there's a chance of that?"

No, she didn't, but she forced an optimistic smile and said, "Maybe. Did you get him a gift?"

She wasn't serious, but he nodded.

"Yes. But I doubt it's enough to make a man who hates the Kingdom want to fly us all the way across the galaxy to the Kingdom's doorstep."

"The wormhole gates make that a less time-consuming trip than it would typically be."

"It's still weeks long. Into territory where he'll be shot at if they spot him. Especially when he very recently blew up one of their freighters." Casmir's expression returned to bleakness.

Kim, not wanting to think about Rache's actions even while hoping he'd had a legitimate reason for them, chose not to respond to that.

"What's the gift? I'll give my opinion on its likelihood of swaying him." Kim looked at the crushers again—maybe he already planned to give one to Rache. Casmir had packed light, with only one bag, so she couldn't imagine he had much room for other gifts.

"I'll show you." He slung his bag off his shoulder.

As he rooted around, Kim sent a new message to Rache. She made herself keep the words calm and casual, though tension knotted in her gut, thanks to the reminder of the ship he'd blown up. The *Kingdom* ship. She couldn't help but feel like a teenage girl running away from home with a felonious boyfriend that her parents had warned her to stay away from.

When may I expect my kidnapping?

"Here it is. I gather someone who works with Scholar Natasha Sunflyer puts these boxes together. They were all over the gift shop, and the signs said that twenty percent of the proceeds go back to help fund her research." Casmir held up a compact rectangular box and lifted the lid. "Mushroom soap, a candle made to look like a morel, a mushroom tea energy drink, and I believe these dried ones are hallucinogenic."

Kim pressed a hand to the side of her face. Casmir would be lucky if Rache didn't throw him out the airlock.

"There were also purses made from dried sheets of *Fomes fomentarius*, which I thought was fantastic—it felt just like suede—but Rache doesn't seem like a guy who would carry a purse."

"Good call."

"I did consider getting it for him anyway and calling it a satchel."

"What made you hesitate?"

"There was a lipstick holder."

"Ah."

Greetings, my future captive. I am near the asteroid holding Stardust Palace Station. We're painting a shuttle with an innocuous hull exterior since I saw the Kingdom shuttle that was ahead of us zip inside. If the knight inside spoke to the crew of the freighter that tumbled into my sights earlier, its owner may not wish to see us.

I heard about that. Kim wanted to stay neutral, wanted to refrain from openly judging him, but she couldn't keep from adding, *Is it necessary to murder people you don't even know simply to put a thorn in Jager's side?*

You can't be surprised, given my reputation, but I'd been informed that the knight was on that freighter, not the shuttle. And that his mission is to retrieve you and take you back to Jorg.

I know. It's Sir Bjarke Asger.

Since you've asked me to kidnap you so you can't be taken back to Jorg, I assume you want me to deal with him.

No. Kim closed her eyes. Had he truly attacked that freighter, believing he was protecting her? If so, the deaths of those men were on her shoulders. *Bonita is distracting him, so we can avoid him. So* you *can avoid him. We're waiting in Ship Bay 2.*

We?

Casmir is with me. As is his...protection. Kim touched the outside of the equipment-filled case she'd been lugging everywhere, ensuring herself that *her* "protection" was still there. Instead of working on a bioweapon, she'd made a few homemade knockout grenades to use if someone snatched her stunner but neglected to relieve her of her laboratory tools.

Yes, I'm well familiar with Zee by now.

Kim did not correct the assumption that there would be only one crusher. *We both need transportation off the station. And we're hoping you can take us with you to your meeting at Dubashi's base.*

There was a pause. Maybe she should have waited until they were on his ship to admit that.

I'm going to assume that neither you nor Casmir is planning to assassinate Dubashi. I'm fairly certain Casmir would have a seizure if he attempted to kill someone.

She frowned, not appreciating the dig at Casmir's weakness. *Mock him, and I'll send him back to get that purse.*

What?

Nothing. We'll meet you in the shuttle bay. Bjarke won't be distracted indefinitely. Kim didn't know how many places Bonita could lead him. It wouldn't take them long to discover that she wasn't in the lab.

I'll head over soon.

Thank you.

"He'll be here soon," Kim said.

"That's imprecise." Casmir tucked his mushroom gift box back into his bag. "I got earrings for my mother. And a dog collar for Princess Oku."

"A *dog* collar?"

"She has a dog."

"Oh." Kim pushed the image of the princess wearing a studded collar out of her mind. "Made from mushrooms?"

"A fibrous textile crafted from them, yes. There are little cards that explain the process."

"These gifts for the women in your life don't *look* like mushrooms, do they?"

"The dog collar has silhouettes of pointers that look a bit like Chasca on it. The earrings are moons and stars."

"I guess that's all right."

"Your zealous approval is a relief to me." Casmir's gaze grew abstracted as he checked something on the network. He lowered his voice to ask, "How soon is soon?"

"I don't know. He's painting a shuttle. I guess it's not as nearly invisible as his ship."

"Even his ship is visible if you're close enough. Remember when it pulled up next to us at the refinery?" Casmir held up a finger, forestalling an answer. "Tristan just walked into the shuttle bay."

"Is he looking for his sparring partners?" Kim waved at the now-silent crushers.

"He's heading toward the *Dragon*."

"Maybe he wants his pertundo back."

Casmir's face grew grim. "Maybe something happened to Bonita."

I'm coming now, my future prisoner.

This might not be the best time, after all, Kim quickly replied to Rache. *Another knight—an ex-knight—just walked in.*

We're docking now. You implied that sooner would be better.

I know, and thank you for hurrying, but two knights and Qin are standing in the bay right now. I don't know what they're talking about, but I don't think we can get past them to your airlock—which one are you docking to?—without them seeing. Kim was about to suggest that Rache go to one of the other bays and that she and Casmir would find a way to sneak over unnoticed, but he replied too quickly.

Perfect.

Pardon?

Your kidnapping will be more believable if there are witnesses. I—Later. There's a problem with the Fedallah.

"Something's happening," Kim whispered. "And Rache is coming now."

"Now?" Casmir trotted to the end of the ship they were hiding behind and peered around it. "Let me see if I can convince that security android to disappear. And…" He glanced back at the silent crushers. "I'll see if I can find controls for the lights."

Kim felt a shaky panic trampling around in her belly. Witnesses were fine, but how would Rache kidnap her in front of Asger and Tristan and Qin without them fighting back? Had Casmir spoken to them? Told them not to fight? She would have to do it herself if he hadn't, though she worried that if Asger found out about their ruse, he would feel duty-bound to tell Ishii or the prince what had really happened.

Before she could send them a message, a *thud-bam!* emanated from one of the airlocks. A shuttle had come in. Hard.

A siren issued an ear-splitting wail.

What the hell? How many *witnesses* did Rache want?

"Combat has been engaged," a computer voice announced. "Stardust Palace Defenders, report to stations. All others, this is a Priority 1 lockdown. Civilians, remain in your quarters."

The wailing continued.

Kim rushed up beside Casmir. Qin and Asger had donned their helmets and were looking toward the airlock the noise had come from, their hands on their weapons. Worse, numerous heads were poking out of the hatches of the other ships in the bay. Some of the crews must have opted to stay aboard rather than pay for lodging. Kim groaned. This was not the stealthy kidnapping she had originally envisioned.

"I'm telling Qin and Asger not to fight, to go in the *Dragon* and stay there," Casmir said over the siren.

"Is it working?" Kim noticed neither of them were moving.

"They want to know what's going on." Casmir glanced at some of the other people now stepping out of their ships, curious about the warning rather than afraid.

"Do *you* know? That siren isn't for Rache's shuttle, is it? He was disguising it so nobody would know it was him."

"I'm monitoring the security network. The station has activated its defenses and is firing at a hostile ship lurking nearby."

"Not pirates again, I hope."

Casmir shook his head. "They know it's Rache. The *Fedallah*."

"Wait, *how*? Isn't it almost invisible?"

“Somehow the station knows it’s there and is firing at it. I’m not sure if the warship is firing back or not.”

Kim groaned. How had this turned into such a mess so fast?

Are you in the bay? Rache messaged her.

Yes.

We’re coming in. We need to get in and out quickly.

Because his warship was being fired at. No kidding. Would they even be able to escape in his shuttle, or would the station defenses target it? How much armor did it have?

“He’s coming in,” Kim repeated for Casmir’s sake.

Boots rang out in the corridor leading into the bay, the noise just audible in the lulls between one siren wail and the next. From her point of view, Kim could see a ways down that corridor, and she groaned again, recognizing the man sprinting their way.

Bjarke.

Unlike with Asger, they couldn’t tell him to step into the *Dragon* and ignore this. Not that Casmir’s command for *that* had worked. Qin and Asger were still in front of the cargo ramp with their hands on their weapons.

“We need to get everyone out of this bay, Casmir.” Kim gripped his shoulder, hoping he could do something.

The door Bjarke had almost reached slammed down, as did the other open doors around the bay. Secondary security doors slid down after them. Kim jumped as they were effectively barricaded inside.

“What—”

“Shuttle Bay Two has a leak of toxic gas,” the computer voice said. “Shuttle Bay Two is being sealed off from the rest of the station. All personnel in the bay must don self-contained spacesuits with supplemental oxygen or seal themselves inside their ships.”

The lighting dimmed, then flashed red, glinting off the crushers’ shoulders.

Kim cursed. Her galaxy suit had a helmet she could put up, but there was only a small amount of emergency oxygen contained inside. She didn’t have an air tank, and neither did Casmir.

“We’ll have to go to the *Dragon*,” she said.

Casmir shook his head. “It’s a ruse. There’s no leak.” He pointed around the bay at the curious people who’d hopped out of their ships. They were all charging back inside now, hatches clanging shut behind them. “I wanted to clear the deck in case there’s a fight.”

Tristan, who wore regular clothes rather than a galaxy suit with a helmet, waved for Asger to go into the *Dragon* as he ran toward one of the exit doors. Tristan tried to get a security panel to work, to override the controls and escape, but the door remained locked.

Casmir raised a hand, as if to warn him he would be fine, but Tristan didn't see them. He sprinted toward a palace yacht that he must have known the code for. Its hatch went up, and he dove inside before it sealed again.

A thud came from the door that was blocking Bjarke, and a dent appeared, bubbling outward on their side. Was he using his pertundo on it? Because he knew Kim was in here? Or because he also knew Rache and the *Fedallah* were here?

"I think a fight is guaranteed," Kim said.

The airlock hatch where Rache's shuttle was docked opened. Asger charged toward it.

"I'm afraid you're right," Casmir said grimly.

CHAPTER 19

DON'T FIGHT, CASMIR'S TEXT WARNING CAME OVER ASGER'S contact. *It's a ruse. There's no danger to us.*

Asger paused uncertainly, the wailing of the station's siren implying there was very real danger here. More than a gas leak was going on. Who was coming in through the airlock that had just opened?

"Get that bastard if he's on that shuttle," Asger's father barked over his comm.

Asger had his helmet on, so the ferocious voice rang in his ear, urging him into motion before he'd figured out what was going on. He resumed his rush toward the airlock hatch.

"I'll be in as soon as I can get through this door," his father continued, a clang punctuating his words. "My contact in station security warned me they're firing at the *Fedallah*, and that shuttle *came* from the *Fedallah.* It might be him. If we catch Rache—if we kill that bastard—there will be hope to redeem your career." Another clang and a frustrated snarl. "How many doors *are* there? What's going on in there?"

"Gas leak. Keep your helmet up."

Asger didn't have an oxygen tank, but he had a few minutes of air stored in his armor. Long enough for this, especially if he reached that hatch before the mercenaries were ready.

Rache. What was the bastard doing here in this system? Joining the thugs being hired into Dubashi's mercenary fleet?

Two smoke bombs bounced out of the airlock tube before Asger reached it. Then a mercenary in black combat armor leaned out with a grenade launcher, pointing it straight at him.

No *danger*? What was Casmir talking about? Was he even in the area?

Asger dodged to the side an instant before the mercenary fired the grenade launcher.

What were the idiots bringing such weapons onto a space station for? There would be far worse than a gas leak in here soon.

The grenade boomed as it struck the far wall and exploded. Asger sprang and landed in front of the mercenary, swinging his extended pertundo toward that black-armored chest. But his foe refused to cooperate by staying in place. He ducked back into the cover of the airlock chamber, and Asger only clipped his shoulder, the blade glancing off.

The mercenary rushed back out with four armored allies at his side. The men scattered more smoke bombs, hazing the air all around the airlock.

Qin caught up with Asger and rushed toward the leader, but someone launched another grenade. Asger dodged out of its path again, but it exploded far sooner than the first, scant inches past his shoulder.

The force hurled him sideways and into the air with so much power that he almost dropped his pertundo. But he clenched it tightly, refusing to let go, and twisted to land on his feet.

Qin had been caught even more fully by the blast. She skidded across the deck on her back, away from the airlock. She wasn't in armor—why would she be, when all she had expected was Asger's father?

Worried she had been seriously hurt, Asger gave up a chance to swing at more mercenaries to jump back to her side. He reached for her, intending to help her up, but she recovered on her own, leaping lithely to her feet.

"I'm all right," Qin promised him.

Surprisingly, the mercenaries didn't charge after them. They weren't even firing further from within the smoke cover they'd created, the gray haze swirling in the dull red of the flashing emergency lights. Boots rang out as the men ran away from Asger and Qin and deeper into the bay. They disappeared behind the cover of the parked ships.

Asger started after them. Clangs kept coming from the door as his father tried to tear his way in. How did the mercenaries think they would get out of the bay if a knight with a pertundo couldn't get in?

"Asger, Qin, stop fighting," came a familiar call from behind one of the ships.

Casmir was leaning out, waving urgently.

It's a ruse, Casmir messaged again, using his chip instead of calling it across the bay. *Back away. Please. And forget you saw this.*

It's Rache! Asger threw back.

What kind of collusion could Casmir have planned with that Kingdom-hating ship-destroying bastard? Asger's father was right. If they had the chance to kill Rache here, they should take it.

Please, Casmir repeated. *I'll owe you one. Go hide in the* Dragon. *Say you were taking refuge from the gas leak.*

A boom rattled the deck. Shapes moved in the smoke again. Asger couldn't tell if more mercenaries were coming into the bay or if the first group was running back to the airlock.

Asger glanced toward Casmir's spot, but he'd disappeared behind that ship.

"Is he here?" Asger's father demanded over the comm, panting now. "Rache?"

"I'm not sure," Asger said truthfully.

All of the black-armored mercenaries looked the same with their helmets on.

Qin took two steps toward the figures in the smoke—was that Zee?—but paused, looking back at Asger. "Do we attack or…?"

Asger stood torn with indecision. "Casmir said not to. What are they doing? Do you know?"

Qin shook her head.

Asger's helmet flashed a warning about low oxygen. He growled in frustration. Was there truly a leak? His helmet display didn't show anything wrong with the air in the bay, other than the contaminants from the smoke grenades.

The smoke cleared a little, and Asger spotted Casmir and Kim jogging toward some of the black-armored men. Not only Zee but numerous crushers were with them. Mercenaries had surrounded them and were pointing guns at their backs.

Damn it, Casmir, are you sure*?* Asger messaged.

This didn't *look* like a ruse.

Casmir didn't look over at him, but he replied immediately. *Yes, yes, it's fine. I'll explain later.*

Asger gripped his pertundo hard, but he didn't rush toward the group. At his side, Qin appeared just as uncertain.

Behind him, metal tore with a wrenching squeal. His father finally shoved himself into the bay through the hole he'd half cut and half ripped in the thick double doors.

"William!" he barked. "What are you doing? Do they have Sato?"

"I'm going to check on them," Asger said, more for Qin than his father's angry shouts.

He jogged toward the departing mercenaries, but his confusion kept him from committing fully. Maybe Casmir had set this up and *wanted* to be kidnapped. Was that how he planned to get to Dubashi's base? With Rache? Or could this be *Kim's* plan?

Realization slammed into Asger. Of course. Kim didn't want to be dragged back to create a bioweapon for Jorg. That had to be it. Why hadn't they told him about this? Had they thought he would tell his superiors? Or his father? That he would be honor bound to do so?

Asger grimaced, realizing he *would* feel honor bound.

"Hurry," his father barked, running up and then passing them. "They've got Sato. Why aren't you *fighting*?"

The mercenaries deployed more smoke grenades, and the lights went out completely in the bay, leaving only a few glowing indicators on the floor.

Asger's night vision activated, but it was hard to penetrate the smoke. All he knew was that the group of friends and enemies and crushers was filing into the airlock tube and the shuttle beyond.

Most of the group. A rear guard held back, turning to face Asger's father. They raised rifles, firing.

Asger lurched into motion. He couldn't leave his father to fight them all alone.

A grenade, this one launched by hand, sailed straight at Asger. He whipped his pertundo across and knocked it aside before it hit him and exploded in the air above his head. The shockwave rattled him again, but he kept going. Qin fired at the armored figures.

One of her anti-tank rounds exploded in the middle of the group, and two mercenaries went flying. Shrapnel hammered into the side of the bay—and the airlock and airlock tube. A new alarm sounded, warning of a rupture.

"Airlock Eight is being sealed off," the computer voice announced. "We have an external breach. Airlock Eight is being sealed off."

The last of the mercenaries helped their comrades to their feet and rushed for the tube. A red light flashed on the wall above the airlock. The heavy hatch started to swing shut.

One of the mercenaries caught it and held it open for his comrades. The remaining men slipped through. The mercenary released it, so it would close, but Asger's father had reached it. He caught the door, grunting as he pushed it open, and slipped through.

Startled, Asger was an instant too late in lunging after him. The hatch clanged shut before he could grab it.

He grabbed the latch and started to pull but caught himself as the sirens screeched all around him. Outside a porthole, he saw the tube flapping, already detached. The mercenaries couldn't have all made it across, but the shuttle was taking off. Reluctantly, Asger let go of the hatch. If he succeeded in forcing it open, it would turn the whole bay into a vacuum.

Instead, he ran to the porthole, his faceplate clunking against it as he tried to spot his father. He saw mercenaries hanging onto the end of the tube, their legs floating free, as it was retracted into the storage around the shuttle's airlock chamber. Several other mercenaries weren't holding onto anything. They must have blown free.

Asger was on the verge of hoping station security would be able to round them up when they fired jet boots and steered at top speed toward the shuttle.

It was turning so that it could head for the tunnel leading out of the asteroid, so they had time to catch up. Where was Rache's ship? Inside the asteroid, or was the station firing external defenses from the outside?

A couple of the mercenaries remaining in the shuttle's airlock helped pull their people in. Casmir and Kim and all those crushers had to already be on there. They'd been ahead of the others. Walking at gunpoint.

The shuttle fired a missile, and Asger jumped, fearing it was heading straight at him. But it slammed into another shuttle docked farther down the bay. He groaned. That was the Kingdom shuttle his father had flown here.

Had he been inside of it? Or on his way there? The missile did a spectacular job of blowing the engine compartment to shreds without damaging the airlock or the side of the station.

Father? Asger tried to message him. *Are you... safe?*

When he didn't get an answer, he tried the comm. Nothing.

Asger twisted his head, looking for his father's galaxy suit. What if the mercenaries had already killed him?

After long seconds of searching the well-lit space outside and not seeing him, Asger slumped and dropped his head. He didn't know if he loved his father—there were times he was positive he didn't like him—but he hadn't wanted him to *die*. Especially if this was some idiotic ruse.

Qin started toward Asger—he was leaning against a porthole, his head slumped to his chest—but jumped, almost firing her Brockinger when drones flew into the bay, whirring over some of the parked ships. But she realized they weren't a threat. They zipped to the blackened wall near the airlock and started oozing a foam patch material.

Right, the hull breach. Qin wondered if they could get that hatch open and chase after the shuttle. Or even if they *should.*

She wasn't positive what she had witnessed, but she was worried since Bjarke had gone out after the mercenaries and hadn't come back. Had he made it to their shuttle and was he even now fighting them? Or was he floating around out there in his galaxy suit, injured or unconscious? One of the mercenaries could have easily shot him when he sprang out after them.

Before Qin resumed her jog to Asger, Bonita climbed through the hole in the door that Bjarke had made. She hobbled into the bay, grimacing and gripping her hip. The sirens stopped complaining, and the red emergency lighting came back on, showing Bonita's hair half fallen—torn?—out of her usual braid, and the seam partially undone at the collar of her galaxy suit.

After glancing at Asger to make sure he wasn't on the verge of throwing himself out the airlock to give chase, Qin rushed to Bonita in case she needed help. She looked like she had been mugged.

What if someone was after her? Qin peered into the corridor, but nobody was back there. Even the security android had disappeared at some point. Because of that leak? An android wouldn't have been affected.

Was there even a leak? Her helmet display said the air was a little thin, after the breach, but that it was breathable. The drones had already finished with the temporary repairs. She didn't see anything about a toxic substance, or any extraneous substances at all, in the air.

"Are you all right?" Qin reached out but didn't grip Bonita, afraid to hurt her further. "Did Bjarke *hit* you?"

Indignation burned in Qin's chest. That bastard had yelled at Asger in front of everyone, then turned whatever that mercenary incursion had been into a worse snarl than it should have been. Not that she'd helped with that. She'd gotten a message from Casmir to hide in the *Dragon* and stay away from the intruders, and she would have trusted him and done so if Asger hadn't charged. She'd been terrified for him.

Now she turned that worry onto Bonita. If Bjarke had hurt her, Qin would strangle him herself.

"What? No, that's not it." Bonita straightened, moving her hand from her hip, though she didn't quite manage to smooth the grimace from her face. "I will blame him for leaving in a hurry when he heard…" Bonita looked toward the airlock, the drones tidying up the last of their foam patch, the scorch marks on the deck, the red emergency lights shining down. "Yeah, that's what he must have heard. He rushed off so quickly, I lost my balance and got tangled in my suit, which was in a different more compromising position at the time. I wasn't holding on to anything but him, you see."

"Holding on to… him?" Qin couldn't help but curl a lip as she *did* begin to see. And wished she hadn't. "You were having *sex*? With *him*?"

"In a lift, yes. Which I do not recommend when you get older and have less padding over your bones." Her hand strayed to her hip again. "Not as bad as the shower, I suppose. It wasn't slick. In most places." The grimace turned into a quick smirk.

"Ew."

Bonita pointed at Qin. "Just uncurl that lip of yours. It's making you look like a snaggle-toothed tiger."

Qin forced her lip to lower and hide the fang it had revealed. "I didn't think you would—I mean, I guess I knew you were going to distract him, but I didn't think you were the type to…"

Qin trailed off, not wanting to insult her captain, employer, and friend. Better to drop it.

"Use sex to get what I want from a man?" Bonita suggested.

Qin shrugged. "Yes."

"I wasn't planning to—I was going to show him the lab, like I said—but then he tried to use sex, or at least kisses, to get what he wanted from *me*. He was manipulating me so I would tell him where Kim *really* was. So I figured it was fair for me to distract him whatever way was easiest.

In hindsight, I should have gotten him farther away from this bay so he couldn't charge back so readily. But by the time we got to the lift, I'm not sure either of us was manipulating the other anymore. I think we were just being horny." Bonita pointed at her. "Your lip is curled again, and your fang is sticking out."

"Sorry." Qin forced her lip down. "It's my favorite one."

"Uh huh."

"And I don't like him. Or trust him, even if he is a knight."

Bonita looked around the bay, her gaze settling on Asger. "Where *is* Bjarke?"

Qin didn't like the way Asger appeared to be mourning the loss of a family member. Had he seen the mercenaries shoot Bjarke? Blow him into pieces outside the airlock?

"He tried to go after the mercenaries," Qin said. "I'm not sure he made it to their shuttle. There was an explosion, and their airlock tube ripped. I think Casmir and Kim made it, but—"

"Casmir and Kim were down here?"

"Yes. The mercenaries marched them and the crushers out at gunpoint."

"Oh. Right. That was why I was distracting Bjarke. Of course. So they could be, uh, kidnapped." Bonita frowned at Qin. "That was Rache, wasn't it? Why did you fight his men? Or was that only Asger?"

"It was really only Bjarke. Asger started to but paused when Casmir told him not to. Then Bjarke burst in—" Qin pointed at the mangled hole in the door, "—and ordered Asger to get Rache. I don't know how he knew Rache was here or… was that the station firing at the *Fedallah*?"

She'd heard some of the words that had come over Asger's comm helmet, but it had been chaotic then, with the sirens wailing, and even her keen ears hadn't caught everything. But the voice on the station comm had announced they were defending against *someone*.

"I don't know," Bonita said. "I was detained."

Qin, convinced there wasn't truly a leak, pushed her helmet back and scratched her head. "I think everything would have worked out fine for them if station security hadn't started firing at Rache's warship. I thought it was invisible to scanners. What if that shuttle can't even get back to it? I wish I knew what was happening out there."

"Me too. Maybe Viggo can update us—he should have some sensor range, even buried in this asteroid." Bonita headed for the cargo ramp, limping noticeably.

Qin reached out a hand in case she wanted to lean on her, but Bonita had always been proud, and she waved away the offer.

"I didn't see the fight," Bonita added, wincing again as she maneuvered up the ramp. She lowered her voice. "Was it… believable? In case someone gets the camera footage later? Someone royal?"

"Bjarke made it look believable, I think. So did Asger and I, inadvertently."

Qin looked toward Asger. He'd stepped away from the porthole, and she could make out that he was murmuring to someone on his helmet comm. Security? Qin was surprised they hadn't shown up yet, but maybe the supposed leak was keeping them out. Or they were busy firing at that shuttle and the *Fedallah.* Qin winced, imagining Kim and Casmir caught in the middle of all that.

She would join Asger and make sure he was all right after she got Bonita settled into the ship.

They were almost to the top of the ramp when the full lights came back on, and the doors rose. All except the one Bjarke had torn his way through. It was too damaged to slide into its pocket and only made it part way up. A security team ducked under it to enter.

Qin paused and looked toward the yacht Tristan had ducked into when the gas leak had been announced. She was surprised he hadn't come out yet. He should have seen by now that the air was clear. Though maybe it was best that he was slow to react. The sultan wouldn't know that Casmir had arranged his own kidnapping and might send Tristan and his security people after the mercenaries in a warship. To get the creator of his crushers back.

"Greetings, Bonita," Viggo said as they entered the cargo hold. "Are you injured?"

"Mostly my pride." Bonita slumped against a crate. "I hope there wasn't a camera in that lift."

"I'm sure station security has other things it's worried about now," Qin said. "Do you want help to sickbay? Or your cabin?"

Bonita lifted a hand. "Viggo, can you fill me in on what's going on out there? Are you able to sense Rache's warship?"

"The *Fedallah*? No. But the station apparently does, because all of the cannons mounted on the exterior of the asteroid have been firing at something for the last ten minutes. If it's Rache's warship, someone either tagged it with a locator beacon, or these people have figured out how to detect a ship through its slydar hull."

"They're still firing at it now?"

"Yes. If it *is* a ship, it's engaged in evasive maneuvers. The cannons keep changing their aim. It does appear that they only have one target, but that may change."

"What do you mean?" Qin asked, her insides knotting.

"My sensors show the mercenary shuttle now exiting the mouth of the asteroid. It's zigzagging its path and flying into the area where the station cannons are firing."

Bonita dropped her hands to her knees. "Those idiots are going to get themselves killed. What were they thinking?"

That they didn't want to be put to use building horrible weapons for their government, Qin thought. She could understand that, but she wished Casmir and Kim had explained the plan better to her and Bonita. They might have done more to help. And they should have told Asger, even if she could see why they hadn't. He might have told his father and his superiors.

"And where is Bjarke, damn it?" Bonita thumped her fist on her thigh. "Tell me they didn't blow him away. If I'd known, I would have tried harder to keep him from leaving. If they'd *told* me exactly what they were doing…"

"Maybe your new hobby with Bjarke made them uncertain that they could." Qin realized Asger wasn't the only one who might have sided with Bjarke, or at least tipped him off.

"My new hobby of having sex? That hardly makes *me* untrustworthy."

"It kind of seemed like your loyalties were divided before." Qin waved toward the level above where they'd met with Casmir.

"I just didn't want to lie to him. I…" Bonita straightened, throwing up her hands in frustration.

A faint clanging reached Qin's ears. She walked back out on the ramp. Was that Asger?

He was still next to the porthole, pacing and talking on the comm, but he stopped and whirled toward the airlock hatch. The clanging sounded again. Someone knocking… from the other side.

Asger tapped a control panel coated with soot from numerous explosions. Nothing happened.

He grabbed the manual lever on the hatch and pulled, muscles straining. Qin hopped off the ramp, intending to help him, but the seal broke with a hiss, and Bjarke stumbled in. The outer airlock hatch was apparently still working and secure behind him.

Bjarke slapped his helmet back as Asger lunged, catching him by the shoulders. Bjarke gasped for air.

"What happened?" Asger blurted.

Bjarke sucked in a few more breaths before recovering enough to pin Asger with a glare. "You tell me. You let them walk out with Sato and Dabrowski."

"There were too many of them to stop them," Asger said evenly.

"You didn't even try. You call that fighting?" Bjarke pointed at something outside the bay. "That bastard blew up my shuttle on his way out. Did you see that?"

Asger dropped his hands and stepped back from his father, his face turning to a stony mask.

Qin wanted to reach out and comfort him with one hand and punch Bjarke with the other.

Asger opened his mouth to say something else, but Bjarke turned his back on him and stalked toward the *Dragon.*

Qin gritted her teeth from the top of the ramp. She had no interest in talking to Bjarke.

"Captain," she called into the hold, "it's for you."

Then she wished she hadn't said anything, because Bonita limped out, reminding Qin of her injury. As soon as she saw Bjarke, she stopped walking, straightening to hide her pain. She folded her arms across her chest and lifted her chin. Bjarke stopped at the base of the ramp and glared up at her. They looked more like combatants than lovers.

"You knew that was going to happen?" he demanded.

"I had no idea that was going to happen," Bonita said, staring steadily back at him.

Not exactly like that, no.

"Do you know where they're going?" Bjarke must not have believed her.

Bonita twitched a shoulder. "To avoid your prince?"

"How far? I have to try to follow them, but they blew the back end off my shuttle. It's nothing but a wreck sitting in its docking bay now."

"You couldn't follow him. His ship has slydar."

"*Someone* knows where it is," Bjarke growled. "I'll talk to station defense and figure out how they detected it, so I can do the same."

"And what would you do if you caught it? In a shuttle or even in some ship here that they lent you?" Bonita waved toward the yacht Tristan had entered—it looked like some princess's pleasure cruiser rather than a combat ship. There weren't any weapons. "Get yourself killed. That's what."

"I have to try to catch up with them. I'll negotiate if I have to." Bjarke spat. "I have a mission, to take Scholar Sato to the prince. And *I* don't give up on my missions. I *complete* them." He glared over his shoulder at Asger, who'd also come over, but was standing a few feet back.

"An epitaph that's sure to look good on your tombstone."

Bjarke clenched and unclenched his fists. Bonita wasn't fazed by his bluster. She merely stood there with her chin up.

"My mission was to retrieve Tristan's pertundo, and that's it," Asger said. "Though I'm now thinking I should follow after him and give it to him. He's going to need it."

"What are you talking about?" Bjarke demanded as Bonita asked, "What do you mean *follow*?"

Qin glanced toward the yacht, but Asger shook his head.

"Tristan commed me a minute ago. He saw what was going on from the yacht. He didn't think he could do anything by himself in a fight against the mercenaries, so he used the smoke as cover to sneak aboard their shuttle."

"He's on there *now*?" Bjarke stared.

"Hiding in a locker. Or he was." Asger grimaced. "He was whispering to me, but then the comm cut out, and I haven't been able to get him back. They may have found him."

"We *have* to go after them," Bjarke repeated and faced Bonita again.

"What do you mean *we*? I have an assignment. I'm off to find a missing scientist. I'm not chasing after mercenaries."

Bjarke took a deep breath. "I'll get a ship from the station then. I'm not going to stay here while that villain takes off with our people."

"Good luck," Bonita said. "I heard the sultan isn't a fan of Kingdom citizens."

Bjarke stalked away looking so frustrated that Qin almost felt sympathy for him. Almost. If he hadn't shown up, Qin believed Kim and Casmir could have slipped out with Rache without any injuries or damage done at all.

"Bonita—Captain Lopez," Asger said quietly. "I know this ship can't battle a warship, but would you be willing to follow them for a while? In case there's a chance to get Tristan back? I admit, I don't quite know what Casmir and Kim's relationship is with Rache—" Asger winced, as if the idea of such a relationship pained him, "—but maybe they can talk him into giving us Tristan back."

Bonita lowered her arms. She might have been a wall against Bjarke's anger, but Asger's quiet, reasonable request stole some of her stiffness.

"I'm sorry, Asger, but we really do have a contract—thanks to you."

"We don't know where Scholar Sunflyer is yet, do we?" Qin had been briefed on the mission, and the last she'd heard, Bonita was only starting to research the missing virologist.

"Not yet."

"We could start out after Rache. Oh, maybe he even has intelligence about Sunflyer." Qin brightened. "We could comm him and ask to trade information. That might give us an opportunity to find out if Tristan… survived."

Asger winced again, but he must have believed he was swaying Bonita, for he waved for his father to come back over.

"I'm not wasting fuel following a ship I can't see all over the system," Bonita said.

"We *know* where they're going," Asger said as Bjarke rejoined them. "Casmir made that deal with Sultan Shayban to capture Prince Dubashi."

Bjarke squinted at him. "You think that means Rache is headed to Dubashi's base?"

Asger hesitated. "Yes."

"Then, Captain Lopez," Bjarke said, facing her again, "I will offer you ten thousand crowns to take me to Dubashi's moon base. Once you drop me off, you can go complete your other mission."

"Isn't that the base that's swarming with mercenary ships right now?" Bonita asked. "Even I saw that invitation. Mercenaries don't tend to be crazy about bounty hunters."

Bjarke clenched his jaw. "Fifteen thousand crowns," he said tightly.

Qin didn't think Bonita was objecting out of a desire to negotiate for more money, but Bonita didn't wave away the offer. She looked at Qin. "What do you think?"

"It's your decision, Captain," Qin said, surprised Bonita was consulting her. "You just steer me where you want me to go, and I'll grab my weapons and go."

"I guess I can research Sunflyer while we're on the way." Bonita pointed a finger at Bjarke's nose. "When we get within firing distance of that moon, I'm kicking you out the airlock. You'll have to use jet boots and a galaxy suit to maneuver your way into the base. There's no way I'm asking for permission to land in that wasp's nest."

"If Scholar Sato is planning to deliver herself into the enemy's hands," Bjarke said, "I'll do what I must to retrieve her."

Qin doubted that was what Kim planned, but she didn't say anything. She liked the idea of going to possibly help Kim and Casmir rather than turning the other way on some unrelated mission.

"Whoever's coming, climb on," Bonita said. "We're taking off."

"You may want to wait," Viggo said, "as it's not yet clear if the shuttle is going to make it back to the warship. The station is turning two of its cannons to target it."

CHAPTER 20

CASMIR WAS FLATTENED TO THE HULL INSIDE THE shuttle, gripping a handhold like a rope dangling from a cliff, and doing his best not to be trampled by Rache's mercenaries or his own crushers. The little ship whipped about more like an Old Earth biplane than a spacecraft. His stomach seemed to pitch about inside his torso as the force of their acceleration threw him up toward the ceiling, down toward the floor, and then smashed him against the bulkhead. He caught Kim's glance—she was hanging from the handhold next to him—and all manner of regret darkening her eyes.

Had they made a huge mistake? Casmir had noticed that the mercenaries hadn't been shooting to kill, but that didn't mean nobody had been injured. He'd tried to hustle Kim and the crushers out as quickly as possible, so Rache's people wouldn't have to linger in the station.

Rache's people who were cursing mightily as the shuttle twisted through impossible maneuvers, threatening to give them all whiplash. The men kept eyeing the crushers, though they were the least mobile things in the shuttle. They reshaped themselves on the fly to put more mass in whichever direction gravity was pushing them.

"Dabrowski, what are all those crushers doing in here?" Rache demanded from somewhere beyond the sea of armored men.

However many people the shuttle was supposed to seat, it had to be fewer than were in it now, assuming one counted crushers as people.

"I am a Z-6000, programmed to protect Kim Sato and Casmir Dabrowski," eleven monotone voices said at once.

Zee—*Casmir's* Zee—said, "I do those things also. With flair."

"Unless one of them is a birthday present to me," Rache growled, "I'm not amused at this unexpected overage. These shuttles have maximum weight capacities, you know."

"I told you that you should have gotten him a crusher for a gift," Kim whispered.

"No, you didn't. You only twitched your eyebrows vociferously at my fungi gift box."

"Eyebrows can't be vociferous. The root of that word means voice. Implying sound."

"Oh, I *heard* your eyebrows twitch."

Casmir's toes rose off the deck during one of the maneuvers, and he momentarily saw over the big mercenaries to where Rache was ducking into the shuttle's navigation area. Gift giving, it seemed, would wait.

The shuttle jolted, as if they'd run into an asteroid.

"The bastards are firing at us," someone growled.

"*Why?* We barely messed up their station."

"And not until they started shit with the *Fedallah.*"

Rache, now up front breathing down his pilot's neck, did not respond to the commentary.

"Can you do anything to stop them from firing?" Kim asked Casmir.

He shook his head. "We've flown out of range of their wireless networks. I didn't think to set something up while I still had access."

"Because you didn't know they could see Rache's ship and would fire at it. And us."

No, it would have been nice if he'd had some warning about *that* new development.

The shuttle veered in another direction, reminding Casmir of the one and only rollercoaster ride he'd gone on as a kid that had involved loops and hanging upside down. He hadn't thrown up that time, but only because he'd been too scared to think of it.

An alert came via his chip, Sultan Shayban requesting permission to contact him.

"Uh oh," Casmir muttered.

He'd told Shayban from the beginning that he would take the crushers to Dubashi's base—that was their deal, after all—but at the time, he'd believed he would be able to finish building the hundred-crusher army first. He hadn't expected to go *with* Kim when she was kidnapped or that she herself would want to go to the base.

A part of him was tempted to deny permission, but no, he would have to talk to Shayban sooner or later.

Casmir Dabrowski, the message scrolled past. *Have you been kidnapped by those mercenaries? Are you in that shuttle? My people are sorting through the footage in the ship bay, but someone hacked into the system, and it's a mess.*

Someone? They hadn't yet figured out that he was that someone? Maybe Shayban assumed Rache had come to the station for inimical purposes and had been responsible for all the trouble.

Yes, Scholar Sato and I are both on the shuttle.

Prisoners! Damn that Rache. I knew he was here for some vile end, but I wouldn't have guessed it was to kidnap you. Does he also want crushers made? The Kingdom knight warned us that Rache had blown up one of their ships and might be gunning for us next. And then we sensed his sneaky warship lurking scant kilometers away from our asteroid.

Casmir didn't want to lie to Shayban, but he accepted that this might not be the best time to straighten out erroneous beliefs.

How did you detect his spaceship?

That was where Rache's—and Casmir's—problems had started.

We purchased a slydar detector from Sayona Station in Cerberus. I wouldn't usually do business with such a sketchy establishment, but this was too good to pass up. The slydar detector is still in the beta-testing phase. I'm so pleased that it worked, since it cost a fortune. I thought we would be using it to detect Dubashi's ships, not Rache's, but now we will know when any friend or foe attempts to sneak up on Stardust Palace.

"A slydar-detector?" Casmir mouthed.

We will stop firing at that shuttle since you are aboard, but what can I do to get you back, Casmir? We have warships of our own that we can send after Rache. They can be out there in twenty minutes. I'm not certain if they'll be fast enough to catch his foul mercenary ship.

Actually, I think he intends to take us to Dubashi's base. Perhaps... we should go along with him willingly, and then find an opportunity to kidnap your nemesis.

I think you will only be shot. There is a bounty out for you, you know. Dubashi wants you dead.

I do know that. I intend to be crafty.

You have not completed the army of crushers. They would have assisted greatly with craftiness.

Indeed. I did leave the one I made for you, and the other eighty-odd should be completed soon. I left the machinery running, and the nanites have already been programmed and injected into the matrices. I hope to return soon with Dubashi in tow.

Casmir didn't get a prompt answer, and he wondered if Shayban was digesting that or if he'd seen through the charade. Maybe some new footage had come in that he was reviewing.

If I am not as crafty as I think, Casmir added, *and I am unable to come back for the crushers, I am certain you will find a use for them.*

As soon as Shayban found someone to reprogram them to obey him. Thus far, Casmir had only made him one.

"Have they stopped firing?" Kim twisted, trying to peer out a porthole.

The shuttle was still zigzagging its path, but the gyrations weren't as wild, and they hadn't been struck again.

I fear you will get yourself killed, Shayban finally replied. *This was less of a concern for me when I did not know you and I thought you were trying to swindle me. But now, I would regret having, however inadvertently, engineered your death.*

Casmir felt guilty since he wasn't being honest about everything with Shayban. *You didn't engineer this, Your Highness. I suspect Prince Jorg wanted the crushers to invade Dubashi's base, and that is why he's lingering in this system, so I would have ended up on this path regardless.*

But you would have ridden into battle on the bridge of one of your people's warships, not cuffed and gagged as a prisoner being dragged into the base by that mercenary.

Kim nudged him. Rache was coming back into the main cabin.

I still have hope that I'll be able to work myself into a better situation than that, Casmir replied. *Maybe Rache would be willing to keep me alive in exchange for a crusher of his own.*

That villain doesn't need any more advantages. Good luck, Casmir. Let me know if I can assist you.

Thank you. I will.

Casmir wondered if that offer would extend to assisting him in getting rid of the invaders in System Lion. He might ask, but only if he managed to defeat Dubashi, as the sultan wished.

"They had us in their sights," Rache said, stopping in front of Casmir and Kim, his magnetic boots keeping him locked to the deck as the shuttle slowed. Were they nearly to the *Fedallah*? "Then they stopped firing."

"Yes," Casmir said. "I requested that."

"From whom?"

"The sultan."

"You and he are buddies?"

"He likes crushers, and I made him one."

"You haven't made *me* one." Rache turned his masked gaze toward the nearest one—Zee. Zee loomed close enough to spring if Casmir needed help.

"See?" Kim mouthed to Casmir.

"I did bring you a gift." Some of the mercenaries were watching this conversation, and Casmir reminded himself that he was nothing more than some odious prisoner to Rache's men. He should try not to blow Rache's cover by suggesting they had a relationship.

"Is it better than a crusher?" Rache asked, deadpan.

"No," Kim said before Casmir could answer.

"It's a nice gift," Casmir protested. "There's not even a lipstick holder."

Alas, the mask hid whatever relief or alarm Rache might feel.

"Scholar Sato," he said formally to Kim with a little bow, "I must inform you that Prince Dubashi requested that I kidnap you and bring you to him."

Casmir arched his brows. Was that true? Or was Rache saying that as an explanation for this side trip for the sake of the men watching their exchange?

"I was going to be disappointed if you didn't kidnap me this month." Kim did deadpan even better than Rache.

"I have no doubt. We will discuss this further in my briefing room once we've docked." Rache headed back up the aisle toward navigation.

"Does he still have a reward out for *me*?" Casmir asked, wondering if Rache could walk the two of them into Dubashi's moon base under the guise that they were prisoners.

Unfortunately, Rache and Casmir had tried that back with the terrorist base on Odin, and it hadn't worked. The former chief superintendent of

Royal Intelligence had known too much about Casmir and Rache to be fooled… and he might have reported all that to Dubashi, if he'd been working with him, as Moonrazor had implied.

No, he *must* have reported that, Casmir realized, thinking about it for the first time since he'd received the new information. That was why Dubashi wanted him dead now, because like that former chief superintendent, Dubashi thought Casmir would be a strong ally of Jager and the Kingdom and a threat to his schemes.

"He just wants you dead," Rache said over his shoulder.

"I'm afraid I can't look forward to discussing that, then," Casmir said.

Bright light appeared outside of the portholes as they flew into one of the *Fedallah*'s shuttle bays. They landed on the pad and took on the ship's spin gravity. Casmir's stomach did a few flip-flops, though he suspected it had more to do with nerves than shifting out of weightlessness.

They would soon be on their way to the base of the extremely rich and powerful man who wanted him dead. The extremely rich and powerful man who wanted the entire Kingdom annihilated. If he was as crafty as he'd promised Shayban he would try to be, Casmir might have the opportunity to keep both of those things from happening. If not, he'd get himself and his best friend killed.

Kim sat at the table in Rache's briefing room, her fingers intertwined on the surface. Casmir paced behind her. All twelve crushers were gazing blandly at him. Kim couldn't tell which one was Zee. Maybe they could get him to wear a tie and a beanie again.

Casmir snapped his fingers and stopped pacing long enough to remove his pack and dig into it. An armored guard stationed inside the door watched him suspiciously. The warship was flying away from Stardust Palace, but Rache hadn't yet deigned to join them. A few announcements had been made about ongoing repairs. Kim had no idea how many shots the *Fedallah* had taken, but it must have been surprising to the crew to have it picked out of the stars.

Casmir pulled out the gift box. Judging by the oddly textured exterior, Kim suspected the container was also made from some mycelium-concoction.

"It's not too late to change your gift." Kim nodded at one of the crushers.

He followed her gaze. "You want me to give him Zee?"

"Is that *your* Zee? How can you tell?"

"I am the original Zee," the crusher stated, "programmed first to protect Kim Sato and Casmir Dabrowski. I am unique."

"Not in appearance," Kim muttered. "I'm going to get you a tie."

"Casmir Dabrowski can pick me out," Zee said.

"How?" Kim looked at Casmir. "Did you give him a mole or something?"

"I can just tell." He opened his box, checked the contents, and must have found everything still in place and unbroken, for he sighed a relieved, "Good."

Kim shook her head, certain Rache would find the gift as bemusing as the underwear.

"What did *you* get him?" Casmir asked. "I didn't see you perusing the station gift shop."

"No, I was busy using my two advanced degrees to make knockout grenades."

She glanced at the guard, wondering what the man thought of this conversation. To his knowledge, had anyone *ever* given his boss a gift?

"You can get knockout grenades in any ship's armory," Casmir said.

"Mine are better. They don't look like weapons." She'd borrowed the containers from the mycology lab, selecting such gems as *dehydrated horse manure*, apparently an excellent substrate for mushroom growing. She doubted anyone searching her case would look inside or touch them at all.

Kim switched to text to add, *I do have a gift for him. I'm not sure what he'll think of it.*

He'll probably be disappointed by the lack of fungi in it.

I doubt it.

Casmir raised his eyebrows. *What did you get?*

I made something.

His face screwed up. *Like a quilt?*

A quilt? Really, Casmir. Have you ever seen me knit anything?

Quilts are sewn, not knitted. My mother does crafts, so I know these things. Oh, but you could knit an afghan.

Why do I tell you anything?

Because I'm your best friend, and this kind of deep intimate sharing is a requirement. He grinned, and then a light went on, and his expression turned to one of understanding. *Oh! Did you write him a story?*

Yes. Even though Kim had planned to tell him, she found her cheeks warming, and she gazed down at her hands. *He likes to read.*

I know. We've discussed his literary interests. Did you make the hero really neat so he'd want to rename his ship after him or her?

The protagonist doesn't have a sex. It's kind of a literary experiment. Maybe Kim shouldn't have brought it up. She'd been inspired to write the story during the long hours in the *Osprey's* sickbay, waiting to see if Casmir would get better, and she feared it was overly maudlin and sentimental because that had been her mood at the time. She hadn't intended to compose a story, feeling rusty after years of ignoring her pen name, but she'd written an essay on the novel Rache had asked her to read, and she'd been inspired to write more after that.

But what if he didn't like it? Or mocked it? When she'd written under a pen name for a vague audience she would never meet, it had all been much safer. There was too much potential for hurt feelings here, vulnerability. She hated vulnerability. She was still debating if she should admit to being the author of the trilogy Rache had read and liked.

Did you make it *really neat so he'd want to rename his ship after it?* Casmir corrected.

We'll see. I'm not sure "The Protozoan" would excite the hearts of the mercenaries serving on it.

You think their hearts are excited by the Fedallah*?*

They probably don't know what that is.

You think they know what a protozoa is?

Yas would.

Yas is not your typical mercenary.

True.

The door opened, and Rache walked in. He dismissed his guard with a flick of his fingers.

"Alone at last," Rache said, somewhat sarcastically eyeing the crushers. Even with his mask on, Kim knew it was a sarcastic eyeing.

"Do you want me to ask them to wait outside?" Casmir asked.

"I am the original and superlative Zee. I must protect Kim Sato and Casmir Dabrowski from within the room."

"The original and superlative?" Rache asked.

"Zee is experimenting with self-identifying appellations now that he has clones," Casmir said. "I imagine you can understand."

"Indeed." Rache walked up to the table, rested his hands on it, and gazed at Casmir. "I just received a comm from Sultan Shayban."

Kim hoped they hadn't been corroborating stories. She also hoped Shayban hadn't been showing off his new crushers to make Rache envious.

"Is it common for enemies to chat with you after they've fired at your ship?" Casmir asked.

"Only when they're demanding my surrender."

"Is that what he was doing?"

"*No*." Rache sounded exasperated.

"Are you irritated with me? Because I have a gift for you if that would help." Casmir pushed the gray textured box across the table. "A thank you for coming out of your way to get us, especially since you probably thought you were only getting Kim, and not me and my entourage."

"That's the truth," Rache muttered.

"And also a thank you for the expensive potion. I didn't sneeze the whole time I was wandering back and forth under the date palms in Shayban's manufacturing facilities."

Rache stared at him. Kim wanted to drop her face in her hand.

"*Potion?*" Rache looked at her. "Don't you educate him on proper medical terminology?"

"I've tried many times to educate him," Kim said. "He's only interested in learning words suitable for describing super villains."

"It's true. I also know a lot of interesting words about the things villains do. Are you familiar with tyrotoxism, Rache?"

"No. I shoot people; I don't poison them with dairy products."

Casmir cocked a brow at Kim. "I think that means he is familiar with it. The word, at least."

Kim swatted away the silly banter. "What did the sultan say?"

"He threatened me." Rache straightened. "If I kill Casmir and drop him on Dubashi's doorstep, he promises to ruin me financially by forbidding anyone to let me bank with them. Given his influence in the Miners' Union, that's a more fearsome threat than if he sent his warships after me. We hold our account in System Cerberus, but I wouldn't be surprised if he has sway there. There are two Miners' Union lords milking the asteroids in the Cerberus belts, and he married one of his daughters to one."

Kim was beginning to understand why Rache was exasperated.

"Do moon bases have doorsteps as such?" Casmir asked.

Rache shook his head slowly, perhaps questioning his intelligence.

Will you be serious? Kim messaged Casmir. *I want as much information as he'll share with us. And not to annoy him.*

Sorry. He still makes me nervous. You know I babble when I'm nervous.

"I'm wondering," Rache said to Casmir, "if I should do exactly that. Maybe roll you up in a carpet, toss you into Dubashi's compound, and stand back to see what happens."

"Unless he has a thing for sexy male roboticists, I don't think much would happen."

"I'm surprised he got the reference," Rache told Kim.

"There's a series of comic books based on Ancient Roman history," Kim said.

"That makes sense then."

Casmir propped a fist on his hip but didn't deny the source of his knowledge.

"I say that," Rache told Kim, "because this is the third government leader in as many weeks that he's won over to his side."

"That's not true." Casmir touched a thoughtful finger to his chin. "It's taken more than three weeks."

"But fewer than three months. You're doing what Mikita did three hundred years ago without a military or even a spaceship." Rache sounded more exasperated than impressed.

"Does a crazy high shaman count as a government leader?" Casmir asked.

"She's among the highest in the organization," Rache said.

"I wouldn't say I've really won Kyla Moonrazor over. She just tried to recruit me to her organization and offered me an android body."

"She tried to shoot the rest of us."

"You did invade her base."

"You did *too*." Rache chopped the air with his hand. "Never mind. Just tell me what you two want to do, now that I have you. I *thought* you wanted asylum, Kim, until Jorg left the system and stopped sending knights after you. Not to be dropped off to do who knows what in

Dubashi's base. With *him*." Rache pointed at Casmir. "And *them*." The pointing finger shifted to the crushers.

Kim grimaced because he seemed to think she'd been disingenuous with him. That had never been her intent.

"Did you even need my help?" Rache asked. "If you'd stood behind those crushers when that knight showed up, couldn't they have kept you from being taken?"

"They didn't exist three days ago," Casmir pointed out.

"My hope," Kim said, "was not to openly defy Jorg, and through him my whole government. That was the reason for the ruse. And I also thank you for helping me. When I asked, I thought I would be able to meet you without fanfare and that you and your crew wouldn't be endangered. I didn't think you'd be attacked for showing up at a non-Kingdom space station."

"I'm usually *not*," Rache growled.

"Oh." Casmir snapped his fingers. "Did Sultan Shayban explain about the slydar detector?"

"No."

"He said he has one."

"I've never heard of such a thing."

"It's new. He's beta testing it."

Rache stared at him. "Are you messing with me?"

"No. I'm trying to be helpful. Do you want to open my gift?" Casmir pointed at the thus-far ignored box. "There's something in there that might make you feel better."

"I doubt that."

Casmir shrugged.

"I'll get Amergin on this supposed slydar detector." Rache shook his head. "I can't believe something like that could exist and we wouldn't have heard of it yet."

Kim resisted the urge to point out that Rache had spent the last several weeks consumed by an unhealthy obsession with the gate and probably hadn't been sifting through the latest intelligence.

"Maybe it's making its debut," Casmir said.

"If one Miners' Union family has it, the others might," Rache said. "I wasn't planning to sneak up to Dubashi's base, but losing the serious advantage that hull plating conveys will be annoying."

Kim wondered if it would be annoying enough that Rache would consider retirement. Would the hunted-by-many *Fedallah* be able to survive in space without camouflage? It wasn't as if there were many places to hide in space itself. There was a whole lot of empty nothing out there between the stars and planets, and sensors had no trouble detecting things that weren't camouflaged flying around in a system.

"Kim wishes to go to the base because of a virologist named Scholar Serg Sunflyer," Casmir explained, steering them back to the last topic. "He went missing three months ago. He has a history of creating bioweapons. Have you, by chance, heard if Dubashi has such a weapon that he plans to unleash on Odin or other Kingdom populations?"

Rache had been considering the box, but his gaze shifted quickly back to Casmir. "I hadn't, no, but I'll get my people on it. We haven't been in this system any longer than you have."

"If Dubashi is working on such a thing," Kim said, "and Jorg heard about it, that may be why he wanted me. To try to develop something preemptively."

"Why would *Dubashi* want you though?" Rache asked. "If you're suggesting he kidnapped this virologist, wouldn't he already have someone working on a weapon?"

Kim spread her hands. "I don't know."

"Maybe we should send a comm and chat with him," Casmir offered. "See if he will tell us anything."

Kim started to give him a withering glare, but hadn't he started his relationships with Shayban, President Nguyen, and High Shaman Moonrazor by *chatting* with them?

"I've been invited to his meeting," Rache said. "I'll chat with him there."

"Are you sure *you* should do the chatting?" Casmir asked. "You're brusque."

"I don't think he's going to respond positively to rambles about comics and super villains."

"No? He seems to be vying for the position of super villain. He even has superhuman abilities. That's always helpful."

Rache frowned. "Like what?"

"Well, he's a high astroshaman and has cybernetic bits. I know you have those, too, so maybe you don't think they're special."

"Who told you he was affiliated with the astroshamans?"

"An astroshaman. Moonrazor."

"A reliable source, I'm sure."

Casmir shrugged.

"As I was saying," Rache said to Kim, waving dismissively at Casmir, "I'm invited to his meeting, and I intend to go and find out what exactly he's offering. My guess would be he wants us to be cannon fodder in his war with the Kingdom, but it's odd that he's only putting that together now. You usually throw the cannon fodder in before the main forces arrive."

"Maybe the main forces haven't arrived yet." Kim shivered at the idea however many ships were blockading the wormhole gate might only be a partial commitment of the prince's forces. How could one man have as much might as an entire government?

"*He's* still here, presumably," Casmir said. "Maybe he plans to go in with or behind the mercenaries."

"To bring his theoretical bioweapon?" Rache asked.

"I'm hoping we can snoop around his base and find out. I promised Sultan Shayban I would." Casmir didn't mention the kidnapping part of his plans. Because he knew Rache, who sought employment from Dubashi, would object?

"You promised to gather intel for him?" Rache asked. "Is *that* why he likes you?"

Casmir hesitated. "Very likely."

"He also found me charming," Zee put in—Kim assumed it was Zee, mostly because the other ones didn't seem to have developed a need to butt into conversations yet.

"He found you formidable," Casmir said.

"Formidably charming."

"I don't think I can argue with that."

"No," Zee said.

"Your crusher is getting weirder every time I encounter you, Casmir," Rache said.

"Will you take us to the base and help us get in?" Kim asked.

"To look for the bioweapon?"

"Yes." Kim kept herself from exchanging looks with Casmir or doing anything that would hint that this was a partial truth. It *was* what she wanted, but Casmir had other plans, and she hated withholding that from Rache.

She reminded herself that they weren't on the same side here. Given his past actions, he probably wouldn't object to bioweapons being taken out of the picture, but he might object to his future employer disappearing.

"We can't let such a weapon be used on Odin," Casmir added to back her up.

Rache grunted. It wasn't at all clear that he agreed.

"I need to think about this." Rache turned toward the door.

"Don't forget your gift box," Casmir said.

Kim expected Rache to keep walking, but he paused, gave Casmir a long look, then swept the box off the table and out the door without looking at it.

"I hope he doesn't feel he needs to take that to a bomb squad," Casmir said. "It's just soap and mushroom delicacies."

Kim shook her head. "Did he seem snippy to you?"

"Maybe. His invisible ship is no longer invisible. That's got to be on his mind."

Among other things. "I didn't mean to thrust all of this extra work on him. Maybe you should have found your own ride to Dubashi's base."

"I didn't realize you wanted to be alone with him for a week."

"Is that how far the base is?"

"From here, yes."

"With all his mercenaries on the ship, I doubt we'd be alone."

"More easily than on a submarine."

"Perhaps." Kim wondered if she should send Rache her story. It existed only in digital form on her chip. She was a little sad she didn't have a form printed in a hardbound book. It would have seemed a more thoughtful gift than digital text.

Maybe it was silly to worry about that now. Rache would be wary of more gifts after opening Casmir's soap and hallucinogenic mushrooms.

CHAPTER 21

BONITA USED EVERY SEARCH TRICK SHE KNEW AS she skimmed network articles, people's public journals, and rumors on the bounty hunter boards she followed. It had been two days since the *Dragon* left Stardust Palace, and she hadn't found anything about Scholar Sunflyer's kidnapping, nor proof that he was in the system at all. How had someone gotten him off Stardust Palace Station without being caught by one of their security cameras?

No, that wasn't that surprising. Their security hadn't been that stellar—Casmir had hacked in easily enough to diddle with the lights and alerts in that shuttle bay.

"I suppose it's not fair to judge them by whether or not Casmir can hack into their network," Bonita muttered, not when he'd gotten onto an impregnable astroshaman network.

"Casmir?" Viggo had been ignoring her while she worked, but he naturally piped up at the mention of his favorite roboticist.

"I bet *he* could find this missing scholar."

"Indeed so. He could also fix the squeak to the middle stall in the lavatory."

"He's a man of many talents."

"Those knights slam the doors too hard."

"I don't need details about what they do in there."

"They're violating my doors, Bonita."

"Ugh."

"Exactly."

Bonita buried herself in her searches again, hoping Viggo would take a hint and stop talking. She would have to refrain from making comments aloud, since that had invited the conversation in the first place.

Unfortunately, the searches continued to come up with nothing. If someone had hired bounty hunters to kidnap Scholar Serg Sunflyer, they had wiped the job from the boards and left no trace. But what if that same someone had tried to legitimately hire a bioweapons specialist before resorting to kidnapping?

She switched over to public job boards in the system—they all had archives so one could see old postings even if they'd expired or been taken down.

"What kind of job posting would you make if you wanted to hire someone to make you a biological weapon?" she asked, perusing but not sure what she was looking for. "I assume someone wouldn't go right out and say in an offering for a position that they wanted deadly weapons capable of killing millions. Maybe in System Cerberus, but Stymphalia has governments that enforce laws and discourage that kind of thing."

"Kim would be a better person to ask," Viggo said.

"Unfortunately, she's not here. I would have much preferred her to the two surly knights that can't be in a room together without shooting ice spears out of their eyes. Kim is appealingly quiet. I like people who don't talk too much."

"How about former people embedded in ships' computers?"

"They're also acceptable if they don't talk too much. Hm, here's a posting from six months ago, someone looking for an expert in bioterrorism and bioweapon *defense*. Who better to hire to build a weapon than someone who's an expert at defusing them?"

Bonita flagged the entry and looked for other postings along that vein. Feeling that she might be on to something, she leaned in, engaged by the work. Since semi-retiring from bounty hunting and switching to hauling freight, she'd forgotten how much she enjoyed the challenge of finding people who didn't want to be found.

"Here's another similar one. The job is being offered by Delta Tech Mining and Manufacturing. That sounds like something that might be owned by a Miners' Union family, doesn't it?" Bonita flagged that one too and kept looking. She didn't want to make premature assumptions.

"I have no opinion," Viggo said after a time.

"On what?"

"Your question. I would not want to be accused of talking too much."

"Ah. Good."

"I will warn you that you have company coming."

Bonita glanced back, hoping for Qin, but Bjarke was approaching. Even though the bruise had healed, her hip twinged at the memory of her fall in the lift.

Viggo issued a low growl that Bonita had never heard from him before.

"Greetings, Toes," she said. "You haven't been showing up to the communal dinners. We've missed your snarky, surly presence."

"Speak with him about his issue, please, Bonita."

"The stall door issue?"

"Yes."

"Don't worry, Viggo," she said as Bjarke stepped into navigation, surprisingly not responding to her comment. "It's my largest concern too."

"May I sit, Captain?" Bjarke gestured to the co-pilot's pod.

He wore his galaxy suit once again, the material revealing enough of his hard form to bring memories to mind. She ruthlessly shoved them aside. She wasn't interested in the hard form of someone who was such a pain in the ass.

"Such formality. Go ahead. I'm sure you would anyway."

Bjarke paused with his hand on the back of the pod. "No, I would not."

"If I shooed you out of navigation, you would go?"

"Yes." Bjarke gazed at her with steady blue eyes. "But if you let me stay, you'll get to hear my apology."

"Oh? Sit down, then."

He did so. "I'm sorry it's taken me a couple of days to remember my manners, such as they are, but I apologize for being gruff and terse with you. I've been angry with the situation, not with you." Bjarke slanted a sideways look at her. "Even if I'm fairly certain you dragged me off to distract me while your… friends escaped."

"I didn't drag you anywhere. I said I knew where Kim had been working, and you followed me. And then you tried to seduce me so I'd tell you everything I knew and help you get her."

She expected a protest of innocence, but he arched his brows and said, "*Tried?* I believe I was at least moderately successful."

"At seduction? Oh, you're not bad. But I didn't tell you anything."

"You were on the verge of it in the lift. I remember you opening your mouth between gasps, about to spill everything you knew."

"All I was going to spill were instructions on what to do with your tongue. Fortunately, you seemed to have a decent grasp of that already."

"*Decent.* Is that all?" A cocky smile that was a little too knowing curved his lips.

"I didn't get to make a full assessment since we were interrupted. You sprang away like you'd been scalded."

"Yes. I do apologize for leaving you so abruptly, but since you were distracting me for the sake of your friends, you can't be surprised that I, upon realizing your treacherousness, had to run off."

"Uh huh. You really know how to warm a girl up, Toes."

"We have several days on this journey. Perhaps you would give me another chance to warm you up."

"This is *not* the discussion I expected you to have with him, Bonita," Viggo said.

Bjarke's eyebrows flew up. "Your ship is… verbose."

"I told you he was human once."

"And that his body was virile and attractive; yes, I remember."

"My ship is also attractive," Viggo said.

"Did he design it?" Bjarke asked.

"Largely," Bonita said. "You can thank him for the sauna and that garish bug-eyed statue in the wall back there."

"That is a figurehead," Viggo said. "Traditionally, it would have been on the front of a sailing ship, but in modern times, tradition has placed them near navigation on the inside of a spaceship."

"Whatever it is, its teeth are scarier than Qin's. It's hideous."

"It's supposed to be," Viggo said. "Its job is to ward off evil spirits."

"We've been boarded by everyone from bounty hunters to mercenaries to uptight knights." Bonita looked at Bjarke. "It's clearly not working."

"There's only so much a figurehead can do," Viggo murmured.

"Uptight?" Bjarke asked.

"I can't believe you would even attempt to deny it," Bonita said. "Viggo has footage of you slamming bathroom doors and stomping around whenever Asger wanders past."

"I'm sure he's doing more stomping and slamming than I am. And if your ship is recording that, it—he—may need a new hobby."

"As far as warming things," Bonita said, before Viggo could jump in with some indignant comment, "maybe you and Asger should use this time to work out your relationship instead."

"That doesn't sound as pleasurable."

"But it would be the mature thing to do, assuming you actually want to have a relationship with him."

Bjarke sighed and gazed at the control panel. "I fear that will be more difficult than ever, given the side he's chosen."

"Kim and Casmir aren't enemies of the Kingdom. Even I know that. They risked their asses to stop terrorists on Odin. And so did Asger. That ought to make them heroes. And if you're not on their side, I'm not sure what that makes you."

She expected him to leave in a huff, especially when long seconds passed and he didn't answer. Then Bjarke settled back in the pod, as if he meant to stay for a while.

Whatever. Bonita went back to looking up the companies that had posted the jobs.

After a few minutes passed, Bjarke surprised her by speaking without the previous snark or bitterness. "William has made a lot of poor decisions over the years. It is difficult for me now to assume anything has changed. Even if I wished to believe the best of him, his superiors—*our* superiors—aren't pleased with him and have made it clear that it's my duty to keep him in line and complete the missions they give us. After being… ostracized for the last few years, I must do my best to fulfill their wishes. The *king's* wishes."

Bonita had a feeling this was a conversation he should be having with Asger—William—rather than her, but her curiosity got the best of her. "Ostracized? Is that why you were posing as the Druckers' accountant?"

"It's a legitimate post for an undercover knight, as the Kingdom keeps tabs on the major governments and players in all the systems, but it was definitely an assignment that was a punishment."

"Because you mouthed off to the wrong person?"

He squinted at her. "Because *William* mouthed off to the wrong person. I admit I've made a few enemies over the years myself with my occasionally sharp tongue—"

Bonita snorted.

"—but his teenage antics paved the way for my recent spate of distant and isolated assignments. I am his father and therefore responsible for him."

"Even when he's twenty-something?"

"He is my son and heir. When I'm in my nineties, and he's in his sixties, I'll still be responsible for him and how his deeds reflect on the nobility, whether we still serve as knights or not." Bjarke flexed a hand and studied the back of it. "I admit I hadn't realized he was so angry with me for not being home. Before the punishment assignments, I was still sent off planet and out of the system frequently. My superiors found that I had fewer moral qualms than other knights and more easily lied and fought my way into shady organizations. They thought this was useful, but I think it's also what made them uncertain that they could trust me fully. I wasn't in the loop with Jager's plans for extending himself—the Kingdom—into other systems, and I was as taken by surprise with the announcement of war and a blockade as anyone. You'd think I'd be old enough now that I wouldn't have to keep proving myself to my colleagues and superiors, but…" He dropped his hand onto his thigh.

"It does sound tedious. Maybe you should quit."

"One doesn't quit being a knight. You train for it all of your life, and then you swear an oath to live and die by the Code and serve wherever the king needs you."

"Definitely tedious. I suggest telling your king and that prince to stuff it and starting your own business in another system."

"And shall I also give up my vote in the Senate and the lands that have been in my family for nearly a thousand years?"

"The chains that bind you." Bonita waved a dismissive hand, even though she couldn't blame him for letting himself be bound. If she had ever inherited anything, especially if it was enough to ensure her livelihood during retirement, she wouldn't be quick to give it up either. Not at this age. Not when she was nearing seventy and was starting over again with saving for retirement. Damn those ex-husbands, and damn her poor choices. She needed to stop making those.

"Chains, perhaps, but they give purpose as well as binding. If I did not work for something greater than myself, I would lose some of my identity."

"Sounds like a personal issue to work through. Try some self-help books."

This time, Bjarke snorted, but he sounded more amused than angry. At least with her. Bonita didn't know if she'd done anything to help his relationship with his son—or save Viggo's maligned doors.

"Delta Tech Mining and Manufacturing *is* owned by Dubashi," she murmured, finishing up her research. "How did I know? We may be going in the right direction, Viggo."

"I am always going in the right direction," Viggo said. "My navigation computations are infallible."

Bjarke, who'd been gazing at the forward display, lost in his own thoughts, looked over.

"One of the other companies that was hiring is also owned by Dubashi. It may have been the same job, essentially, just a differently worded posting. The third… I'm not sure. It's a private corporation, not publicly traded, so it's harder to dig up information."

"A job posting by Dubashi?" Bjarke asked.

"Seeking an expert in biodefense and bioterrorism. I was surmising that if he wasn't able to attract a suitable candidate legitimately, he might have kidnapped one."

"Such as the scholar you were contracted to find?"

"That's what I'm thinking. Which means we could be flying to the right place."

"And that we might encounter a bioweapon already in existence there," Bjarke said grimly.

"Another reason for me to punt you out the airlock and wait with the *Dragon* outside of firing range." She winked at him.

"You expect me to pick up your missing scholar while I'm in there?"

"Yeah, if you wouldn't mind. I'll cut you in on the bounty."

"Your mind works in odd ways."

"Practical ways."

The clang of boots on the ladder rungs floated up to them. Bonita glanced back as Asger came into view.

"Captain?" Asger stepped into navigation. "I've been messaging Casmir, and he says he hasn't seen Tristan. Have you had any luck contacting the *Fedallah*?"

Bjarke swiveled the pod to look at his son.

Asger jumped. "I thought you were Qin."

"Yes, we're so obviously similar," Bjarke said. "You're in contact with Professor Dabrowski? What about Scholar Sato?"

"I haven't messaged her before. I don't know if she would accept me as a contact, given whom I travel with."

"No fighting in navigation," Bonita said, worried they would be at each other's throats in a minute. With her caught in the middle.

"I didn't come to fight." Asger ignored Bjarke's cool stare and looked at her. "Will you try contacting the ship again, Captain? I don't know if Tristan is still stuck in a locker in that shuttle or if he's been killed. Casmir said he could ask, but if he did, Rache would know he's got a knight stowaway, and that might not go over well."

"The implication that Dabrowski is working with Rache is disturbing," Bjarke said. "And is Sato *also* there voluntarily?"

"They didn't tell me their plans," Asger said. "I would guess they're using Rache to get where they want to go rather than working with him. Casmir is good at getting people to go along with his schemes."

"But that *murderer*!" Bjarke lurched to his feet.

"I said no fighting." Bonita held up a hand. "Don't make me get Qin to kick both of your asses."

The men glared at each other.

Bonita rose to her feet, pushed past Bjarke, jabbing her hip into his side, and planted her hands on Asger's chest. She pushed and did some glaring of her own. He was almost a foot taller than she, but he allowed himself to be maneuvered out of navigation.

She turned, intending to do the same to Bjarke, but he gave her a stiff bow and headed out on his own. To her surprise, he paused and rested a hand on her shoulder, fingers brushing her bare neck just long enough to put titillating memories in her mind, then walked out. He closed the hatch behind him.

Bonita sank back into the pilot's seat. When had her life gotten so complicated?

Kim sat with Casmir in one of the two guest cabins they'd been assigned, each more utilitarian than the ones on the *Osprey.* They had bunk beds built into the wall, stools without any padding, and lockers containing galaxy suits with oxygen tanks, weapons, emergency rations, and equipment-cleaning kits. The weapons surprised her, especially since guards stood outside their doors, albeit the men hadn't done anything to keep them from visiting each other or going to the mess hall.

The last time she'd passed them, they'd been fondling their guns and staring at the crushers. All except Zee were lined up in the corridor.

Casmir had started out with all of them in his cabin, but even he had agreed it was too tight with twelve hulking crushers standing around. Kim couldn't imagine sleeping with them all staring down at her. Or even staring at a wall. The new ones weren't as chatty as Zee—yet—but it wasn't as if they were cuddly and cute.

Now, she and Casmir were watching news footage from back home, this time video and sensor readings of the fighting near the wormhole gate. She found that easier to stomach than the earlier glimpses they'd had of bombings in the capital, but the System Stymphalia news anchor hadn't mentioned if the ships attacking Odin had been driven off or not. Nothing more than snippets were getting through the blockade, and only when a fast, armored courier ship made it past Dubashi's combined forces and through the gate.

"We should have more ships than that available to fight these guys." Casmir watched with his chin in his hand. "Why isn't Jager or Admiral Whoever-is-in-charge throwing everything they have at the invaders to drive them out of our system and free up the gate so we can get more allies in?"

"Maybe they were already destroyed." Kim shifted her weight on her hard stool. She could have sat on one of the bunks, but the mattresses weren't much softer.

Casmir didn't seem to mind. He was sitting cross-legged on the bottom bunk with his boots off.

"That's a grisly thought," he said.

"Or maybe our ships were sabotaged ahead of time? Or, if there's fighting throughout the system, they could be busy defending Odin and all of our moons, stations, and habitats."

"Those thoughts aren't any less grisly," Casmir said.

"War doesn't induce cheerful musings."

Casmir flopped back on the bunk. "It makes me uneasy that we're flying away from the System Stymphalia gate instead of toward it. Even though I logically know that taking Dubashi out of the equation is the best thing we could do for our people, I feel like we're fleeing rather than helping."

"We'd have to go through *that* if we tried to make it home." Kim pointed at footage of a courier ship trying to thread the needle on its way into the system, but two Miners' Union warships zipped in and riddled it full of holes. The thrusters died, and half the hull plating was blown off. "I hope that was an unmanned ship."

Casmir shook his head. "I just thought we had more might than this. Why has Jager been out picking fights in other systems if he doesn't have a massive fleet to back him up?"

"Some of the Fleet is stuck outside the system. The attack and the blockade must have come as a surprise to Royal Intelligence."

"It's only the four warships that we know of."

"That we know of." Kim doubted anyone would bother mentioning other stranded ships on other missions to civilian advisors, advisors who had gone rogue, at least from Jorg's viewpoint.

Casmir gazed intently up at the frame of the bed above him. "Royal Intelligence is a sprawling organization, and I assume that we have spies in all the systems—we even had someone in System Cerberus. How could an invasion fleet have taken our people by surprise?"

Kim spread her hand. She didn't know.

"Something isn't adding up," Casmir said. "I feel like if we were back home, we would have an easier time gathering intelligence and ferreting out answers."

"Or we'd be in jail."

She would be, at least, for running away from Bjarke—from Jorg. Strange that with one choice, she had likely become more of an outright criminal in the Kingdom than Casmir, with all of his twisting and bending of the orders he'd been given.

"That is possible," Casmir said. "And I didn't have a network signal down in the castle dungeon, so information gathering was difficult."

"I think we're in the best place we can be to help our people."

A message came in on Kim's chip from her mother.

Kim, I have seen some of the footage coming out of the Kingdom. I hope you are not still on one of those warships and in the middle of all that. If you are, I advise you to escape as soon as possible. A war is not a healthy place for a scientist. They'll either shoot you by accident or use you for amoral purposes.

Kim laughed shortly.

"Enh?" Casmir looked over.

"Message from my mother."

"Does she agree we're in the best place to help our people?"

I lament that my stance may mean that I won't be welcome back in the Kingdom, the message went on, *but I have been offered a position on Tiamat Station, heading up research on the piece of the gate that the station ship was able to bring back. Did you know President Nguyen used to be an archaeologist and that we have met before? How strange that she is a political leader now, but it's beneficial for me. Should you escape from the Kingdom, she is willing to give you and Casmir work and lodgings here for however long you wish. I invite you to come. I do not know how the war in System Lion will end, but I fear to be associated with the Kingdom any longer, regardless.*

If you do make it back home... give my regards to Haruto and his boys.

"Not exactly," Kim said. "She suggested we escape from the Fleet promptly and come stay with her on Tiamat Station. She'll be researching the gate and can get us jobs."

"We did escape. Maybe she'll approve."

"Probably not of us going off to risk our lives infiltrating Prince Dubashi's base." Kim shifted again on the hard stool.

"We survived infiltrating an astroshaman base."

"You *barely* survived."

"But you didn't get so much as a hangnail. That evens things out."

Kim thought of all the worry and regret and questioning of herself she'd done when Casmir lay there in sickbay and she hadn't been sure whether he would live or die. She didn't want to experience that again. Nor did she want to die herself when she had so much work left that she wanted to do. There were so many projects that might help humanity that she longed to pursue, and, if she was honest with herself and acknowledged her ego, she also longed for a place among the famous scientists known throughout human history.

"I wonder if Rache would take us back to System Hydra if we asked," she murmured wistfully.

She wouldn't abandon this course, not when there might not be anyone else who could deal with Dubashi's theoretical bioweapon, but it was hard not to see the appeal in her mother's suggestion. Her corporation even had a lab on Tiamat Station—or would once that building was cleaned up—so she could go back to her old work. Her *useful* work.

"We've been flying the other direction for three days, and you haven't even flirted with him. You'd probably have to offer him a shoulder rub to get him to consider it."

"He hasn't come by." Kim didn't know if Rache was busy, avoiding her, or giving her space in case she needed it. Maybe he was waiting for her to come to him? But his quarters were behind the briefing room that was accessed through the bridge. She would feel conspicuous walking past his officers to knock on his door, especially when she was fairly certain they all believed she and Casmir were prisoners.

"You could send him flirty videos."

"I thought you didn't approve of me having a relationship with him."

"Oh, I don't, but if you're going to ask him for favors, your chances might be better if you did favors for him first."

"Such as sending flirty videos?" Kim didn't even know what a flirty video looked like. Her putting on lipstick and making kissing sounds? She curled a lip.

"Not with that face. You look like you took a bite of an orange and found out it was a lemon."

That effectively summed up her experience with relationships thus far.

"I did send the story I wrote," she admitted. "Yesterday. It took me two days to work up the courage."

"You launch enemies across shuttles with side kicks, but sending someone a story is what takes courage?"

"Yes. Is that weird?"

"I think it just means we've identified your only vulnerability." He smiled at her.

"Not only, surely," she murmured, then rose to her feet. "I'm going to see if we're allowed to use the gym."

"Kim?"

She paused. "Yes?"

"I have to go to the moon base and try to get Dubashi because I promised Sultan Shayban I would, and because… I'm coming to believe that I have the power—in the cerebral computer-hacking-and-robot-building sense of the word—to effect change. For the better. But I wouldn't blame you or think any less of you if you went and joined your mother. I think your power is to make bacteria that are beneficial for mankind as a whole, not to deal with failures of politics."

"There's not a definition of power that mentions computer hacking or robot building."

"Maybe not *yet*." He winked.

"If there's a bioweapon, someone who understands biology better be there to deal with it."

"Yas has a medical background. Maybe you could make him a nice cheat sheet or flowchart to take into the base. I'm sure he could get in as Rache's guest."

Kim's mind fell in a pothole at the thought of someone holding a flowchart while trying to disarm a bioweapon.

The door chime rang. Since she was nearest, she waved at the sensor to open it.

Rache stood there in a black galaxy suit rather than his usual black combat armor. He wasn't wearing any visible weapons, though the form-fitting attire made it clear that his *body* was a weapon, and she thought of the time he'd rolled up his sleeve so she could draw his blood. Strange that she should admire a man's physique when she had so little interest in a physical relationship. Or was it akin to buying a sculpture purely for aesthetic purposes? He was nicely… symmetrical.

"You weren't in your cabin," he remarked blandly.

"We were watching footage from the war," Kim said, refusing to be embarrassed by the direction her thoughts had strayed.

Rache gazed past her to Casmir, who was still flopped on his back on the lower bunk, prodding the slats above him with one socked foot. "I gave you separate rooms because I thought you might like privacy."

Kim twitched a shoulder, not sure how to read the comment. Had he *wanted* her to be alone?

She *was* pleased to have a private place away from his ship full of hulking strangers, but Casmir was familiar and comfortable. They were in a star system she'd never visited before and far from their home that was under attack. She would rather have a friend to commiserate with than hunker down alone in a strange place.

"May I speak with you in private?" Rache held a hand out toward the corridor.

Casmir, his head now upside down and dangling off the bunk, watched them curiously.

"I assume the corridor is not your destination." Kim waved at the crushers and the guard by the door. There was no privacy out there.

"No."

"Do you wish for me to accompany you, Kim Sato?" Zee was also watching them. His head was in the upright position, and he was, as always, poised to spring into battle if needed. "You may be in danger."

"She's not in danger," Rache said to the crusher. He sounded more amused than irritated today. That was good. "And you and your small army are receiving free room and board on my ship, so you would do well to consider me an ally."

"My army is ideally sized for infiltrations." Zee, on the other hand, sounded a tad indignant. "And we do not require board. We only take up room. If you are the one responsible for providing this, then I believe that makes you our landlord or perhaps hotelier, not our ally."

"Hotelier, right. I'll have some towels and little soaps delivered later." Rache looked toward Casmir. "Your crusher is lippy."

"Yes, isn't he wonderful?"

"Your life's crowning achievement, I'm certain."

"I am a glorious achievement," Zee agreed.

Kim, afraid Casmir's lippy crusher might offend Rache, stepped into the corridor.

"Are the other ones going to be lippy too?" he asked as they walked past them. They lined the corridor like statues, but their hollow eye-like indentions followed Rache.

"I think it depends on how much time they spend with Casmir, learning from him. Zee didn't speak much in his early days."

"It must have been like the air was perfumed with serenity."

They passed one of the guards, and the man's eyebrows flew up. Maybe Rache didn't typically speak of perfume with them.

"We were being harassed by bounty hunters, terrorists, and law enforcement, so not really."

"I only had the bounty hunters looking for you to protect you from the terrorists."

"Me or Casmir?"

"Casmir, I suppose. I didn't know you at the time. I hadn't kidnapped you yet."

"Which is, naturally, how all good relationships start."

Rache stopped in front of her guest cabin and waved the door open. Kim wasn't sure whether to be relieved or disappointed that he'd chosen the staid spot instead of his own cabin. If he had to sit on those awful stools, she could be certain he wouldn't overstay his welcome. But it would have been more comfortable to relax on an actual chair, in a room with books and art.

"Will you be offended if I point out that my cabin on the *Osprey* was more posh?" Kim asked when they were alone.

"If the Kingdom outfits its ships with posh cabins, that may be why it's losing the war."

She halted mid-step.

"*Are* they losing?" Kim wouldn't be surprised if he had more intelligence than the news anchors were sharing. "In that last footage, it looked kind of even. But I suppose if ships have gotten through to Odin… I wouldn't have expected that."

"Nor I. I'll be curious what Dubashi says at this meeting. I know he has allies involved in the invasion that are from some of the systems' governments as well as other Miners' Union families, but it's mostly his ambitious project, I gather. He's funding everything, and a lot of those ships in Lion are his. I'm surprised the Kingdom hasn't quashed the blockade and the entire force."

"Casmir was saying something similar, that the math doesn't add up."

"Jager doesn't like showing his work either," Rache said dryly, and Kim smiled, remembering Casmir's comments about showing his work—or not—on the submarine. "Thank you for sending that story. Will you sit down?" He gestured to the bunk and unlocked a stool from the deck for himself. "I am more interested in talking to you about your writing—especially since I had no idea that you *do* write—than Jager."

He tilted his head in what she assumed was a curious look.

"Will you take that off for the discussion?" She waved at his mask, wondering if she'd have to offer to rub his head again to get him to comply. His hair had been soft, so she hadn't minded. Touching was more acceptable when she initiated it and was in control. Which would probably make her a horrible and bossy lover. But she hated surprise touching. The one and only time she'd gotten in trouble in school had been when she'd punched a kid who'd thought sneaking up on her and *tickling* her—as he'd called it—had been fun.

"Of course. I planned to." Rache tugged off the hood and mask, his hair ruffled underneath, and poked into one of the pouches on his utility belt. "I also brought this, in case you want to relax."

"Relax?"

Rache pulled out a pouch she recognized from Casmir's gift box. "Mythic and Mystical Mushroom Mixture," he read from the label. "A blend of dried psilocybin mushroom, cacao nibs, and special berries to offer a tasty treat and a transcendental and enlightening experience." He held them up for her perusal and arched his eyebrows. "Casmir is trying to drug me."

"So naturally you brought them here to share."

"I had Yas run some tests on them. He said they didn't contain any toxins other than naturally-occurring psychoactive and hallucinogenic compounds."

Kim raised her eyebrows. "You thought he might poison you?"

"No, but I could see him happily giving money to some huckster selling gifts, not realizing that it was a setup for someone to poison *him*."

"I suppose. I'm more worried about the *special* berries. What does that mean?"

"That they're genetically modified or engineered for superior taste?"

"More likely their entheogenic potential."

Rache opened the top of the package and sniffed. "We could eat around them."

"Are you actually proposing that we consume them?" Kim wouldn't have guessed that Rache would drink alcohol, much less take psychedelic drugs. Or any kind of drug that would affect his mind. Didn't a mercenary captain have to be alert and at the top of his game at all times, lest some mutinous coalition assassinate him and take over his ship?

"Don't you trust Casmir's taste in gifts?"

"*No*."

He laughed shortly, a smile tugging at his lips, and she remembered how much she liked that expression on him. How rare it was. Too bad it was fleeting.

"And I'm not eating them," Kim added. "You're not trying to muddle my mind to get me in bed are you?"

"Nothing so crude. I would prefer that your mind be fully present if we ever engage in such activities." He looked around, didn't see what he sought—a table?—and pulled over another stool to set the bag on. "I did think it might loosen your tongue if you munched on them. I'd even be willing to munch with you if it meant you'd answer a question I have."

"You don't think I'd answer it without being drugged?"

"I don't know. You haven't brought it up yet, and if what I'm thinking is true, then its existence suggests a desire for secrecy."

She squinted at this vagueness. This wasn't the conversation she'd expected to have with him. He hadn't said anything more about her story or the essay she'd sent with her thoughts on the book they'd read.

"You wouldn't worry about mutinous assassins trying to kill you and take over your ship if you were drugged yourself?" she asked.

"Not at the moment. None of my men want to come down this corridor with Casmir's army looming outside. A number of them have fought Zee. It was a memorable experience. He hurt us even through our combat armor. We blew him up twice, but he put himself back together." Rache's dark eyes grew flinty. "I'm wounded, offended, and even disgruntled that Casmir is building an army for that pissant Jorg instead of for—"

"You?" Kim raised her eyebrows.

"I can see why he wouldn't give them to me, but why not for himself? He doesn't need to be the crown lackey."

"He did program them to obey him first and foremost. I'm skeptical that he'll hand them over to Jorg without contingencies."

"No? Does he plan to use them to march on Drachen Castle, slay Jager, Jorg, and Finn, and take the crown for himself?"

"I'm not sure how you can ask that with a straight face." Kim decided she wouldn't say more about the crushers or Casmir's deal with Shayban, not to Rache. As friendly as Rache was with her, he was still a threat to the Kingdom and at odds with what she and Casmir wanted to do. Was this the intelligence he'd hoped she would deliver under the influence?

"I let hope guide my tongue," Rache said.

"You'd truly want Casmir in charge of the Kingdom?"

"Sure. He's not going to hurt anyone, and he'd probably give me a pardon."

"Is that what you want? You scarcely seem a man repentant and regretful of your sins."

"I know. I didn't think I'd miss the Kingdom or Odin after Thea was gone. I wasn't that close to my foster brothers, and Lord Lichtenberg was always a distant, hard-to-please figure. Lady Lichtenberg was nice enough. I'd be upset if I learned she died. I don't find myself missing people that much, but I miss the forest, the evergreen branches dripping after a rain, the grasses full of dew, and the damp, gray beaches and the smell of the sea and the salt air misting my cheeks. Maybe it's just hiraeth, but since learning that Odin is being bombed, I've caught myself thinking that I'd be sad if I never got to walk barefoot on the beach outside of Lichtenberg Manor again. I should have done that when I was there to help you."

Kim didn't know what to say to his voiced nostalgia. It was hard not to suggest that he'd brought it on himself. Even though she understood why he was so very angry with Jager, she couldn't see it as justification for all that he'd done. She hated that he was so willing to kill soldiers to hurt Jager, men whose only crimes had been being born into the Kingdom and finding work that suited them.

She dropped her chin, feeling it was a betrayal to all those dead that she was here talking to Rache. That she'd come to care for him.

"Casmir isn't noble or anywhere in the line for succession," she murmured. "The Senate would laugh if he attempted to proclaim himself king."

"Conquerors don't worry about succession lines," Rache said dryly.

"The Senate would also laugh if he tried to proclaim himself a conqueror." Kim almost choked, imagining what Casmir's parents' reaction would be. Even as a mental exercise, this contemplation boggled her mind.

"I wonder," Rache murmured.

"You didn't mention Oku. Does she also need to be slain? Because I'm positive Casmir won't sign on for that."

He wouldn't sign on to slay *anyone*, not even people who deserved it.

"No," Rache said. "We were never close, but she wasn't the whiny brat that Jorg was. I did my knight's training with him. What a joke that he could even pretend he would selflessly sacrifice himself for someone, which is one of the core tenets in the Knights' Code."

Kim almost pointed out that selfless sacrifice didn't seem to be Rache's modus operandi either, but that was perhaps not fair. He might risk his life for someone he cared about. Or for some*thing* he cared about. He'd been willing to risk it all to keep Jager from getting that gate. She wondered if he'd managed to get any pieces for himself after all that, and if he had, what he would do with them.

"For my vision, Oku would simply have to step aside," Rache decided. "Which she might. She was always far more interested in examining beetles on the sidewalk and capturing fireflies in jars than in listening to Lichtenberg and her father talk politics."

"How old was she when she was doing that?"

It hardly seemed fair to judge someone's leadership potential by their age-seven antics.

"That was at all ages I knew her, I believe," he said dryly. "Though by her teens, she was capturing the fireflies so she could breed the ones with a predisposition toward eating the larvae of slugs, thus to keep slugs from infesting her gardens."

That story made Kim want to spend time with Oku, not dismiss her as someone to be pushed out of the way. Not that Rache's fanciful imaginings had anything to do with reality or would come to pass. It was odd that he was voicing such things. Maybe he'd sampled a few of the mushrooms before coming in.

"What I wanted to ask you," Rache said, "is about your story."

Nerves rattled in her belly like autumn branches bare of leaves. She'd expected this, and even wanted to talk to him about literature, but maybe she'd been silly to share something of hers. Even though he'd professed to like the fantasy trilogy she'd published under a pen name, what if he had more critiques than accolades for the short story?

"I liked that you gave your parasitic protozoan intelligence and had it wrestle with its urges, knowing that it was, in destroying its host to feed, destroying its home and ultimately itself. In my arrogance, I did wonder if you wrote it for me and were giving me a message." His eyebrow twitched.

Kim decided it was a vociferous twitch. "As a professor of mine once said, it matters not what the author intends but what the reader takes away."

He chuckled. "True enough."

"Is that the question you feared I wouldn't answer?" She admitted that she *hadn't* answered it, not really.

"No." Rache gazed thoughtfully at her. "I also noticed a lot of scientific vocabulary in the story. Which makes sense given your background and that it *was*, at least on the surface, about a biological matter. But I remembered another author I read who used a similarly scientific vocabulary in what was a fantastical story set in a made-up world."

"Ah." The single syllable came out dry. Or maybe that was her throat.

Had the short story truly been enough to link her to her allegory-writing pen name?

"Since I was curious," Rache continued, "I ran a software program to analyze and compare the works. Your short story and the published fantasy trilogy by this author. I suspected you were familiar with the work, since I saw the signed copies in your mother's apartment and you reacted to me lifting one off the shelf. At first, I thought you might also be a fan of the author and have modeled your writing after his. His, as I assumed from the initials, though I suppose there was no reason for me to assume that, other than there were few bathing scenes."

Kim blinked. "Few what?"

"I've noticed that female authors tend to write more about sybaritic pleasures, at least in that genre, than men. Hot springs in caves were frequent occurrences in my childhood reading."

"But only by female authors?"

"It was a noticeable trend. The male authors always wrote of battles and sleeping on the ground if the characters slept at all. Anyway, I ran the software program, and the computer estimated with eighty-seven percent certainty that the short story and the trilogy were penned by the same author."

"Interesting."

Rache gazed at her. No, it was more of an intense scrutiny than a gaze.

A part of her wanted to keep her secret, even though she didn't think he would react poorly to the revelation. He'd liked the work, after all; he'd said as much. Right now, Casmir was the only one who knew of her secret fiction-writing hobby. But she decided Rache would appreciate being trusted with the knowledge.

"I wrote them during my summers off while I was going to graduate school," Kim said. "They didn't sell that well, so my publisher didn't ask for anything else in that genre. I tried a thriller the following summer, sort of a mindless let's-write-something-that-might-actually-sell project. My editor took out all my five-syllable words and replaced them with five-letter words. Or fewer. It didn't do badly. I have a standing invitation to write more of those, but I've been too busy with work, and I'm more fond of stories that actually have something to say."

Rache continued gazing at her through the admission. She couldn't tell if he was stunned or rapt or simply thoughtful. He'd been fairly certain when he walked in, after all. Eighty-seven-percent certain, anyway.

"I think that if I fell at your knees and asked you to autograph my copies, you'd be uncomfortable rather than flattered," Rache finally said. "So I'll refrain."

"Yes. Thank you." Kim decided he'd grown to know her fairly well in their short times together, but she realized she shouldn't refuse to sign them. She'd signed her mom's copies, after all. But that had been as a joke that they had both been in on. It hadn't been an attempt to pass herself off as someone else. This felt… weird.

"Are you all right? You look like you're panicking. I didn't mean to make you feel awkward. That's why I brought the mushrooms."

Kim snorted. "No, it's fine. It just seems borderline dishonest to sign as a fake entity. Obviously, I did it for my mom, but that was different. Maybe if I had more experience, I wouldn't feel that way. You caught me off guard." She realized he might not have spoken literally. "Do you actually have physical copies?"

If he didn't, she couldn't sign anything.

"Yes." He smiled lopsidedly. "That's why I'm distressed that someone has developed a way to see through the ship's slydar hull. This is my only home, so my books are here. I would be upset to lose them. The ship and the crew, too, of course, but mostly my books. Some are very old and were hard to obtain."

"Maybe you could get a safe deposit box on some neutral planet."

"Then I couldn't admire them and read choice passages again from time to time. As I do with yours."

Kim looked at the deck, uncomfortable with that look of admiration. She'd never been comfortable with admiration, but having it come from someone she'd developed feelings for made it all much more complicated. And—yes, he was right—awkward.

"Sorry, I'll stop staring at you with rapt adoration now."

"Good. Thank you."

"I suppose I'd better get back to trying to find blueprints for that moon base."

Kim looked at him again. "Are you going to help us… get in?"

She'd almost said *help us kidnap Dubashi*. But Casmir had been careful not to mention that, and as much as she wanted Rache to be on her side in this, she feared he wouldn't be.

He took a deep breath and shifted his gaze to the wall above the bunks. "I haven't decided what I'll do. I want to protect you, and you seem determined to fling yourself into danger with Casmir, who is for some reason on a suicide mission for a random Miners' Union leader he can't know that well. But I've been hoping I could use the chaos of this war to more easily get to Jager. I've had the thought that Dubashi might even offer me that gig."

"Assassination?" Kim tried to keep her tone neutral, but an icy chill zapped her nerves.

"Yes. I'd do it for free, naturally, but… I mentioned my fears to you the last time we spoke. I think I'd be more fully committed if it was a job. In ten years as a mercenary, even though I've been injured and almost killed and taken losses of equipment and men, I've never failed to complete a job."

Was it a betrayal that Kim hoped Dubashi *didn't* offer him that contract?

Rache stood, but before heading for the exit, he bowed deeply to her, as if he were the knight he'd once trained to be. "I understand you're busy with your career, but should you ever wish to write more books of any kind, and you're not interested in your publisher's mandates, I would happily open a publishing house to print them for you. Across all the Twelve Systems, should you give me the rights to do so."

"Because starting a publishing company is a small matter." Kim smiled to hide that she was flustered. She should have thanked him instead of making a snarky comment.

"In the grand scheme of businesses, it's not too complicated, not in this day and age. You don't even need to buy a press. Pequod Holding Company has started and invested in numerous businesses, so I'm not without means."

"Thank you." Kim stood, feeling she should see him out, or maybe hug him for his offer, even if she couldn't see herself taking him up on it. Having her work published by a criminal and enemy of the Kingdom was scandalous at best. "I'm glad you've enjoyed my stories."

She clasped his hands. For once, they weren't enshrouded in gloves, just as his face wasn't hidden behind that featureless mask. His skin was warm, his palms calloused, and she realized his face wasn't far from hers. Maybe standing up had been a mistake. Getting this close had been a mistake. What if he kissed her? What if *she* kissed *him*?

His gaze traced her face, her lips, and he lifted a hand to her cheek, but it hovered an inch away. He arched his eyebrows. A question. Could he touch her? She had a feeling he'd never asked a woman before, had just assumed that anyone holding his hands would want it—would want him.

Did she? And if she did, would it be a betrayal to her people and all those he'd killed?

She felt a tension and frustration that she wasn't sure was sexual or just stress. She closed her eyes and slumped forward, pressing her forehead to his shoulder instead of kissing him.

"Why did you have to say you're thinking of assassinating my king, David?" she mumbled.

He sighed softly. "Because he's an asshole. And I apparently don't have the knack of wooing complicated women."

She shook her head but didn't pull away from him. "I'm not sure *I'm* the complicated one here."

"Maybe we both are. Maybe that's why I brought the mushrooms."

She laughed, and some of the tension seeped from her. She leaned into him, and after a moment's hesitation, he wrapped his arms around her. It wasn't unpleasant. Which was the problem.

"Clearly, I made a mistake in not trying them," she said.

"I thought so," he said mildly and stroked her hair.

She let him.

CHAPTER 22

CASMIR SWIGGED HIS ANTI-SEIZURE MEDICATION WITH A SWALLOW of water, sanitized his teeth, and went back to the bottom bunk in his cabin.

Kim hadn't returned since wandering off with Rache. He tried not to think about them doing lurid things together in her cabin—or his. It was too disturbing. In part because Rache was still a criminal, even if he'd helped them, and in part because she'd always so firmly dismissed any interest in touching or close-up human contact—it warped his reality to think of her doing lurid things at all. He'd always assumed she would one day find some brainy scientist who was equally indifferent to touching, and that they would have a nice wholesome relationship where, if they had children, they would employ test tubes and artificial wombs. Rache was neither nice nor wholesome.

If he was honest with himself, it bothered him that she might consider Rache as a mate when she'd never looked at him with even vague romantic interest. She was far more likely to be exasperated than interested if he wandered around the house shirtless, and tell him he was scaring the squirrels on the back fence. He'd accepted from the day they first met that she wasn't interested in a relationship with him—she'd made sure to establish the no-touching rule right up front—and that had never bothered him, but it didn't seem… *right* that she could have zero interest in him but be attracted to someone with the same face. Yes, Rache had all those muscles, but of all women, surely Kim should be able to appreciate someone for his mind. Rache's mind *couldn't* be an appealing thing to peer into. It just couldn't.

Sighing, Casmir dimmed the lights for the night. But he didn't slide into the sleep sack that was supposed to keep him comfortable while protecting him should anything happen to the ship's gravity. He hadn't yet figured out what he was going to do when the *Fedallah* reached the prince's moon base.

He'd considered waiting for Rache to disembark for his meeting and then sneaking off with his crushers to hunt for and kidnap the prince, but he suspected the moon base would be full of guards. Even with the crushers, Casmir feared he would need an ally to get into the base and find Dubashi. If Rache planned to accept a contract from Dubashi to go fight against the Kingdom, he wouldn't agree to help Casmir kidnap his putative employer.

Rache might even lock him in his cabin or the brig if he realized what Casmir planned. Casmir didn't *think* Rache would hand him over to Dubashi, now that they had a relationship of sorts, but he wasn't entirely positive about that. He dared not put his fate in Rache's hands.

"I'm going to need autonomy," he murmured, now wondering if it had been a mistake to leave the station with Kim. She probably would have been fine alone with Rache, and it wasn't as if Bjarke had been after *him*. He could have finished minting the rest of the crushers and then found another ride to the base. Maybe. It did seem like it would be best to make his move during this big meeting. Presumably, there would be a lot of ships and people coming and going, so it would be easier to sneak onto the base.

"If there is somewhere on this ship that you wish to go," Zee said from his spot by the door, "I will accompany you and ensure you are not deterred."

"Thank you, Zee. I was thinking more of how I'm going to find the freedom to complete my promise to the sultan once we get to the moon base."

"You now have a mighty army to command. We can protect you and take you anywhere."

Casmir smiled. "Have you had any promising conversations with any of them yet?"

Zee hesitated. Casmir didn't think he'd ever noticed him hesitating. Much like an android, Zee could process options a thousand times faster than a human being, so it wasn't as if he needed time to think.

"They have not yet developed interesting personalities," Zee said.

"It did take you a while to do that yourself. And for me too. You'd be waiting even longer for a freshly birthed human to develop into anything except a squirming, crying little creature. Though I've heard watching the process can be fun." He smiled wistfully, wondering if he would ever have children. He'd always thought it would happen someday, that he'd meet that perfect someone and have at least two kids—as he could attest, being an only child could be lonely—but with his fate so up in the air, dare he continue to expect that future?

Even if something came of his video exchanges with Oku—alas, he hadn't received a new one since arriving in System Stymphalia—was he foolish to imagine a future in which they might be permitted to get *married*? And have children? He knew it was silly to speculate about such a thing with someone he barely knew, but he feared the king would forbid his daughter from marrying some scruffy clone.

"I have had occasional exchanges with Tork, but since messages must be carried through the wormhole gate on a ship, they are delayed by days," Zee said, apparently having no opinion on babies. "It is not an efficient way to compete in a network game."

"Nor to flirt with a woman, I'm afraid."

"Tork is not a woman."

"No, I meant Princess Oku. Sorry, I'm thinking of my own problems instead of yours. That's selfish."

"Are humans not selfish by nature?"

"Not entirely, I'd like to believe. I suppose our genes do compel us to spend an inordinate amount of time thinking about mating, since that's traditionally been a requirement to reproduce, and if we don't reproduce, our genes don't get passed on—genes are *definitely* selfish. But there's a little brain space left over to think about the needs of others." Casmir hoped his actions hadn't led Zee to form that opinion about human selfishness.

"Humans seem paradoxical. I have observed that they are inherently social creatures and seem to have a physiological need to co-exist and work together in communities, but they also celebrate individualism and self-reliance, often seeking to obtain personal glory."

Casmir realized this was the kind of conversation he'd caught Zee having with Tork and might not reflect on anything he'd actually done. Maybe Zee missed his philosophy buddy. A buddy who was, in a sense, as alien as he was and could study the species around him without personal bias.

"That's more true in some societies than others," Casmir said. "Cultural tendencies toward individualism or collectivism usually date back to monolithic events that took place on Old Earth and caused certain beliefs to be widely adopted into the religions of the time. Many have been carried into space to these new systems."

"Tork and I have discussed this too. It is fascinating that some societies have changed very little in their centuries in a new star system with new events to shape them, whereas others have forgotten their roots and created new cultures as a reflection of the space habitats or moons or planets that have become their homes."

"Perhaps we should try to get Tork back one day," Casmir suggested. "He seems to have become a friend for you."

"Tork is an inferior android. I will wait until one of the crushers becomes interesting."

"While continuing to play games and chat with Tork in the meantime?" Casmir smiled, knowing Tork would take just as many potshots at Zee if he were here.

"It is acceptable to play games with a lesser being."

"Does he ever win?"

"Only if well-established rules and tactics will suffice. I am the more creative thinker. I am fluid."

"It does take a creative and fluid soul to avoid the notice of security guards by turning into a couch."

"Yes."

Casmir, a message came in from Asger, reminding him of the three earlier messages and Asger's insistence that Tristan was somewhere on the *Fedallah*. *Are you there?*

Yes. Casmir looked at the time stamp on the message, noted the lack of significant delay in the delivery, and decided the *Stellar Dragon* had to be close. Had Bonita learned that the missing Scholar Sunflyer was in Dubashi's base?

Maybe it would be possible to get Rache to slow down and let Casmir switch ships. Though he would have to come up with a more plausible reason than "I don't think you're going to let me kidnap Dubashi, so I want to ride with someone who will."

Any update on Tristan? Asger asked.

No, but per your instructions, I didn't let Rache know he might be on the ship.

I'm concerned. It's been several days. Is he just going to hide until the Fedallah *gets to the moon base? Does he even know where Rache is headed?*

Are you sure *he's here?* Casmir asked.

He told me he sneaked aboard that shuttle right before you took off. There's nowhere else he could be. Either he's still on that shuttle or he's slipped off into the rest of the ship.

But you haven't been able to contact him since?

No. I thought he might be worried about Rache's communications people picking up on unauthorized transmissions. Maybe he turned off his chip. Can you look for it?

I'd have to know his chip ID. Especially if it's offline. Someone shouldn't be able to locate one at all if it's offline, but I know a few tricks.

I thought you might. I contacted Princess Nalini. She has his chip ident. I'll forward it to you.

Thank you. I'll check again. Uh, what should I do if I find him?

Keep the mercenaries from killing him. Asger's grimace appeared in Casmir's mind as if he'd sent it with his words. *I know how Rache feels about knights.*

Right. I'll see what I can do.

Are you a prisoner there?

There's a guard at my door that follows me when I go to eat or use the lav.

Casmir. *Why did you* go *with him?*

I didn't want Kim to go alone, and I wasn't sure when my next chance would be to get to Dubashi's base. It was always possible Jorg would send more people to the station to ensure I was complying and ensure I'd go nowhere except back to his ship with the completed crushers.

I hope you're able to get to him. And I wish I was walking in with you to help. Tristan would be useful too.

A good reason for me to find him.

Before Rache does, please.

I'll do my best.

The door opened. Casmir lurched up in his bunk, worried some intelligence officer had detected his transmission and didn't approve.

The lights flared to life, and he squinted at the dark figure who walked in. The dark hooded figure.

"You're supposed to ring the door chime and wait to be invited in," Casmir said.

"It's my ship. I own all the cabins. That means I can go where I wish without an invitation." Rache strode in, unlocked a stool from the deck, and sat down to face him.

"What if I'd been naked?"

"What if you had?" Rache twitched an indifferent shoulder.

"We would have ended up comparing penises rather than discussing whatever pressing matter you have on your mind." Casmir didn't want to do either. Something about Rache's stiff pose made him think he was about to be questioned. And that he might not want to answer the questions. Zee took a couple of steps closer to the stool, an act Rache didn't miss, and loomed near him.

"I doubt there's much difference."

"I don't know. The nobility isn't known for practicing circumcision, even though it makes hygiene easier."

Nervous babbling, nervous babbling… Casmir clamped his lip in his teeth and forced himself to take a slow inhalation and exhalation.

Meanwhile, Rache dropped his masked face into his hand and rubbed his temple. "I can't believe Kim voluntarily spends time with you."

Casmir bristled at hearing her first name on his lips. Thus far, at least in his presence, he'd usually called her Scholar Sato. He reluctantly reminded himself that the relationships she pursued were none of his business.

"Crushers do not have genitalia," Zee announced. "And thus no need to clean them. However, I do occasionally rotate my molecules as part of a dust-sloughing procedure."

Rache lifted his head, looked at Zee, then looked at Casmir. "Your crusher is getting weirder by the day. I don't think you should let the other ones spend time with you and get imprinted with your personality."

"No? Maybe Jorg wouldn't want them then."

"Thus your master plan is revealed." Rache dropped his palms onto his thighs and studied him. "What are you *really* doing here, Dabrowski?"

"Casmir."

"And why did you bring them? For the supposed intelligence-gathering mission you're on. Please tell me you don't have some deluded plan of infiltrating Dubashi's base and killing him."

"I don't kill people. I have qualms about that. I'm already upset enough that others have died because of decisions I've made."

"So what are you doing?"

"Maybe I came along as Kim's chaperone."

"You and your twelve killer robots."

"It's not as if I alone could stop you if your intentions toward her weren't honorable."

"I think *she* could stop me if my intentions weren't honorable. She side-kicked one of my armored men across a submarine and knocked him out."

"Good. I approve."

"For someone who doesn't like violence, you're smiling rather gleefully."

Casmir decided it wouldn't be appropriate to envision Kim side-kicking *Rache* across a shuttle. "I don't object to self-defense."

"She was hijacking my submarine."

"She's a complicated woman."

"Yes." Why did Rache sound like he was smiling when he said that?

Casmir scooted himself around on the bunk to sit cross-legged and face him. What could he divulge that wouldn't be an outright lie and that would prompt Rache to help him rather than impede him?

"I mostly left because we were tipped off that Bjarke—Sir Bjarke Asger—was coming to get Kim to take back to Jorg's ship. I didn't know if he also planned to pick up the crushers that were ready." That was true. Casmir had no idea what Bjarke had intended or been ordered to do in relation to him and the project. "In a couple more weeks, the rest would have been done, but I automated production, so I didn't technically need to stay."

"*Rest?* How many are you making?"

"One hundred and one. The extra one was for Sultan Shayban, in exchange for the resources he gave me to make the others."

"How much were those resources worth?"

"He allowed the use and retooling of a portion of his manufacturing facility for free, so there was no cost there. I didn't check the current market price for the metals used in the alloy, but the raw materials that went into the project would have been worth roughly five million crowns."

"Five *million*? And he gave you all that in exchange for one crusher?"

"Surely a good deal. You can't imagine that Zee would go for less than that in an auction, can you?" Casmir had no idea what a crusher would go for, but he'd heard of wealthy entrepreneurs spending millions on old sports memorabilia, so it seemed plausible. Zee was worth far more than a football signed by a sweaty athlete.

"I don't know. Is he going to discuss genitalia when he's up there?"

"Demonstrations of Zee's personality would only increase the bidding frenzy."

Rache removed his mask and hood, either so they could have a frank conversation with eye contact or so he could push a hand through his short hair. It had been a while since Casmir had seen his face, and he decided anew that it was disconcerting to have a twin who was so different from him, so hard and angular and quick to glare. He wondered what Kim had found out about his past. She'd said she wouldn't share.

"Dabrowski—Casmir—tell me what you hope to accomplish here? With these." He waved at Zee and toward the corridor, though the door was shut on the rest of the crushers.

"On your ship? Nothing. I've actually realized that it's unlikely that Kim needs a chaperone and that I have no purpose here."

"Is that *really* why you came along?" Rache leaned back on the stool, indignation flashing in his eyes.

No, Casmir almost said, but maybe it would serve him if Rache believed that. He couldn't tell Rache the *truth.* "She's my best friend. And you kill Kingdom subjects whenever you get the chance. Even now, aren't you going to Dubashi's meeting because he's offering to pay people to attack the Kingdom? How can I not be concerned for a friend who's… talking to someone like that?"

He prayed Rache didn't tell him they'd been doing more than talking. He didn't want to know.

"She'll be kicked out of the Kingdom if someone in Royal Intelligence figures out she's your buddy now," Casmir added, feeling hypocritical since he'd come up with the plan that had brought Kim here. But Rache seemed willing to go down this line, to believe it was the reason Casmir had come.

"What did you intend to do to stop it? Throw your crushers at me?"

"I just want her to be safe. *You* should want her to be safe too. If you care, why let her risk her career to spend time with you?"

A muscle jumped in Rache's jaw when he clenched his teeth. But he looked away instead of rebutting. Was it possible he agreed on some level?

Whatever he thought, Rache didn't answer.

Casmir cleared his throat. "Anyway, I know it's her choice. Would you mind if I contacted Bonita and asked if she would come pick me up? I can take my crushers with me. She's heading this way, I believe, so it shouldn't be hard to arrange a rendezvous point."

"I've noticed." Rache recovered his equanimity and dry tone. "I'd ask if she also has the capacity to track my ship, but I suspect we're just heading in the same direction."

"She's trying to track down a missing scientist. All roads lead to Dubashi's base, it seems."

"Is that why you want to join her? To help her collect some bounty?" Rache sounded doubtful.

"I will certainly try to retrieve the scholar for her if I chance across him. But I'm going to stop a war."

Rache's snort was skeptical, but the follow-up squint appeared to be more contemplative.

"I'll let your freighter find us and hook up for an exchange," Rache said, "but you promise me that if Kim doesn't want to go with you, you won't try to talk her into leaving."

Kim wouldn't leave anyway. She wanted to check the base for a bioweapon, and she'd more easily gain access to it with Rache, even if she had to play the role of his prisoner.

"You have my word that I won't try to talk her into leaving," Casmir said, delighted Rache would let him go, though maybe it wasn't a surprise. What mercenary would want twelve Zees on his ship who weren't obedient to him? "I shall assume that I don't have to ask for your word that you won't tie her up and force her to stay."

"How respectful of you to assume I have integrity." Rache stood and pulled his mask back on. "Contact your ship. If you want to leave behind any crushers programmed to obey me, I'll allow that."

"Considerate of you."

"Yes."

Asger donned exercise clothing and headed to the *Dragon*'s lounge to use one of the treadmills, but when he neared the hatch, he heard the whir of the belt and the rapid *clomp, clomp, clomp* of someone already running on one. He stopped in the corridor. Yes, it was cowardly, but he didn't want to pull out the adjacent treadmill if his father was in there.

A part of Asger wished he had stayed on Stardust Palace instead of coming along when his father had chartered—manipulated Bonita until she'd complied and taken him on—the *Dragon*. But he was worried about Tristan as well as Casmir and Kim. There was no way he could have twiddled his thumbs and waited for someone else from Jorg's fleet to come pick him up while his friends were in trouble.

He stepped inside, resolving to get a drink and leave if his father was there.

But Qin was the one running on the treadmill, her long legs traveling faster than most people could manage at a dead sprint. She was barely sweating, her hair still soft and dry, back in a tail and bouncing between her shoulder blades. Her two pointed ears protruded from the dark locks, and one swiveled toward him slightly. Somewhere in their travels, that had stopped seeming weird.

"Hi, Asger." Qin lifted a hand though she hadn't looked back.

He supposed her ears were good enough that she could identify him by his gait. Or maybe she'd smelled him coming. An odd thought. He resisted the urge to give his armpits the sniff test.

"Did you come to run?" She barely sounded breathless, despite the fast pace.

He wondered if he could keep up. He'd always worked hard to maintain his fitness, but he wasn't genetically engineered. Still, his competitive spirit made him want to suggest a few races.

"I think so." Asger pulled out the other treadmill and maneuvered it beside hers.

"You're not sure?"

"The last time I came up here, I ended up getting slightly inebriated and flapping my lips to Casmir." Asger stepped onto the treadmill instead of heading over to examine the contents of Bonita's liquor cabinet. Tonight, he felt less like getting smashed and more like burning off some of his tensions.

"He probably didn't mind."

"No, he seems to like talking."

Asger strapped himself in, glanced at the setting on Qin's machine, and decided he needed to warm up before attempting that speed. He also noticed that she had chosen a forest trail to show on the display as she ran, ferns and mossy tree trunks blurring past. He remembered her leaping from branch to branch in the park in Zamek City and wondered if he could talk Casmir into creating a program for the treadmill that emulated such a journey.

One of Viggo's robot vacuums whirred into the lounge and did a few laps around the perimeter, then positioned itself in front of Asger's treadmill. Though it had no eyes, it seemed to gaze at him, indicator lights blinking in some kind of idleness pattern.

"Now I'm really tempted to sniff my pits," he muttered.

"What?" Qin glanced at his face, then at his armpits.

"I thought you might have smelled me coming when you guessed who it was without looking."

"I did."

"Because of my armpits or just my overall scent aura?" Was there such a thing? He didn't know.

"It's true that armpits are strongly scented areas. And, uh, certain lower areas." She glanced at him, her cheeks red, but he didn't know if it was only from the exercise or if she was embarrassed to bring up his lower areas. He would only be embarrassed if she told him they were offensive to a sensitive nose. "But when I smell someone at a distance, I guess you could say there's sort of a collective aura. I'm going to do some sprints if you want to join me."

"I thought you already were sprinting."

Her eyes crinkled. "No, warming up."

"The clock says you've been on there for an hour."

"Yes."

Asger shook out his arms and increased the speed. "I'm ready. Are we racing or just encouraging and supporting each other?"

"Whatever you like." She smiled and turned up her treadmill to max, which was faster than he would have guessed possible. Maybe someone already had put in a custom program.

Asger went along with it, glad for the excuse to push himself. Lately, his muscles had been so tense that it had been all he could do to keep from lashing out at his father when they passed in the corridors.

As he warmed up and sweat began to flow, the vacuum that had been staring at Asger whirred around his treadmill. It took him a moment to realize it was mopping up his sweat instead of sucking up lint and dirt. Versatile thing.

During a supposed rest period—Qin slowed down to eight miles per hour—Asger sneaked a few glances at her. She wasn't sweating as much as he was, but there was a sheen to her pink cheeks, and her hair—and the fur on the back of her neck—was damp.

Somewhere along the way, he'd started to find that fur, and all the rest of her, exotic and intriguing instead of a demonstration of the horrors of genetic engineering and why it was outlawed in the Kingdom. It didn't hurt that she kept fighting at his side and standing up for him to his father. She was a good friend. More than that, he admitted. Lately, his thoughts had been prone to imagining things they could do alone together *besides* running.

But if he truly wanted that, he had to tell her. Did he?

He'd been trying to put distance between them since that kiss, because there were so many reasons why it would be difficult for them to have a future together—he couldn't imagine it unless he gave up his career and his home and everything that came with it, including all of his responsibilities as his father's heir. But to lead her on for a fling wasn't fair, to pretend they could be something and then later say he had to return to a world that had no place for her in it. She didn't deserve that. But she didn't deserve getting the cold shoulder now either. She deserved… He snorted. Probably someone who would treat her better than he could.

Qin glanced over. "Are you all right?"

"Yes. Just thinking about how amazing you are."

Her eyebrows flew up, and an ear swiveled toward him. "What? Why? Because I can run faster than you?"

"I don't think we've definitively proven *that* yet, but that's only one of the reasons. You're very, uhm, nice." Asger waved at her, intending to imply that all of her was great, but she looked down at her boobs, and he realized he might only be suggesting she had nice lady bits. "Pretty, I mean, but also a good person. Loyal and kind and… *nice*."

Dear God, *Casmir* was probably better than this at flirting with women.

"Thank you." She faced forward and ran for a while before adding, "I thought maybe you thought it was a mistake that you—we—kissed."

"No. I mean, maybe it was, but I liked it."

Her next glance was a little wary, but she said, "I liked it too." She offered a quick grin. "You're sexy."

Heat flushed his face—and other parts. And here he'd thought he was as warm as he could be after all that running.

"Thank you. I don't regret kissing you, and I'd like to do a lot *more* with you, if I'm honest about it, but I've been worrying… Well, you saw what it was like for you on Odin. I couldn't imagine you living there, and I couldn't imagine me *not* living there, assuming I don't get kicked out of the knighthood and my father doesn't disown me." He grimaced, not wanting to let his mind wander down that path again. "I didn't want to, er, have sex with you and then leave when the war is over and I can go home. I didn't want you to think I was like those pirates and just wanted to see what it was like because you're, uhm, different."

He was botching this. Maybe he should pull out some alcohol after all.

"You're *nothing* like them, Asger. You actually kissed me. They usually went straight to shoving things in."

He curled a lip. "Gross."

"I thought so. And I know you care. I just wasn't sure if… Well, if you want to have sex or kiss more or whatever normal things men and women do, I would enjoy that. I never expected…" She slowed her treadmill down to a walk. "I guess I've read a lot of those fairy tales and sometimes have unrealistic thoughts, but I would never expect you to want to get married to a—to me and make me Lady Whatsit in your castle."

Asger was encouraged to hear that, especially the part about wanting to have sex, but it did make him sad that he couldn't give her the fairy tale.

"I'm assuming you have a castle," she added.

"Three stories, six towers, a moat, and almost twenty thousand square feet of living space. Though technically, it's my father's castle, and I just have rooms there."

"Are there a lot of trees?" she asked wistfully.

"There's a whole forest out back. Some of it was logged centuries ago, but the trees have all grown back, and wood isn't used much for building anymore, so they're probably safe."

"A forest. It sounds dreamy."

He grinned, amused that she was more interested in the trees than the towers. "I'll show it to you someday, all right? If we all end up back on Odin again."

"I'd like that." Qin turned up the speed on her treadmill again. "We better finish up our workout."

"Oh, were we not done?" He'd been hoping they could move on to other things now that she'd admitted she wanted to.

"No." She grinned, a little wickedly this time, and leaned over to increase the speed on *his* treadmill.

After eight sprints and eight rest periods that were too fast to be considered even vaguely restful, Viggo cleared his throat.

"Bonita has received a comm."

Asger slowed down. "For me?"

He was breathing hard, sweat dripping down his face and off his chin, and he didn't care that his voice sounded hopeful.

A faint spritzing sound drifted up, along with the scents of lemon and vinegar. Was that vacuum using air freshener? Or maybe that was some sanitary fluid for the deck. Viggo did care about his cleanliness, didn't he?

"Sort of," Viggo said. "Bonita told me to tell one of the Asgers to, ah, get up here and deal with it. Your father is sleeping in his cabin, so I chose you. Also, you looked like you were about to collapse."

"Depending on who the comm is from, that could still happen." Asger grimaced and removed the waist strap.

"Do you want me to come along?" Qin asked.

"It's the Kingdom," Viggo said.

"Never mind," Qin said.

Asger patted her arm and headed up to navigation, though he had a feeling he would regret it. Whoever it was would want to know why he was haring off on an unassigned mission. Or was he? Had his father gotten permission for this trip? If he was supposed to find Kim, and they were chasing her, maybe he didn't need permission.

"Here's one of them," Bonita said, waving Asger in.

He didn't recognize the crisp, clean-shaven officer on the forward display, but the man wore captain's rank on his Fleet uniform. When Asger glanced at the identification of the ship comming them, dread waltzed into his stomach. It was the *Chivalrous*, Prince Jorg's ship. He should have woken up his father to deal with this.

"I'm Sir William Asger." He wished he were in his knight's armor and not sweaty exercise togs.

"Hold, please." The captain looked to the side.

Prince Jorg himself replaced the officer in the display. Asger gaped—he hadn't expected the prince would address him directly—then remembered to bow deeply.

He started to introduce himself, but Jorg spoke first.

"What are you doing on that freighter, Sir Asger?"

"Assisting my father, Sir Bjarke Asger. He was sent to Stardust Palace to retrieve Scholar Sato and…"

And what? Asger didn't want to get Kim in trouble by reporting that she'd fled with Rache. Oh, but wait. Was *that* the plan? Casmir and Kim had told him so little.

"…she wasn't there when he went to look for her," he finished to be safe.

And it was mostly true.

"She wasn't *there*? Did she not transfer to the very freighter you're on and go to the station? Do you have her there now?"

"No. We're chasing the ship that we believe has her."

"And what ship is that? The sultan wouldn't tell me anything that's been going on there." Jorg's eyebrows drew down. "I'm half-tempted to return to his station and show him what happens to those who defy the Kingdom."

If Jorg's orders had truly been to gather allies and bring more ships back to System Lion to fight off the invaders… he had a strange way of asking people for help.

"Tenebris Rache has her, Your Highness," Asger's father said, stepping into navigation, frowning at him, and then bowing to the prince. His hair was tousled from sleep, but he wore a galaxy suit with his knight's purple cloak—far more appropriate attire for speaking to royalty. Had Viggo warned him?

"Oh, good," Bonita muttered. "All of my favorite people are crammed into navigation with me."

Asger's father quirked his eyebrows at her, but focused on Jorg when he raged, "Rache!"

"I'm not clear on what exactly happened, Your Highness—" his father glanced at Bonita again, his expression wry this time, "—but it appears he knew I was coming and kidnapped her himself."

"Are you able to track his ship? I heard there's a way now, but we haven't been able to get anyone to sell us this technology." Jorg's eyes flared with indignation.

"No," Asger's father said, "but we believe he's going to Prince Dubashi's moon base for a meeting."

"A meeting? You mean the gathering of an invasion force. We've seen all those lowlife mercenary ships flying there, and we plan to do something about it while they're all in one place."

Asger kept his face neutral, but he frowned inwardly. What if the prince meant to take all of his forces and attack the base while Casmir was trying to fulfill his promise to the sultan? A promise Jorg would know nothing about. Should Asger tell him? He glanced uncertainly at his father.

"You'll take control of that freighter you're on and fly over to join us," Jorg said.

"Uh." Bonita, still in the pilot's pod, lifted a finger. "That's not going to happen."

"We'll need all the forces we can muster to go against so many. My hope is that the mercenaries won't show any loyalty or be willing to take on much risk. I'm sending coordinates for a rendezvous point."

"What about Sato, Your Highness?" Asger's father asked. "We can't let her end up working for Rache. Or Dubashi—if he's taking her to him."

"Leave her for now. This is more important. I expect to see both of you at the rendezvous point."

The comm went dark.

Bonita folded her arms over her chest and glared at them—no, at Asger's father. "'Take control of that freighter?' Does your idiot prince know I'm not a Kingdom subject, that this freighter isn't registered in the Kingdom, that he has no right to touch it, and that I think he's a steaming pile of dog shit?"

Asger shook his head. *He* wouldn't try to take over Bonita's ship—his stomach curdled at the thought of fighting Qin for control, or for anything. He fought *with* Qin, not against her. But what if his father decided he had to obey orders? Had to try to take the *Dragon*?

His father clasped his hands behind his back and gazed thoughtfully at the display, distant stars glittering where Jorg's face had been. "I need to consider this."

"Yes, consider how you're *not* going to take control of my ship."

"I've paid for passage," he remarked calmly.

"Not to rendezvous with some war party that's going on a suicide mission. And certainly not to *join* them."

Asger grimaced. It had sounded like Jorg wanted to add the *Dragon* to his little fleet. And use it for cannon fodder against the mercenary ships? It wasn't as if the freighter's single railgun made it formidable in battle. Besides, Bonita and Qin had nothing to do with this war and shouldn't be asked to sacrifice themselves for the Kingdom.

"Neither of you is Casmir," Bonita added. "Even if you locked me up and somehow bested Qin and threw her in the cell with me, you'd have to hack Viggo to get the ship to go anywhere."

"Not a simple matter, I assure you," Viggo said. "My computers have recently been upgraded and have numerous sophisticated encryption security measures. Also, I can electrocute you with surges from my outlets."

Asger thought of the vacuum mopping up sweat in the lounge, but he didn't remark on whether it connoted sophistication. Bonita was far too tense to laugh.

"We can join Jorg's fleet, as ordered," Asger's father said, glancing at him, "or we can continue to the moon base, which may soon be attacked by Jorg's fleet. Neither destination would be safe. But it would be better for my career and my duty if I obeyed Jorg." He gazed at Bonita. "Is there a price at which you would take me to him?"

"No. I'm about five seconds from returning your money and shooting you out the airlock for associating with questionable people."

"Do continue on course then, Captain," Asger's father said. "But I must insist that you wait until we reach Dubashi's base to shoot me out the airlock, per our deal." He bowed to her and walked out, hands still clasped behind his back, his purple robe swishing against the hatch jamb.

"I don't know what to make of that man." Bonita looked at Asger. "Do I have to worry about him stunning me and Qin in our sleep and trying to take the ship by force?"

"I… would like to think not." Asger couldn't imagine his father doing that to Bonita, no matter how much of an ass he could be at times, but he also had a hard time envisioning him not doing everything in his power to obey a royal order.

"Your certainty is comforting."

"Sorry."

She shook her head and walked out, leaving the flying to Viggo. Asger worried about the ramifications of not doing what Jorg asked, and he also worried about what would happen to Casmir and Kim if they were on that base when Jorg's fleet attacked.

CHAPTER 23

YAS HURRIED INTO THE SHUTTLE BAY, WORRY TIGHTENING his hand around his medical kit. It was the night shift, and he'd been asleep for an hour when the comm had bleated in his cabin.

"In here, Doc." One of Jess's engineering officers waved from the hatchway of a shuttle.

Yas ran over, his slippers not making a sound on the deck. "What happened?"

"I'm not sure. I left to get us both some coffee. I came back, and the chief was passed out on the deck inside."

Yas hustled inside and down the aisle, afraid Jess had blacked out from extreme pain or some complication of those painkillers she took. What if she'd sneaked down here to consume some and had overdosed by accident? Or *not* by accident?

Jess lay crumpled on her side in the back, her face pressed against the black matting, half of her dark hair fallen out of a bun and covering her cheeks.

He knelt down and touched her shoulder, checking for responsiveness, even as he dug into his kit. She did not groan or move in the slightest. He rested his fingers on her throat, relieved to find her pulse steady. Relieved, but puzzled, since he would have expected it to be slower than typical if she'd passed out from an overdose of a painkiller.

Once he had his medical scanner out, he let it more accurately check her vital signs. His own fingers had a tremble to them and couldn't be trusted. He'd never had that with patients he'd operated on in the emergency room, but he hadn't *known* them. Hadn't cared about them…

He brushed her soft hair back from her face, telling himself it was only so he would see when she woke up, but his fingers encountered a surprising lump. "What the—"

Yas pushed her hair back and scowled at a swelling bruise. "She didn't overdose; she clubbed herself in the head."

The engineer was in navigation reporting to someone on the bridge, so he didn't hear the revelation.

Yas searched around, wondering what Jess could have struck so hard that it knocked her out. Then he stared in realization at an open locker door in the back—a locker large enough that someone could have been hidden in it.

He lurched to his feet. "Lieutenant? Tell the captain I think we have an intruder."

Yas bent and lifted his patient in his arms. Rache could deal with the intruder while he took Jess to sickbay for better treatment.

But he glanced around warily as he left, wondering why she'd been attacked in here. This was the falsely painted and unregistered shuttle that Rache had taken over to Stardust Palace to pick up Casmir and Kim, the one that had been damaged as it fled the station. It made sense that Jess would have been down here repairing it. But who could have been hiding in here, and why? And why had the person chosen that moment to leap out?

"Nobody keeps the ship's doctor in the loop," he grumbled, carrying her out.

Kim sat in a chair in Rache's cabin, reading the first couple of chapters of a weathered hardback she'd pulled from a shelf in his case. *A Brief Biography and an Analysis of the Tactics and Strategies of Admiral Tarik Mikita.*

She'd chosen it from his mixed collection of nonfiction war histories and dark and depressing classic novels from Old Earth and the Twelve Systems. She had skipped past the military stuff and was reading the biography in the back, not because she wouldn't find it interesting to learn exactly what kinds of tactics the admiral had employed but because the biography was short enough that she could finish it that night. She was aware of the *Fedallah* hurtling through space toward their dubious destiny and what might be limited time for reading.

"Are you comfortable enough?" Rache asked. He was sitting on his bed, leaning against the wall, and drawing in a sketch pad. His mask lay on the sleep sack next to him—she hadn't even had to ask him to remove it this time. "We can switch if you want."

"It's fine. An upgrade to the metal stool in my cabin. There's a backrest."

"The epitome of luxury." Rache waved toward an empty corner of the cabin. "I used to have a large cushion filled with foam pellets that I read in. My old first officer gave it to me as a gag gift, but it was surprisingly comfortable."

"Old first officer? So not the bald man we passed on the bridge whose elaborate mustache drooped in shock when I walked toward your cabin with you?"

"No. My old first officer is dead. I haven't let myself get that close to any of my officers since then. It's too hard when they die, and in this line of work, death is inevitable."

"So, it's better not to have any friends." She raised her eyebrows.

"Not among the crew. I thought I might be safe befriending a civilian scientist, but she's also good at putting herself at risk."

"You're thinking of Casmir. I keep getting yanked into dangerous situations against my wishes. I would much prefer to be back home working in my lab." Kim thought of the footage she'd seen of the war. Was that lab still standing? Were her colleagues at work, or had the populace been urged into bunkers? Did bunkers even exist anymore in the city? She remembered touring some of the subterranean safe houses from centuries past, most now forgotten or turned into attractions to be visited by children on school field trips. Many generations had come and gone since a real threat had penetrated System Lion.

"You're kind not to bring up that I was the one to yank you into one of your first dangerous situations," Rache said.

"That *was* rude, but now you're helping me, and you made me dinner."

Kim waved to the small table where they'd sat after he invited her up for a meal, scrounging enough greens from the ship's small hydroponics room to make a salad. It had been smothered in nuts and dried berries and a rich dressing that was fairly impressive given the mostly shelf-stable stores aboard. The main course of Lamb Protein Puck cowering under brown gravy had been less fresh, and he'd apologized that he didn't have the ingredients to cook her anything, but had promised he made their salads himself.

"I have to add those terms into the equation as I consider my feelings for you," she added.

"Naturally." He returned to his drawing.

Kim thought about bringing up his plans again, and maybe trying to change his mind, but she found herself disinclined to nag or wheedle, even if he would only get himself killed on his current course. And she was enjoying sitting here quietly, him drawing and her reading.

"Are you looking for me in there? Or Casmir?" Rache asked without looking up. He'd noticed her choice earlier but hadn't commented on it.

"I'm looking for…" Even though his tone was neutral and she struggled to read him as much as she struggled with everyone else, she suspected he wanted the answer to be him and not Casmir. But she had picked it up because she'd thought she might give Casmir some advice based on what she found. The book, according to the title page, had been published in System Hesperides, one that Mikita had conquered toward the end of the Kingdom's expansion, and one that had been among the first to free itself in the centuries that followed. The book's origins, and the fact that Rache had chosen it for his collection, suggested it a more likely source of unbiased information than most. "The truth," she finished. "I'm sure you've seen the Kingdom's interpretation of Mikita."

"Yes. Though I actually read that first. Jager gave it to me."

That startled her, not that it had been given but that Rache had kept it. "And you haven't since burned it?"

"It did cross my mind several times. Not to burn it—what kind of troglodyte burns books?—but to abandon it somewhere."

"When did he give it to you?"

In other words, how long had he known about his famous progenitor?

"When I was thirteen and developing my first rebellious streak. He came to Lichtenberg Manor and told me what he expected from me and what wouldn't be acceptable. Which was anything except training to become a knight, acing every test put in front of me, and becoming a walking encyclopedia on military matters. Thus to fulfill my role as his loyal general someday."

"If your tone were any drier, your tongue would spark and catch fire."

"You can imagine how delighted I was to learn that I'd not only been created to be his pawn but that my future was set in stone."

"Did it make you rebel more?"

"It made me resent him, but I did as he directed. At thirteen, I didn't loathe the idea of becoming a great war hero, destined to bring back the former glory of the Kingdom—those were his words—but I did resent all the work. I had little free time. My rebellion was sneaking away to ride my air bike at night and later entering into races. But I did all of the schoolwork, passed all of the tests, memorized the writings and speeches of great knights and admirals of the past." His tone managed to turn even drier. "After all that, I was delighted to meet Casmir and have him get the best of me twice in a row. Which is, I suppose, three times in a row now, since I have five gate pieces in my hold instead of five hundred, and I'm convinced he was responsible for all those ships showing up."

Kim knew Casmir had been but didn't confirm it. Not when Rache already sounded resentful.

"According to this," she said, "Mikita grew up in a poor family with only his mother and grandmother around to take care of him. He started selling baubles on the street at age eight to bring home money to help feed younger brothers and sisters, and he was determined to enter the military service academy and become an officer and maybe even find a way to become a knight. He believed that was the best way to ensure his family would have a better life. He had medical issues—the specifics aren't mentioned here—that kept him from being accepted into the military service academy. But he wouldn't accept that as the final answer, so he found a knight and proved himself over and over to him until he was accepted as a squire. Mikita eventually was also accepted as a knight, and when King Ansel started trying to expand, he was finally permitted to enter the military, where there were numerous opportunities for him to prove himself and gain rank."

"Is something in that supposed to explain Casmir's… I was tempted, for the sake of my ego, to call it luck the first time. I don't think I can at this point."

"I think his victories, if you want to call them that, have come because of his friendships with others. Wasn't it Asger returning to help him on that cargo ship that kept you from getting the gate then?"

"Asger and Zee, I suppose."

"And on the refinery, Bonita and Qin came back for us when we didn't expect them to."

"Kim, I have a hundred men that I pay to be loyal and serve me."

"Which isn't quite the same as friends who will do anything for you. I won't deny that he has an unorthodox way of looking at things that probably startles classically trained tacticians—"

Rache snorted.

"—but he's also good at turning enemies into allies, when he puts his mind to it. When I first met him, I had zero intention of becoming his roommate. I was positive it wouldn't work out. Yet somehow, after a couple of hours with him, I ended up moving in the next week and never left, even after I could have afforded a posh flat with a view of the ocean." She twitched a shoulder.

"So his charisma is what's besting me?" Rache sounded skeptical but not outright dismissive. Maybe he truly wanted to figure this out.

"I'm not sure it's as much charisma as being genuine with people and wanting to help them with their problems. That tends to come through." Kim tapped the open page of the book. "I think that you also grew up at a disadvantage." She smiled, expecting that to goad him a bit.

His brows arched. "Having only the best schooling and tutors and martial arts instructors."

"Having no adversity to overcome and no reason to be driven to succeed. If this is right, when Mikita was young, he wanted to scrape his way out of poverty. Later, he chanced across Princess Sofia and longed to win her hand in marriage, but he had to prove himself to the king to be able to do so. And so he did, over and over and over. He refused to let obstacles stand in his way. He was driven, not by something so hollow as revenge but by love."

Rache didn't snort this time. She'd expected him to laughingly dismiss the power of love. But he appeared more contemplative.

"I didn't learn until much later that I'd been gene-cleaned and that the original Mikita couldn't have been. That has made me wonder if something about that has made a difference for me. It's hard to imagine that a great admiral would have had seizures on the bridge of his flagship, but…" Rache waved his fingers in the air.

"The seizures may be unique to Casmir. This doesn't mention what Mikita's medical disabilities were, but there's usually an epigenetic component in what expresses itself. But yes, I'm sure whatever kept him from originally qualifying for the military was another form of adversity. There are all manner of variations on the 'that which doesn't kill us makes us stronger' quotation, and science backs that up with the well-established concept of hormesis. Casmir probably wouldn't have created the crushers if he hadn't been driven earlier in life to build a robot to protect him from bullies in school. I don't think he's driven in the way Mikita was, at least not yet, but he's certainly had to learn to accomplish things in ways that don't rely on strength, athleticism, money, or beauty."

"I wonder if the queen had all that in mind when she kept him alive and gave him a simple home."

"I've never met her and don't know her outside of her media facade. It's possible she just didn't want Jager to get rid of the supposedly imperfect baby and felt she owed him a chance at life since she and her husband brought him into the world." Kim wondered if Casmir would ever get the meeting with the queen that he'd wanted since he'd first become aware of her influence.

Rache tapped his pencil on his sketch pad, gazing off at nothing, and Kim went back to reading.

"You don't mark up the pages," she said after a while, noting the unblemished interior. None had even been dog-eared.

"No. Do you?"

"Sometimes I underline passages I want to remember and scribble notes. Not often. I usually read electronic books, so it's easier to annotate them."

"I don't like to leave marks on physical books, especially rare ones." Rache went to the bookcase and pulled out a notebook. "But I do sometimes take notes when I read. I always feel I remember things better when I write them instead of simply thinking them into my chip's memory."

"So do I."

Rache offered her the notebook. There were sections for many of the books on the shelves, each carefully organized by a table of contents.

She started to read his thoughts on the Mikita book, but the door chime interrupted her, ringing shortly, almost uncertainly.

Rache sighed and donned his mask and hood. "I suppose it's good that you're not naked."

"I thought you might request that when you got the sketch pad out. I was prepared to indignantly tell you that women with advanced degrees in the sciences don't pose naked."

"No need. I'm capable of using my imagination when drawing." He handed her the sketch he'd been working on before he headed to the door.

It was indeed a picture of her—she hadn't wanted to assume, but she'd caught him glancing at her face a couple of times—but instead of being naked or reading in his chair, she was wearing combat armor and kicking an armored man in the gut. She chuckled, but she was secretly touched that he'd been amused by—maybe even pleased by?—that story.

"Sir!" a young officer blurted, glancing behind Rache and looking relieved by the lack of nudity. "There's an—"

The lights went out, and the thrum of the engines stopped reverberating through the deck. Kim set the sketch pad and books down and rose to her feet. An alarm beeped from the bridge.

"—intruder," the officer finished grimly.

Rache snatched a DEW-Tek rifle from a rack above his bed.

Casmir, Kim sent a message. *You're not doing anything, are you?*

Who, me?

Does that mean yes?

No, I'm in my bunk reading reports.

What about your crushers? she asked as Rache rushed through the briefing room and onto the bridge.

Kim followed him.

Emergency lighting glowed red, and then the main lights came back online, but the thrum of the engines did not return.

"Engineering?" she heard Rache ask someone. "I'm on my way."

"He's fighting our men, sir," an officer said.

"Then I'm definitely on my way." Rache sprinted for the lift.

Worried that this had to do with one of Casmir's crushers, Kim raced in and joined him before the doors shut.

"You could have stayed behind," Rache said. "Unless you seek to practice your side kicks again."

"Do you know what's going on? Who's responsible?"

"Not yet. Do *you*?"

I checked on them, Casmir messaged. *All of my crushers are still in the corridor. But the guard that was keeping an eye on me—and them—disappeared.*

Kim shook her head. "I thought one of Casmir's crushers might have wandered off, but he says not."

The lift stopped, and the doors opened, revealing shouts and the sounds of weapons fire coming from ahead. Rache charged out with his rifle in hand. He wore his galaxy suit but not armor, and Kim frowned with concern.

If Casmir's crushers weren't stirring up trouble, who was? One of Rache's men? *Many* of his men? Or some stowaway who wanted to kidnap her? What if Jorg had gotten a spy or saboteur aboard? Or what if someone was hunting down Casmir for Dubashi's bounty?

Advancing more slowly than Rache, Kim followed the corridor toward engineering. She didn't know the ship well, but she'd been on this level several times now, first as a prisoner and then as a guest. The shuttle bays were down here, and so was engineering.

More weapons fire sounded, and someone shouted, "I got him!"

A crunch and a boom followed the words.

Smoke poured out of the open doorway to engineering as Rache ran in.

"And he got you," someone said. "Idiot."

"I'm wearing armor. He isn't."

Footsteps pounded the deck. Kim inched closer until she could peer through the doorway, but she didn't go inside, not with energy bolts streaking left and right through the smoke. Bangs sounded, and she made out someone springing behind the engine housing for the ship's main drive. The dark figure must have climbed up the back, for he appeared on the top and sprang off, heading straight toward her.

Kim flattened herself against the wall, glimpsing short dark hair and a bearded face in the smoke. As the man ran toward the exit, Rache appeared behind him, sprinting after him. His prey had a rifle, but it wasn't pointing at Kim. The man looked like he only wanted to escape.

Kim stepped into his way and kicked him in the chest. He was fast and almost evaded her boot, but she clipped him enough to stop his flight.

As he stumbled back, Kim recognized the bearded face, but Rache caught him around the waist before she could say anything. He tore the rifle away as he hefted the man from his feet and hurled him back into engineering. He flew all the way to a side wall, crunching hard against it.

Rache sprang after him, as did the other mercenaries in engineering.

"Wait!" Kim shouted, rushing into the room. "Wait, please. I know him."

Rache was kneeling atop the man—atop the ex-knight *Tristan*—a hand around his throat, but he did pause and look back at her. "You kicked him. That can't hint of a friendly relationship."

"No, it does. I met him on the station, and he's..." If Kim said he was a knight, Rache would kill him without hesitation.

"Who?" Rache asked. "He's trying to sabotage my ship."

Kim licked her lips, lifted her hands and walked slowly toward them, hoping Rache would give her a moment to explain. Though she couldn't explain Tristan's presence. Or who he was, not without risking his life. Should she try to lie?

Casmir, she messaged. *Hurry down to engineering. The intruder is Tristan, but I'm not sure how to keep Rache from killing him.*

Be right there.

"He *did* sabotage the ship, sir," one of the engineering officers said, his rifle pointing at Tristan. "We're on auxiliary power and decelerating. He took the main engine offline. We're also spewing some kind of gas vapor. Hantz, check on that, will you?"

"Yes, sir."

Tristan, Kim saw as she inched closer, was conscious, and he looked like he wanted to fight Rache, but there were three other men with weapons aimed at him now. Tristan also wasn't armored. He was wearing the same green and gray clothes she'd last seen him in at the station.

One of the engineers scurried off to check on the gas leak.

Rache's fingers were tight in Tristan's shirt, the collar twisted and his face growing red. Tristan glanced at Kim—it was the only movement he could manage with Rache pinning him down.

"Bridge," Rache said coolly, "is anyone following us?"

"Prince Jorg's fleet is about a day behind us," came a reply over the comm. "It's not clear if they're following us or heading to the moon base to crash the meeting."

"How many ships are there?" Rache asked.

"All of the ones Prince Jorg has managed to get on his side, it looks like. His ship, four Kingdom Fleet warships, and about a dozen smaller ships with weapons. They'll catch up with us quickly if we keep decelerating."

"We won't," Rache said. "Hantz and Rigger are on it."

He nodded toward one of the men pointing his weapon at Tristan, and the officer slung it over his shoulder and joined his comrade who was already checking the damage.

"Kim." Rache sounded like he was struggling to keep the cold out of his tone when he addressed her. "Who is this guy, where did he come from, and why am I not breaking his neck this very second?"

Heavy footsteps sounded in the corridor outside, several sets of them. If that was Casmir, he'd brought his buddies.

Rache glanced toward the noise. Tristan tensed, as if he might take advantage and try to escape Rache's hold. Kim shook her head minutely, hoping he was looking at her and would heed the warning.

But it was Rache who glanced at her and probably noticed the gesture.

Four crushers jogged into engineering, the fading smoke stirring around their dark forms. Casmir poked his head inside before following them in.

Rache rose to his feet, hefting Tristan up with him and twisting his arm behind his back while shifting him like a shield to stand between him and the crushers. Rache adjusted his grip on Tristan's neck but didn't release it.

Casmir blinked a few times. "What's going on?"

"That's what I'd like to know," Rache said. "You know this guy? Where'd he come from?"

"Yes, that's Tristan from Stardust Palace. He's Princess Nalini's business partner, and he was also testing my crushers. But, ah, we didn't invite him along on our kidnapping." Casmir looked at Kim. "Did we?"

She shook her head, noting that Casmir was walking slowly into engineering. His arms spread, he attempted to look innocent. Since he wasn't armed and was in pajamas, that might have worked, if not for the crushers walking beside him, staying close enough to protect him if someone got twitchy with a rifle.

"Business partner?" Rache asked skeptically. "Why is some real-estate analyst sabotaging my ship?"

"I don't know," Casmir said. "Are you competing in the property-buying sphere currently?"

"No."

"Perhaps he could explain if you released his neck. He looks like he's going to pass out."

"I'm thinking of killing him," Rache said. "And stop right there. You're making me mistrustful of your intentions."

Casmir stopped. "If you kill him, he can't explain anything."

"Darn."

"Rache," Kim said. "Can you just disarm him and put him in a cell until we figure this out?"

Rache must have been accessing the network and running a face identification program, for he growled low in his throat. "Tristan Tremayne, until very recently a knight of the Kingdom."

"Yes, but now working for the sultan and the princess," Casmir said. "No?"

"We can get the main drive back online, sir," one of the engineers said. "He turned everything off, but it doesn't look like he had time to damage anything. And we've stopped the gas venting out our hull. I think he was hoping someone could track us down with it."

Rache glared at Kim and Casmir. Though his mask covered his eyes, Kim imagined them very hard.

"We didn't know he was here," Kim said, hating the idea of him mistrusting *her*.

"But since he is here, we should definitely use him," Casmir said. "And let him talk. And breathe. Tristan, how did you *get* here?"

Rache loosened his grip enough to let Tristan suck in a few painful breaths.

"I saw that you were being taken prisoner," Tristan rasped. He glanced at the crushers. "I thought that was what was happening. I snuck aboard the shuttle and have been there for days. I came out looking for you but couldn't find you in the brig."

"So you decided to look next for them in engineering?" Rache asked. "Inside my fusion drive's housing?"

"Once I realized whose ship I was on, I knew I was in over my head. I thought if I could sabotage it, the Fleet could catch up and rescue you." Tristan's brow furrowed. "But I think I may have been mistaken that you needed rescuing."

Kim tugged at her ponytail, feeling awful that he'd done this for her and Casmir. What if they couldn't talk Rache out of killing him?

"Didn't you get kicked out of the Kingdom?" Kim asked. "Why would you risk yourself so?"

"To protect good people from being kidnapped by mercenaries?" Tristan gave her an incredulous look, as much of one as he could manage with Rache still gripping his neck. "I *had* to."

"Does Nalini know where you are?" Casmir asked. "She's going to be worried. The sultan too."

"I turned off my chip so I couldn't be tracked."

"Well, this is great. Rache, I can use him for my plan. Or you can use him for *your* plan. A trained knight isn't someone to be tossed aside carelessly." Casmir smiled, clearly hoping to touch on something that would convince Rache to keep Tristan alive.

Seconds passed. Kim wasn't sure whether to be upset or relieved that she couldn't see Rache's face, especially when he spoke next.

"I've received word from a bridge officer and my doctor that your trained knight knocked out my chief of engineering." Rache's tone was dark, protective, and his fingers tightened again.

"Thoughtful of him to knock her out rather than killing her," Casmir pointed out.

"I wouldn't do that," Tristan bit out, struggling once more to breathe. "I didn't know her. She opened the locker where I was hiding. I reacted."

"You reacted by cracking her on the skull," Rache said. "You *could* have killed her."

"Do you wish me to stop this violence, Casmir Dabrowski?" one of the crushers asked—Zee, presumably.

"If any of those things touch me, you're going out the airlock, Dabrowski," Rache growled, opting for the surname with his men watching on—or because he was angry.

He looked at Kim—she lifted her chin and gazed back at him, not defiantly but hopefully with an expression that said he was being deliberately obtuse and difficult about this. He didn't make the same threat to her. He didn't say anything at all.

Casmir lifted his hands. "I can understand why you're upset, but you've stopped him, and your doctor is taking care of your engineer, right? Murdering him now in cold blood won't do anything except make you look like a nefarious villain in front of a lady and four impressionable crushers. Zee already has preconceptions about you, thanks to all those dramas he watches, but the other three don't have opinions yet. And then there's my plan. I'm realizing Tristan could really help me out. Do you want to hear about my plan?"

"No," Rache said.

"I do," Kim said.

She'd deliberately been vague with Rache about what Casmir wanted to do, because she'd thought he wished to keep it a secret. So what was he alluding to now? Something new?

The engines started up again, the faint reverberation emanating from the deck under their feet. Kim willed Rache to accept that his ship was on the mend and that nothing irrevocable had been done. If he killed Tristan in front of her… Casmir was right. It wasn't in the heat of battle now. It wasn't self-defense. It would be murder. Again.

A part of her wanted to stalk out so she couldn't see it if he did it. But a bigger part of her hoped he wouldn't do it if she was there.

Rache growled, this time in frustration, then shoved Tristan away from him. He might have crashed into Casmir, but Zee stepped out and caught him. Tristan bent forward, inhaling deeply.

"I don't know if you've figured this out yet, Dabrowski," Rache said, "but I highly doubt you and I are after the same thing on that base. That I'm giving you a ride there is ludicrous."

Rache looked at Kim one more time, but the only additional words he spoke were for his engineers, ordering them to send him a full report on the damage and the repair estimates. Then he was gone, leaving the two men with rifles still pointing them loosely at Tristan.

"Do you want to lock him up with me in my cabin?" Casmir offered them when they exchanged uncertain looks with each other.

The word *lock* seemed to appeal to them. They nodded.

Kim walked with Casmir and Tristan to the lift as the guards marched them at gunpoint, though thanks to the way the crushers arranged themselves, the weapons pointed at them rather than Casmir or Kim. She didn't see Rache again. It appeared that date night was over.

CHAPTER 24

CASMIR SAT ON HIS BUNK WITH HIS HANDS clasped between his knees, listening as Tristan decanted the story from his point of view. And wincing at the knowledge that it was his fault that the poor guy was here. Kim, who'd also joined them in the cabin, sat with her face in her hand as he spoke.

"I knew almost right away that it was a mistake," Tristan said, "or at least… ill-advised, given my lack of armor and weapons, but when I saw those men marching you at gunpoint to their ship, I reacted. I knew I'd barely have enough time to slip out there, and it was only because of the smoke that I was able to sneak aboard. I thought I could bide my time and find a way to rescue you. But as soon as Nalini told me—" he waved at his chip, "—that it was Rache's people, I knew I was in over my head. I figured I wasn't going to make it back to the station alive and that I should at least try to lead others to take down his ship. Maybe if the whole fleet came, they could rescue you."

Tristan, seated on one of the uncomfortable stools, looked back and forth from Casmir to Kim and then to Zee and the other three crushers that had joined them inside. The rest of the crushers, after some arguing and frustrated comm calls from the two mercenaries who'd escorted them up here, had been ordered into Kim's cabin. They hadn't *gone* into it until Casmir had asked them to please wait inside.

"*Are* you prisoners?" Tristan asked uncertainly. "It seemed so obvious when I made my snap decision, but upon reflection, I wondered how the men—*Rache's mercenaries*—" he said the latter with such distaste that Casmir wondered how he'd kept his tongue civil enough to avoid having his neck snapped down there, "—could have taken them all against your wishes."

"Well," Casmir said lightly, "if we weren't prisoners before, I think we are now."

Kim shook her head ruefully.

Casmir doubted Rache would be mad with *her* over this, but he feared he would be blamed. Would Rache still rendezvous with the *Dragon*? Casmir had sent Bonita coordinates and promised that Rache would give some signal so that she could find his ship. Now, he feared Rache would space him—and Tristan.

"Do you want to explain the rest to him or should I?" Casmir asked her. "It seems we owe him that much after he risked his life to try to rescue us."

"It was your scheme. You can explain it."

He bowed to her from his seated position. "You're kind, as always."

Casmir gave Tristan the story, emphasizing Kim's desire to avoid building bioweapons and Jorg's insistence that she do so, but he didn't say anything about his own plans, not aloud. Given the night's events, he assumed Rache had someone monitoring their cabin.

"I wish I'd known," Tristan said. "Jorg is an utter ass. He's the reason my career is over. I would have helped hide you on the station, so you wouldn't have had to join *him*." Tristan pointed in the direction of the bridge, but there was no doubt who *him* was.

"I couldn't stay on the station," Kim said. "It's possible Dubashi already *has* a bioweapon. If so, someone needs to find it and make sure it can't be used against the Kingdom." Her expression was bleak as she touched her own chest.

"Rache agreed to take you to the base?" Tristan started to rub his bruised neck but must have decided it hurt too much, for he turned it into a tender probe. "And help the Kingdom?"

"He was going there anyway." Kim opened her mouth, as if she would say more, but hesitated.

"To sign on with Dubashi *against* the Kingdom, I believe." Casmir looked at her. "Unless he's changed his mind. I don't suppose he told you anything different? Or that, due to his undying ardor for you, he's agreed to stop being villainous?"

The strong, agile, and athletic Tristan… fell off his stool.

Casmir gaped at him. Tristan scrambled to his feet and sat down again before Casmir could reach over to help.

"Was that a joke?" Tristan asked in bewilderment.

"Sort of," Casmir said, as Kim firmly said, "*Yes*."

"You were gone for three hours with him, and there was no ardor?" Casmir raised his eyebrows. "Are you sure? Maybe you're not that familiar with ardor since you always eschew it."

"Can you be serious?" Kim asked.

"I wasn't being entirely *un*serious. Men change for women. It happens all the time in literature."

"Not in the literature he reads."

"A lack of romances on his shelves, I take it?"

"War and revenge novels."

"Typical. Maybe you should get him a copy of *The Masked Spaceflyer*."

"Because that's… a romance?"

"Oh, one of the best. And it has a hero with a mask. If you don't buy it for him, I will. I know he loves my gifts."

Tristan touched his throat again. "I find this conversation disturbing."

"You probably should have stayed stuffed in that locker on the shuttle," Casmir said. "Safer for your sanity."

"I believe you."

Casmir smiled, held his gaze, and tapped his own temple. He hoped that Tristan would take the hint and bring his chip online so they could message each other without anyone overhearing.

"I guess we'll have to wait and see if he's still willing to transfer me—and all of my friends here—over to Bonita's ship," Casmir said to Kim.

Tristan gave him a single nod. Casmir sent a request for permission to contact him.

"I'm skeptical that he wants to help you on your quest," Kim said, "but I'd be shocked if he didn't want to get rid of you and your posse. The question is whether it'll be onto Bonita's ship or out into space to die."

"I'm hoping we've bonded enough that he no longer wishes to kill me," Casmir said.

The noise that Kim made in the back of her throat wasn't reassuring.

Tristan, Casmir messaged, *you know I agreed to try to kidnap Dubashi and bring him back to the sultan, right? Will you help me?*

Yes. I owe the sultan much. Also, Dubashi tried to kidnap Nalini. I would do almost anything to ensure he's no longer a threat to that family.

Good. Thank you. I have a plan. I'm just thinking about how I can make it work without getting Bonita or the Dragon *in trouble. Do you think Dubashi has any idea who you are?*

I met his son in person and thwarted his kidnapping attempt, so probably.

Oh? Damn. Casmir drummed his fingers on his thigh. Maybe he wouldn't be able to make use of Tristan, after all. *Dubashi has a bounty on my head. Don't ask why. It's an even longer story than the last one. A while back, I was thinking of asking Rache to pretend to bring me to Dubashi's meeting to turn me in, but that wouldn't work if Dubashi already knows we have a relationship. Also, it turns out that Dubashi wants Kim now, too, so I bet Rache plans to pretend to turn her in.*

Should my head be hurting?

Probably. You weren't getting much oxygen to it for a while. When you showed up, I thought you, as some unknown ex-knight who could perhaps be believed to have turned to the bounty-hunting life, could pretend to turn me in. But we'd still need another ship. I'm afraid of going in on the Stellar Dragon *because it could get Bonita in trouble, and it's also likely there are records of me flying here and there on it by now. Dubashi might assume that we're allies instead of enemies.*

I'm not sure I fully understand your schemes, but I'll help you any way I can. Especially since I don't think I'd be alive now if you and Kim hadn't intervened.

Casmir thanked him and didn't point out that his life had only been in danger because he'd tried to help *them*.

Another message came in, Bonita asking if he was still alive, and he answered it eagerly.

Captain Laser, I've missed you!

There was a long pause before her response came. *Uh, El Mago. Viggo has missed you.*

Only Viggo? Disappointing. Perhaps his enthusiasm had been too much.

We heard from Rache, Bonita messaged. *He said the Kingdom Fleet is on his ass, and he doesn't have time to stop to rendezvous with us. To be honest, I'm relieved. I've been sweating since you sent that plan to me yesterday. Do you know I've got Asger* and *Bjarke on board? Bjarke would fling himself at Rache with his oversized axe if he caught sight of him, and my ship isn't so big that guests won't notice that we've docked with another ship.*

Ah.

Casmir bit his lip, disappointed that Rache had changed his mind. Was it truly because of the fleet and Tristan's stunt? Or had he simply decided not to let Casmir go and possibly get in the way of his plans?

What if I can get a ship and come to you? Casmir asked, mentally adjusting his plan. *A shuttle.*

Could he talk Rache into lending him that one with the lack of identifying marks? Did it have enough fuel to get to the moon base from… wherever they were now? He would have to find out. And convince Rache that it was a good idea. Not daunting at all…

That would be fine, Bonita replied, *if Rache doesn't come with it.*

I was thinking of myself, my crusher army, and Tristan. Do tell Asger we've found him, will you? If Tristan hasn't already gotten in touch with him.

I'll tell him. Asger will be glad he's alive. You do know things would be simpler if you'd arranged a ride on my ship to start with.

Tell me about it. I had no idea you'd end up going to Dubashi's base.

Nor did I. I'm hoping nobody looks too closely at us and notices we're a freighter instead of a warship.

You say Bjarke is with you? A new idea percolated into Casmir's mind. *What was his background story again? He was working undercover as a pirate?*

Yes, a pirate accountant for the Druckers in System Cerberus. He was supposedly reporting in to your Knight Headquarters on the goings on in that system. Hey, Casmir, answer something for me, will you?

Always.

If you have knights all over the systems spying on people, how did the Kingdom get caught with its pants down when those ships popped into System Lion to blockade your wormhole gate?

I've wondered that myself. Do you think someone like Dubashi would know anything about Bjarke's secret-agent status?

I can ask him, but I don't know why they would have crossed paths before.

I believe I've figured out my new plan. I just need—

The door opened, but the four crushers swarmed it before Casmir could see who was trying to come in.

"And here I thought *one* was annoying," Rache growled. "Let me in, Dabrowski."

Casmir exchanged a look with Kim, wondering if they should be worried or glad that Rache had come to see them.

"Step aside, please, Zee and other Zees."

Tristan had no weapons, but he stood with his fists ready as the crushers moved to let Rache in.

Rache barely glanced at him, instead focusing on Casmir.

"I got a message from Dubashi," he said. "The meeting has been moved up, thanks to Jorg heading to his base. Dubashi said he wanted to get contracts hammered out before the Kingdom ships arrived, presumably so he has a bunch of mercenaries willing to fight them."

"Will *you* fight them?" Kim asked quietly.

"Do you really need to ask that?" Rache asked, equally quietly.

"I suppose not."

"So I came to tell you," Rache said, switching back to Casmir, "that there's no time for your rendezvous with that freighter. You'll have to come along."

"Are you inviting me to the meeting?"

"No, I'm inviting you to stay locked in this cabin and out of trouble while I go to the meeting." Rache eyed the crushers.

"Can I posit an alternative?"

"What now?" Rache asked in exasperation. "I'm already sparing your saboteur's life." He flung a hand toward Tristan.

"Are you? You've just said you'll fly into war with us locked in here. What if you lose? We could all die."

"I'll weep terribly as my own death finds me."

"Or—" Casmir waved his hand with a flourish toward the rear of the ship and the *Dragon* trailing behind, "—you could let me, Tristan, and all the crushers borrow one of your shuttles—that one that has been painted to look anonymous, perhaps—and we'll get out of your hair completely. Doesn't that sound delightful?"

"You out of my hair? Yes."

"I'm noting the complete lack of hesitation. Does that mean you agree to the loan?"

"Why would I give you a shuttle?"

"To get us all out of your hair. Kim, too, if she wishes. It sounds like you're not sufficiently displaying your ardor to her."

"I didn't say that." She frowned at him.

Casmir lifted an apologetic hand. He shouldn't interfere with—or make fun of—their relationship, even if its existence distressed him.

"I could accomplish that by punting you out the airlock," Rache said.

"I believe you'd find that difficult." Casmir waved at Zee, who loomed next to Rache's shoulder. "I'm sure you would rather focus on your upcoming meeting and battle with the Kingdom than deal with my squad of crushers."

Rache fell silent, and with the mask on, Casmir couldn't tell if he was glaring at him or closing his eyes in meditative contemplation.

"What are you going to *do* with my shuttle?"

"Use it to get to the *Dragon*."

"That's it?"

"Yes." Casmir's left eye blinked. "At first," he amended. "And then I'll take it to the base so Bonita doesn't have to get close and endanger her ship."

"And remind me what you're doing on Dubashi's base," Rache said flatly.

"An errand for Shayban." Casmir smiled. That one was the truth.

Rache stared at him for a long silent moment, and then he looked at Kim for just as long of a moment. To see if she would nod or plead on Casmir's behalf? She merely gazed back, her expression neutral.

"Who would *fly* it?" Rache looked at his misaligned left eye, though he probably also knew Casmir didn't have piloting experience.

"It has an automatic system, doesn't it?" Casmir snapped his fingers. "Oh, and I can have Zee download the necessary software in case there's a hiccup."

Rache dropped his chin to his chest and shook his head slowly.

"Do you promise not to puke in it?" he asked.

"Why does everybody ask me that before lending me equipment?" Casmir asked Kim. It wasn't as if he could roll down a window and stick his head outside if he got sick.

"Because they've traveled with you," Kim said.

"Hm." Casmir extended his palm toward Rache. "I don't know how long it will last, but I haven't been experiencing much motion sickness since taking your potion. If that changes, I promise to clean any messes I make."

Rache turned toward Kim. "Will you go with him? Or stay?"

"Stay," she said quietly and without hesitation.

Casmir kept himself from shaking his head. As he'd pointed out, he wasn't here to be her chaperone, and she could take care of herself. And if he was honest with himself, he doubted Rache would let anything bad happen to her, if it was at all in his power to keep her safe.

That didn't keep him from messaging her. *Can I leave a couple of the crushers to act as bodyguards for you? If you're going onto the station, you'll need help.*

Kim eyed Zee a little dubiously, and then considered Rache. *No. I'll be fine. Thank you.*

He thought that might be a mistake, but she'd never warmed up to the crushers as much as Casmir had, so he didn't push it.

"Pack up, Casmir." Rache headed for the door. "I'll have the shuttle prepped."

Qin stood in the cargo hold, her boots locked to the deck, as the *Dragon* extended its airlock tube to link with the shuttle Casmir and Tristan had borrowed, stolen, or begged from Rache. She hadn't gotten the full details and wasn't yet sure.

Even though they were supposed to be getting Casmir, Tristan, the crushers, and nothing more, she wore her full combat armor and carried three weapons. Just in case this was a trap. She didn't know why it would be, but she still didn't trust Rache.

Boots rang on the rungs in the ladder well in the corridor on the other side of the hold, and Qin inhaled, catching Asger's warm, pleasant scent along with the tang of blade-cleaning oil. He was also armored, with his pertundo in hand, as he walked across the hold.

"Expecting trouble?" He nodded to her weapons.

"When accepting a shuttle that was sent from Rache's ship? Always. You?" She nodded to *his* weapons.

"Always."

He smiled, holding her gaze. "Maybe we'll get to fight together soon."

"Does that mean playing with my pop-up puzzle palaces was too sedate for you?"

He'd come by her cabin the night before, asking if she wanted to play a game of cards or dice. She'd been delighted. Even though he was dour whenever his father was around, he'd been much more open and prone to smiling at her since their talk on the treadmills. Unfortunately, she hadn't *had* any games. Her childhood hadn't involved such things, and all she'd been able to offer was a puzzle book that Bonita had given her as a gift because of the unicorns and dragons in it.

"It was a little sedate. Very unmanly. I felt the need to go polish my pertundo after braiding that unicorn's tail."

"That's one of the best puzzles. You were surprisingly adept at it."

"Surprisingly? I'm athletic, competitive, and determined to win at all costs. That makes me adept at many things."

"And a little haughty."

"You saw how quickly I braided that tail. You can't deny my skills."

She smiled at him. "I like you when you're making jokes."

He raised his eyebrows. She blushed, not sure she should have said that aloud. It had popped out, unedited.

"I guess I've been a little humorless lately."

"Humorless, grumpy, surly, glowery."

"Glowery?"

"Definitely."

"He just makes me crazy." Asger extended the shaft of his pertundo, pressed the butt to the deck, and leaned on it. "For the longest time, I thought it would be nice to spend a few days with him and get to know him now that I'm not a kid anymore. Now I know better."

"I've barely seen you talk at all."

"Exactly. I thought if we had time together, maybe we could do that. Talk. As adults. But he doesn't see me that way. He sees me as a child and a screw-up. He—" Asger shook his head. "Sorry, I told myself I wasn't going to complain about it anymore. I already got drunk and blathered about my feelings to Casmir." He curled a lip.

"I'm a girl. It's okay to blather about feelings to girls."

"Is it?"

"Sure, we like it. Especially from grumpy, surly, glowery men with big weapons."

He gazed thoughtfully at her. Did he think she wasn't being honest? Or that she was teasing him?

She smiled, hoping to convey her sincerity. She hadn't had that many opportunities in her life to be someone's confidante, and she wouldn't mind it, not with Asger.

"I didn't say it before, back when we, uh—" He waved to the spot where they'd been standing when they kissed. "But I really appreciate it that you think I'm a better knight than my father. I can't honestly agree that it's true, but it's nice to have *someone* believe it."

She reached out and rested a hand on his cheek. He grew still at her touch, his gaze holding hers.

"If I say he's a jerk who doesn't deserve such a loyal son, will you kiss me?" She meant it as a joke, but she forgot to smile as she brushed her fingers from his cheeks to his lips.

His eyelids drooped half shut. "Yes. You don't even have to say it."

He stepped closer, but a clank came, and the control panel beeped to announce the airlock tube was fully hooked up.

Qin jumped, dropping her hand.

Asger smiled ruefully.

"Maybe later," he offered as more sounds came from the tube. Casmir's crushers or a pack of Rache's mercenaries striding over?

"Only maybe?"

"Definitely?"

"I hope so."

A knock sounded on the hatch, and Qin forced herself to focus on it. She peered through the little porthole to see the top of Casmir's head and a bunch of crushers lined up behind him. She unlocked the hatch, and they tramped in. Tristan came in at the end of the queue, without armor or weapons, and appearing rumpled and tired.

Several of the ship's robot vacuums appeared out of nowhere and whirred toward Casmir. A few of the crushers stepped forward, as if worried they represented some menace. The vacuums skittered back, somehow sensing the looming threats.

"They're fine, my friends." Casmir patted the air. "They'll clean your toes if you let them."

"Crusher toes are self-cleaning," one of them announced—was that Zee?

Casmir came forward and patted Qin on the shoulder as the vacuums whirred around his legs. "Thanks for meeting us." He gave Asger a similar pat. "I have a plan."

"I'm worried," Asger said.

"Me too," Qin said.

"It involves your father," Casmir told Asger.

"Then I'm *definitely* worried."

"Can someone ask him to come down?"

"I can ask." Qin had last seen Bjarke in navigation with Bonita, so she sent a message to her.

Bonita said they were on their way down.

"You all right, Tristan?" Asger asked. "You look rough."

Qin noticed bruises on Tristan's neck.

"I tried to sabotage Rache's ship," Tristan said. "He didn't appreciate it."

"I'm surprised you're not dead," Asger said.

"I almost was." Tristan touched his neck. "Kim and Casmir showed up and talked him down from, er, murder. I haven't quite figured out why they have that ability to influence him."

"It's more Kim than me," Casmir offered.

"Nonetheless, I feel that rescuing the two of you wasn't needed."

"Just be glad all he said when we left was for me to keep my knights out of his hair."

"*Your* knights?" Asger asked.

"I'm collecting them, you see," Casmir said. "It's handy to have large, muscular, well-trained men around me."

"The crushers aren't sufficient?"

"They're also nice. They have those self-cleaning toes."

"Yes," Zee said with his chin up.

If he'd had feathers, he would have preened. Qin was sure of it.

"How did you get one of Rache's shuttles?" Qin asked. "It *is* one of his, isn't it? When Bonita checked, it didn't have identifiable markings, and its ident was registered to System Cerberus."

"It is," Casmir said. "He gave it to me because I promised not to throw up in it."

"Is that generally enough to prompt people to give you expensive things?" Asger asked.

"No. It's a long story." Casmir brightened when Bonita and Bjarke walked into the bay. "Just who I need to see."

"Casmir," came Viggo's voice from a speaker. "I thought you were here to see me."

"Naturally, and I'll be happy to fix or upgrade any of your parts while I'm here. But it's Sir Bjarke Asger—technically Johnny Twelve Toes—who can help me with my plan."

Bjarke eyed him dubiously. Qin didn't think they'd spent much time together.

"What can Johnny do to help?" Bjarke asked. "And what's your plan?" He looked toward the airlock hatch. "Is Scholar Sato in the shuttle?"

"No. She stayed with—uhm, Rache kept her."

"Damn it." Bjarke clenched a fist. "I'm ready to ram my pertundo into that bastard's chest."

"Would you settle for kidnapping Dubashi, stopping a war, and returning peace to the Kingdom?" Casmir asked.

Bjarke squinted at him. "You're a civilian advisor, who, last I heard, was assigned to manufacture robots on Stardust Station. I'm positive you haven't been given orders to do any of those things."

"No, but don't you think Prince Jorg will be appreciative if we accomplish them?" Casmir smiled charmingly. A robot vacuum whirred between his legs.

"*We?*" Bjarke turned his suspicious squint briefly toward Qin and Bonita, but he let it settle longest on Asger.

Asger lifted his hands.

Qin doubted he knew anything more about this than she did. She wanted to step forward, growl, and protect him from Bjarke's unfair glare, or at least clasp his hand in support, but Casmir drew Bjarke's attention back first.

"You and I, Sir Knight." Casmir pointed to Bjarke's chest, then his own. "Dubashi has had a bounty on my head for weeks now. I want to be bundled up and delivered to him—with my twelve crushers here. If he's waiting to greet us in his shuttle bay, the crushers can snatch him up. If he's not, once I'm in his base, I'm hoping I can hack into his system and find him. Then we'll snatch him up." Casmir waved toward the shuttle linked to the *Dragon*. "I think I've been seen in Rache's and Bonita's orbits too often for it to be believable that either of them would be bringing me in to collect the bounty, but an opportunistic Drucker pirate might be a plausible captor who would turn me in."

Bjarke stared at him as if he'd hatched robots out of his nostrils. "My orders are to bring Kim Sato to the prince."

The man had a singular mind, didn't he? Qin rolled her eyes.

"Perfect." Casmir's smile broadened. "She'll be there."

"Where? The moon base?"

"With Rache, who's going to the meeting for mercenaries. At the moon base."

"He's taking her in there with him?" Bjarke asked. "Is there a bounty on *her* head too?"

"Actually, there is. It came up on the network recently." Bonita waved toward navigation. "Casmir is wanted dead. Kim is wanted alive and uninjured."

"So Rache is taking her to turn her in and gain favor with Dubashi?" Bjarke curled a lip.

Casmir spread his hands, as if he had no idea. Right.

Asger glanced at Qin, but he didn't say anything. Neither did she. If Bjarke hadn't yet figured out that Kim and Rache's relationship wasn't antagonistic, it wasn't Qin's place to mention it.

"You'll help me find her if I take you there?" Bjarke asked Casmir. He glanced toward the airlock tube. "Is that why you brought that shuttle?"

"So we can go in without endangering Bonita and the *Dragon,* yes." Casmir nodded.

Qin was glad he'd acquired a ship. She worried that their freighter would be too obviously out of place among powerful mercenary warships, and that someone might notice it, shoot it, and try to loot them.

"And I will absolutely try to get back together with Kim while we're there," Casmir said. "She's my best friend."

Bjarke returned his squint to Casmir, then considered the crushers. "You actually did build some. Huh."

"Oh yes. And I believe the complete complement of one hundred that Prince Jorg ordered will be ready by the time we return to Stardust Palace. I automated the manufacturing after doing my first run." Casmir waved at his troops.

Bjarke's lowered brows gradually lifted. "I admit I didn't think you would actually do it. When you sneaked Scholar Sato off the *Osprey* with you, I doubted your loyalties and commitment to the mission."

Casmir touched his chest, his brows raising in an innocent "who, me?" expression.

Again, Qin kept her mouth shut. She wouldn't do anything to get Casmir in trouble, though she'd learned by now that, while his loyalty to his people might not be in doubt, his willingness to strictly obey orders from his king was. But he wasn't a soldier. Why should he have to follow some dubious military chain of command?

"Do you really believe they'll be enough to overcome Dubashi's defenses?" Bjarke waved to the crushers. "He likely has cybernetically enhanced security men and robots of his own."

"The crushers are very effective, sir," Tristan said. "I can attest to that."

"I'm also hoping that Dubashi won't have an entire platoon of troops waiting to meet us," Casmir said. "If we leave promptly, we can arrive about the time that meeting is starting up. He should be distracted."

"Tristan and I can go to help," Asger said.

Tristan nodded. "As long as someone can loan me a galaxy suit and a couple of weapons."

Qin wanted to volunteer to help, too, but she couldn't leave Bonita.

But Casmir shook his head. "I'm sure they won't be so distracted that they won't scan us as we approach. If they see extra men inside, they may believe Johnny Twelve Toes is being dishonest with them."

"Won't they sense the crushers?" Bjarke asked.

"No. They were designed not to give off significant heat or energy signatures."

Bjarke returned to considering Casmir thoughtfully. Still deciding if he trusted him?

"I'll do it," he finally said.

"How are you going to play Toes without your tattoos?" Bonita asked.

"I'll have to hope they don't have pictures of Johnny Twelve Toes in this system. Unless you have a way to apply fake tattoos."

"I have a makeup kit." Bonita's eyes twinkled.

"I have nail paint," Qin added, "and some stuff for stenciling skin."

Bjarke appeared more horrified by these suggestions than anything Casmir had mentioned, but he let Bonita lead him off by the hand.

"What are *we* going to do?" Asger asked Tristan.

"Where is this ship going?" Tristan waved a finger to indicate the *Dragon*. "Back to the station? Did you come out here looking for us?" He shifted his finger to include himself and Casmir.

"Just you, actually," Asger said. "I knew Kim and Casmir were up to something."

"I wish I had."

"Sorry, Tristan," Casmir said. "Had I known you were the type to fling yourself into danger to rescue a near-stranger, I would have tried to warn you not to."

"I was a knight," Tristan said, as if that explained everything.

"Yes, I should have realized." Casmir smiled.

"Bonita was hired to find Scholar Serg Sunflyer," Qin pointed out. "We've been heading this way, in addition to looking for Tristan, believing that Dubashi might have kidnapped him, and he might be in the base."

Casmir scratched his jaw. "If Dubashi had Scholar Sunflyer—or has him now—why would he need Kim?"

"Are you suggesting," Qin said, "Scholar Sunflyer might be dead?"

"Or escaped?" Casmir sounded wishful.

"*We* could go look for him," Tristan said, waving at himself and Asger, "if we can find a way to sneak in with Casmir and Bjarke. I agree that a simple freighter should stay away from the mercenaries."

"This is not a *simple* freighter," Viggo announced. "I am complicated, emotionally sensitive, and have hidden depths."

"And you're a big snoop," Qin said.

"You're standing in the middle of my cargo hold. It's not as if I'm using special spy equipment to listen to your conversation."

"Casmir," Asger said. "If we stowed away in your shuttle, could you make some kind of scanner-scrambling box we could hide in?"

"Uhm." Casmir gazed around the cargo hold, which was mostly empty since they had unloaded their last freight at the station, and then toward engineering. He tapped a rhythm on his thigh as his gaze kept roving, finally coming back and landing on… his crushers? A smile curved his lips. "Zee, you make a fantastic couch."

Qin blinked. What?

"I am a capable chameleon," the crusher said.

"A large hollow box should be a simple matter," Casmir said.

"Extremely simple."

Asger's eyebrows rose. "That's not the scanner-scrambling material I had in mind, Casmir."

"And yet, it could work if he makes the sides thick enough, and I wouldn't have to build anything. The crushers are already designed not to register on scans."

"I don't understand," Tristan said.

Zee melted like candle wax, then expanded and formed into a box as tall as Casmir. The top opened like a regular lid on hinges that appeared identical to the rest of the tarry black material.

Tristan's jaw dropped. Even Asger, who had seen Zee transform before, gaped. Zee opened and closed the lid a couple of times, sealing the seams the last time so that his hollow box was impermeable.

"Oh man," Tristan said, understanding dawning. "I just spent three days stuck in a locker on a shuttle. At least that wasn't airtight."

"How did you go to the bathroom?" Qin asked.

"A couple of times, after the mercenaries got off, I was able to sneak out and use the shuttle's lav. A couple of times… I wasn't."

"Ew."

"And here Rache was worried about me throwing up in there." Casmir patted the Zee-box on the side. "Zee, can you make air holes?"

Zee melted and re-formed into his original bipedal shape. "It is possible a scanner would detect something inside of me if there were holes."

"Bonita has air tanks," Asger said, "and Tristan can borrow a galaxy suit, I'm sure. I'll get your pertundo so you can use it for one more mission."

Tristan had grown ashen at the sight of the box-without-airholes, but he lifted his chin at this last sentence. "My pertundo? I would like to put it to use one more time."

"I assume we won't have to share a box?" Asger asked.

"If Zee can make a box, the others can," Casmir said.

"I will instruct them in the ways of versatility," Zee said.

"We do not need instruction on how to form a box," another said, with a touch of Zee's haughtiness.

"I believe we have a plan," Casmir said.

Asger drew Qin aside as Casmir and Tristan went off, perhaps to hunt for a galaxy suit. "A third crusher could probably make another box if you want to come along."

"I've been considering it. Cats love boxes, you know."

He blinked. "What?"

"I see you didn't have pets growing up."

"Not cats. I had a dog when I was a kid. He mostly *ate* boxes. At least when he was younger. When he got older, he was more likely to lift his leg and, uh, never mind."

"That is one thing I would not suggest doing to a crusher."

"No," Asger agreed. "I think not."

Qin was tempted to ask Bonita if she could go on the mission—if Scholar Sunflyer was inside the base, she could get him herself—but if Bonita and the *Dragon* ran afoul of some of the mercenary ships and got into trouble, Qin wouldn't forgive herself if she wasn't there to help. She remembered that captain Bonita had tricked when they first came into the system. Would those ships be at the meeting?

"I'll stay here," Qin said, then gripped his hands. "But I want you to be careful, so you can come back to me and braid my unicorn's tail again."

He studied her hands, then lifted them and held them to his chest. He glanced around the hold—only the crushers remained, and they were busy turning into practice boxes—then eased closer to her.

"I want you to know how much your support means to me," he said, gazing into her eyes. "You're very special."

As she gazed back into his beautiful blue eyes, her heart captivated, she mumbled something incoherent, momentarily forgetting how to form words. Then, before she lost her courage, she leaned in and kissed him. He smiled against her lips and kissed her back.

Nearby, the lids of box-shaped-crushers thunked as they experimented, but she had no trouble ignoring it.

"Qin," Bonita called sometime later, her voice drifting down the ladder well from above. "I need you to come stencil a pirate."

Asger drew back, his smile crooked. "How much would I have to pay you to paint a penis on his cheek?"

"I don't have one of those in my stencil kit."

"I guess you don't have the erotic collection. Or the anatomical education collection."

"No. There are forest creatures and ponies."

Asger's smile grew wicked. "I'd also pay well to see Johnny Twelve Toes walk into the enemy base with a pony on his cheek."

"I'll see what I can do."

CHAPTER 25

YAS WAS CHECKING THE PROGRESS OF THE MEDICAL nanites and waiting for Jess to wake up when Kim Sato walked hesitantly into sickbay. A guard loomed in the corridor but didn't follow her in, nor was Rache anywhere in sight. Yas didn't know if she was guest or prisoner or some mix of the two, but it seemed nobody was worried she would attack him if left unsupervised. Likely true, but it did make him wonder if Rache had forgotten about her proclivity for kicking his mercenaries.

"Good morning, Dr. Peshlakai," Kim said, her gaze shifting to the prone Jess on one of the sickbay beds.

"So formal. We've mutinied together. I think you can call me Yas."

"I'm not one of his crew, so I didn't mutiny. I attempted to escape while suborning you."

"I'm not sure which scenario is least flattering for me."

"I hope you weren't punished." She gave him a probing frown.

"Not by the captain. The mercenaries were not pleased with me. I've been forced to remind them that it's unwise to threaten a man who may one day be standing over your unconscious body, with access to all manner of deadly drugs."

"Are you allowed to do that? Threaten to kill patients? It seems contrary to the Hippocratic Oath."

"I believe I can threaten them all day long. I can't actually harm them. But *they* don't know that."

"That seems like a loose interpretation," Kim observed.

"All of the modern interpretations are loose ones. The original oath involved swearing to Apollo, Asclepius, Hygieia, and Panacea. That's not as trendy as it once was."

Kim came to stand beside him and look down on Jess. “Is she going to be all right? It’s been a day and a half. I didn’t expect her to still be unconscious.” She grimaced and lowered her voice. “Did Tristan inadvertently do serious damage?”

“Tristan?”

“It’s a long story, but that’s the ex-knight who was stowing away in Rache’s shuttle. I think she surprised him. He only sneaked aboard because he was trying to rescue us.” Kim grimaced and touched her chest. “I’m sorry Chief Khonsari was injured.”

Yas felt pleased on Jess’s behalf that Kim remembered her name. As far as he recalled, they had only met during that unpleasant sojourn on Skadi Moon when Rache had kidnapped Kim, and they’d all been afflicted by the gate’s pseudo radiation.

“I’m less sorry,” Yas said.

Kim blinked a few times. “What?”

“Of course I don’t wish anyone to be injured, but as I mentioned to you on the sub, she’s one of the ones who refuses to come in for exams. And she’s… the one I’ve most wanted to examine. To see if there’s a medical reason for what seems to be lingering physical pain from the cybernetic surgeries she underwent to save her life.”

“So you scanned her while she was out?” Kim guessed.

Yas nodded and waved to his full-body scanner. “She’s not still unconscious from the intruder’s—er, your knight’s—attack. The concussion was relatively simple to fix. The numerous fractures and compressed disks along her spine are what I’ve had nanites working on repairing. Since it was clear the injuries pinched nerves and were painful, I’ve kept her under a light sedative while they work.”

“He damaged her spine?” She frowned again. “Or was it some kind of whiplash from the head trauma?”

“No. Sorry, I wasn’t clear. These fractures have been there for a while. I believe they’re the cause of the ongoing migraines and nerve pain she hinted at.” His fingers curled into a frustrated fist. If only she’d come to him *months* ago. “And I suspect they came about because she was given cybernetic prostheses for the limbs and organs that were too damaged to repair, but someone didn’t think things out fully. Her hand on that side has increased gripping strength, her arm increased lifting capacity, her leg increased pressing capacity.” He mimicked squatting and hefting something. "And as an engineer, she has probably used her extra strength. Often. But not only were her upgrades not symmetrical, since she retains most of her biological body on the other side, but whoever did the surgery didn't think to strengthen her spine or replace the bones with synthetics, so she could more easily support the greater weight she has no doubt been lifting, the greater force she's been applying. Most of the mercenaries with cybernetic upgrades did that, but I'm sure whatever surgeons they went to knew the men were seeking enhanced strength and intended to use it. With Jess, the surgeon was presumably just trying to do enough to save her life."

"Talking about my condition to strangers, Doc?" Jess slurred from the bed. "That's a little rude."

"This is Kim Sato. You remember her, right? She saved our lives. She's not a stranger. She's—"

"The captain's girl, I know. I was just teasing."

Kim's eyebrows flew up at being called the captain's girl. Yas was glad she'd heard that and not some of the more lewd and speculative commentary that he'd caught in the mess hall.

"Still, you could at least rub my feet if you're going to spill all my secrets to *near* strangers."

"Do you *want* your feet rubbed?" Yas would if she did. His fingers twitched in that direction of their own accord.

"Usually. Sometimes, it helps the rest of me hurt less."

"I'm hoping the rest of you will hurt less naturally now. At least until you injure your spine again."

"My spine," Jess mouthed, and then she squinted. "Did you do an *exam*, Doc?"

"Just a full-body scan to assess your injuries. And a blood draw for various tests. A check of your vitals."

"That *sounds* like an exam."

"Does it? Huh."

"Maybe you should pray to those ancient Greek gods now," Kim murmured. "She looks like she's thinking of strangling you."

"The patients on this ship are on the surly side, I've noticed," Yas said.

Jess wrangled the indignation off her face—and did not strangle him. "What about my spine?" She swallowed. "Is it something that'll keep me from working? I don't know… This is the only home I've got anymore, Doc."

Yas lifted his hands. "Your spine is on its way to being fully healed. You should feel better than you have in some time." He didn't mention that she might be able to more easily wean herself off the trylochanix now. One battle at a time. "However, I am going to recommend you see a cybernetic surgeon with an excellent track record, because I think you'll need some spine enhancements to keep from hurting yourself again."

She crinkled her nose. "That sounds invasive."

"It is an invasive surgery, but most of the mercenaries have done it and survived it, if that helps."

"Not really. I've seen those guys eat bullets and pull each other's fingernails out on dares."

"You could try a girdle."

"A what?"

"A girdle designed specifically for back support."

There was that nose crinkle again. As a professional, he shouldn't point out that it was cute.

"I think that would get me teased a lot in engineering," she said.

"Instead, you should hurt yourself and deal with pain all the time."

"It's the mercenary way."

"I hope you're joking."

Jess lifted a hand. "Yes, yes. I'll try to find someone to look at me. Someday."

Kim clasped her hands behind her back. "I know of an excellent cybernetic surgeon in Zamek City who works with implants and prosthetic limbs attached for medical purposes—cybernetic implants and enhancements for athletic or combat purposes are frowned on in the Kingdom, but she's very experienced and good. I also know an excellent physical therapist who specializes in those who've newly received prostheses."

"A girdle *and* a physical therapist. Just get me a cane or a float chair now." Jess flung a dramatic arm over her face.

"Chief Khonsari appreciates your input, Kim," Yas translated. "She's just feeling grumpy and distraught at the idea of needing these therapies since she's only twenty-nine."

Kim didn't seem to know what to make of the comments. "The physical therapist is Casmir's mother. She bakes *hamentaschen* for her clients."

"Hamen-what?" Jess lowered her arm.

"Uhm, kind of a stuffed cookie."

"Cookies sound promising. Especially after all the protein-puck meals I've eaten on this ship."

"They're quite good," Kim offered.

"Too bad there's no way this ship will ever go to the Kingdom." Jess grimaced. "Unless it's to bomb it."

Kim's eyes darkened, but the door opened before she said anything else.

Rache walked in wearing his combat armor, the helmet tucked under his arm. "Chief Khonsari, you're conscious. Good."

"I woke up so the doc can rub my feet, and Kim promised me cookies."

"If you come to Odin," Kim murmured. "Sans bombs."

"*I* wouldn't bomb anyone." Jess laid a hand on her chest.

Rache did not comment on the cookies—or foot rubs—instead turning to Kim. "We'll be there soon. If you're still determined to come over with me…" He might have raised his eyebrows behind his mask.

"I am," Kim said.

"Then prepare anything you want to take with you. I don't know if he'll search you or allow you tools."

"He?" Nobody had given Yas the story of why they'd picked up Kim, though her being the *captain's girl*, at least according to the rumors around the ship, had seemed reason enough.

"Prince Dubashi," Rache said, "is in the market for a bacteriologist."

"Why do I have a feeling nothing good can come from that?" Yas asked.

Kim sighed. "Because it can't."

Oku paced the paths of the tiny garden in the Citadel, longing for her greenhouse back in the capital, and the small laboratory where she worked on her projects. Frustration made her steps fast and agitated.

She'd gone into the king's offices that morning and tried to get an update from Senator Boehm on the war and what was happening with

Jorg—and Casmir—in System Stymphalia, but he and the rest of her father's staff had shooed her out, promising she was safe and didn't need to concern herself with any of this. She'd crossed her arms, attempting to be stern and stubborn, even though it wasn't in her nature, and had refused to leave until someone gave her some information. Boehm had merely walked away, saying he had a meeting. At a loss and with nobody to be stern to, she'd slunk out.

Oku wished Casmir would send her a message and let her know what was happening in System Stymphalia—and with him. But she hadn't heard from him in more than a week. She didn't even know if her message had made it through the blockade on one of the automated courier ships yet.

"You need something to do, Your Highness," Maddie commented as Oku walked past for the twentieth time.

The Citadel was as safe as the castle, but nobody was willing to entertain Oku's suggestion that she didn't need a bodyguard here. Maddie had drawn the short straw that morning.

"I pulled all the weeds in the garden." Oku waved to what had been a tidy pile of discards and what was now a scattered pile surrounding a hole. Chasca was digging for who knew what.

"You need something to do that a robot couldn't do."

"Robots can do a lot." Oku was sure Casmir would agree.

She understood Maddie's point though and was about to ask for suggestions when she spotted Casmir's mother, Irena, walking through the courtyard with an older woman who had also come in on the bus. They paused, and Irena directed her friend to do a few stretches.

The guards were keeping an eye on them but didn't insist that they return to their rooms. It had been two days since any ships had gotten through to the city with bombs. Oku hoped that meant everyone was safe, and they could all go home soon, but it might only signal the calm in the eye of the storm.

She headed toward Irena, not sure what she wanted to ask, but curious if Casmir had sent his mother any messages. Maybe it was because she was stuck here without access to her work, but she found herself missing his chatty updates. However, she was scared of what his response would be to the one her father had recorded, so maybe it was good that she hadn't heard back.

"Good morning, Princess Oku." Irena curtsied.

"Good morning, Mrs. Dabrowski," Oku said.

Irena's friend also offered a greeting, then walked to one of the garden benches to sit down.

"I don't suppose you've heard from Casmir?" Irena asked.

"No. I thought you might have."

"He wrote several times when he was in System Hydra, I believe it was, but I haven't heard anything in a couple of weeks. And it's always hard to tell how he's actually doing when he *does* communicate. He jokes around and uses humor to downplay the seriousness of things instead of telling us what's *really* going on." Irena shook her head. "I remember him coming home from school as a boy with a swollen eye and a bloody nose. In a fit of parental worry and indignation, I demanded to know what happened. He neatly sidestepped the question by saying he'd decided to do an experiment to see if a person's blood pressure affected the rate at which blood flows from a wound."

Oku, not certain if Casmir's parents knew about his run-in with the Great Plague yet, didn't mention it—though this story possibly explained why he'd neglected to tell Oku about it. "Did you ever find out what happened?"

"Yes, but only because another boy's mother commed to force her son into apologizing to Casmir for *tripping* him, as he called it." Irena's eyes narrowed at the memory. "As if you can give yourself a black eye while falling. He didn't even have any scratches on his hands. Oh, well. It's the distant past now, and fortunately, Casmir was never the type to hold a grudge or plot revenge on someone for a wrong. His father isn't either. After such events, Aleksy would always come up with a lecture for Casmir about how forgiveness, not anger, would help him resist *yetzer hara*, and that it would make him a boring target to his tormentors. That may have been true, or it may simply have been that as Casmir got older, he got crafty about finding ways to protect himself."

"He mentioned the robot bodyguard he built." Oku looked up *yetzer hara* on her chip instead of asking for a definition, not wanting to remind Casmir's mother that she wasn't of their faith. She wondered what his parents would think if they found out about her father's… offer. Could she truly call it that? Her father's *manipulation* was more like it.

"Yes." Irena smiled. "He got good at using his humor to deflect attacks too. If you make people laugh, he'd say, they'll forget they want to punch you. He learned to use it like a shield, which helped him, but it can be hard to get a serious answer out of him if he doesn't want to give it. You're never quite sure when he's really hurting inside."

Oku looked down at her feet. She knew about shields. She'd learned to make them herself, not to keep people from hurting her but to keep them from realizing she existed at all. It had seemed the safest way to avoid being used or drawn into political quarrels, but after so many years of that, she feared she'd hidden herself so well that she'd given up all the power and influence inherent in her position. Nobody consulted her, confided in her, or kept her in the loop, and it was frustrating now that so much was going on.

"I hope he's not hurting, wherever he is," Oku said when she noticed the pensive expression on Irena's face. "I've been trying to get updates about what's going on in System Stymphalia, but I'm not…" She bit her lip, hesitant to admit how powerless she was. But would Irena judge her? Wasn't she in the same position? "I don't have a lot of power in my father's court. It's been hard to realize I don't know how to change that. I've tried to, ahem, assert myself, but it didn't go well."

She had influence among other academics, but that did her no good here.

"Assert yourself?" Irena raised her eyebrows.

"Yes. Sternly. With one of the senators."

"If my years of marriage and treating male clients have taught me anything, it's that they're more likely to respond to empathy than sternness, at least from women."

"I'm not sure how to empathize with Senator Boehm."

"Is that the frazzled man with the gray hair that stalks the corridors, talking about how he's too old for all of this?"

"Mm, possibly." Oku thought that described *most* of the senators.

"The secrets one will withhold from enemies one will give in confidence to a friend," Irena said, sounding like she was quoting something.

"I'm not an enemy."

Irena's eyebrows drifted upward again.

"They may consider me a pest," Oku admitted. At least this week. "You think if I try to… make friends with some of the senators or maybe people in Royal Intelligence, they'd be more likely to talk to me?" She supposed that was obvious; she just didn't know *how* to make friends with people thirty and more years older than she and with no interest in science. She'd always found it much easier to connect with academics than her father's political peers, people who always had some agenda and who it seemed safest to avoid. "I don't have a lot in common with them."

"You're human, and we're in the middle of a war." Irena spread a hand. "That's enough."

Oku was about to say she would keep the advice in mind when Senator Boehm walked out the front door, heading for a vehicle in the parking lot. He *did* look frazzled. Maybe he would appreciate someone to rant to…

"Excuse me, Irena."

"Of course," Irena murmured.

With new determination, Oku headed over to intercept Boehm. No, not to intercept him. To walk at his side.

CHAPTER 26

KIM CLASPED HER HANDS BETWEEN HER KNEES AS Rache's shuttle whipped into one of several tunnels in the moon base, heading toward the coordinates they'd been given. He was sitting next to her in one of the banks of pods, but they had barely spoken since launching from the *Fedallah* a half hour earlier. Eight of his armored mercenaries filled nearby seats, in addition to the pilot up front.

As far as Kim knew, Rache had been invited in by Dubashi himself. That wasn't keeping him from going in without backup.

Kim wished *she* had backup. The plan was for Rache to drop her off with Dubashi's people, collect his reward, and head to the meeting while she… figured out the rest for herself. He'd asked if that was truly what she wanted or if he should look the other way and let her sneak out of the shuttle while he attended the meeting.

As much as she would prefer to stay hidden, she doubted she would be able to gain access to the rest of the base without Casmir there to hack into networks and open locked doors. She'd end up stuck in the shuttle bay. By letting Rache turn her in, she ought to be taken directly to the medical laboratories and briefed on what Dubashi wanted done. At which point she could find out what had *already* been done. She just hoped her homemade knockout grenades would prove sufficient when the time came to escape.

Fortunately, Casmir, Bjarke, Asger, and Tristan were also on their way to the base—she'd checked in with Casmir during the ride over—so she ought to be able to hook up with them eventually. But she had no idea if they would be directed to the same docking area or would be anywhere near her in what was doubtless a giant subterranean complex.

Kim glanced at Rache—he wore his armor but hadn't donned his helmet—tempted to ask if he would come back to check on her after the meeting. But she'd been hesitant to address him since the incident with Tristan.

It was her fault that Tristan had been there to injure Jess and damage the *Fedallah*, and Rache certainly knew that. He'd radiated tension since then, somehow palpable even with the mask hiding his features, and it made her regret causing the change. She missed the comfortable evening they'd spent reading and drawing and chatting in his quarters. He hadn't snapped at her, or voiced any blame, but she wasn't sure how to interpret this new edge.

Casmir was never like that. She couldn't remember many times in the years she'd known him that he'd lost his temper or even displayed real anger. Frustration, occasionally, but if he hit his thumb with a hammer, he would apologize to the hammer for using it inappropriately instead of slamming it down on something.

It wasn't fair to compare Rache to Casmir and vice versa, but it was hard to resist the temptation. Scientific studies on twins often yielded interesting results, so maybe it was natural for her mind to make comparisons. She wondered if Rache would let her test his neurotransmitter levels and compare them to Casmir's. Not that Casmir could be considered a baseline for normal.

Rache glanced at her and sent a chip-to-chip message. *Are you admiring my handsome profile or having pensive inner thoughts while looking vaguely in my direction?*

She blushed, realizing she had been looking at him while thinking. *Your mask blurs your profile. I was wondering if you would let me test your neurotransmitter levels.*

He tilted his head as if he were scrutinizing some strange new life form. Kim blushed harder. She'd just requested to turn him into a science experiment.

Do they seem that unbalanced? His customary dryness came through with the words.

No. They're fine. Kim clasped her armrests and faced forward. *And your profile is handsome even when it's blurry.*

Thank you. I think.

She decided against asking for help. It wasn't his job to keep her out of trouble. She would find a way out on her own. Besides, she didn't want to ask Rache for any more favors, not when this last one had almost turned disastrous.

Her insides tightened into a knot as she imagined what would have happened if Rache had killed Tristan. Could she have forgiven him for that? Could she forgive him for all he'd done and all that he might do? She knew the answer, from a moral and law-abiding point of view, should be a resounding no, and yet… he'd helped her more than once. And he'd helped others on her behalf. And he liked her books and wanted to start a publishing company for her.

She leaned her elbow on her armrest, dropped her face in her palm, and wondered if her life would ever return to normal. And, if it did, would she be disappointed by the absence of a criminal mercenary captain in it? Why couldn't he just be some attentive scholar she'd run into back in the capital? Having a relationship with him would have been a far simpler matter then. But would she have been attracted to such a man? Or was some rebellious part of her soul attracted to the villain? No, she didn't think that was it. She'd had no trouble turning away jerks in the past. The problem was that he was a villain, but he wasn't a jerk.

"I don't know," Rache murmured, "if that forlorn position means you want a hug, you want a neck rub, or you're mourning what can only be the execrable state of my neurotransmitters, and you'd be horrified if I touched you at all."

She didn't know either. None of them quite fit. "I'm more of an essay than a multiple choice kind of person."

"Complicated."

"I know."

"Do you give partial credit for earnest effort even if the answer isn't right?"

Kim started to nod and say that she appreciated his concern, but the craft slowed for some checkpoint, or maybe for a forcefield to be lowered, and he leaned into the aisle, shifting his attention toward navigation. She couldn't see the forward display over the high seat back in front of her.

"Almost there, sir," the pilot called back. "They're letting us in."

"Good," Rache replied. "Land wherever they tell us. We're all allies here."

One of his officers looked over at Rache, glanced at Kim, then looked back to him. "*Are* we allies, sir?"

"Our meeting with the prince will determine that," Rache said.

"We must have passed nearly a hundred warships on the way in. Looks like he's hiring the whole galaxy."

"Yes," Rache said.

"You may get your wish, sir. An end to the Kingdom."

"Yes," Rache said more softly.

An end to *Jager* was what Kim thought he wanted. But to create that end, would he partake in an invasion force that would kill millions? And what if, after all that, Jager got away?

The thought made her want to cry.

Don't do it, she thought silently. It wasn't until he looked at her that she realized she'd sent the message, not just thought it. She wouldn't take it back. *If you must kill Jager, then so be it. But don't help destroy a world.*

Would you forgive me if I killed him?

A faint clunk reverberated through the shuttle as it settled onto a landing pad, but Rache's masked face didn't turn away from her. She sensed his intentness as he waited for a response.

I don't know. Kim knew what Jager had done to him, at least his side of the story, and Jager had thrown Casmir in the dungeon and was a threat to him—to both of them—but her entire body chilled at the idea of condoning murder. Or at looking the other way while it was done. But she would accept it over genocide. *I do know that I wouldn't forgive you if you helped kill my family and my colleagues, and Casmir's family and his colleagues, and everyone we know in Zamek City and on Odin.*

I'll keep that in mind.

It sounded like the kind of thing one said when one didn't plan to comply but didn't want an argument. She didn't try to keep the bleakness off her face.

Rache unfastened his harness and stood, joining his men in the rear as they selected weapons from racks. Kim had her galaxy suit, her case of laboratory supplies, and a stunner that he'd given her. She assumed someone would take it as soon as she left the shuttle, but for now, she made sure it was at the bottom of the case, just above the innocuous-looking tins from the mycology lab.

She found Rache waiting for her in the back. The side hatch was already open, and she glimpsed his men fanning out defensively on a rough stone floor. It didn't look like anyone was there to meet them yet.

"Rache?" Kim asked, then lowered her voice to correct herself. "David?"

"Yes?" he replied equally quietly.

"I didn't get a chance to…" She hesitated when one of the men glanced back inside, no doubt waiting for his boss to join them. "Can we have a second before we go out?"

He drew her into the airlock, held a finger up to the senior-ranking man outside, and closed the exterior hatch. The pilot was still in navigation up front, but he wouldn't see them unless he came back. He wouldn't see them at all if Rache closed the inner hatch, as he once had so they could have a private moment, but she wouldn't ask for that. They probably only had a few seconds until Dubashi's people arrived.

"Before we go out and part ways," she said, "I want to thank you for coming to get me. And for not killing your stowaway. And for giving Casmir that shuttle."

"I *lent* him that shuttle. He better not get it destroyed. *Or* puke in it."

"Yes, thank you for lending it to him." She debated whether she'd said enough for the situation. For some reason, it was always hard for her to express gratitude. Maybe because she didn't like needing help—it always seemed a weakness—and thanking someone was admitting it, in a way. "And thank you for wanting to start a publishing company for me."

"That latter being the most important?" He sounded amused. Good.

"It's up there." Kim smiled and rested her hands on his shoulders. With his armor on, there was nothing but the hard carapace to feel, and she was disappointed—she should have done this when they'd been in her cabin together, and he hadn't been wearing armor. And he'd been hugging her and stroking her hair. But she'd been too busy being conflicted then. That hadn't changed much, but she had this uncomfortable sense that they were picking different sides and she might not see him again. She didn't want to walk away without…

She lifted her hand to touch his face through his mask and was about to ask if she could push it up, but he must have sensed that was what she wanted, because he did so, but he seemed a little puzzled. Because he couldn't read her intent? Or because he could and thought it was the wrong time?

"I'm sorry," she said. "I'm not very experienced at this."

"Thanking people?"

"No."

She leaned forward slowly and saw the understanding in his eyes a moment before she kissed him. She feared it was a horrible kiss, because all she could think about was that she wanted him to like it and not regret that she was so complicated, so much work. What sane man would want a relationship with a woman who was so inept—incapable?—of returning affection?

He lifted a hand to the side of her face, then stroked it through her hair, fingers brushing deep enough to tease her scalp. *That* felt a lot better than the tongue contact. It was even relaxing, and she stopped worrying so much about doing the right thing with her mouth. She found herself tempted to touch his head and slide her fingers through the soft coolness of his hair.

Someone rapped on the hatch.

She flinched away, like she'd been caught doing something inappropriate. He was much slower pulling his hand away, and he brushed her cheek with his knuckles before pulling down his mask, donning his helmet, and grabbing his rifle.

"Thank you. It was good." He gently gripped her hand. It occurred to her that they'd never done that, never held hands. It would be weird to walk out like that when she was supposed to be his prisoner. Too bad. "I wish you'd done it a week ago," he added, "so we could have practiced some more along the way."

"I thought you were mad most of the trip."

"Not with you."

"Just with Casmir and Tristan?"

"Yes, but I don't want to kiss them, so I assumed that was acceptable."

Rache sighed and released her hand, then opened the hatch.

Kim braced herself as the bright white light of a hangar carved out of moon rock flooded the airlock. Rache put a hand on her back to guide her out, like a captor asserting his presence and guiding her, she supposed, but it felt more like a friend's touch. A lover's touch? Since he was in full armor, she doubted a stranger would make that assumption.

"That's her," a male voice said. "Excellent."

Kim identified the speaker, a lean sharp-nosed man with black eyes that seemed ancient, though his body appeared to belong to someone who, had he been from the Kingdom with no access to anti-aging therapies, would have been about sixty.

A lean woman in a black military uniform stood next to him, her gray hair pulled back in a severe bun. A dozen black-and-silver bipedal robots with anti-tank guns like Qin's were fanned out around the two people, their weapons aimed at Rache's mercenaries, who were also fanned out, though their weapons were pointed at the speaker. He—Prince Dubashi?—appeared indifferent. If he was armored, it wasn't obvious, but he might have something under the loose brocade sherwani and gold pants he wore.

"Scholar Sato," Rache agreed.

"Scholar Sato." Dubashi bowed to her. "I am Prince Dubashi, and this is General Kalb." He waved for his officer to take her case.

Kim wanted to fight that but knew it would only tip them off that she had weapons inside. She hoped they would bring it along wherever they took her.

"I have some work that I need you to finish composing for me, ma'am," Dubashi said.

"I usually get paid to do work," Kim said. "Established professionals in the field don't expect to be kidnapped."

"No? Surely rank amateurs have no appeal. You should be honored."

"No."

"Unfortunate, but I must insist that you work for me. Only for a short time, until the completion of a project, and then I will release you." Even though he'd bowed politely, his eyes were hard, like chips of obsidian.

"What happened to Scholar Serg Sunflyer?" Kim asked, more to find out if he'd been here than because she was certain of it.

Kalb opened her case and searched it, quickly removing the stunner and pocketing it.

"You can attempt to ask him if you wish. Come." Dubashi gestured toward an exit framed by columns complete with a carved architrave and friezes. The decorative accents made the hangar feel more like an ancient temple than a modern space installation.

"I'll insist on payment before relinquishing her," Rache said.

"Do you not believe I'm good for it?" Dubashi chuckled without humor.

Kalb closed the case and handed it to one of the robots to carry.

"Only a foolish mercenary accepts a new mission before being paid for the old," Rache said.

"You'll be paid, Rache. And I'll offer you the mission I believe you've been waiting a long time for."

Rache didn't react.

Kim licked her lips. Was Dubashi hinting at Jager's assassination? Did he know Rache that well?

Dubashi headed for the exit with Kalb and two of his robots trailing behind. They were of a similar size to Zee, but they had hard angles and lacked his liquid movements. They appeared heavy, sturdy, and formidable. Kim wouldn't want to try to side kick one.

Rache, his hand still on Kim's back, walked after Dubashi. She barely felt his touch through her galaxy suit, but she didn't mind his closeness, not here. If they ended up fighting, she wanted him at her side. She was less certain about the mercenaries who tramped after them, but at least they were obstacles between her and the remainder of Dubashi's robots—they followed Rache's group, hemming them in.

As they walked, Dubashi's back occasionally visible between the robots, it sank in that this was the man who'd started a war with her people, had ordered the bombing of Odin, and had almost gotten Casmir killed with that bounty. If she found the opportunity to stick a dagger—or the scissors she had in her kit—between his shoulder blades, shouldn't she take it?

Kim noted the hypocrisy of judging Rache for wanting to kill Jager when she was contemplating murder. But she feared she would regret it if the chance came up and she didn't take it. If she could, by putting a stain on her soul, save millions of people, wouldn't it be worth it?

But would killing Dubashi truly end the threat to the Kingdom? Or did Dubashi have a dozen family members or other underlings ready to step in and carry on? For that matter, what if he'd already uploaded his consciousness into an android body in preparation for his eventual death?

They wound through the gilded corridors, up several levels in a lift tube that pushed their platform aloft on a burst of air, and into a part of the base that had the familiar antiseptic smell of a hospital. Dubashi's walk had a slightly mechanical precision of gait to it, and she wondered how human he was. Perhaps scissors to the back would do nothing but reveal circuits or implants.

Dubashi stopped at a door and leaned into a control panel for a retina scan. After a few seconds, a soft click sounded, and a very thick door slid slowly into the even thicker wall.

Kim grimaced at the security measure. Whatever was designed to keep people out could as easily keep her in.

"Only Scholar Sato and Rache will come in with me," Dubashi stated.

His robots maneuvered to protect the entrance from anyone thinking of springing inside.

"Sir?" one of Rache's men asked.

"Wait here," Rache said, then guided Kim inside.

Two of the robots detached from the group to follow Dubashi and Kalb.

Kim started to compose a message to Casmir to let him know where in the base she was, but a jolt of alarm zapped her as she realized there wasn't a network signal. Not a single one. She would have expected numerous networks on a base of this size, even if they were all secured, and also access to the system-wide public network. Maybe they were too deep in the moon for that, but what about the rest?

Her mouth went dry as they walked into a modern, brightly lit room with sleek black marble floors. To the sides were several biolabs, complete with airlocks, showers, vacuum rooms, and ultraviolet rooms to ensure nothing that the researchers worked on inside would escape out. Powerful ventilation rumbled, pulling out and filtering the air even in this outer room.

Dread settled into Kim's gut like bricks before Dubashi said a word. He wouldn't need this degree of safety precautions if his people weren't working with seriously deadly agents.

Dubashi only said a couple of words about the labs, then led them to the back to show them a number of rockets in complex racks. Or was that a track for moving them through some hidden passage for loading?

Kim swallowed. Everything she had feared she would find was here.

"The delivery mechanisms." Dubashi waved a hand at the rockets, then pointed to the closest of the sealed biolabs, the inside visible beyond a thick Glasnax wall. "The virologic weapon that Scholar Serg Sunflyer started working on but wasn't quite able to complete is in there."

"What stopped him?" Rache asked in a flat disinterested tone.

Was that tone an act? Back when she'd first met him, he'd destroyed the bioweapon that someone had ordered to use on the Kingdom. Surely, he wouldn't approve of this one. But would he disapprove enough that he would refuse to work for the man dangling the one mission he'd ever truly wanted before him?

"Fatal moral qualms, unfortunately."

"He decided he couldn't finish it, and you killed him?" Kim asked.

"Not exactly." Dubashi guided them to another lab, this one with a corpse laid out on a table, as if being prepared for entry into a morgue cabinet. "I did inflict a small amount of pain on him, to incentivize him, if you will—such crude methods are not my preferred way of dealing with people, but I was running short on time. It was he who chose to take his own life. A lethal injection of some chemical or another. It wasn't the virus. Which would have been rather poetic, I thought, but I understand it's quite painful."

Kim stared glumly at the dead man who Bonita had been hired to find. Poor Natasha Sunflyer wouldn't be getting her father back.

"My time is even shorter now, Scholar Sato." Dubashi faced her with his obsidian eyes even harder than before. "I need you to figure out what remains to be completed in the bioweapon and to complete it. I know you're not a virologist, but you have an ecumenical background from what I've deduced. I'm positive you're capable of this."

"I'm not," she muttered.

"I trust you will figure it out. After my meeting, I'll be leaving in a ship designed to safely carry those rockets. I need them to be operational and ready to deploy."

"And if I refuse?"

Rache shifted to stand at her side. He was watching Dubashi, but he seemed to be watching her, as well.

She lamented the lack of a network, since she couldn't send him any silent messages. And with his mask on under his helmet, she had no chance at guessing his thoughts. His stance was protective. But was he offering to kill Dubashi to protect her? With his men outside, they were outnumbered. Could they win?

Kim wasn't sure if Rache was even offering to try. He wanted a contract from Dubashi.

"I'm prepared to drug you and upload all your knowledge and all your memories into my computer banks. That lab over there has all the equipment for the transfer." Dubashi pointed toward another equipment-filled room, this one without an airlock, simply a Glasnax door and wall.

A piece of furniture that reminded her of a dentist's chair with straps for holding down one's ankles and wrists was mounted in the back. Cables and probes and what reminded her of electrocardiogram electrodes dangled near the head. A shiver of fear coursed through Kim as she imagined needles thrusting through her skull.

"At which point," Dubashi continued, "I'll have no use of your body, Scholar Sato. My robots have orders to strap you into that unit there and turn it on, if it's clear you're not working on the project. It's paramount that this be completed soon."

The stony-faced officer said nothing. Kim also couldn't tell if she was fully human.

Dubashi's gaze flicked toward Rache, who was standing very still, watching him intently. "Whatever you're thinking, Rache, know that I am one of the people who purchased the experimental slydar-detecting technology, and thanks to my spies at Stardust Palace, I know that it works. My moon's extremely powerful weapons are targeting your ship right now. *Do* cooperate with me. You will be rewarded, as promised."

"I'm still waiting for the transfer of funds for Sato's capture." If Rache was worried about the threat to his ship, he didn't give anything away.

Irritation flashed in Dubashi's dark eyes. "Very well."

He walked to a desk near the front door, pulled out a tablet, and plugged a cable into a network port. He tapped a few commands.

Rache turned his back to Dubashi and faced Kim. Kalb was keeping a close eye on them, and so were the two security robots.

"I'm not leaving you here after that threat," Rache murmured. "What do you want to do?"

What would Rache *agree* to do?

"Can you beat them in a fight?" Kim breathed, not wanting Kalb to overhear. She hoped Rache had some auditory enhancements along with everything else he'd had implanted.

"Depends on if he's expecting it and has planned for it."

She grimaced. Dubashi had to have planned for all manner of trouble. They were deep within his lair, and he had all the advantages. It would be foolish to fight him here.

And more than that…

Her gaze drifted to the rockets and all the biohazard warnings around the labs. This was the last place they wanted to hurl men and robots around, breaking things in a fight.

Rache followed her gaze.

Kim shook her head slightly. If she appeared to be complying with Dubashi, the robots shouldn't have a reason to strap her into that chair. She hoped.

"It's done." Dubashi stepped away from the desk.

Rache faced him again. "So you say. As I'm sure you know, I can't check my bank without network access. I haven't even been able to comm my ship since arriving."

"Yes, it's a shame that the dense layers of rock make wireless connectivity an impossibility," Dubashi said blandly, not sounding like he believed it a shame at all. "There is a comm tower on the surface. After we complete our business, I'll take you to it if you wish. But for now, I must insist that we leave the good scholar here to work while we join the mercenary captains who are waiting for us in my conference room. The Kingdom ships are on the way. They will provide a good test for my new mercenary fleet, but we must have time to iron out details and sign contracts first."

Dubashi extended his hand toward the door.

Rache looked at Kim again, as if to ask if she was sure. She nodded once.

He walked out with Dubashi, who paused to murmur orders to Kalb as they passed. Kalb nodded and sat at the desk.

Apparently, it wasn't only the robots that would guard Kim. Maybe Kalb was the one who would determine if Kim was working sufficiently… or needed to be thrown in that chair.

As Rache disappeared into the corridor outside, walking side by side with Dubashi, Kim felt relieved that he'd trusted her capable of keeping herself alive without his help, but an illogical and scared part of her also felt like he was betraying her by leaving her. And going with *him*. The man who'd ordered her kidnapped. The man who was trying to get Casmir killed.

The man Rache wanted to work for to destroy the Kingdom.

CHAPTER 27

CASMIR COULDN'T KEEP FROM DRUMMING HIS FINGERS ON the side of the co-pilot's pod. They were less than an hour from Dubashi's base. The forward display was zoomed in on the moon, the exterior reinforced with something akin to armor—it looked like a big metal cue ball bristling with weapons platforms and towers. Dozens if not hundreds of large warships floated in space all around the moon. Shuttles were flying into tunnels—entrances to the base—presumably delivering attendees for the meeting.

On the way here, Casmir had located and acquired a copy of the blueprints from the original builder's secured files. He knew where the meeting was likely taking place as well as where the living areas were located, but he couldn't help but feel that leaping out with his crushers and three knights wasn't enough of a plan.

He'd considered trying to send the virus he'd used on the pirates back in System Hydra, but he was still haunted by what he'd inadvertently caused by doing that. The deaths of hundreds, maybe thousands, of people. Even if his virus would work on someone as tech savvy as an astroshaman leader, Casmir hated the idea of knocking out the power to the base and possibly opening the door for the Kingdom fleet to swoop in and destroy it. Dubashi might be guilty of many crimes, but who knew how many normal people were inside that moon?

What Casmir did plan to do was hack into the base's networks as soon as they were close enough for access. Hopefully, he could gain control of critical systems. But something about this prince, this only vaguely known nemesis who had been after him since this all started, unnerved him.

This was a guy who'd been around a long time, doubtless surviving countless attempts on his life from people who wanted to steal his wealth. And he was still here. Here and powerful and influential enough to start a war on an entire Kingdom. Casmir worried he wouldn't be smart enough or have the necessary resources to kidnap him.

Drum, drum, drum...

Bjarke looked at his fingers. Casmir put his hand in his lap and grabbed it with his other hand. His left eye blinked twice.

"Would you like to see the blueprints for the base?" Casmir asked, hoping to stave off Bjarke voicing regrets about trusting someone as goofy as he. Or pointing out how ridiculous and obvious the two large boxes secured in the back next to the rest of the crushers were. They might pass a sensor scan, but what if there was a visual inspection before the shuttle was allowed to fly in?

Bjarke raised his elegant eyebrows. Casmir had been startled when Bonita had patted Bjarke on the ass when they parted ways, but he decided the senior Asger was as handsome as his son, even being thirty years older and even having his face covered, once again, in garish barbed-wire-dagger tattoos. Had Dubashi been female, Casmir might have opted for a different strategy in approaching him. Perhaps putting Bjarke in sexy attire and sending him strutting in as a distraction. Or bait.

But Dubashi wasn't likely to fall for that. Even if he did like sexy knights.

"You have the blueprints?" Bjarke asked.

"I got them from the architect's site, yes. They are, uh, forty years old, it looks like, but it's the best I could do. There's very little published on the network about the moon base or Dubashi. I found rumors about how people who visit never get to leave again, but they didn't seem substantive."

"Let's see them." Bjarke didn't comment on the rest.

Casmir forced himself to stop talking—babbling. Bjarke wasn't as intimidating as Rache, but the fact that he was painfully loyal to Jager and Jorg, and Casmir was taking an unapproved and roundabout way to do their bidding, made him worry. He had to be careful what he said around the knight.

"I'll put them up on the display." Casmir waved, and the view of the moon was replaced by the blueprints.

Bjarke slanted him a sideways look. "You shouldn't have access to the navigation computer from that seat."

"I know."

"You shouldn't be able to put things on the displays."

"Don't worry. I'll do it to Dubashi, too, if I can."

As Bjarke scrutinized the twenty-three levels of the base, all deep underground inside the moon, Casmir wondered if he *could* do that. If they arrived in time for that big meeting, he might be able to make up a presentation to play on some big display in the meeting hall.

But what could he say or promise that would rivet all of those mercenaries? A kinder, gentler Kingdom that would stay put and not offend the other systems further? No, he could hardly promise that. A crusher to everyone who *didn't* go to war with the Kingdom? He almost laughed aloud at the idea. Unfortunately, he couldn't count on everyone out there sharing Sultan Shayban's interest in metals and robots.

"It's huge." Bjarke pointed at one level. "There are a bunch of conference rooms. And there are guest quarters. Private quarters. A control room—we should make note of that. An auxiliary control room. And, uh, four more auxiliary control rooms. This looks like someone with a paranoid streak. He might be hard to find."

Casmir nodded. "That occurred to me too."

"I don't suppose there's any way to track him down by his chip or whatever he's got? The intelligence report I was given says he's got a lot of cybernetic upgrades."

"I know, but none of the details are published on the public network. If I can get into *his* network, maybe I can get some better intel, but…" Casmir paused as another thought came to mind. "Give me a minute. I may have someone I can ask."

Was Kyla Moonrazor still feeling thankful to him? It hadn't sounded like she had any love for her co-high shaman. But would she do something to betray him?

For that matter, was she even still in the system?

Casmir sent a message. *High Shaman Moonrazor, I'm going to visit your colleague, but I fear he may not wish to speak with me. Which is puzzling, since I'm an enjoyable conversationalist versed in many topics that might interest an astroshaman.*

He paused, feeling he should offer her something before asking for a favor, but he didn't know what it would be. He half-hoped she would respond and banter with him, so he could more easily segue into the request, but it had been more than a week since their last conversation, and he didn't know what part of the system she was in. If she'd left, then his message wouldn't reach her in time for her to even consider helping.

Unfortunately, a response did not come. He decided to ask straight out. If she wanted something for the information, she would let him know. Wasn't there negotiating advice about starting low so you could go higher if needed?

I was hoping you would be willing to share his chip ident, if you know it, or some other method of tracking him by his implants, so that I can find him and speak with him. Guilt at the lie surged to life, and he reluctantly added, *Technically, I hope to kidnap him and deliver him to a rival. Thus to put an end to the war he's decided to wage against the Kingdom. If you could help me*—inspiration came between one eye blink and the next—*perhaps I could help you find your people a place where you could stay until you've finished your studies of the gate, have built a new one, and are ready to leave the Twelve Systems.*

Casmir remembered her admitting that her people preferred to stay in hiding, something that would be challenging now that their secret under-the-ice base had been damaged and made known to all.

I've recently made the acquaintance of a renowned real-estate developer who might have suggestions, but if that doesn't work out, and you've got some chutzpah, I happen to know of an astroshaman base in a national forest on Odin that was recently vacated. The former chief superintendent kept it hidden from all the satellites and technology of the Kingdom, so I know it's possible.

Casmir hurried and hit send on the message before his morals forced him to delete those last sentences. It wasn't as if he could legitimately give her land. All he was doing was sharing a potential hiding place. On the home world of one of the most insular and unwelcoming cultures in the Twelve Systems…

He sighed.

Noticing Bjarke watching him, Casmir said, "I'll let you know if I hear back in time."

That earned him a grunt. Bjarke studied the blueprints a while longer, downloaded them to his chip, and put the moon back on the display.

A message came in for Casmir. Not the text response from Moonrazor he expected, but a video from Oku.

He sat up, his boots thunking onto the deck, and Bjarke glanced at him. One of the Kingdom couriers must have gotten through the blockade and distributed fresh mail.

Casmir was tempted to run back to the lav or another quiet corner of the shuttle, yank out his tablet, and watch the video in private. But they weren't that far from the base. He ought to stay in navigation in case something happened.

Reluctantly, he let it play on his contact, resolving to watch it later on a larger display. He hoped it would be something light to bolster him before he started this mission in earnest, but as soon as Oku came into focus, with her father, the humorless King Jager, standing beside her, fear replaced the pleasure that had been burgeoning in his heart.

Had she been caught communicating with him? Would Jager refuse to allow that? Was Jager about to deliver some threat?

Casmir couldn't imagine a possible scenario where Jager sending him a message—or standing nearby while Oku delivered one—was a good thing. The monarch he should have thought of as a leader and protector of the Kingdom and his world was a source of fear now. Had he done that to himself? Or was Jager the bully picking on him for no reason?

No, Jager had his reasons… Casmir couldn't pretend he hadn't made choices to create this scenario.

His dread grew when Jager spoke first. Oku tried to smile but it looked forced. Very forced.

As Jager detailed all he knew of Casmir's deviations from his orders, Casmir sank into his pod, as if he might disappear into another dimension if he burrowed deeply enough. Especially when Jager said, "I'm concerned by my most recent report, which hints that you might not be precisely obeying my son either. I don't know what it is you hope to gain out there by working against us, but if you fancy yourself some future ruler of the Twelve Systems, know that assassins will find your back and you'll never sleep."

Ruler of the Twelve Systems? Dear God, how could anyone think he aspired to that? Did *Oku* think that? She appeared more stunned and startled as her father rattled off Casmir's crimes. No, none of them had been *crimes*. Jager had no more right to that gate than anyone else, and he certainly had no right to choose the president of Tiamat Station. Casmir wasn't the criminal here, damn it.

But assassins? Assassins more competent than Dubashi had sent after him?

Casmir imagined his life like a wine glass dropped on the stairs, shattering further with each bounce down to the landing.

"I'm offering you one last chance to come back into the fold," Jager continued in the video, "to take your place as court roboticist—you requested that position, as I recall—and to work at my side. Should you return to Odin and prove your loyalty, I'm even willing to offer you a prize."

Casmir's stomach churned. There was that word again. Prove. Prove your loyalty. Prove your worth. What kind of man was Jager that he insisted everyone prove that they had a right to exist in his realm? Couldn't people just be allowed to be?

Still, he sat a little straighter, less at the idea of some vague prize, but more because there might still be a chance to return home to his old life. And to ask Oku for that coffee date? Casmir didn't know yet why she was in the video. She hadn't spoken. Had Jager usurped her—and her chip—as a way to get a direct message to him?

She wore a grimace as Jager continued on.

"Princess Oku is not yet betrothed, and I gather you have some interest in her. Royal Intelligence has been kind enough to decrypt the videos you two have been sending back and forth and share them with me."

Blood rushed to Casmir's head, and his heartbeat pounded in his ears. Betrothed? Was Jager saying that he knew of Casmir's incipient feelings for Oku and… wasn't going to forbid a relationship? More than that, he was *offering* a relationship, Casmir realized as Jager continued on. If Casmir played the part. Court roboticist. Loyal subject. Obedient servant to the king.

His heart soared at the idea… and then crashed. He couldn't marry Oku as some *prize*. How could that even be a possibility in this modern age? He knew the royals and some of the nobles still arranged marriages for their children, but nobody in the *real* world did that. He couldn't marry someone who didn't want to marry *him*. And nothing about the wan, shocked expression on Oku's face suggested she was pleased by any of this.

Finally, her father nudged her, and she spoke. But it wasn't to say anything about marriage. She very formally said she looked forward to seeing him again and mentioned Chasca. After hesitating, she added that his family was safe in the Citadel, and relief flooded him. Had she done that? Ordered them retrieved? Or—no, she must have gone out to get them herself. She mentioned a childhood picture of him that he knew was in his parents' apartment.

Tears threatened to film his eyes. A reaction to the relief he felt that his parents were safe and that she'd been willing to go out and retrieve them at whatever risk to herself.

If only *Oku* were the one suggesting marriage. He would be far more tempted by that, tempted to dance on her father's puppet strings for that opportunity. But they hadn't spent enough time together for him to assume they would have some idyllic fairy-tale future if they got married. The rational part of his mind knew that. It was just hard not to speculate and dream.

The video finished with Jager speaking again, threatening again. "Support the Kingdom, and you'll have a place in it forever. Become its enemy, and you'll regret it."

No room for misinterpretation there. As the recording ended, Casmir lamented that there hadn't been a private addendum from Oku. But he feared, from that comment about Royal Intelligence intercepting their previous correspondence, that there might not be any more. Even if her father didn't forbid it, she might feel inhibited, knowing other eyes would see anything he sent.

The idea of not hearing from her again until he—somehow—managed to return to Odin stung his battered heart. As did the realization that he *couldn't* return to Odin unless he obeyed Jorg and helped the prince's fleet win the day.

Dare he hope that his present mission, however self-assigned, might turn out in such a way that it would please Jorg and Jager instead of ruining his chances of returning home forever?

Casmir wiped his eyes, glad for the high sides of the pod that kept Bjarke from seeing his face. He needed a moment to regain his focus, his clarity.

He looked back to check on the crushers—and the two boxes. Poor Tristan and Asger had been locked up in them for the last hour. They hadn't wanted to risk being out when they got within scanner range of Dubashi's moon.

When the shuttle was within forty minutes of the base, the comm beeped for the first time. Bjarke checked the identification before answering it.

"It's from the moon. Here." He unhooked flex-cuffs from his belt and tossed them to Casmir. "Look captured."

"Right." Casmir hesitated before snapping them around his wrists, reminded that Bjarke hadn't liked this plan, didn't like that they were acting without orders, and might not like Casmir much either. What if he decided to change things up?

Bjarke reached for the comm button but frowned over at Casmir.

Casmir snapped the cuffs on. If he needed to, he could have Zee break them. Casmir had to remind himself that, as strange as it seemed, given Bjarke's brawn and his own extreme *lack* of brawn, he was the one with the power here. He not only had Zee, but he had the eleven others. Casmir glanced back to make sure the crushers wouldn't be visible to the comm camera. They had all glided out of sight. Dark silent ghosts. Not even the boxes were visible.

"This is Johnny Twelve Toes," Bjarke answered. "As I messaged earlier, I've got something you want. Where should I land and drop him off?"

Casmir was disappointed but not surprised when someone other than Dubashi answered. A young female officer in a black military uniform came up on the display, frowning at Bjarke. Some trusted lieutenant? Maybe Casmir's sexy-knight plan could be put into play after all. Alas, she didn't look like someone who would be led astray by a pretty man.

"We read two human life signs in your shuttle, Twelve Toes, and that's not a craft registered to the Druckers."

"Most of their ships aren't officially registered," Bjarke said dryly.

Casmir trusted that the shuttle, whatever its registry, also didn't point to Rache.

"And myself and Dabrowski are on here," Bjarke said. "What else did you expect?"

As he shifted the camera toward the co-pilot's seat, Casmir closed his eyes and slumped his head against the side of the pod, as if he'd been drugged or knocked unconscious. He made sure his cuffed wrists were in his lap and would be visible.

"He's supposed to be dead," she said coolly.

"I can make that happen." Bjarke twitched a shoulder. "It'll cost you two thousand extra."

"It should be less work to bring us a body than a living person."

"Not really. He's already unconscious. If I shoot him, there might be blood to clean up. Extra work on my part."

"Just bring him in. I'm sending directions and a code that'll lower the forcefield for thirty seconds. You'll have to fly in fast."

"I can do anything fast, but I prefer slow, precise, and ensured to be enjoyable by all parties involved."

Casmir opened his eyelids enough to see Bjarke offer a sultry smile.

"The only parties involved will be the security androids in the bay. If you don't come out with Dabrowski dead, they'll have orders to shoot you."

Bjarke abandoned the smile. "So long as the money hits my account before we do the exchange."

"You'll get your money, pirate." She sniffed and cut the comm.

"She was kind of condescending," Casmir said.

"She works for a prince. I'm just a scruffy pirate accountant."

"I'm half-surprised your Druckers aren't here for the meeting."

"Pirates don't get involved in other people's wars. Their whole schtick is to be powerful enough to take what they want without risking themselves. That doesn't work when you're battling entire government fleets."

A soft beep sounded.

"We've got directions and the code," Bjarke said.

Casmir nodded. Nothing to do but wait.

After a few minutes, a message came back from Moonrazor, and Casmir scanned it eagerly, hoping for some useful tidbit.

I'm sending along his chip ident, Professor, her note said, *but I don't think you'll find it very helpful.*

He paused, wondering why that would be.

What may be of more interest to you is that Dubashi asked for a loan from several members of the astroshaman high council earlier this year. We were surprised, since it's always been assumed that he's the wealthiest among us. It's possible he just didn't want to spend his own money on his war, but who knows? I don't believe any of us gave him that loan. Money is so plebeian, so human.

Good luck and don't get yourself killed. I'm on the other side of the system, so hardly in a position to offer you an android body this time.

Casmir sent back a *thank you*, read the message twice more, and burned the ident into his mind in addition to saving it on his chip. He would look for it on the network as soon as they were close enough to access it.

Bjarke shifted in his seat and checked the instruments. Casmir thought about sharing what Moonrazor had given him, but since she'd warned him the ident might not be useful, he was hesitant to suggest he'd gained some advantage.

"In case this all goes to hell and we both get killed," Casmir said instead, "thanks for being willing to try it. To work with me. I know my methods are a little unorthodox, but I really do want to stop the war and make sure everyone back home is safe. Even if this wasn't exactly what Prince Jorg had in mind, it seems like it could work. Remove the head and the warmongering snake dies, right?"

"It depends what kind of power infrastructure he has in place," Bjarke said without commenting on the rest. "I do wish I had some men at my disposal." He glanced back at the crushers. Zee was back in sight, keeping an eye on Casmir, as always. "I'm not sure I can count on William and Tristan. And you're—" He glanced at Casmir but didn't finish the sentence.

Casmir tried to keep himself from finishing it in his mind with derogatory and dismissive words.

"*I* believe we can count on Asger and Tristan. They're good fighters. Tristan helped break in my crushers."

"Glad the boy is good at something," Bjarke muttered.

Even though Tristan was the one who'd been kicked out of the knighthood, Casmir was sure the comment pertained to Asger. Poor guy. Why couldn't his father see Asger for who he really was?

"He's good at a lot of things. Have you two fought together? Other than during that rather brief cluster of chaos in the astroshaman base?"

"We used to spar when he was younger."

"But not since he became an adult? A knight? I hope you get a chance to spend some time together out here. And, uhm, work things out."

"We *are* working things out," Bjarke said in a terse I-don't-want-to-discuss-this-with-a-near-stranger tone.

Usually, Casmir would take the hint and back off, but he cared about Asger. And he still felt guilt and worried that, through association with him, Asger was worse off with his superiors now than he had been before they'd met. Maybe even worse off with himself. Though Casmir remembered him reading that philosophy book when they'd first met, trying even then to make sense of the universe. And his place in it.

"Are you?" Casmir made his smile hopeful, not skeptical. "Because I know he would like that."

Bjarke frowned at him.

"You think he's made some mistakes, right?"

Bjarke grunted. "He told you about the calendars?"

Was *that* at the heart of all this? Casmir reminded himself he didn't know the details and that he didn't have any right to judge. "He told me he's made mistakes—what teenager doesn't?—and he doubts his self-worth now. Because somewhere along the way, someone led him to believe *he's* a mistake."

Bjarke squinted at him. "He said that?"

"I'm paraphrasing. He was drunk at the time."

"I never told him he was a mistake."

"He believes it. I keep telling him he's great, because he's a loyal friend who stands up for me, even at the risk of his own life, and he tries so hard to do the right thing. But there's only so much your peers can say to help. It's the people above you, the people you fear and respect and want to please, who have power over you. Maybe it's not fair, but what they say matters more. You can destroy someone with that kind of power."

Bjarke stared at him, his face hard to read.

"You can also build them up with that kind of power," Casmir offered.

Could someone who believed in and followed the Knights' Code truly not have the capacity to understand and care about his son?

"You're really an engineer?" Bjarke finally asked.

"A mechanical engineer specializing in robots."

"Do they like your therapy sessions?"

"I don't think Zee is in need of therapy, but he would happily chat about human relations and social dynamics with me."

"Let's save that for later." Bjarke focused on the control panel. "We're heading in."

Casmir's stomach did a flip-flop as they went from skimming above the dull gray surface of the moon to dipping down into a well-lit tunnel. Fortunately, the usual queasiness did not take root.

Another shuttle flew ahead of them. Indicator lights flashed on the side walls—a scanner system checking the ships?

At a spot that appeared no different from the rest of the tunnel, the ship ahead slowed, thrusters flaring orange, and hovered. Was that where the forcefield was?

Casmir realized they should be within range of the base's networks and that he should have been working on getting onto them rather than talking about relationships with Bjarke. He closed his eyes, letting Bjarke handle the flying, and searched for a signal so he could let his programs loose and find a way in.

After a long minute, he frowned. His chip was searching… and still searching for a signal.

As they plugged in their code for the forcefield and flew deeper into the base, into a range where Casmir should definitely have had access, he realized with gut-sinking certainty that there was no network. Not a *wireless* network.

Even worse, the moon rock walls blocked out access to the system-wide network. He couldn't hack into Dubashi's base, and he couldn't even send a message to Kim to find out where she had ended up.

He groaned.

"What?" Bjarke asked.

Casmir imagined running around with cables, trying to find physical ports to plug into a hard-wired network while the knights and crushers were battling enemies all around him.

"My job just got more formidable."

CHAPTER 28

BONITA SAT IN NAVIGATION IN THE *STELLAR DRAGON*, watching the busy moon base from afar. She'd turned off the thrusters to avoid attracting attention, and the freighter floated between two previously mined asteroids, their surfaces gouged with deep pits and as tunneled as honeycomb. Her long braid kept trying to float free from her pod.

While she watched, she was also monitoring the unsecured communications flying between the mercenary ships, as well as between them and the comm tower on the surface of the moon. The computer was running a search on it all, looking for mentions of Scholar Sunflyer and also of bioweapons. So far, nothing had popped up.

Qin clomped into navigation, setting her boots carefully so the magnetic soles caught with each step. She wore her combat armor, though there was no threat to the *Dragon* at the moment, and she eyed the distant base wistfully. Bonita knew she'd wanted to go with Casmir and the knights and was now second-guessing her decision not to let Qin join them on their incursion. She'd asked Bjarke and Casmir to look for Sunflyer on their way in, but Qin could have made that her priority.

Yet… Bonita had a niggling feeling that the situation would explode, and she'd been reluctant to let Qin get caught in the middle. The Kingdom fleet was on the way, the mercenary warships numbered in the dozens, and the moon base itself had weapons platforms all over the surface. This meeting might as well have been taking place on a rusty old land mine poised to explode at the slightest brush of pressure.

As much as she wanted to complete her assignment and return triumphant to Stardust Palace, it wasn't worth getting Qin killed over it, especially when she wasn't certain Sunflyer was in there.

"Thank you for staying with me," Bonita said. "If trouble finds us behind this asteroid, I'll need you."

"I know. Would you be upset if I hoped for that?" Qin flexed her fingers and extended her nails, as if to say she hoped for some action.

"Trouble?"

"Yes. It feels like we're hiding while our friends go into danger."

Because that *was* what they were doing. "If they were smart, they'd be hiding too."

Qin shook her head. "They want to help their people. It's worth personal risk to oneself to potentially save a great many."

Bonita's mouth twisted. With thinking like that, Qin wouldn't live to see twenty-five. But she couldn't fault her idealistic friend for caring.

"I know," she said, "and if they need help getting back out, we'll help them. Or if they find Scholar Sunflyer but can't get him alone, I'll have to send you in." Somehow. Bonita eyed the hornet's nest on the display with distaste.

Qin's pointed ears perked with interest.

"Just don't pray for that, please," Bonita said. "On the off chance that God is listening to you."

"I've never prayed in my life." Qin shrugged. "Neither the scientists nor the Druckers thought it was important to instill a sense of… spirituality into us."

Before Bonita could comment, the comm panel flashed. So much for hanging back with the thrusters off and avoiding notice.

"Ugh, it's that Fleet ship again."

"The *Chivalrous*," Viggo said helpfully.

"I don't want to talk to that prissy poodle or any of his minions," Bonita said.

"We don't have any knights left to call up to speak to him," Qin said.

"Which he might consider a problem, if he didn't assign them to their current mission." From what Bonita had gathered, Casmir had assigned *himself* his current mission… and talked Tristan, Bjarke, and Asger into going along with him.

"Can we ignore it?"

"We can. I'm debating if there could be repercussions." Bonita eyed the scanners. "That ship, as well as… eighteen others are going to be at the base before long. Four of them are those hulking Kingdom warships.

They could pulverize us without ever firing a weapon. They could just run us over."

"One would expect them to be busy with other matters," Viggo said.

"Are they going to fight the mercenaries meeting with Dubashi?" Qin asked.

"They neglected to file their flight plan and itinerary with me," Bonita said, "but my guess is they're going to try to break up that meeting. Unless they're smart and want to hire the mercenaries for themselves before Dubashi does. That would actually make sense, since they're outnumbered, assuming the Kingdom can outbid a wealthy Miners' Union prince. You'd think an entire planetary government would have such resources."

"Maybe we *should* talk to them and find out what they're doing." Qin scratched her jaw with one of her claws, her skin tough enough to withstand it. "And pass that information along to Casmir. If the Kingdom is hiring mercenaries, that shouldn't be a problem, but what if a fight starts while our friends are inside?"

"That's what I've been sitting here worrying about."

The incoming-comm button flashed again. Insistently.

Bonita reluctantly answered it, reminding herself that she wasn't a Kingdom subject and would be under no obligation to do anything the snobby prince requested—or attempted to *order*.

She groaned inwardly when his face filled the display. She would have preferred to speak to one of his minions, some random comm officer relaying a message.

"Where is Bjarke Asger?" Jorg asked without preamble.

"This isn't his ship," Bonita said, happy enough to avoid greetings.

"Summon him to speak with me."

Summon him? What was she? A witch?

"He's not here. He went to the moon base." Bonita wouldn't share their plan, but out of a sense of self-preservation, she would point out that Jorg's knights weren't aboard her ship. She didn't want to give him a reason to come visit her.

"He *what*? His orders were only to get Sato."

Bonita shrugged. "He didn't confide in me. He just left."

"*How*?" He squinted suspiciously at her. "Our Intelligence agent learned that his shuttle was destroyed on Stardust Palace Station."

"He flapped his wings and flew. Look, I'm not your Intelligence agent. If you want to—"

"'Ware your tongue, bounty-hunter peon," Jorg snarled. "You do not want to make an enemy of the Kingdom."

"*Peon?*"

Qin rested a hand on her shoulder before she could follow that up with the curses that wanted to spew out. "Sir Bjarke Asger and William Asger are trying to *help* the Kingdom, uhm, sir. Are you going to try to hire some of the mercenaries?"

"It's *Your Highness*, not *sir*." Jorg curled a lip. "And I'd chew off my own arm before hiring mercenary scum. Where are the Asgers now? And even more importantly, where is Kim Sato?"

Qin shrugged. "Maybe in that base? We don't know for sure. We're on another mission."

"What could you possibly be doing rubbing the belly of that ugly freighter on an asteroid?"

Bonita grew chill at the knowledge that he'd taken the time to find out exactly where they were.

"*Ugly*?" Viggo protested. "The *Dragon* is sleek with the lines of an elegant mythical creature swirling through the skies."

"We've been hired to look for someone," Bonita said. "It's none of your business who. You'll have to look elsewhere for your wayward knights."

She cut the comm before the sneer on Jorg's face could devolve into further insults. What an ass.

"It doesn't sound like he's planning to hire those mercenaries," Qin observed.

Bonita grunted. "The Kingdom didn't put their most diplomatic leader in charge of rounding up allies, did it?"

"I believe he's simply the person who was stuck outside of the system when their gate was blockaded," Viggo said. "Shall we warn Casmir that the Kingdom fleet is only… six hours away now?"

"He probably already knows—Rache knew they were coming, and that's why he wouldn't rendezvous with us—but yes, I suppose so."

Bonita sent a message to Casmir with the details, but after a minute, it bounced back with an alert.

Unable to deliver message. Recipient offline. Will try again in one hour.

"His chip is offline." Bonita looked at Qin. "Can you contact Asger?"

She tried sending the same message to Bjarke. The same error came back.

Qin shook her head. "No. What does that mean? They're all locked up somewhere with network access blocked off?"

"Or they're all dead," Bonita muttered grimly.

Casmir peered at the displays as Bjarke settled the shuttle onto the landing platform. They were deep in the moon base, and the scanners struggled to read their surroundings, beyond what was in the hollowed-out hangar around them. He hoped to see one of Rache's other shuttles, a sign that Kim was down here and not far away. All he saw were some battle bots waiting outside, large bipedal robots with bug-like heads and arms and hands that held rifles as easily as humans.

"They must have been sent to another bay." Casmir slumped with disappointment.

"Not surprising. There are lots of bays around the base." Bjarke powered down the shuttle and rose to his feet. "Let's let Tristan and William out and see if any human beings, or maybe Dubashi himself, come into the bay, before leaving the shuttle. If he delivered himself into our hands, that would be convenient."

Casmir doubted they would be that lucky, but he said, "True."

Bjarke looked over as Casmir rose from his pod, slinging his tool satchel over his shoulder. "Do you have a weapon?"

"No. I have twelve crushers."

"I saw some rifles in the back. I guess we can't give you one of those, if you're supposed to be my dead prisoner, but you could fit a pistol in your purse there."

"It's a satchel, a manly satchel, and I'll pass. Even if I didn't have an aversion to carrying deadly weapons, I'd consider it especially unwise right now." Casmir remembered that Bjarke hadn't caught up to their group in the astroshaman base until *after* he'd had his seizure, so he might not know about them. He was always reluctant to admit his weaknesses to people, but Bjarke should know in case it happened again here. Casmir dearly hoped it wouldn't—under the best of circumstances, a seizure left him tired and disoriented, and under the worst… Well, shooting an ally was only one of the many problems it might cause. His enemies had a knack for timing their attacks on him—and his unreliable brain—well. "I have a tendency toward seizures. They were controlled back on Odin, but space has added some variables that my medication doesn't compensate for as well."

"Oh." Bjarke digested that. "Don't have one while you're hanging over my shoulder pretending to be dead."

Was that how he planned to carry Casmir out? Lovely.

"I'll do my best." Casmir called back to the crushers. "Zee and friends, please release the knights. It'll be time soon to do battle."

The boxes re-formed into bipedal crushers. Even though Tristan and Asger had air tanks, they sprang to their feet like swimmers lunging to the surface after holding their breath underwater for too long.

"I will remain close to protect you, Casmir Dabrowski," Zee said, "while the others go out to fight. What is our goal?"

A good question. Unless Dubashi came to them, they had to go find him. Casmir, as Moonrazor had subtly warned, couldn't locate the prince through his chip when there was no wireless network, so he would have to make guesses about where Dubashi was likely to be. Already at his meeting? Preparing in an office or his quarters? Showing guests to suites?

First things first. "We'll have to subdue whoever comes to meet us and disable the robots waiting in the hangar out there." Casmir pointed to the hatch they hadn't yet opened.

He was glad he'd had the foresight to download the blueprints on the way here, *before* losing network access. At least they had a good map. He perused it and found a route to the likely locations of Dubashi's office and quarters, as well as the meeting rooms and other shuttle bays. Meanwhile, Bjarke remained up front, monitoring the scanners, waiting to see if Dubashi, or that officer who'd commed them, showed up. Asger went up and looked over his shoulder.

Tristan waited with the crushers. He'd borrowed a galaxy suit and a rifle from Bonita's armory, and Asger had given him back his pertundo, but he wasn't as well-protected as Bjarke and Asger, both in their knight's liquid armor. Since he still seemed very knightly in demeanor—Casmir couldn't believe he'd rushed aboard Rache's shuttle by himself to attempt a rescue—Tristan would probably eschew advice to stay back with him.

"Two of the robots are walking toward our hatch," Asger called back softly, as if he might be overheard outside of the shuttle.

"No sign of the female officer or Dubashi yet." Bjarke peered back at Casmir. "Should we walk out, pretending I'm going to hand you over to those robots, or fight now? I doubt we can get much further with the prisoner ploy. It got us in and through the forcefield, so that's good, but since Dubashi is keen on you being dead, his robots might have orders to shoot you as soon as they catch sight of you."

"Comforting," Casmir murmured.

A rapping sounded at the exterior hatch.

"I think we're being invited out." Casmir took a deep breath, nervous for his friends and nervous for his crushers too. Other than sparring with Tristan, this would be their first real combat. "We'll drop the ruse. Let my crushers go out first and handle the robots."

Tristan lifted his head, a defiant spark in his eyes. Asger and Bjarke wore similar expressions. They clearly did not want to hide behind robots.

Casmir shrugged and spread a hand. "It's why I made them."

The rap came at the hatch again. Since a robot was doing the knocking, it was probably only in Casmir's mind that the second version was more insistent.

"Go get them, boys." Casmir nodded, then stepped back so he wouldn't be in anyone's—anything's—line of fire when the hatch opened.

Bjarke took one last look at the scanner display, but he must not have read any humans heading their way. He jogged back to join Asger and Tristan at the rear of the squad of crushers as Zee opened the hatch. Casmir's creations tramped out. Bjarke tried to shoulder one out of the way, so he didn't have to go last, but the crushers were like walls. Walking walls.

Weapons fire buzzed right outside the shuttle, then heavy thuds and clanks sounded as crushers and robots came together in hand-to-hand combat.

Casmir resisted the very stupid urge to stick his head out and watch the battle. He put his helmet up and poked into his satchel, hoping he had a few cables along that would work for plugging into Dubashi's hard-wired network. Would the prince have had some proprietary system constructed over the years? If so, Casmir would have to hunt around for the equivalent of a maintenance or systems administrator's office so he could find cables designed to work here.

The thuds and clanks were replaced with squeals and horrible wrenching sounds, along with the clatter of robots—or pieces of robots—hitting the landing pad. Casmir lamented that he couldn't take over the battle bots instead of destroying them.

"Not this time," he whispered.

The combat noises faded, and a few silent seconds passed.

"Clear," Bjarke called from the hangar.

Casmir ventured out, grimacing at the carnage—it looked like a robot graveyard, with nothing but pieces of the defenders remaining. But he nodded in satisfaction at the twelve crushers standing by the closed metal exit door. Whatever damage they had taken, they had already repaired themselves. There was a reason so many people desired crushers for themselves.

As Casmir joined the others, he looked along the walls, hoping to spot some network ports, but there were only panels for environmental and hangar controls. Two other ships occupied the cavernous space, but they were powered down, no sign of life inside or outside. As the scanners had told him, neither was one of Rache's shuttles—Kim hadn't come this way.

"Which way first? The conference rooms?" Bjarke waved at his chip—he'd also downloaded the blueprints. "And are you leading or am I, Dabrowski? I'm still trying to figure out where we came in."

Yes, the levels and levels of corridors and rooms and hangars and all the wiring and environmental infrastructure made the blueprints more confusing to read than a simple map.

"They'll know we're here soon, if they don't already," Asger said. "Casmir shouldn't go first."

Casmir spotted a camera high up on a wall. Yes, if someone was monitoring that, Dubashi would indeed already know that his pirate bounty hunter had turned into a knight invader. Especially since Asger and Bjarke wore their telltale armor and carried their pertundos.

"Zee and I will lead. If we run into more battle bots, I'll hide behind him as you all storm past. Let's try to find Dubashi's quarters first. I'm curious about… a lot, really." Casmir looked thoughtfully at Tristan, wondering if Princess Nalini's new real-estate-development partner would have a good eye when it came to looking over a prince's finances, assuming Casmir could hack into his records.

The door didn't open for them, but the crushers easily forced it aside. Casmir jumped at the squeal of weapons fire as two of them strode into the adjacent corridor. The rest of the crushers rushed inside, and Casmir couldn't see around them to ascertain who was shooting at them. He trusted the crushers to handle it, even as he felt useless.

Seconds passed, crunches and crashes and thuds echoing from the corridor. Casmir worried they would have to fight all the way to Dubashi's quarters, which were several levels down from this hangar, and that Dubashi would come up with something more daunting to throw at them. How he longed to get to a computer station so he could plug in and, he hoped, gain access to everything.

No, not everything. He wouldn't be able to control these robots or anything that wasn't itself hard-wired in. And he wouldn't be able to locate Kim, even knowing her chip ident. He hoped that wherever she was, she wasn't in trouble.

"Clear," Bjarke barked.

Casmir entered the corridor, stepping around more broken pieces of robots on the floor, and headed toward a lift. Zee and another crusher walked beside him, with Bjarke, Asger, and Tristan right behind. The remaining crushers trailed after. He felt like a general leading an army.

Not surprisingly, the lift doors did not open for them. Zee startled Casmir by lifting an arm he'd torn off one of the robots. He waved it at a sensor, and the doors opened.

"How'd you know there was a security chip in there?" Asger asked Zee.

"My creator, in his vast wisdom, uploaded schematics for all of the common military robots that we might encounter," Zee said.

Vast wisdom, hah. Casmir had forgotten what all was in the original programming.

"Casmir, why do all robots talk about you like you're a particularly fine lover?" Asger asked.

"I didn't get that from Zee's comment." Casmir stepped into the lift, noting the size of its interior and the size of his army. "We have a platonic relationship."

Asger, Tristan, and Bjarke followed him inside.

"Casmir Dabrowski cannot produce offspring with a robot," Zee announced. "He seeks to court Princess Oku."

"What?" Asger blurted, gaping at Casmir.

"No, no." Casmir groaned—this was not the moment he would have chosen to admit that to Asger, who was besotted with the princess, or had been at one time. "I'm just hoping to ask her for coffee when we get home. And to discuss her bee project."

"Princesses don't have coffee with commoners," Asger said stiffly.

"Casmir Dabrowski is a delightful coffee companion," Zee stated.

"Please stop helping," Casmir whispered as Zee stepped in beside him.

"We're not all going to fit," Bjarke said, indifferent to coffee dates.

But Asger kept staring at Casmir. *Glaring* at him?

The crushers outside of the lift morphed and half walked, half flowed into the car. They flattened and molded themselves to the walls, and one stuck himself to the ceiling, the light dimming as he covered the panel.

The doors slid shut after the last one was inside. Being surrounded by their tarry black re-formed bodies made it feel like they were in a large coffin.

"Those things are creepy as hell," Bjarke said.

"They're versatile, nearly indestructible, and an asset to our team," Casmir corrected him.

"I don't think it's that much of a mystery why they like him," Tristan murmured to Asger.

Asger, a pensive glower still on his face, did not respond.

Zee waved the robot hand at the sensor on the panel inside the door. The panel had a display, but nothing came up. There weren't any physical buttons to press.

"Tell me we aren't trapped in here with two thousand pounds of metal," Bjarke said.

"Better than two thousand pounds of sweaty enemy troops," Tristan offered.

"Actually, the crushers weigh more than that combined." Casmir scooted his way to the control display and used a screwdriver to open a panel underneath. There, he found his first network port. And it used one of the four universal connectors from around the Twelve Systems, one he had a cable for. "Hah."

Casmir would have hugged it if he could. He plugged in with his cable, the other end inserted into his tablet.

The system was locked tighter than a bank vault. Fortunately, more by accident than design, he had his hacking programs backed up on the tablet. Unfortunately, this was much clunkier and slower than interfacing directly.

“This will take some time,” he said.

“We could force the doors open and look for stairs or a ladder,” Bjarke said.

“We could split our forces to cover more ground and have a better shot at finding Dubashi,” Asger said.

“We could wait and let Casmir finish what he’s doing,” Tristan said.

“I’m starting to like you, Tristan,” Casmir murmured distractedly. He took the robot hand Zee still held, flipped it to find a serial number, and then tapped it into the lift program for access. Their car started moving. “It’s going to take time to get into the secure portion of the network where everything important is, but the lifts and most doors require only that someone be a human or robot resident of the base.”

The lift car creaked ominously as it descended. Protesting the weight of all the crushers? Just because they could squeeze themselves into small spaces as effectively as a cat didn’t mean it lessened their overall mass.

The car groaned to a stop on the level Casmir had plugged in, and the doors slid open. Crimson energy bolts shot into the lift, bouncing off armor and crushers and the walls.

A bolt ricocheted off Bjarke’s chest and slammed into Casmir’s shoulder. Zee yanked him farther away from the door as he gasped. Even though the galaxy suit provided moderate protection, it felt like a hammer against his muscle. He stumbled as the crushers and knights rushed out, jostling him as much as the energy bolt had.

Zee remained inside, acting as a shield between Casmir and the exit. He also kept his foot in the way so the door wouldn’t close.

Casmir used the time to work on the network. He couldn’t stay plugged into the lift port all day, but if he could get in once, he could create a log-in and passcode for himself and jump on more easily the next time.

A grinding sound floated over the din of the battle. Someone cried out in pain. It sounded like Asger.

Since their enemies weren’t firing into the lift now, Casmir risked peeking around Zee. Something that looked like a large grenade hurtled through the air toward Bjarke, who jerked aside, avoiding it by scant centimeters.

It struck the wall behind him. Instead of bouncing off, spider-leg-like grippers sprouted, and it suctioned to the wall. The grinding noise sounded again as a powerful drill protruded from the object’s body and drove into the metal wall. Smoke wafted from the hole.

Asger hollered from farther down the corridor, “Get it off me!”

Casmir couldn’t see him through the crushers and battle bots—there had to be another dozen out there attacking his team—but he could guess that one of those flying drills had struck him. Or stuck *to* him. And was burrowing through his armor?

Bjarke pushed his way past the crushers to reach him. “Hang on, William!”

Asger roared in anger and pain.

One of the battle bots fired something akin to Qin’s anti-tank gun. Casmir didn’t see the shell land, but the explosion boomed, and the floor in the lift quaked. Bits of one of his crushers flew in all directions. The view cleared long enough for him to glimpse more robots with more anti-tank guns striding toward their group.

Casmir thought the crusher would be able to reassemble itself and regain its integrity and form, but if they were struck enough times with explosives in rapid succession, it could overwhelm their ability to repair. It was also possible the blows would knock out the nanites and thus the programming instructing the crushers *how* to reassemble.

Zee gently pushed Casmir’s helmet back so that he couldn’t see out—and a stray energy bolt couldn’t come in and hit him. “Trust in the crushers to take victory from those inferior robots, Casmir Dabrowski.”

“I know. I will. Thank you, Zee.” Casmir believed the crushers *could* win. He worried more about his knight friends. It would be better if they stayed back and let the crushers take the brunt of the attacks, but that didn’t seem to be in their DNA.

Casmir forced himself to return to his tablet and the network. He’d gained access to an interface for a systems administrator.

“Making myself an account,” he murmured to himself—or perhaps to Zee. “Want me to download any network games while I’m in?”

“I believe this should not be a priority now.”

“True.”

“Did I make a mistake by speaking of your interest in Princess Oku, Casmir Dabrowski?” An energy bolt bounced off Zee’s chest as he finished that sentence, but it didn’t faze him.

Speaking of things that shouldn’t be a priority now…

“No, it’s fine. Asger will remember that he’s intrigued by Qin, and he’ll get over any disgruntlement. I hope.”

“Clear,” Bjarke called back.

Casmir reluctantly unplugged the cable—at least he'd made some progress—and hurried out after Zee. Several of those projectile drills were stuck into the walls, holes gouged out, and as Casmir passed, one of the crushers reshaped his body away from one sticking into him. The drill clunked to the floor. The crusher stomped it into a thousand pieces.

Asger was still standing and, with Bjarke's help, had removed the drill assaulting him. But blood dripped down the front of his silver armor, a hole revealing a gouge in Asger's shoulder. The armor appeared to have thickened in that spot, the intelligent sensors reacting to the threat, but it must not have been enough. Maybe the weapons had been built precisely for this, to stick to armor long enough to drill holes.

"The prince's quarters are supposed to be up here." Bjarke led the way, running now that they were close.

Asger didn't acknowledge his pain, only hurried after his father.

They had to fight a few more robots before they reached the prince's quarters, with Casmir flattening himself to the wall behind an ornamental column and Zee. He was surprised they hadn't yet run into any people. Did Dubashi live here alone with that female officer? That was hard to believe. Casmir would expect a prince to have a huge family around him, like Sultan Shayban did, and to have his palace—or moon base—filled with servants attending to his every whim. Admittedly, robots could do that, and perhaps an astroshaman preferred mechanical company, but the utter lack of people seemed odd. Maybe they were all hiding. Or were at that meeting.

They turned a couple of corners and into a corridor that only had one set of double doors at the far end. Dubashi's quarters. The doors were framed by the most ornate columns they'd seen with an architrave and frieze above, battling spaceships carved into the marble. Old spaceships. They looked like relics from the Kingdom's first expansion, reminding Casmir of Dubashi's supposed age.

Bjarke stopped in front of the doors. They looked like wood but were made from a hard metal that didn't budge when he pushed at them. Or when Tristan joined him and they both pulled.

"I'll open them," Casmir said, noticing a panel with a port.

"I hope so, because this is a dead end until we can get in." Bjarke made room for him to squeeze in with his tablet.

Casmir didn't point out that it would probably be a dead end even after they were open, unless secret passages led out of the prince's quarters. Secret passages that they could find.

Not surprisingly, the account he'd made for himself in the system didn't give him access to the lock on Dubashi's doors. He'd given himself full administrator powers, but there had to be a special level above that, one he hadn't found on his first perusal. He needed full *prince* powers.

A rumble emanated from the corridor behind them.

"*Now* what?" Asger groaned.

"We'll soon find out," Bjarke said, sounding fearless until he added softly, "I wish I'd kissed Bonita before I left."

"I wish I'd kissed Nalini," Tristan said.

"I wish I'd kissed…" Asger glanced at his father and must have decided he didn't want to say. "Someone."

Casmir was busy and felt no need to point out that he had no one to kiss.

"Any chance you're almost in, Casmir?" Tristan murmured as the rumbling grew louder. The floor reverberated under their feet.

"There's a chance," Casmir said.

"A good one?"

"No."

CHAPTER 29

KIM DONNED A BIOHAZARD SUIT OVER HER GALAXY suit, already certain before she looked at the first slide or computer display that such was a wise course of action. Viruses aside, there were doubtless things in this facility that could eat through SmartWeave and kill her.

General Kalb, who had yet to speak, wore only her military uniform, but unless Kim found Scholar Sunflyer's work and dumped it on the floor, it shouldn't matter. If a completed virus *was* in here, it would likely be in one of the biosafety level-four labs with alarms that would squeal if someone tried to take it out.

If Kim's case had made its way in here, she could have tried to get one of the knockout grenades out to use on Kalb, but the robots had disappeared with it. Unfortunately.

Kim did her best to ignore Kalb and the guard robots as she poked into one of the lab computers. Though she was tempted to mulishly do nothing, she had better find out what she was dealing with. This was why she had come, why she had delivered herself into the enemy's hands. How far along had Scholar Serg Sunflyer gotten in developing his bioweapon before his conscience had turned fatal on him?

None of the workstations had passcodes or required retina scans. Maybe it was assumed that if one got this deep into the base, one was expected to be here.

Scholar Sunflyer had taken meticulous notes, and dread sank deeper and deeper into Kim's gut as she read them. He'd been modifying the Orthobuliaviricetes virus, which was horrifically scary and deadly even in its natural form, if not as readily transmitted as something like the Great Plague.

It had been used before by militaries and terrorists, and she thought she recalled a vaccine being created at one time. She checked. The computer wasn't hooked up to the Stymphalia System public network—nothing here was—but someone had downloaded vast amounts of biological and medical data.

Yes, there *was* a vaccine, but it only worked if all six shots were administered before exposure. Without it, there was a 100 percent chance the virus would destroy the brain and result in death. Similar to the Old Earth virus rabies, the original needed to be transferred by saliva getting into an open wound or mucous membranes, but in Sunflyer's notes, he talked about how he'd modified Orthobuliaviricetes not only for airborne transmission but to be able to survive outside the human body for up to a week. He believed the new virus was, as Dubashi had demanded, deadly enough to be filed with the other viruses under the classification of *planet killer*. Something that could theoretically wipe out the entire population of a planet, moon, or habitat.

Kim's body shook as she read the details, struggling to focus as she imagined this being unleashed on Odin.

There was a confession at the end of Sunflyer's notes.

He really intends to use this. Dear God. I can't... can't let him do it. He brought in a bunch of rockets today—the delivery mechanisms to drop it over the continents of Odin. He wants to use it to wipe out human life on the entire planet. *So he can bring in his people and claim the fertile world for his own and populate it from scratch. I didn't know... I had no choice, but I didn't realize he intended to use it for more than some scare tactic in military maneuvers against the Kingdom. I can't go through with this. I can't.*

"Wish you'd had that realization earlier," Kim muttered.

The notes didn't say, but from the molecular structure floating on the display beside them, she feared he'd completed the project. But if that was true, why had Dubashi wanted to bring her in? Was it possible he didn't know? Or had he wanted the virus tested before loading it into those rockets and taking them to the Kingdom?

Kim had never had that series of vaccines, not that they would be effective on this modified version anyway. She was the last person who wanted to test the stuff. She didn't even want to be in the laboratory with it.

Kim poked around in refrigerators and found carefully labeled and dated vials. She walked to the back of the main room where the rockets waited in their track to be swept through a hole in the wall and to some waiting ship.

Aware of the officer following her and keeping an eye on her, Kim found an electronic screwdriver and opened the panels in one of the rockets. An alert flashed on an interface inside, warning her of a deadly biological element inserted into chambers deep within the bowels of the rocket. She almost dropped the screwdriver.

Were the rockets already *loaded*?

What if Scholar Sunflyer had finished? What if he'd only told Dubashi the project wasn't complete to keep him from trying to use it?

Kim closed the panel and checked the other rockets. They were all loaded.

Willing her hands to remain steady, she removed one of the sealed containers from the bowels of a rocket, very careful to unmount it from its housing without bumping anything. The opaque cylinder didn't appear to be easily breakable—not until the rocket itself detonated and spread the contents over who knew how many square miles—but she didn't want to risk anything. She *did* want to know if Sunflyer had actually loaded his altered virus. Maybe he'd put harmless dummy canisters inside.

"I hadn't realized they were loaded," Kalb said, watching.

"I'll check to see if it's the substance he was hired—kidnapped—to complete or if he stuck something else in there."

"I'd like to know that too." Kalb's tone went dry as she added, "And we *did* try to hire someone at first."

"Nobody wanted to come build you a bioweapon that could destroy entire population centers? How odd."

"If the Kingdom cooperates with Prince Dubashi's demands, that won't happen."

"Are you sure? That's not what Scholar Sunflyer believed." Kim glanced toward the lab holding the dead man's corpse.

"If they don't cooperate, then it will be unfortunate for them. Ajish has desired a planet, a lush planet where man can walk outside without a spacesuit or breath mask, for a long time. Not just for himself but for all the people in the little empire he's created. There are millions of them out there, living on his asteroids and habitats."

Ajish? Was that Dubashi's first name? Kim had no idea. And she didn't much care.

Carefully carrying the container with her, she passed through the decontamination chambers and into one of the level-four biosafety labs. Kalb didn't follow her. Good.

Kim turned on the fans, checked her suit to ensure she was fully encapsulated and on independent air, then cracked the seal of the container. Time to examine the substance inside under the electron microscope.

An alert went off as soon as she broke the seal, and the hair on the back of her neck rose. She'd worked with stuff this deadly before and found that she could keep her calm as long as she didn't think of the ramifications to Odin. Her hands and her movements were steady as she prepared a negative stain slide with phosphotungstic acid she'd found in a cabinet.

Her hand paused as she was returning the bottle to its shelf. There was some chloral hydrate right next to it, a chemical reagent that she used in her knockout solution. By itself, it wouldn't be as effective, but if she could inject a dose, it ought to work…

Kalb was watching, so Kim didn't linger. She finished preparing her slide and eased it into the microscope, then turned to the computer display and waited for the identification it could make far more easily than she. Even before the readout came up, she was fairly certain this was the altered virus—the alarm system certainly believed it was deadly.

It was right.

Kim stared at the results longer than required for identification as she considered what to do. Dubashi's weapon was loaded and ready for transport, but he didn't know it. Unfortunately, his loyal minion General Kalb was watching her through the Glasnax wall. Kim didn't think Kalb could see past all the equipment to the microscope display. Kim either had to lie to her—and do it well enough that Kalb believed her—or admit that the rockets were ready to go. At which point, Dubashi might be able to load them onto a ship with the press of a button. Maybe it wouldn't even take his touch. Maybe Kalb could do it.

"Well?" Kalb asked.

Kim shook her head slowly, not looking back, not wanting her eyes to leak her lie. "This isn't the virus. I think he was hoping to fool you. Do you have any idea where he might have stored the actual samples? Or is it possible all he put together were computerized models?"

There was a long silence. The faint clacks of the robot defenders changing position drifted back into the silent lab. Kim wondered how much time she had until Jorg's fleet got here and attacked. This lab with this slide was the last place she wanted to be if the ceiling caved in.

"Show me," Kalb said, her voice cold.

Had she detected Kim's lie? Damn it, Kim had kept her voice steady and calm. Maybe she should have tried to add some faux puzzlement.

"Of course. Come in, if you like."

Kim waved at the airlock and sterilization chambers that Kalb would have to pass through. She opened her mouth to warn her to put on a biohazard suit, but caught herself. If she said that, Kalb would know the air was infectious. But if she didn't, Kalb would be infected with the virus when she entered. That would be a tempting, if horrific, way to deal with her enemy if the virus would take her down in minutes instead of twenty-four to forty-eight hours, but since it wouldn't, Kim didn't contemplate it for more than a second.

The decision was taken away from her when Kalb walked to the cabinet to pull out a biohazard suit. She clearly didn't trust Kim. As she shouldn't.

While Kalb dressed, Kim disposed of the telltale slide in the lab's incinerator. She also sealed the original container and placed it inside to destroy it. She had no intention of taking it back out and returning it to the rocket. No, she wanted to figure out how to distract or fool Kalb so she could remove the rest of the containers from the rockets. And destroy *everything,* including Sunflyer's formulation and notes.

She just had to remove Kalb from the picture first.

The officer glanced over several times while she dressed, but she had to also focus on what she was doing, to ensure her suit was airtight. And virus-proof.

When she wasn't looking, Kim pulled out the bottle of chloral hydrate and hid it out of sight. She pulled open drawers until she found syringes. There. Perfect. She filled a syringe and put the bottle away.

As Kalb stepped into the airlock chamber, Kim hunted for an innocuous substance that she could use to make a new slide for Kalb's perusal, but Kalb was facing her now, so she had to be careful. It would be suspicious if she was throwing open cabinets to hunt for things.

Kim waved a slide under the sink out of Kalb's sight, collected a drop of water, and put it under the microscope. Maybe that was for the best. If she'd placed something with an elaborate composition under the microscope, Kalb might not have been convinced that it wasn't the virus.

As Kalb moved into the lab, Kim slid her syringe into the pocket of her suit. She wasn't sure when she would get the chance to use it.

Kalb was armed, bringing her stunner *and* her rifle into the lab. The suit didn't have a belt for the stunner, but it had a pocket, and she slipped it inside. She kept the rifle in her hands.

Maybe when she tried to take the weapons back out, the computerized sanitation system would object. A rifle, with its long barrel and nooks and crannies, would be difficult for the decontamination chambers to fully sterilize. But if Kim let her get back out, the robots would be able to see them. Right now, they were around the corner, standing guard by the exit. This might be her only opportunity to do something.

Kim stepped back as Kalb entered, waving her to the microscope.

As the officer headed over, Kim eyed her biohazard suit, trying to calculate the force she would have to apply to puncture it with her needle. It was sturdy, but not nearly as impenetrable as armor or a galaxy suit. And all Kalb wore underneath was a uniform. Her neck was protected by the oversized helmet, but her thigh might work, especially if Kim could hit the femoral artery.

If the needle went through, the virus might get through, too, but these suits had positive pressure interiors designed to keep contaminants out in case of damage. It should only be the needle itself that was a threat, and Kim hadn't yet removed the sterile cap. Also, the laboratory's ventilation system had been running, so the air was probably clear by now.

Kalb kept her rifle pointed at Kim, unaware of the thoughts racing in Kim's head, as she walked to the microscope. Kalb had to look away to study the display.

"This is what's loaded in the rockets?" she asked.

"Yes." Kim moved closer under the guise of pointing at the bland water molecules floating on the display. She stopped just to the side and behind the woman's shoulder.

"What is it?" Kalb asked.

Another time, Kim would have laughed at the idea of someone not recognizing the molecule, but she was too focused on her task. "A simple saline solution."

Kalb started to turn. Kim leaped for her back.

The rifle whipped around, but Kim knocked it aside with a raised knee as she grabbed Kalb's shoulder and pushed her into position so she could wrap her arm around her neck from behind. The helmet got in the way and kept her from applying the right pressure, but she stepped in close, securing the hold.

Kalb thrust backward, trying to throw Kim, but Kim had practiced these tactics on her larger, stronger brothers. She drove her knee into the back of Kalb's knee and knocked her to the floor as she reached around with her free hand. She jammed the syringe into Kalb's inner thigh.

Kalb bucked and struggled, so her aim wasn't as precise as she wished, but she thumbed the plunger down before Kalb managed to twist away.

Kim let her go, jumping back into a fighting stance. Afraid Kalb would shout out for the robots, she sprang right back in, slamming a palm into Kalb's solar plexus. The woman stumbled back, bumping against a wall. Kim winced at the noise.

Kalb opened her mouth to shout, but her eyes were already glazed, and she seemed confused about her own intent. Kim snatched her stunner from her pocket and prepared to shoot if Kalb yelled. Would it be effective through the suit? Kim didn't know.

But it didn't matter. Kalb's eyes rolled back in her head, and she pitched to the floor.

Kim dragged her into a corner of the lab, though there was nowhere that she could completely hide the unconscious body from view. She hurried into the decontamination chambers, shifting from foot to foot as they ran through their painfully slow cycle. She wished she could override the system. Nobody else was in the lab, and it wasn't as if a virus would hurt those robots. She wanted to get rid of the containers in all of the rockets before Kalb woke up—and before those robots twigged to the fact that Kim had taken her out.

As soon as she stepped out, the two robots faced her.

Kim's heart was pounding in her ears, but she made herself ignore them—and the weapons they had pointed at her. She turned back to the lab and called, "See if you can find the real virus in there. I'm going to remove the containers of the fake ones from the rockets, so we can reload them with what your boss wants."

Of course, Kalb did not answer.

Kim had no idea how intelligent the robots were, but she had to assume they were akin to androids or crushers. Praying they would give her a few minutes before thinking to check on the general, Kim hurried to the rockets. There were seven more that she had to dig into so she could remove the well-secured containers.

This would take time. More than a few minutes, she feared. And dare she try to carry all seven containers back to the lab for disposal at once? She glanced around as she worked, wondering if there was an incinerator out in the main area that would work well enough.

As she imagined her colleagues yelling at her for improper lab etiquette, Kim removed the canisters and set them on the floor one by one. Despite her galaxy suit temperature-modulating fabric, she felt like a yeti in the double suits, and sweat dribbled down the sides of her face and the back of her neck. Her hands were damp and slick inside her thick gloves.

A comm chimed, and she swore under her breath. She had removed all but two of the canisters.

"General Kalb," came Dubashi's voice over a speaker. "Report."

Kim looked at the robots. "I don't suppose you can answer that? It'll take the general five minutes in the decon chamber before she can get out of that lab."

She was certain she'd seen a comm panel in that lab, but maybe the robots wouldn't think of that.

"General Kalb, report," Dubashi repeated. Was that suspicion in his voice?

One of the robots walked toward the lab.

Kim set down the canister in her hand and hurried to intercept the robot. "Never mind. I'll answer the comm for her."

The robot reached for her shoulder. She almost dodged the grasp, but the thing was faster than it looked, and she was wearing the clunky biohazard boots over her own. She caught her heel and stumbled.

Its mechanical hand crunched down hard. Unfortunately, a side kick to the groin would do nothing to a heavy robot that *had* no groin.

The other robot strode past them, heading straight for the lab where it was sure to see Kalb on the floor.

Hell.

CHAPTER 30

WHATEVER WAS RUMBLING AROUND THE CORNER DREW CLOSER, a grinding and whirring that made Casmir think of some giant tunnel-boring machine. He was focused on finding a way to unlock Dubashi's secured doors and had his back to the noise, but he felt its ominous presence drawing nearer. Fortunately, all of his crushers and Tristan, Asger, and Bjarke were between him and it. They ought to be able to handle almost anything.

But when he thought of the projectile drill that had cut a hole into Asger's armor—and his shoulder—doubt filled him. Casmir was on the verge of calling Zee to try to force open the great metal doors, even though Tristan and Bjarke had already tried, but if he successfully got into Dubashi's office, he would need time in there. It would be ideal to be able to re-lock the doors behind him.

"It's a tank," Bjarke said, the armored vehicle finally making its way around the bend. "Who puts tanks in tunnels?"

"It's spewing something out of that hole," Asger warned, even as the crushers surged forward to attack the vehicle.

"Gas? We've all got our helmets on."

"No, my helmet scanner says it's an acid."

"An acid that can eat through crushers? Through *armor*?"

Casmir's tablet beeped.

"Yes," he whispered, waving for the doors to open. They did so with ponderous slowness, as if this were some tomb that had been sealed for thousands of years, rather than the prince's office that he'd been in that morning.

"Better destroy it before we find out," Bjarke said and ran after the crushers.

"Wait," Casmir blurted. "We're in."

Asger and Tristan, who'd been about to take off after Bjarke, paused.

"Do what you need to do in there, Casmir," Asger said. "We'll make sure you're safe."

Casmir eyed a gray-blue vapor hissing out of the top of the tank. The armored vehicle was narrow, designed for these tunnels, but it had gun turrets in addition to whatever that acid was. "Or we could all hide inside."

"It'll break down the doors if we don't deal with it," Asger said, the crushers already swarming the tank.

"All right, but leave me Tristan. And Zee, please."

Zee hadn't taken off after the other crushers—he remained protectively close to Casmir. But Tristan was poised to charge with the others.

"What can I do?" he asked.

"Help me with the financial stuff. You're a numbers guy, right?"

Judging by the longing way he looked toward the battle, Tristan still considered himself first and foremost a combat guy.

"I'm going to need help in here." Casmir could already see a plethora of displays and computer equipment that would have daunted even an analyst from Royal Intelligence.

Tristan hesitated, especially when a weapon fired, and one of the crushers flew backward from what appeared to be the nearly indestructible tank. But he finally nodded and ran inside.

"Knock if you want in," Casmir yelled to everyone else.

They were too busy to glance back. Asger cursed, pain leaking into his words. He was already injured, and if that was some corrosive acid making its way into the gap in his armor…

Casmir forced himself to trust that the men and the crushers could handle themselves, and closed the doors. And locked them. They were buying him time. He would put it to the best use that he could.

"I'm not sure how long we'll have." Casmir waved for Tristan to follow him to the multiple desks and wall of displays.

They were showing footage from the war in System Lion and business news and market updates from all of the systems. The war reports riveted Casmir for a few seconds, especially since a couple seemed to be tactical displays from ships' computers rather than information being filtered through the media. They looked like real-time reports, but he knew that wasn't possible.

"I'm not sure I can be of use in here." Tristan, who'd faced countless killer robots, looked daunted as he scanned the displays, text and numbers scrolling down some of them.

"If I can get in, you can help me sift through everything." Casmir plugged his cable into the first port he found and used his access to find Dubashi's personal files.

"I'm not that good at sifting. At reading."

"Aren't you training to be a real-estate mogul?"

"Not by reading. There are lectures." Despite the booms coming from beyond the door, Tristan looked embarrassed as he shrugged and avoided Casmir's glance. "I'm a slow reader," he mumbled.

"With numbers too? Or just letters?"

"I'm not bad with numbers."

"Let me see if I can find his financial records. I got a tip that he might have some problems in that area. I need you to interpret them while I… I'm not sure yet, but I'm going to see if I can crash that meeting without actually walking in there."

"Walking in behind your crushers might not be suicidal."

"But that tends to start a battle." Casmir tapped at his tablet furiously, again lamenting how much slower it was than his chip, but he was gaining familiarity with the network now. The same access he'd had to acquire for Dubashi's door got him into his secure financial reports. "I want to *stop* a battle."

Tristan glanced at Zee. "Are you sure? I think Sultan Shayban would be pleased if you destroyed Dubashi's entire base—and him too. He has a bloodthirsty side."

"I don't." Casmir didn't explain that even destroying the *robots* here bothered him. "Here's some recent financial data. I'd have to do more work to gain access to his bank accounts, but it looks like he's recording everything in his books." He put the data he'd found on one of the displays, ticking boxes for graphs and charts in case that helped Tristan.

Barely glancing at the information himself, he switched his attention to finding the conference room Dubashi was using on the network. He hoped the meeting was still going on. It seemed possible that Dubashi, realizing an enemy was invading his base and destroying his robots, would have ended it early to go deal with the problem. He might even now be leading some huge army to his office…

"Huh," Tristan muttered.

Casmir, experiencing a *huh* of his own, didn't look over. He'd found the only conference room with the computers powered up and online. Remembering the security camera he'd seen in the hangar, he flagged it and went hunting for access to the cameras for the entire base. Was there one in that conference room?

"If this is right, he's in the red," Tristan said. "For his personal accounts and his business account, at least his main one, the one he appears to be using to fund the war. He has plenty of assets—asteroids, refineries, mining ships, and a whole bunch of warships he must have purchased for the blockade—but those aren't the kinds of things one can easily find buyers for or sell off quickly. His cash flow is severely limited right now. Not at all sufficient for his current demands. Damn, do you know how much it costs to pay mercenaries? And there are… are those bribes?"

As Tristan continued to mutter to himself about what he was discovering, Casmir found the software running all of the cameras in the base and surfed around until he located one in the conference room. He put it up on one of the displays. It gave a view of a massive wood table with numerous men and a few women sitting around it, all wearing combat armor or galaxy suits in a mishmash of colors and patterns. It was clear these were independent operators and not members of a single team.

Casmir's breath caught as he recognized the familiar black armor of Rache's mercenary company. The person wearing it was leaning against a wall instead of sitting, and he looked about Casmir's height. Rache, then.

But where was Kim? And for that matter, why hadn't Rache brought more of his men?

Was Kim hunting for Scholar Sunflyer and the theoretical bioweapon? By herself? Casmir's heart shriveled at the idea. As competent as she was, she shouldn't be alone in this place. What if she was locked up and being forced to work on some vile project? Why had Rache left her? Had Kim assumed she would be able to communicate with Casmir? Damn the lack of a wireless network.

What if Dubashi was with Kim at that very moment? Casmir didn't see him sitting at the table.

Further, several of the people spoke to each other and gestured agitatedly. Impatiently. Because Dubashi hadn't arrived yet? Or because he'd left them to deal with the intruders? Casmir grimaced and glanced at the door, but whatever trouble was going on outside it, Asger and Bjarke and the crushers were handling it. So far.

"I need sound," Casmir whispered.

He wanted to hear what the people in that meeting were saying, and even more, he wanted to be able to talk to them.

As he was tinkering, Dubashi walked into the conference room. The conversations around the table halted, all eyes turning toward him.

A display above the one that Casmir had requisitioned flashed, and he jerked his gaze away, envisioning Dubashi playing some seizure-causing light show. But it was just a report coming up, brighter than what had been an empty backdrop of stars. Before he could read the report, it shifted back to stars, this time with ships flying toward the camera.

The other displays in the row showed footage from the war, and at first, Casmir thought this was another recording sent from System Lion, but he recognized those ships. The *Osprey*, the *Eagle*, and was that Prince Jorg's *Chivalrous*?

A banner displayed an alert, warning that the ships were coming and would arrive in two hours. Maybe that was why the people in that meeting were agitated. Did they know?

Casmir reached up to rub his neck and clunked his fingers against his helmet. He pushed it back, trusting Asger and Bjarke to warn him if the office was about to be overrun. He rubbed his neck and shook his head and wished he could rub his aching brain. They were about to be in the middle of a war zone. He couldn't imagine Jorg was coming for the meeting. Dubashi was sure to defend his base… or order his new mercenary allies to help.

"But *will* they help? Mercenaries expect to get paid." Casmir looked over at Tristan, caught him moving his lips as he read something.

Tristan swiped at a display, pulling up new columns of numbers.

"Can you make me a report showing that he's in financial trouble and can't pay those mercenaries?" Casmir asked. "Something very simple that could be interpreted at a glance."

"I… should be able to. Yes. I am an expert at simple."

"Good. I'm going to see if I can impose myself on that meeting."

Dubashi had started pacing, lifting his arms, and talking. Making his pitch.

Casmir didn't have sound yet, but he could guess at what the man was saying, what he was promising. If he didn't figure out how to impose himself quickly, those mercenaries would rush back to their ships in a fervor and sail off to attack the incoming Kingdom fleet.

The two robots wrestled Kim toward the reclining chair surrounded by hooks and dangling sensors, unbreakable metal straps gleaming on the arm and leg rests. She fought, kicking and yelling her frustration, but her metal assailants were as strong as Zee. She systematically ran through all the escapes she knew, escapes that worked well against humans with weaknesses in the joints and the ability to feel pain, but she couldn't break their mechanical grips. Panic made her desperate and even less effective, but it was so hard to tamp it down.

What would Casmir do? He was never the strongest in the room, so he rarely tried a physical fight. He would talk to the damn robots. Would that work?

"Wait," she panted, glancing back and groaning at how close she was to ending up in that chair. "You need me. Dubashi needs me. The rockets aren't loaded right now. This uploading of the consciousness might not work. Or—" another argument struck her, one that was actually true, "—it'll take too long! Isn't the Kingdom fleet on your doorstep?"

The robots slammed her into the chair. One tore her hood off as a metal strap snapped around her left wrist. She managed to keep her legs from settling into the leg rests, instead kicking out and clubbing one of the robots in the torso. She'd broken boards and bones with those kicks, but the five-hundred-pound robot did not budge. It pushed her legs down while the other pressed a hand against her chest.

"Your Highness," a groggy voice said.

General Kalb. She'd woken up and escaped from the lab.

Kim doubted she would have any more luck pleading her case with the officer, not after tricking her and knocking her out, but she raised her voice to try. "General, you don't have time to do this to me if you want me to help you with the rockets."

"Shut her up," Kalb growled to the robots. Then she lowered her voice. Speaking on the comm? To Dubashi?

Despite Kim's ongoing struggles, the robots got her fully snapped into the chair. One pressed her head against the rest, and a cool band with a viscous layer of some cool slick material slithered across her forehead like a snake. It snapped into place, and she could no longer lift her head.

She wanted to be defiant and brave, but tears of fear pricked at her eyes. Nobody except Rache knew she was here, and he was in that damn meeting, trying to get this asshole of a prince to pay him to assassinate Jager. Screw him and his cursed obsession.

And she was just as frustrated that she hadn't arranged to meet up with Casmir before she'd gotten in here. But how could she have guessed there wouldn't be a wireless network anywhere in the whole base and that they wouldn't be able to communicate?

What she *could* have done was accept Casmir's offer of the crushers. It had been foolish to come here with only Rache as backup. He was more unpredictable than Zee.

"She took a bunch of containers out of the rockets," Kalb said. "She said they were a salt solution, but they had to be the completed virus. She wouldn't have cared about removing them if not. Sunflyer completed them weeks ago, and we never knew. We've been sitting here on this."

Kim could hear the muted tones of Dubashi's voice, now that she was no longer struggling—no longer could struggle—but not the words.

"I'm not touching them," Kalb said. "You come down here and do it yourself. Or convince *her* to deal with it. But I wouldn't trust her to, even with a gun at her back. I've got her strapped in that chair right now. How long does that transfer take? Could we ensure the android version would be any more likely to comply?"

Kim curled her fingers around the edges of the arm rests, tightening them painfully as she imagined being an android, just like her mother. An android who could no longer taste coffee, enjoy the warmth of the sun on her skin, kiss David… She didn't even know if she'd *liked* that, but she liked him and wanted another chance. He would never kiss an android.

"How long do we have?" Kalb asked quietly, responding to some new comment. After a moment, she said, "Can the base stand up to them?"

Kim wished she could hear the answer. Or maybe she didn't want to know.

The tears threatened to fall as she imagined being strapped in here as Jorg's fleet dropped its bombs and destroyed the moon, and her along with it. Killed by friendly fire, her body blown out into the vacuum of space. Who would even know that she'd died here?

CHAPTER 31

ACID ATE INTO ASGER'S WOUNDED SHOULDER AS HE smashed his pertundo down onto the armored tank again and again, lightning streaking from his nearly indestructible blade. Unfortunately, the tank was just as indestructible. What was this thing *made* from?

The acid it kept spraying did not eat away its own hull. Meanwhile, alarms flashed on Asger's helmet display, warning him that his armor was in danger of being compromised. *Further* compromised. Already, it felt like a hole had burned all the way through the front of his shoulder to the other side.

One of the crushers leaped onto the top of the tank, trying to find some panel to rip off. He almost grabbed the hole that was spewing the acid vapor.

Asger clambered closer to the spot and swung his blade at the hole. Maybe *that* was a weakness.

The blade clanged off the armored hull, not small enough to connect with the delivery mechanism inside. He shifted his position and the shaft of the long weapon in his hands. Instead of trying to cut, he drove the long tip of the pertundo into the hole.

Metal crunched as it sank in with satisfying give. He rammed it in as deeply as he could, then twisted, hoping the thing's computer brain was back there.

Smoke wafted from the hole around the pertundo's shaft. Not acid vapor this time but genuine smoke.

Something pushed up on his pertundo, startling him. The crushers were working together to heave the tank over in the tunnel. Asger yanked out his weapon before it was torn out of his hands.

"Look out!" he warned, since his father wasn't in sight. Was he attacking the tank on the other side?

The crushers lifted, then pushed, and the nose of the tank cleared the ceiling—one gun bent as it scraped along the surface. The vehicle tipped over to land on its back, studded treads whirring uselessly as it lay like an upside-down turtle.

Asger spotted his father on the other side of the tank. He'd gotten out of the way, but he would have been pinned if he hadn't been paying attention.

He gave Asger a curt nod through the smoke. Asger nodded back. The crushers fell upon the less sturdy underside of the tank, like scavenger birds tearing apart some hapless roadkill.

His father glanced down the hallway, looking the way they had come, checking for more threats. He must not have seen anything because he climbed past the crushers and joined Asger. They walked back to the big metal doors that Casmir and Tristan had disappeared behind. Asger's shoulder throbbed with each step, or maybe with each heartbeat.

He leaned against one of the doors and waited, expecting another attack to come. Whatever Casmir planned to do, it was a foregone conclusion that Dubashi would try to stop him.

After watching the carrion-crushers finish demolishing the tank, as if they were tearing off pieces to recycle for some other purpose, his father leaned beside him against the other door. Asger considered knocking and asking to be let in, but there was nothing he would be able to do when it came to hacking networks. This was his place. Guarding the door and hoping Casmir could work magic. And that it was a type of magic that would turn the war in the Kingdom's favor, so that Asger would be allowed to go home.

As seconds passed, and the crushers settled, Asger looked over at his stone-faced father. Was he homesick after more than a year away? Or had Odin long since stopped seeming like home to him? It had been so long since they'd both been home on the family estate together. Asger decided he would prefer to stay in town at the knights' barracks if they were both on Odin at the same time. Even now, he wished he were here with someone else. Qin.

Was she back on the *Dragon* worrying about him? He knew she'd wanted to come.

Asger caught his father looking over at him. Judging him, no doubt. Wondering why he wasn't a better fighter, a better knight, a better son.

"William?" His father pushed back his faceplate and wiped sweat from his brow. "I'm sorry I wasn't around more when you were growing up."

Asger felt his jaw hit the deck—or at least the bottom of his helmet. That was the last thing he'd expected. He couldn't remember his father *ever* apologizing to him.

"You know my father was a knight, too, a great war hero in the Lunar Riots. He wasn't around much when *I* was growing up. Because he was so important, he was trusted and called on to go off-planet frequently. Whenever he *was* around, he instructed me on combat and quizzed me on the Code and the Kingdom's history. He always seemed to keep testing me until I got one wrong, and then he'd let me know I needed to study harder. The Asgers have always been great knights and protectors, and I was expected to be one too. I got frustrated with trying to measure up to his standards and—you'll find this surprising—developed a sarcastic streak."

A biting streak, Asger would have called it. He'd felt its bite often.

"My superiors didn't appreciate it any more than my father did, if you can imagine. I dug myself a hole that I had to work hard to climb out of. By the time you came along, I'd earned some respect, though it never seemed like enough. I felt I had to prove myself over and over again. Because my father was extraordinary, and *his* father was extraordinary, I couldn't be anything less. And I…" He looked away. "I couldn't have a son that was anything less."

Asger swallowed, afraid this startling openness was going to turn into another lecture.

"Because that would reflect poorly on me," his father said. "And after my rocky start, I'd fought hard to not be anyone's failure. I thought you were coming along well until your mother died, and then… well, you know what happened."

"Yeah, nobody was around, and I wanted someone to pay attention."

His father grimaced. Asger didn't know if it was because he regretted not being around or if he was still embarrassed by the memory.

"I'm just trying to say that, when you did those things, made those mistakes, I could have handled it better. It's hard for me to admit—my father *never* would have had a conversation like this with me—but I was, still am, absorbed in proving my worth. My worth to the king and to the old man and to all those ancestor heroes of the past. And when I was given piddling assignments in forsaken places, it was hard for me to imagine that it wasn't because my value had been tarnished in their eyes."

"I'm sorry what I did embarrassed you. Or affected you." Asger never would have believed, especially back then, that his father *could* be embarrassed or affected by anything he did. This conversation felt surreal even now, a dream he would wake up from. Only the biting ache in his shoulder convinced him this was reality. "Do you think there's something wrong with us that we're obsessed with pleasing a king who's kind of an ass, worrying about what our peers think, and living up to the expectations of past generations?"

"It is part of belonging to the nobility. It's what we endure in exchange for the land and the right to a say in government. It's our duty to dedicate our lives to serving the crown, to being exemplary."

"I don't think all nobles feel that way." Asger could think of more than a few of his peers who'd dedicated their lives to drinking, whoring, and gambling. Admittedly, they usually weren't firstborns and heirs. They were the lucky sods who had older brothers to shoulder the burden of carrying on the family tradition.

"The ones worth anything do."

Asger wondered if his father included him in that category.

"Anyway, I want you to know—" his father shrugged in his armor, "—I don't think you're a mistake because you've done some dumb things. I've done dumb things too. All things considered, maybe I've judged you too harshly."

Asger wanted to nod vigorously in agreement, but all he said was, "I'll try to do better."

"Good. Me too."

Clanks emanated from the corridor around the bend. Asger touched the hole in his armor—and his flesh—and grimaced. The battle wasn't yet done.

Qin paced behind Bonita in the *Dragon's* small navigation chamber, her hands clasped behind her back as she watched the Kingdom ships flying closer to the moon base—and all the mercenary ships anchored in space around it.

A battle appeared inevitable, but she didn't see how the Kingdom could win. Their fleet numbered only sixteen or seventeen vessels. There had to be at least fifty mercenary ships out there. Fifty *visible* ships. Since Rache's *Fedallah* was out there, who knew how many more vessels with slydar hulls were invisible to the *Dragon's* scanners? Further, the moon itself had weapons platforms scattered across its dark surface.

The question was whether all the mercenaries would fight, or if they would watch. Had Dubashi already paid them?

"I hope they get out of there in time." Bonita gripped the side of her pod, fingers loosening and tightening. Was she feeling as useless as Qin?

"Me too."

"Even if they left now, that shuttle could become collateral damage if they got in the way of the fight."

"I know," Qin said.

"Ah, Bonita?" Viggo's tone had an odd note to it.

"Yes?"

"I was monitoring your conversation with Prince Jorg, and I don't recall you inviting him over for dinner. Is that correct?"

"I think I invited him to stuff his head up his ass." Bonita frowned and tapped the scanner controls.

Qin shifted uneasily. "You didn't say exactly that, but it probably came through."

"I *thought* that. Uh, is that his ship?" Bonita pointed to a blip on the scanner display.

"The *Chivalrous* has left formation and is veering toward us instead of the base," Viggo verified. "It's accelerating rapidly."

Bonita swore and pulled the navigation arm to her temple. Qin gripped the back of the co-pilot's pod. Could the *Dragon* escape? Bonita had maneuvered them in close to an asteroid, practically sitting in one of its craters, so that they wouldn't be noticed. So much for that ploy.

"I'll get my weapons." Qin tapped her claws against the chest plate of her armor.

"Wait," Bonita said. "We're going to try to flee."

"There isn't time, Bonita," Viggo said. "If I had realized sooner that they were coming toward us, I would have warned you. Even if we maneuver away from this asteroid, they would overtake us rapidly."

"Doesn't that prince have a fleet to lead into war?" Bonita demanded in exasperation. "Why is he pestering *us*?"

She fired the thrusters, getting them away from the asteroid. The force threatened to send Qin's legs sailing out behind her.

"Maybe he doesn't know that admirals—and princes—are supposed to lead their fleets from the front." Qin bit her lip, torn between pulling herself into the co-pilot's pod so she wouldn't be hurled around the ship, and running down to her cabin for her weapons.

"He probably considers himself non-expendable," Viggo said.

The comm chimed.

Bonita glared at it. "Do we ignore that or try to chat them up to buy time?"

Qin didn't think Bonita had it in her to *chat up* the Kingdom. Throw invectives at them, possibly. Which would accelerate the time table instead of delaying it.

"What do they want?" Qin wondered. "Their missing knights? Do you think they believed you when you said they weren't on board?"

"How would I know?" Bonita thumped her palm down on the comm panel.

A crisp female voice said, "This is the *Chivalrous*. Prepare to be boarded. If you attempt to flee, we will fire on your ship."

"*Why?*" Bonita demanded.

Qin's magnetic soles almost flew free again as Bonita angled the *Dragon* around the curvature of the asteroid and fired its thrusters. Maybe she hoped she could get around to the back and use it as a shield between them and the Kingdom ship as she flew deeper into the belt.

"You have aided men who are wanted by the Kingdom. Surrender immediately."

"Screw off." Bonita closed the comm.

The *Chivalrous* fired a weapon that had no trouble curving around the asteroid. The scanner display lit up with a warning: INCOMING FIRE.

Bonita tried to maneuver out of the way, but one could only maneuver so quickly in space. Two missiles slammed into the rear of the *Dragon.* Alerts shrieked, and the force threw Qin into the bulkhead behind her pod.

"I'm getting my weapons," she said, wishing she'd made that decision earlier.

"Viggo." Bonita patted the navigation panel in vain. None of the controls responded.

The last thing Qin saw as she maneuvered herself toward the ladder well was the thruster display flashing OFFLINE.

"I'm sorry, Bonita," Viggo said sadly. "With time, perhaps I could fix them, but…"

Bonita swore and followed Qin down to their cabins, going for her own armor and weapons. "They're not taking my ship without a fight," she announced.

Already in her armor, Qin reached the cargo hold and the airlock chamber first. The panel by the hatch showed the *Chivalrous,* looming like a moon compared to them, aligning itself with the *Dragon* and extending an airlock tube.

Qin rushed to the armory and grabbed a few innocent-looking explosives she could plant on the deck. They were similar to the ones she'd used weeks earlier to fend off the boarding party on the *Machu Picchu* and would blow upward instead of damaging the deck. With luck, they'd damage the Kingdom boarding party.

As Qin set the last of them around the airlock hatch, Bonita entered the hold in her armor with a rifle in hand and wearing a bandolier of smoke bombs and grenades. She nodded approvingly at Qin, though her face was grim. Did she doubt they could repel these people? They'd fended off forced boardings before, but not from a ship so large. The *Chivalrous* probably had a crew of a hundred or more. How many thugs would the prince send over?

"Might I suggest hiding, Bonita?" Viggo suggested.

"No," Bonita snarled.

A clank came from the airlock hatch.

"I assume we're not letting them in?" Qin tucked herself into a nook in the hold that provided cover while allowing her to lean out to fire.

"Hell no." Bonita slipped into a similar spot and pointed her rifle at the airlock hatch.

Qin thought about turning off the magnetic soles of her boots and trying to surprise the intruders by firing down from the ceiling, but there was no cover up there, and the angle wouldn't let her shoot into the airlock chamber.

"Really, Bonita," Viggo said in mild reproof. "They've already damaged my engines. You're going to encourage them to torch holes in my hatches?"

"Maybe if we delay them, some of those mercenaries will saunter off and give them a hard time."

"I'm afraid I can tell you that no other ships are in the vicinity."

"Maybe the sun in this system will experience a solar flare and toast all of their equipment."

A wrenching sound almost startled Qin into firing, but it came from the exterior airlock chamber door, not the interior. Not yet.

"They tore it clean off," Viggo said mournfully.

"*Off?* Those hatches are reinforced with four layers of…" Bonita shook her head. "Bastards."

Qin remembered times when that hatch had been forced open before, but previously, it had involved a space-rated blowtorch and ten or fifteen minutes.

The wrenching sound came again, louder than before, and Qin gaped as the inner hatch was forced open, its thick hinges warping as if they were made from the softest metal rather than the sturdiest of alloys. Qin couldn't smell her enemies, not with her helmet on, but the realization of what they were dealing with thundered into her mind before she saw the tarry black figures.

Bonita fired first, probably expecting her energy bolts to bounce off combat armor. They did bounce off, but the crushers that strode into the hold were not armored. They didn't need to be.

Qin fired one of her explosive rounds at the first of two, four, six… no, damn it, ten crushers that strode in. The head of the construct transformed to liquid so quickly that the round passed over the spot where its head had been. It exploded next to the exterior hull, and a breach alarm rang out.

"Captain, I'm sorry," Qin cried out as the crusher's head re-formed.

Two other crushers stepped on the explosives and were blown upward, their bodies warping. They struck the ceiling but merely twisted and pushed off, heading back to the deck. The rest of the crushers, their soles as magnetized as Qin's boots, rushed in. Four headed for Qin and four headed toward Bonita.

"Bonita…" Viggo warned over the speaker. "You must surrender."

Reluctant to risk blowing a hole in the hull, Qin leaped into the crushers, using punches and kicks to attack them. She knew it wouldn't be effective on them, but her weapons weren't effective either.

Frustration lent her even more speed than usual, and she connected, knocking her foes backward, but more surrounded her, and she knew fighting was futile. The last time they'd battled crushers, she, Bonita, Asger, Kim, and Casmir had only managed to get rid of the handful that had tried to get Casmir because they'd had Zee to help. Qin and Bonita had nobody this time, and there were too many.

That didn't keep her from fighting as hard as she could. She was *engineered* to fight, not to give up.

But one finally slipped around behind her and caught her by the shoulder. Even with her great strength, she couldn't break its grip. She kicked out, having the satisfaction of slamming a boot into a dark torso of one in front of her and sending it flying back into the airlock chamber. But another crusher grabbed her from behind, and they soon had her immobilized.

Qin's weapons were ripped away, but she snarled, refusing to acknowledge fear as the crushers twisted her arms behind her back and marched her toward the airlock. Bonita was enduring the same treatment. The crushers had them completely surrounded. There was no escape.

"Hold them there," a man said, appearing in the tube.

A breach alarm pulsed from the bulkheads in the cargo hold. Qin hoped it was for a tiny easily repairable leak, not that these brutes were likely to let them do repairs.

An officer strode into the hold wearing armor, his features obscured by his faceplate. He looked around, then waved for four armored men to enter.

"Search the ship," he said. "We're looking for Kim Sato, Casmir Dabrowski, and William and Bjarke Asger."

"None of whom are here," Bonita growled.

"We'll find out soon," the officer said, then extended a hand toward the crusher. "What do you think of the prince's pets, Captain, I assume it is?"

"Captain Lopez, yes, and they're a lot uglier than Casmir's pets."

Qin frowned. Were these different crushers or had Jorg already gotten ahold of the ones Casmir had been building for the sultan?

"Are they?" the officer asked as his men fanned out to search the ship. "These are some of the originals. I think he helped build them too. Prince Jorg likes them."

"I bet. Why send men in to brutalize women when ugly robots can do it?"

"I'll grant that you're certainly a woman, Captain, but you travel with strange company." He looked at Qin.

Qin growled at him. Bonita smiled.

An armored man chanced on one of the explosives Qin had set. She smiled to herself when he was blown into the air, cursing in pain as his armor was breached. The officer told him to quit screwing around and finish the search. The Kingdom soldiers were a sympathetic lot.

Several minutes later, the Kingdom troops returned. "We didn't see anybody else, sir."

"That's what I told you." Bonita glared.

"Where are they?"

"On that base, trying to help your people. I don't know why they're bothering. You're not worth it."

The officer gazed at her. "Has anyone ever advised you, Captain, that it's not wise to antagonize the people holding you captive?"

"Never heard that, no."

"Bring them along." The officer waved for the crushers to follow him.

Qin took a long look back as she was herded first into the airlock, and she wondered if she would ever see the *Dragon* again.

"You're seriously kidnapping us from our own ship?" Bonita demanded, the crushers shoving her after Qin. "I've committed no crimes, and you have no jurisdiction here."

"You're not being imprisoned because you're a criminal, Captain, though I would be shocked if a little research didn't turn up some indiscretions. But as an incentive to motivate others."

CHAPTER 32

JUST AS CASMIR FOUND THE SOUND CONTROLS FOR the camera in the conference room, so he could hear what Dubashi was saying in that meeting, the sound of guns firing rang out in the corridor. He jumped. Something clanged off the door of Dubashi's office. Muffled thuds came through, and Casmir heard Bjarke shout. He had to trust that the crushers and the knights would take care of the new threat.

Casmir switched to the computer station at one of Dubashi's desks. Even with such formidable allies defending the office doors, he feared he didn't have much time.

As he searched for a way to take over one of the displays in that conference room, while keeping the people inside from turning it off once he started transmitting, Casmir spotted a file name that startled him. *Jager*.

That was all it said, with the file extension telling him it was a video clip.

He tapped it open, unable to resist, even as another bullet clanged off their door.

"Just a quick look," he whispered.

Tristan was organizing the financial reports into graphs. Casmir should have a couple of minutes.

Jager's face, little different than it had been the day Casmir had spoken to him in the dungeon, appeared on the comm display. "Not only are we disinterested in trading with some self-proclaimed prince whose supposed royalty only comes from the crowns he's lied, cheated, and swindled others out of over the centuries, but we will see to it that your little empire is wiped out when we take System Stymphalia for our own."

The clip stopped playing. That was it? Some snippet from a longer conversation that Dubashi had saved as… what? Motivation?

"Why would Jager have goaded someone so powerful and influential?" Tristan had paused his work to watch the video play.

"I don't know. It almost seems like…"

"What?"

Casmir hesitated to say the words, since this snippet had clearly been trimmed from some surrounding conversation—maybe Dubashi had been blustering and threatening just as much as Jager had.

"Casmir?" Tristan prompted.

"That Jager wanted this, wanted Dubashi to start a war with him. With *us*."

Tristan didn't point out that he wasn't a part of the Kingdom any longer. "But what about the news footage that's made its way here? Unless it was faked, Odin—Zamek City—is being bombed. Jager couldn't have wanted that."

"I wonder." Casmir remembered the message he'd gotten from Oku of her standing at her father's side in what had looked like a windowless secured complex, not old Drachen Castle. Basilisk Citadel, he guessed, though he'd never been inside. A forcefield was known to protect the Citadel from all threats ancient and modern. So even if the city was in danger, Jager and his family were safe.

Tristan poked him. "Wonder later. I'm ready with your file."

Casmir glanced back at a graph and a simple bank statement with the negative numbers circled and bolded in a large red font. "Good. Give me a moment."

Casmir pulled out his tablet and plugged it into the nearest port, bringing up a program that should help him take over the comm system. An explosion roared outside the doors, and he almost dropped the tablet. Somewhere nearby, rock snapped, reminding him ominously of the astroshaman base. How many levels of stone were above their heads now?

"I hope they're not buying us time with their lives." Tristan stared at the door.

"You can join them if you want. But first tell me if there's anything else you found that would help me convince a bunch of mercenaries not to work for Dubashi."

"He hasn't paid any of the people he's got blockading the System Lion gate in over a month. It's probably only the fact that they're stuck in that system that they haven't realized their pay is overdue. And since Dubashi is a Miners' Union prince, they must assume he's good for it."

"Why *isn't* he? I know war is expensive, but…" Casmir trailed off as he got the access he wanted. He was ready.

"He bought a *lot* of the warships that he sent on the blockade mission, and it looks like he's got some more here in the base or elsewhere in this system too. Maybe he bought them to sacrifice them to this venture. I'm sure he's lost dozens by now to the Kingdom Fleet. Maybe he thought he could do it all himself, but he's realizing he needs even more firepower." Tristan waved to the conference room still on the display, to Dubashi walking about, hands raised like a preacher delivering a sermon.

"Why would he invest so much in such an all-or-nothing venture?"

"That's not atypical for entrepreneurs, I'm learning. They take big risks and fail often, but sometimes, those risks can pay off in a big way, and the rewards are vast."

"Like a planet?" Casmir asked.

"I imagine so."

"All right. Thank you. Wait, one more task, please. Can you cycle through those camera displays and try to find Kim? I think she might be stuck in a medical lab somewhere."

"I'll look."

Casmir toggled on the sound from the camera in the conference room, and Dubashi's voice filled the office. It wasn't, he could tell right away, the voice of a smooth orator, but he was indeed promising great wealth to whomever joined him.

Casmir would never get a better opening. He took over the speakers in the room as well as one of the displays.

"Ask to see that money," he said.

Dubashi whirled toward a speaker.

Realizing he might destroy them or be able to wrest control back, Casmir spoke quickly.

"You're being swindled, my friends. My name is Casmir Dabrowski, a roboticist working for Sultan Shayban—" Vaguely true, and Casmir hoped these mercenaries would be more likely to believe an ally of Shayban than a loyal minion from the Kingdom, "—and I'm looking at Prince Dubashi's bank account right now. It's empty, my mercenary friends." He tapped a button to place the pretty chart Tristan had made on the display in the conference room. "*Worse* than empty. He's in the negative. This war has bankrupted him."

"Lies," Dubashi barked.

He rushed toward the display, yanking out a DEW-Tek pistol. But Rache, bless his cold mercenary soul, intercepted him, catching his wrist before Dubashi could fire at the display.

"Since you don't know me or have any reason to take my word for it," Casmir went on, inspiration striking as he glanced at Tristan, "allow me to have Princess Nalini's new business partner—if you travel often in this system, I trust you have heard of her—detail what he found in Dubashi's bank files."

Casmir waved the startled Tristan forward to expound on the chart. He had no idea if mercenaries would have heard of the sultan's entrepreneurial daughter, but he didn't think it would matter. Establishing her—and Tristan—as business people might be enough.

Despite being surprised, Tristan offered a solid summing up of what he'd found, managing to encapsulate Dubashi's financial straits in a few succinct sentences. They were delivered without passion—he didn't sound at all like he was trying to sway someone to his side—which served to make the words more believable.

Meanwhile, Dubashi struggled against Rache and shouted for his guards. Armored robots, not men, rushed into the conference room, but the mercenaries, who clearly wanted to hear more, interfered with their progress and kept them from assisting their boss.

Dubashi spun toward Rache and whispered a string of harsh words that Casmir's purloined camera on the far wall couldn't pick up. Whatever he said—A threat? A promise?—prompted Rache to release him. Dubashi threw something to the floor, and smoke rose up.

No, more than smoke, judging by the coughing that started up. Rache raised his armor's helmet, as did several of the other mercenaries.

Dubashi leaped onto the table and flung himself over the tangle of robots and men, displaying strength and alacrity shocking in someone that age—shocking if he'd been fully human, that was. He bypassed the crowd and rushed out the doorway as the smoke filled the room.

"How much do you want to bet he's headed up here to strangle us himself?" Tristan asked.

"A distinct possibility." Casmir bit his lip, considering the chaos in the conference room.

Rache had disappeared. Was he chasing after Dubashi? If he wanted Dubashi, why had he let him go?

The remaining mercenaries were still fighting robots. Or maybe each other. Or both.

"I'm surprised that was so easy," Tristan admitted.

It *had* been easy. "I bet they'd already seen a lot of signals that Dubashi might not be quite as wealthy as they'd previously believed. If it's true that the mercenaries that got sucked in for the initial blockade haven't been paid in a while…"

"Word might have gotten out." Tristan nodded.

"Also, you were convincing. You sounded like an accountant."

"And everyone believes accountants?"

"Unbiased ones."

Tristan's lip twisted, as if he didn't believe there were many unbiased accountants out there. But what he said was, "Do you think they'll go back to their ships and get out of here before Jorg's fleet arrives?"

"Good question." Casmir looked at the displays showing the mercenary ships floating in space around the moon base. "There are so many warships out there, all apparently available to hire, for someone with the money to do so."

That was definitely not Casmir. It could be Jorg if he was smart enough to do so. Should Casmir attempt to send the prince a message from here? Did the Kingdom *need* to hire these mercenaries? Or would it be enough if they didn't show up to reinforce the enemy fleet already in System Lion?

"That almost could have been me." Tristan offered with a rueful smile.

"Because you're the princess's business partner?" Casmir tapped through the idents of the incoming Kingdom ships and sent a comm to Jorg's *Chivalrous*, wondering if a message originating at Dubashi's base would be accepted.

"No. My mentor, Sir Sebastian Hanh, tried to leave his estate to me back when I was still a knight in good standing. He had a son and a family, so that didn't go over well. If I ever show up back on Odin, they'll drag me before a judge to sign away any interest in it. If it hasn't already been signed away by the king or the Senate. They don't care for non-nobles receiving estates."

"I can imagine. Can you try to find Kim?" Casmir waved Tristan to the displays featuring internal cameras. "And, uhm, it would be good to know if Dubashi is about to storm in."

"Yes. Sorry, I got distracted earlier."

"Don't be sorry. You were great. I'm glad you agreed to help me instead of flinging yourself onto that tank with the others."

Tristan shrugged. "I spent a lot more years training to be a knight than to be a financier. Flinging comes naturally."

"Well, you should work on overcoming that. You've got a brain."

"Would you be embarrassed if I admitted that means a lot coming from you?"

"Puzzled but not embarrassed. I only get embarrassed when I have seizures in front of cute girls. Come on, Jorg. Answer the comm. Your wayward roboticist wants to talk to you."

Tristan blinked at the abrupt topic shift.

Casmir glanced at the camera zoomed out to show the Kingdom fleet. Where *was* the *Chivalrous*? He leaned over and ran a quick search. The camera swiveled and locked onto two ships near an asteroid. One was the *Chivalrous* and one was—

He sucked in a startled breath. The *Stellar Dragon.*

What were they doing *together*?

Casmir assumed Bonita had found the asteroid to hide behind to stay out of the way of the action, but why in the universe would Jorg be taking his ship over to harass hers? Did he think Kim was aboard? Or that his knights were? He couldn't want Qin or Bonita. *Why?*

The *Chivalrous* finally answered the comm, and Casmir lurched back in time to see Jorg's face pop up on the screen. A second of panic welled up as he forgot what he'd intended to say in light of this new information. Should he ask what the hell the prince was doing over there? Or maybe if he gave Jorg a new direction to go, he'd leave Bonita alone.

Jorg started to open his mouth, and Casmir rushed to cut him off.

"Oh, Your Highness. Thank you for answering me personally. I'm honored. And comming, you may have noticed, from Dubashi's office inside his base. An ally and I—" Casmir caught himself before mentioning Tristan by name, recalling that he and Jorg were mortal enemies now, "—managed to break into Dubashi's finances and learn that he's lacking a certain cash flow right now and can't pay any of the mercenaries he's hired or is trying to hire. Naturally, we crashed their meeting and let these new mercenaries know. I think it's possible that you may be facing fewer enemies when you arrive. I'm sure that will please you." Casmir *hoped* that would please him. "But it occurred to me that you might wish to take advantage and hire these ready-at-hand mercenaries to help evict the ships blockading the System Lion gate."

Prince Jorg's face went through a half a dozen emotions as he listened to Casmir's rapid-fire speech. Or perhaps it was a nervous-burbling speech.

"Hire mercenaries!" Unfortunately, his face settled on the last emotion, rage. "We do not hire those bottom-feeding lowlifes. We don't need them."

"Uhm." Casmir wanted to argue, wanted to convince the prince otherwise—the weeks the blockade had been in place suggested the Kingdom needed to hire *someone*. But before he got two more words out, Jorg continued on, his voice raised to drown out Casmir's.

"And you! What are you doing on that base? You're supposed to be delivering crushers to me."

"Yes, Your Highness. But I assumed you'd want Dubashi thwarted first. I have twelve crushers—" Casmir hoped he still had twelve crushers, "—and left the manufacturing facility at Stardust Palace building more. The one hundred you asked for. Sultan Shayban agreed to—"

"That ass. You left the manufacturing facility unmanned? He'll try to keep them all for himself. Dabrowski!"

"I do plan to go back to retrieve them." Casmir smiled and tried not to unravel in the face of this illogical anger. He was here helping the prince, the entire Kingdom. How could Jorg truly be upset?

To the side, out of view of the camera, Tristan shook his head slowly, as if he'd expected nothing less from the unstable prince.

"And I'll bring them to you, of course, Your Highness," Casmir continued, forcing good cheer. "Just give me a rendezvous point. Or even better, if you could come pick us up—" while leaving the *Dragon* alone… "—that would expedite things. I don't actually have a long-range craft available to take me all the way back to the palace."

"No?" Jorg's anger faded into something cooler, his eyes closing to slits. "Are you certain you hadn't planned to get away with my knights and all your crushers in this freighter we found lurking near an asteroid?"

Casmir tried not to quail under that scrutiny. Was that why Jorg was over there? Had he believed Bonita was going to be his pilot in a wild escape from the base and the fleet? That didn't make sense. The *Dragon* wasn't as fast as most of the ships Jorg had gathered.

"The *Stellar Dragon*? No, we parted ways with it. The captain is on her own mission, trying to find a missing scientist."

"We'll see about that." Jorg leaned in, tapped a button, and the camera view shifted to a stark brig cell.

Casmir couldn't keep from swearing under his breath. Qin and Bonita, both stripped of their armor, both bruised and bleeding, stood behind bars, glaring defiantly.

"Why?" Casmir whispered, confused, his heart aching for his friends. He hadn't wanted them to be caught up in this madness.

"Because they mean something to you," Jorg said. "And to Sir Bjarke and Sir William Asger, I understand. You've all made grave mistakes in not following my orders."

"But we *were* following them. Especially Bjarke! He's loyal to you, Your Highness."

"An odd emphasis. Are you saying that you and William are not?" Jorg's lip curled.

"No, Your Highness." Casmir wondered if Jorg knew anything about the message Jager had sent with Oku. If he did, wouldn't he believe that Casmir didn't need any other levers applied to him? "I simply thought I could find my own path with the crushers, and I know you didn't ask me to take over Dubashi's moon base, but I assumed you would want him captured and out of the fight."

Jorg tilted his head. "*Have* you captured him?"

"Not exactly yet, but he's here somewhere. We *can* capture him." Casmir hoped so, since that had been his promise to the sultan.

Jorg grunted. "Do so, and I'll spare the lives of your friends. Or trade their freedom for yours, I should say. You, as far as I'm concerned, are a wanted man. I plan to take you back to the Kingdom to face my father. In cuffs."

Jorg, Casmir decided as he stared numbly at the display, was not as good at manipulating people as Jager.

"Bring Dubashi to me," Jorg said, "alive or dead. I don't care which, but I want him. If you fail, you'll all regret it."

The comm went dark.

"When did our government leaders turn into super villains out of a comic book?" Casmir croaked, the image of Bonita and Qin injured and locked up burned into his mind.

Tristan sighed. "I think Jorg always has been. He's always liked seeing people hurt. Jager is… I'm not sure. More subtle, at the least."

"Yeah." Casmir rubbed his face with a shaking hand, trying to focus on what he needed to do next. "We need to find Kim *and* Dubashi. And we need to do it quickly, because the rest of Jorg's fleet is almost here."

"I found her." Tristan's voice was grim. He pointed to one of the displays.

It featured a sprawling medical laboratory with an alarming wall of rockets gleaming in the back, like shark teeth jutting up from a rack on the floor to a high ceiling. Kim was in a side lab, strapped into some madman's torture chair. And a bunch of robots and a woman with a rifle were pointing their weapons at her.

"We have to go," Casmir said. "Now!"

***

Hope whispered through Kim when she heard the door to the laboratory complex open, but General Kalb merely glanced aside without reacting and kept her rifle pointed at Kim's chest. With the two robots looming beside her, and the metal fasteners of the chair keeping Kim from even moving her head, she found the rifle almost laughably superfluous. But there was nothing in her now capable of laughter.

Dubashi walked into her view, his sherwani ruffled and his face flushed. Kim hoped someone had punched him.

Despite the dishevelment, his voice was calm when he spoke. "You said a couple of the rockets are still loaded and that the virus is indeed inside?"

Kalb nodded curtly.

"Watch her." Dubashi jogged out of sight. "I'll get them onto the ship. We're evacuating."

Kalb looked sharply in the direction he'd gone. "What happened to the mercenaries?"

The faint hope returned, though Kim feared that whatever was going wrong for them wouldn't help her.

"They found out that finances are tight," Dubashi said, a soft clank sounding from the back of the lab, "and surprisingly few were willing to work for physical assets."

Kalb snorted. "Were any of them?"

"Rache."

Kim closed her eyes.

"We've got Rache. *He* knows the value of assets. He's going to assassinate the king and that idiot prince, too, if he can. And if we've got two rockets, that may still be enough to clear off Odin for our people's use."

Clear off Odin. He truly intended to use the virus. Not just bluff. Not bargain with the power those rockets would give him.

"We just have to get them safely to System Lion," Dubashi added. A faint rattling started up. "There, the rockets are on their way to my ship."

Kim opened her mouth, not sure what she would say but knowing she had to say *something*. She had to try to sway them somehow.

A computerized voice came from the speakers, drowning out her attempt. "Alert, alert, the base is under attack. Moon shields have been deployed, and Automated Weapons Sequence One is firing."

A faint shudder reverberated through the lab, and vials and equipment clinked and clanked in cabinets. On a station, everything would have been secured against the possibility of it losing its spin gravity, but on a moon, with its constant gravity, nobody had taken such precautions.

A hot flush of fear went through Kim as she imagined stored containers of Scholar Sunflyer's concoction tipping over and breaking. Not that the virus was the immediate concern. If these megalomaniacs shot her, what did it matter if it escaped into the air?

"Do we need her?" Kalb jerked the tip of her rifle toward Kim's chest.

The galaxy suit underneath her biohazard suit would protect her from a couple of shots but not from sustained fire.

"No," Dubashi said, walking back into view. "Ironic that we never did. Shoot her."

Kim trembled with anger and fear, but she refused to beg for her life. She glared at Kalb, willing the shields to fall and for the base to be destroyed before they could escape.

The door opened and someone in black armor bowled into Kalb an instant before she fired. Rache. It could only be Rache in that armor.

His momentum carried them out of Kim's view, Dubashi leaping back before being taken down as well. Clatters and thuds echoed from the walls, armored punches against armored bodies. A wrenching squeal sounded as Rache roared in anger.

Dubashi reached for a weapon as his two robots rushed away from Kim's side and toward the fight, but he must have thought better of engaging. He hurried out the door.

Kim almost roared *Coward!* after him but clamped down on the word. The fewer opponents Rache had to battle, the better.

General Kalb yelled in pain, but then the noise was cut off with a sickening crunch. Something was hurled across the lab and crashed into a Glasnax wall. Her body? Or Rache's? Kim had lost sight of everyone, even the robots.

"There are containers full of a deadly virus over by the rockets," she yelled, realizing that the fight might break open the ones she hadn't had a chance to incinerate.

"I'll do my best not to break them," came Rache's voice, surprisingly calm amid what sounded like wrecking balls clashing together.

"Thank you." She rolled her eyes at her ludicrous response.

An even more ludicrous, if only for its extreme politeness, "You're welcome," came back.

Another shudder went through the lab, rattling equipment and vials. It was fiercer than the first one. Kim imagined Jorg's fleet firing relentlessly at the moon's surface while the mercenary ships scattered, doing nothing to impede the Kingdom attack.

Two more men ran into the lab, and Kim groaned. Dubashi had sent reinforcements.

But, no, she realized as her mind processed what she'd seen. The two men wore the silver liquid armor of knights and carried the trademark pertundos. An entire stream of crushers came in after them.

"Don't kill the guy in black armor," came Casmir's voice from the doorway.

Kim sagged in relief. She'd never been so pleased to see him walk into a room.

Tristan came after him. Good. She was relieved that his team had all made it.

"That's Rache!" Bjarke roared.

"Who we're definitely not worrying about picking a fight with right now," Casmir said firmly as he looked around. "You and he can punch each other senseless once we get off this base."

"Over here." Kim couldn't wave but lifted a few fingers.

Casmir rushed to her chair. "One second. Let me find the controls."

Another shudder coursed through the complex. A snap came from the ceiling, and Kim watched in horror as the cement split and a crack ran to the wall.

"I think Dubashi's shields are failing," she muttered.

"They just need to hold long enough for us to get back to our shuttle," Casmir said. "And for me to bask in the glory of getting to rescue you. I *never* thought this would happen."

Kim rolled her eyes. "I'd rather hoped it wouldn't."

But she couldn't bring herself to feel embarrassed. Not now. She just wanted to get out of this alive.

"*I'm* rescuing her," Rache said, stepping into view. "I was here first."

"You were busy wrestling with robots like some super villain's cannon fodder." Casmir found the controls that released the chair straps. "Look, I hit the button. That makes me the rescuer."

"Please, you're the damsel in distress. Zee probably carried you here." Rache sprang forward to grab Kim's arm and help her out of the chair.

"I ran all the way on my own two legs," Casmir said.

Kim tried to wave away the help—it wasn't as if she'd been injured—but Casmir gripped her other arm.

"Rache, did you see Dubashi?" Casmir asked.

"See, yes, but he ran away while I was tackling the woman aiming a rifle at Kim's chest."

"Damn, I was supposed to kidnap him. But I do see why you prioritized Kim."

"I thought you would."

"Let's get out of here." By the time they reached the exit, Kim managed to extricate herself from their overly helpful grips. "Wait!"

She remembered the canisters she hadn't had time to incinerate and rushed back, relieved to find them on the floor where she had left them. While the men waited, she destroyed them, trying not to think about what might have happened if Rache and the others had broken them during their battle.

Bjarke and Asger, having utterly destroyed the two robots, surged out ahead of the group and took the lead, racing through the corridors toward a lift. Tristan came behind Kim, Casmir, and Rache, followed by the squad of crushers.

When Casmir reached the lift, he waved at a sensor, and the doors opened. Even without a wireless network, he must have found a way to give himself access to everything.

The entire group crammed in, which Kim wouldn't have thought possible, but the crushers melted and flattened themselves against the walls.

"Are we going to hunt for Dubashi?" Bjarke asked, surprisingly looking to Casmir. Deferring to him?

The lift lurched to a stop, and the lights went out as more tremors wracked the base.

"We better get out of here while we can," Tristan said.

Casmir hesitated. "The blueprints show more than ten ship bays in the base in addition to the one we came in through. Even if we had time to look for him, he would probably have taken off before we guessed right."

The lift groaned, then lurched back into motion as the lights came back on, dim emergency lights.

"Better to survive and fight another day," Rache said.

Casmir shook his head bleakly but didn't object.

They exited the lift on the top level of the base. Huge pieces of rubble scattered the floor and the lights flickered. Kim and Rache started off in one direction, then paused when Casmir and the others headed the other way. Kim realized they'd been brought in through different hangars.

"This way, Kim." Casmir waved for her to follow as the knights and crushers pounded off ahead of him.

Rache looked back at her. "Are you coming with me or him?"

Kim remembered Dubashi's words that Rache had taken his offer, that he was on his way to assassinate the king. She shook her head. She would not go with him on that mission, and she highly doubted she could talk him out of it. Maybe she would try, but not from his ship. If she had *any* chance of clearing suspicion and doubt from her name back home, she couldn't spend any more time with him.

"I can't come with you." Kim didn't mean the words to come out laced with disappointment or condemnation, but she feared they did. "I'm sorry."

She waved, then turned and didn't look back as she ran after Casmir and the others. It wasn't as if she could have seen the expression on Rache's masked face even if she had looked at him.

CHAPTER 33

CASMIR SAT IN A POD ON THEIR SHUTTLE, his elbows on his knees, his hands gripping the back of his head. They'd kept Dubashi from hiring all those mercenaries and sending them off to invade System Lion, but Kim had just filled him in that Dubashi had likely gotten away with two rockets filled with a virus so lethal it fell into some special *planet-killer* category.

"There's more," Kim admitted from the pod next to his.

Casmir groaned and lifted his head. "What?"

They were flying away from the base, with Tristan, Bjarke, and Asger up front in navigation, the men cursing and gasping and oohing as the Kingdom ships pummeled the moon. Automated weapons on the surface fired back at them, but the efforts seemed half-hearted.

Casmir couldn't care less about the moon, not if Dubashi had already gotten away. Bjarke, who was piloting their shuttle, hadn't said anything about another ship escaping the base, but Casmir assumed the formerly wealthy Miners' Union prince could afford slydar. He might have slipped away with ten ships, for all they knew.

Kim spoke in a voice so low Casmir almost couldn't hear her. "Dubashi said that Rache accepted his contract, to assassinate Jager and also Jorg if he can."

"He'd do that *without* a contract or any money, wouldn't he?" Casmir asked. "The answer must be yes, because he was in that room when Tristan informed all the mercenaries that Dubashi is out of funds and can't pay."

"Is that what happened? I wondered where all the mercenary ships went." Kim waved vaguely toward the forward display. "Dubashi said he still had assets and that Rache was willing to accept some of them. Maybe he's getting an asteroid belt or mining ship in exchange." She hitched a shoulder. "I gather he had a… *thing* about going to assassinate Jager and that he'd been waiting a long time for someone to give him this mission."

Casmir flicked his fingers and dropped his head back into his lap. He didn't want to say assassin-Rache was inconsequential, but he cared a lot more about the possibility of horrific biological weapons being deployed on his home world than he did about the king's life. Jager had bodyguards. Casmir's family—everybody he knew and cared about—did not. Few of them even had galaxy suits or other self-contained suits that could protect them from a virus.

"We have to warn Jorg." Casmir grimaced, remembering his *last* attempt to interact with Jorg. And that Jorg had Qin and Bonita now.

"About Rache?" Kim asked.

"About Dubashi and the rockets."

"Ah. Yes. We should warn Jager, too, even if there's no way to know if a courier ship will be able to get through the gate before Dubashi does."

"At the least, any messages should get to Odin before he does."

Kim leaned back, a brooding expression on her usually expressionless face. She was probably worried that Rache would get himself killed trying to get to Jager. If Royal Intelligence had picked up one of the same slydar detectors that Shayban's people had, it was very possible.

Casmir wondered if he should comm Rache, now that they were away from the moon and had access to the system network again, and suggest working together to get Dubashi. Would Rache even consider it? Probably not. Not if he'd accepted a contract from him.

Still, Rache might be their only way out of this system. When Kim had made her choice at the lift not to go with him, Casmir had almost pointed out that both shuttles might end up going back to the *Fedallah*. He didn't want to be stuck with Rache or ask him for another favor, but he *had* borrowed this shuttle and should return it. Further, he worried they didn't have a way to get to the gate or even back to Stardust Palace. This shuttle didn't have the fuel to reach either destination.

He hoped, perhaps vainly, that Jorg had left the *Stellar Dragon* adrift and that it wasn't too badly damaged. Maybe they could fly *it* to the palace.

And then what? Casmir rubbed the back of his neck. How was he supposed to get Bonita and Qin back? Could he barter the information about Dubashi and the virus for them? Somehow convince Jorg to drop his friends off at Stardust Palace? Didn't he have to go there, anyway, to pick up the crushers?

Casmir smiled thinly, imagining Jorg's frustration when he found out that the pristine new crusher army wouldn't take orders from him. He might be delayed for days there while he tried to figure out how to reprogram them.

Unfortunately, neither Dubashi nor Rache would be delayed. Casmir assumed they both had fast ships, ships with slydar that could run the blockade without being seen, and would continue straight on to Odin.

He sat up as a thought occurred to him.

"What is it?" Kim asked, watching him.

"Maybe nothing. Maybe something."

Casmir composed a message.

Kyla Moonrazor, I thank you for the tip about Dubashi's finances. We were able to dig into his banking information and convince a lot of mercenaries that they don't want to work for him right now. Unfortunately, he slipped away from us with... How much should he admit? What would an astroshaman from another system care about the Kingdom and its citizens? But she would probably find out anyway. She could surf the networks as easily as he could. *A weapon that could wipe out all human life on Odin. I don't know where you are or even what you're doing in this system, but you mentioned having the ability to take control of the wormhole gate for your people. Is there any chance you're willing to do so now? Or in the next couple of days? I'd like to keep Dubashi from escaping this system and invading ours. At least until we can get to the gate and deal with him.*

Casmir debated before sending it. He'd already promised to help her find a hiding place for her people. What more could he offer? A crusher? He doubted she would be impressed; she could probably make them or something similar herself. But it was all he had to bargain with.

There's little I can offer you for your assistance, but I have been making new crushers and giving them out as presents. If you're interested in one, let me know. Thank you.

He signed it and sent it, expecting a delay again. Wherever she was, it wasn't anywhere close to Dubashi's base.

"Wow," Tristan murmured from navigation. "They blew up that entire half of the moon. And then some. I knew Prince Jorg was a vengeful bastard, but wow."

"I doubt anyone was even left on it." Bjarke growled. "I've located the *Stellar Dragon*, and it's damaged. There's no life on board. Damn. What did Jorg say when he spoke to you, Tristan? To Casmir?"

Casmir sank back, a weariness almost as deep as he'd felt when he'd had the Plague seeping into him. The infiltration hadn't been that hard, not his part, nor had it taken that long. Maybe his weariness came from this constant worry that he wouldn't be able to make things right and go home. He'd never be able to hug his parents again, or go to gaming nights with his friends, or see one of his students graduate and get a great job.

Or ask Oku for that coffee date. She wouldn't want to have anything to do with him now that her father was offering her up as some prize. Who knew if Casmir was even the only one Jager had made that offer to? Maybe they had called up a few admirals while they'd been at it.

He couldn't forget that caged look in Oku's eyes. For the first time, he couldn't bring himself to replay one of her videos.

Fortunately, when Casmir didn't reply right away, Tristan, who had heard the gist of that conversation, summed it up for Bjarke.

"I can't believe he would do that, kidnap innocent civilians." Bjarke sounded so disappointed.

Casmir wondered if this might be the first waning of his steadfast loyalty toward the crown.

"I can," Tristan said.

"Do we go to the *Dragon*?" Bjarke looked back at Casmir. "Or try to join up with the fleet?"

Casmir raised his eyebrows, shocked that Bjarke would defer to him or ask his opinion. He'd expected to have to wrestle the knight—or have Zee wrestle the knight—to get him to go to the *Dragon*.

"Are you only asking me because you're afraid the fleet will shoot us down if we zip in close in one of Rache's shuttles?"

"That did cross my mind, but I can comm them. And this is his unmarked shuttle." Bjarke's gaze shifted to Asger, then to Tristan, and then back to Asger.

Casmir waited before giving his answer, sensing that Bjarke was trying to figure something out. Or maybe his heart had already figured it out, and he was trying to rearrange his rational mind in a way that could accept it.

"Even though we didn't manage to catch Dubashi," Bjarke said slowly, swiveling to look at Casmir again, "I'm not convinced we did the wrong thing by disobeying orders. Dubashi would have escaped that regardless." Bjarke waved toward the demolished moon. "And if he'd succeeded in hiring those mercenaries, mercenaries with ships totaling more than double what Jorg brought to the battlefield, I think Jorg and everyone out there would have been killed. No, not Jorg. He was over here, picking on Bonita's ship." Bjarke clenched his jaw, indignation and rage burning in his eyes like hot embers in a fire.

Nobody else was surprised by Jorg's actions. Not now. Bjarke had been late to arrive at his conclusions.

But Casmir didn't blame him. Bjarke had spent his whole life loyal to the king, loyal to the system that rewarded him. If anything, Casmir was delighted that he seemed willing to consider another option now.

Tristan cleared his throat. "If it's at all possible, I would like a ride back to Stardust Palace. I don't regret coming, but I… didn't even say a proper goodbye to Nalini."

Casmir nodded. "Take us to the *Dragon*, please, Bjarke. Let's see if the ship is repairable. If not, we'll *have* to turn ourselves over to Jorg."

Or Rache, Casmir added silently. But Rache may have already taken off on his mission. Even if he hadn't, would he welcome Bjarke and Tristan onto his ship? Even his relationship with Asger was iffy. Kim was the only guarantee, and would she, knowing what she knew of Rache's plans, even be willing to go?

Casmir did not ask.

"El Mago!" Viggo's voice rang from the bulkheads as Casmir and the others stepped out of the airlock and into the cargo hold.

The *Dragon*'s damage had been apparent from the outside, including an exterior hatch door that had been ripped off, but they had managed to dock the shuttle to it. As they'd come aboard, they had passed some of Viggo's repair bots working on sealing breaches in the hull—fortunately the inner airlock hatch had not been completely ripped off—but Casmir was already creating a list of things he would have to do to make the freighter space-worthy again. Right now, the *Dragon* was floating like a derelict in the shadow of an asteroid.

"I'm so relieved to see you," Viggo went on. "They stole Bonita and Qin. That dreadful officer and a bunch of crushers."

Casmir missed a step and almost floated free when he didn't get his magnetic sole down in time. He still had *his* dozen crushers. Could Jorg have gone to Stardust Palace Station after they'd left and picked up the next batch? No, there wouldn't have been time, even if Sultan Shayban had let him onto his station. Jorg or one of the other Kingdom ships must have had some of the originals.

Ice chilled his veins at the idea of any of his crushers being used to capture his friends. To *hurt* his friends. He remembered how battered Bonita and Qin had been in that video, and he had to take a deep breath to calm himself down, to keep himself from hating Jorg and wanting revenge on him. That was Rache's schtick. Not his. The thought of becoming like Rache in any way terrified him.

"I'm sorry they were taken, Viggo," Casmir said. "I'll do my best to repair you, and then we can go find them."

"I certainly hope so. *Thank* you, Casmir. For ages, I've been wasting away with worry and feelings of abandonment, fearing I would tumble into some asteroid, be smashed beyond repair, and meet the end of my existence."

"Hasn't it only been three hours since they were taken?" Bjarke asked.

"Four, thank you."

Casmir started toward the engine room, but before he'd taken more than a dozen steps, Viggo said, "Oh, dear."

"What?" Casmir asked.

"There's another ship approaching. A very *large* warship."

"Mercenary? Or Kingdom?" Casmir looked toward Bjarke.

If it was a mercenary, Casmir might be the best one to try to make a deal, but if it was the Kingdom, Bjarke would be the logical person to speak with them.

"It is the *Osprey*," Viggo said.

"Oh. Hm." Casmir didn't know how to react to that. He liked to think he'd built a relationship with Ishii, but if Ishii had been punished for letting Kim go, he might be more bitter than ever. What if Jorg had sent the *Osprey* to finish them off? As a test or a chance to *prove* themselves? Casmir was so tired of that word.

"Let's see what Ishii has to say." Asger headed for the ladder well.

"What if that ambassador has taken charge and Ishii is in the brig?" Casmir muttered, but he followed after Asger.

Kim, Tristan, and Bjarke must have been curious, for they came up to navigation too. They passed a few forlorn vacuums along the way, cleaning up in case their captain came back.

In navigation, Viggo toggled between the cameras to put the *Osprey* on the forward display, the warship huge as it approached.

"Is your comm working, Viggo?" Casmir asked.

The comm panel flashed, alerting them to an incoming message, and Ishii's dyspeptic face appeared on the display.

"Never mind. I see that it is." Casmir forced a smile, but maybe it would have been better if he'd appeared badly beaten and the recent victim of a seizure. Those were the times he'd managed to get sympathy from his old robotics-camp nemesis. "Hello, Sora. Did you enjoy blowing up the moon? I hope you appreciated the lack of mercenaries there when you arrived."

Normally, Casmir wouldn't rush to take credit for a good deed, but as with Jorg, he hoped it would keep Ishii from exploding at him. He and his friends *had* helped.

"Yes, Dabrowski, we appreciate that you told the mercenaries that he was broke. And that for whatever reason, they actually believed you."

Casmir almost gaped, surprised he'd found out. Had Ishii—or Jorg—had a plant in that meeting? "That was Tristan who reported on the finances. He's very good."

Maybe if Ishii reported that to someone, Tristan would get out of some of the hot water he was in with the knighthood.

"I don't know who that is, and I don't care right now. Tell me, did we manage to blow up that self-proclaimed prince, or did he get out alive?" Ishii didn't sound angry. He sounded tired. Casmir wondered what he'd endured this past week as a loyal captain in Jorg's little fleet.

"I'm positive he got out." Casmir looked behind him for Kim, but Zee had followed him up and loomed behind him, as if to lend an intimidation factor to Casmir. "We're not sure with how many ships, but uhm…"

Kim squeezed around Zee to face the display. Casmir watched Ishii for signs of fury toward her. He would butt in if Ishii was an ass about her refusal to obey Jorg.

"He had me strapped down and spoke freely in front of me to his officer," Kim said in her flat deadpan voice. "From what I heard, he got away with two rockets loaded with an altered version of the Orthobuliaviricetes virus, and he plans to use it on Odin."

"Is that as deadly as it sounds?" Ishii asked.

"Even more so."

Ishii swore, the fury that Casmir had expected coming to life. At least it wasn't directed at them. Yet.

"He must have slydar," Ishii said. "We didn't see any ships getting out of there except for your shuttle and the shuttles that went directly to the mercenary ships. I'm going to assume he had his own vessel and wasn't hitching a ride with someone."

"I'd assume so too," Casmir said. "We were going to tell Jorg about the rockets, but, maybe you can pass along the word."

Ishii snorted. "No, you can still tell him. You're coming with us."

"We can't abandon the *Dragon* here." Casmir held up a hand, aware of Bjarke trying to push his way to the front. "Did you know Prince Jorg boarded it and took Bonita and Qin prisoner?"

"I know what he did," Ishii said. His flat tone sounded disapproving, but that didn't mean he would disobey orders. "We'll tow that ship along until it can fly on its own. I'll send engineers over to repair it since *we* did the damage."

Not you, Ishii, but Jorg, Casmir thought. But if Ishii was willing to take the blame and felt guilty enough to send men to repair it, Casmir would keep his mouth shut.

"You, Kim Sato, Sir Bjarke Asger, and Sir William Asger will come aboard the *Osprey* with us until we figure out how we're going to get through the blockade—and stop Dubashi from destroying our home."

"Ah." Casmir didn't look at Kim, but he had a feeling she would prefer to stay here, lest Jorg still want her to make a bioweapon. And Casmir would certainly prefer more autonomy himself. How could he negotiate with Jorg for his friends if he was a prisoner in Ishii's brig? "I have formed a bond with the ship's intelligence, and I could be useful in repairs."

"This is indeed true, Captain Ishii," Viggo put in politely. "I would prefer if Casmir were the one to repair my damage. Have you seen the excellent work he does on vacuums?"

"Casmir Dabrowski also does excellent work on crushers," Zee stated, speaking for the first time. "As you can see from my exquisite stature, which has recovered from the great damage delivered to it during the battle in the moon base."

Casmir resisted the urge to drop his face in his hand. His helpful non-human allies were as likely to get him in trouble as his enemies.

"Yes," Ishii said, "but I'm going to have to insist everyone I named come aboard the *Osprey*. In exchange, I will do as I said and send men over to fix that freighter. I will also *attempt* to help you smooth the prince's ruffled feathers so you can get your friends back."

Casmir doubted the gruff and quick-to-anger Ishii would be able to smooth anything, but he didn't see that they had much choice. With the *Osprey* looming above the hapless *Dragon*, they could force the issue. He looked at Kim, and she nodded, though he could tell she also didn't want to return to the *Osprey*. Casmir hoped they could figure out a way to work everything out.

"We accept," Casmir said. "Thank you, Sora."

"Don't thank me," Ishii grumbled and closed the comm.

"Does anyone else," Asger asked, "want to pluck the prince's ruffled feathers rather than smooth them?"

Even Bjarke said yes.

A message came in on Casmir's chip.

I accept your offer of a crusher, it said without preamble. The sender was Moonrazor.

Does that mean…?

The majority of his comrades filed out of navigation before the lagged response came in. *The gate is temporarily inoperable, until it's my pleasure to make it otherwise. Let me know when it'll be my pleasure.*

Casmir had no idea what she'd done or how—more details would likely pop up on the news network soon—but he trusted that she spoke the truth. *Thank you. I will.*

He wasn't sure what kind of deal he'd just made, or if Moonrazor truly wanted a crusher or would ask for some greater favor, but for the moment, it appeared that Dubashi wouldn't be able to make it to System Lion. Odin would be safe, at least from that virus, at least for now. And Dubashi would be stuck here in System Stymphalia. As would Prince Jorg. And that Ambassador Romano.

“All my favorite people in one system together,” he murmured.

But if they were here with him instead of making trouble for the Kingdom back home… that was something. He would take it.

EPILOGUE

KIM LAY ON THE BED IN HER GUEST quarters on the *Osprey*. It was the same cabin she'd had before. At least it wasn't the brig.

She'd wondered if Ambassador Romano or Ishii himself would insist on a cell after her unauthorized departure. But Ishii had only escorted Kim and Casmir to their previous cabins and told them not to make trouble. She wondered if Asger and Bjarke had been given the same command.

Tristan had stayed aboard the *Dragon*, partially to help with repairs and partially because Ishii hadn't mentioned him when he'd ordered everybody else aboard. He hadn't seemed to mind. They were all heading to Stardust Palace, the last Kim had heard, to collect Casmir's crushers and regroup. The system news had been reporting that something was wrong with the wormhole gate and nobody had been able to leave for the last two days. Teams of specialists had been dispatched to study it.

Kim wanted to ask Casmir if he knew anything about it—why did she suspect that all quirky things that happened originated with him?—but the Jewish new year had come upon them, and he was in his cabin, fasting and supposedly not talking. She wondered if he would be able to refrain with the chatty Zee and all the other crushers in there with him. Maybe so. There had been a haunted look in his eyes when he'd mentioned praying for forgiveness and contemplating atonement.

She thought *Jorg* should be the one doing those things.

A message came in on her chip, startling her. She had been trying to find a way to compose one to Scholar Natasha Sunflyer on Stardust Palace to let her know that her father had died. Or taken his own life. Kim wasn't sure what to say and had been waffling for an hour.

My dearest Scholar Sato, Rache messaged. *Do you know anything about this broken gate? Correct that. Does* Casmir *know anything about it?*

What makes you think that? she asked, though she'd been wondering the same thing.

Speculation is that it's astroshaman work, and he's the only one I know who's been lip wrestling with high shamans.

Interesting. I can't ask at the moment. He's not speaking, in observance of his religious holiday.

So message him.

That's probably against the rules. But you *can message him if you wish. If he did arrange it somehow, I'm sure it was to stop Dubashi from killing everyone on Odin, not to inconvenience you.*

But if Rache couldn't fly off to assassinate people, Kim couldn't lament that.

Just so long as the gate gets un-broken before long. If I had to pick a system to be trapped indefinitely in, this wouldn't be the one.

Kim hadn't minded Stardust Palace. It had smelled nicer than most stations, and she could have found some interesting work to do with Scholar Sunflyer. But she also longed to go home.

I did reach out for more reasons than to complain, Rache continued. *I want to apologize for leaving you to go to that meeting. I had a bad feeling about that lab and that chair, and I left anyway. I regret that. I'm aggrieved that I almost didn't make it back in time.*

I told you to go, but thank you. And thank you for returning to rescue me. Rescue. That word was harder to get out than a confession. Kim hated to admit that she'd gotten herself into that situation and had needed rescuing. She would feel better about it if she had succeeded in removing the virus from *all* the rockets.

You're welcome, came Rache's reply. *And I'm pleased that you realize that it was I who got there first, not Casmir, who merely pushed a button.*

I am considering it a joint effort. I also thanked him.

I suppose that's acceptable.

You're magnanimous.

Yes, Rache replied. *I believe that's mentioned in the dramas that Casmir's crushers have been watching about me.*

I haven't seen any yet, so I can't say.

A part of Kim wanted to keep their conversation to banter that had nothing to do with her current problems or Rache's new mission, but with him stuck in the system, he might decide to go after Jorg. Dubashi had mentioned Jorg specifically as a target he'd given Rache. What if the *Fedallah* was, even now, speeding after the *Chivalrous*?

David, in case you're thinking of... harassing Jorg's ship, could I convince you to wait? Or not do it at all, she thought silently. Jorg, asshole that he was proving to be, was still their best bet at raising a significant enough force to help with the war back home. *He took Captain Lopez and Qin prisoners, and they're in his brig.*

What followed was a silence longer than the lag from distance would have accounted for, and Kim's gut sank with the certainty that Rache was indeed flying after Jorg now. Did he have any feelings for Bonita and Qin? He hadn't interacted with them nearly as often as he had with Kim and Casmir. But they had been a part of that memorable dinner, at which Casmir had given Rache underwear and pizza.

That sounds like a reason to *"harass" him, not one to stay away,* Rache finally responded, the quotation marks around harass suggesting he'd had something more inimical in mind.

But not to blow up his ship with them aboard. Let Casmir and me deal with Jorg. Please.

Deal with? Is Casmir going to give him fungi gifts?

Perhaps even underwear. I understand the gift shop at Stardust Palace Station is well-stocked.

Are the underwear made *from fungi?*

That is a possibility. It's quite versatile, I understand. You almost got a purse.

A purse? Men don't carry purses.

Casmir was going to call it a satchel.

What stopped him?

The presence of a lipstick holder. He feared that would give away his ruse.

Hm. I'll make a deal with you, Kim.

She braced herself as another pause followed the words. What would he require? A neck rub? Another kiss? A proclamation of love?

If Casmir promises to buy a purse for Prince Jorg, and records himself giving it to him, with lipstick already inserted into the holder,

I'll refrain from attacking his ship until you've retrieved your friends.

She puffed out a relieved laugh. *Will you require a copy of the recording?*

Do you really need to ask?

Perhaps not. I agree to your deal.

THE END

Printed in Great Britain
by Amazon

46306155R00249